The Goddess' Teardrop

The Chronicles of Ragnorak Book 1

A novel by

Christiano Prime
https://www.facebook.com/profile.php?id=1000333
01249234

Cover Art by Julie Tyslicky
https://www.facebook.com/profile.php?id=1000070
33579275

Foreword from the author:

This is a work of fiction. All the characters, organizations, and events portrayed in this novel are either products of the author's imagination or used fictitiously.

I'd like to thank Connie Lesoski and Christy Sawyer, without their love, and constant faith in my dreams, this story would never have been told. This book is dedicated to the Upsilon Delta Chapter of Tau Kappa Epilson. My brothers taught me to be confident and have faith in myself. This story is a love letter to those many people who have inspired me on my journey to become a self-actualized human being.

Chapter 1
Move-In

The campus of Bay Valley State University was in the northern woods of Bay City, Michigan. The city was nestled at crook of the Thumb of the Michigan mitten, resting at the edge of Lake Huron. Lake Huron was one of the five Great Lakes of Michigan, the largest bodies of fresh water in the world. The campus grounds were adorned in the classical manner with stone fountains and sculptures. The campus was surrounded by forest, with the main road, State Park Drive, cutting through the university dividing it into two halves. The university had a secluded, natural feel, with downtown just minutes away.

Virgil Pitcher cruised onto campus with his navy Chevy Blazer, making his way to the freshmen parking area on the outskirts of the school. Campus was flooded with students, new and old, making the move into the dorms. Some parents were present "over helping" their children in an embarrassing fashion. Virgil had driven to Bay Valley by himself, not wanting his mother there to dote on him. His hometown of Caseville was an hour northeast into the west side of the Thumb, home to one the best beaches in the area. Growing up in a small town could be stifling, especially for someone like Virgil who had always felt different from his peers. He was looking forward to the opportunity to meet new people.

Bay Valley was a D-II university, nowhere near as big as the D-1 schools like Michigan or Michigan State. Virgil didn't want to be at a huge university. The college had an average student population of twelve thousand with a large commuter base. The campus had been built on land formally used as a state park. Investors had made a deal with the State of Michigan in the 1940s after World War II, buying the land to build a state funded university. Bay Valley State University was founded thereafter.

Virgil parked his Blazer grabbing his backpack and duffle bag. Virgil would be eighteen at the end of September. He stood just shy of six feet tall, with a frock of wavy dark black hair. His eyes were the color of sapphires. He had full lips, with a strong jaw line, and a nose that was just slightly too large. Virgil had a strong physique, and a toned build. He had played soccer and ran track in high school, and lifted weights on a regular basis. Virgil had a Libra personality, typically polite and compassionate, and often indecisive.

There were four large freshmen dorms forming a ring around the commons area, a large patch of grass where students could sit or play sports. Virgil was placed in the Living Center North, or LCN for short. He went inside, got his key, making his way to his room, 231B on the second floor. He skipped the crowd near the elevator, squeezing pass parents and students making his way to the stairs. His dorm room was conveniently placed next to the stairwell.

The room opened into a dinning/living room area. A table and chairs were in the corner, bland furniture was arranged around an empty entertainment center. A large window was in the living room, looking out onto the sidewalk, and a small faculty parking lot. A kitchen was to the immediate right of the entrance that could fit maybe two people in it. The dorm had been painted sterile white and looked starkly plain. Virgil made his way to the back of the living room, and down a hall off to the right. There were two full bathrooms, and four bedrooms in the hall. Virgil was dismayed to find that he was the first roommate to arrive. He walked over to his bedroom door, last on the left, unlocked it and went inside.

The room was small and simple. Virgil paid the extra money to have one to himself. There was a twin extra long bed in the corner along with a desk, dresser, closet and a small stand. He put his bags on the ground and jumped on his bed enjoying the sheer pleasure of finally living on his own. This was the first time he'd moved out, and his adrenaline was pumping. He could do anything he wanted! Heading back down the congested halls, he stepped outside into the fresh air, running into another guy knocking them both down.

Virgil quickly stood up, "Hey man I'm really sorry about that," Virgil said helping the other guy to his feet.

He chuckled and said, "It is not a problem bro." He was a few inches taller than Virgil, with brown hair and plain features. Virgil noticed that he had Greek lettering on his shirt. "Are you in a Frat?" Virgil asked.

The man's face darkened a little, and Virgil felt he said something he shouldn't. "We don't call it that, as Frat is a derogative term. I am in a fraternity," he admonished.

"Oh, I'm sorry, I didn't mean to offend you," Virgil said feeling a bit foolish.

"We're good just don't make a habit of saying it." He extended his hand out, "The name's Paul."

"I'm Virgil," he said shaking Paul's hand. Paul had a firm handshake. When they touched a large crack of static shot up his arm. Virgil noticed on Paul's hand a golden-brown tattoo symbol he didn't recognize. He had a ring with a blue gemstone, on the same hand, that glowed when they touched. Virgil furrowed his eyebrows and let go, the ring going back to normal. Paul got a curious look on his face, noticing Virgil looking at the tattoo on his hand. Virgil stood there not knowing what to say when another guy approached them with the same letters on his shirt, carrying a few boxes.

"Paul lets finish helping this kid and move onto the next one," Paul's brother said.

"Jesse this is Virgil. Virgil this is my brother Jesse," Paul introduced them.

"Nice to meet you Jesse," Virgil said extending his hand. Virgil noticed a similar tattoo on Jesse's right hand. His was red, the symbol was different yet the same kind of style, it almost looked like a sword.

"You too," Jesse said shaking his hand. The moment they shook hands the blue gem on his ring lit up. Paul and Jesse exchanged a look that lasted barely a second.

They offered to help Virgil finish moving and he accepted. "What fraternity do you guys belong to?" Virgil asked.

"Our actual name is longer, but we call ourselves the Betas," Jesse said. "I'm a third year here, been in since I was a freshman."

Their conversation was mostly small talk, such as how the Detroit Tigers were fairing. Though they were polite, Virgil felt the hand tattoos were strange.

"Thanks for helping me move my stuff in guys," Virgil said as they made it back to his room.

"It was our pleasure!" Paul said earnestly. "We've been helping people all day, doing a favor for a cool guy like you is no problem."

"We're having a party later tonight, if you're looking for someplace to hang out," Paul said pulling out an invitation. Virgil's roommates choose that moment to walk in and introduce themselves.

"What are you fellas up to?" asked the shorter of the two guys, a red head with freckles, and pale white skin.

"We were just inviting your roommate here out to our fraternity house," Paul handed them both invitations. "We're the Betas and we're not your run of the mill fraternity. We are an elite collegiate group of men seeking only the best to join. We're throwing a party at our house tonight if you feel like coming out," he said. Jesse shook each of their hands and the two Betas left the room. The guys walked further into the room, and the three men all grinned at each other.

"Boyd and Damian?" Virgil asked them.

"I'm Boyd," the red-haired guy answered. Boyd was a short man standing only 5'5. His red auburn hair was cropped close to his head. He had a rather small head with dark beady eyes. He still had some of his baby fat, with a pudgy belly and face. He seemed loud, opinionated, with a hyper personality.

"I'm Damian," the other guy said. He had dark blond hair, with a small straight nose, and pale blue eyes. Although he seemed like the preppy type, he had a shy personality.

"Virgil," Virgil replied with a smile.

"Where you from?" Damian asked.

Virgil held up his hand in reference to the mitten of Michigan, like many people did in the state when explaining where they lived. He pointed to his thumb, "I'm from the west part of the Thumb, Caseville," Virgil explained.

"Have you got all your stuff moved in yet?" Damian asked him.

"Yeah those Beta guys helped me," Virgil nodded.

"They seemed cool, are you in pretty good with those frat guys? Think you could introduce me to them?" Boyd asked.

"Not really," Virgil said putting the party invitation on his desk, "I only just met them."

"Well at least we have a party to go to, and this flyer says its five dollars a cup for the keg," Boyd said excitement filling his voice.

"You guys party much?" Damian asked giving the other two a questioning look.

"I have a couple times," Virgil said shrugging his shoulders, never having "partied" in his life.

"Guys I'm telling you what, I got wasted every night back in high school," Boyd exclaimed rather boastfully. "I was on the soccer team, and my buddies and I were raging alcoholics!"

"Impressive," Damian replied sarcastically. "Next you're going to tell us you were dropped on your head as a baby, we never would've guessed," Damian said mockingly serious. Damian asked, "You guys want to go get something to eat? Our meal plans start today."

"Damn man, I forgot about that. I'm going to kill that cafeteria!" Boyd exclaimed.

The three newly acquainted roommates finished unpacking their rooms, talking to each other from across the hall as they did. Boyd turned on some music, blaring it to emphasize the kind of music he liked. After the three new friends finished they were all hungry and went to the living room where another dormmate, James, was sitting with his girlfriend, Stacey. They were holding hands talking softly to one another. They went to the cafeteria as a group, as James and Stacey were meeting up with her friends there. They all sat together and asked each other questions to break the ice.

"What are your guys' majors?" Virgil's roommate James asked the group.

"I'm a secondary education major," Damian replied.

"Pre-Law," Boyd said.

"I'm Pre-Med," Virgil answered.

"Oh well that's nice. James here is a secondary education major AND he's here on a full ride scholarship," Stacey boasted emphasizing the phrase full-ride.

"Really what for?" Virgil asked.

"My grades. I graduated Valedictorian of my class," James responded. He sounded proud of himself but not arrogant.

Boyd snorted, "What are you some kind of nerd?"

"Hey!" Stacey said her brows furrowing into an expression showing them she was clearly offended. "He is not a nerd!"

"No offense, if James is a lame nerd I don't really care," Boyd said in a mocking tone.

"He's not lame," Stacey said interrupting James, and replying for him in a whiny voice. Great, I hope this isn't any indication as to how these two are going to get along, Virgil thought. Virgil was starting to get the inkling Boyd was a loudmouth that liked to start stuff. He cleared his throat breaking the awkward silence.

"I don't think you're lame," Virgil said to his roommate, "I'm here on a full ride for academics as well."

"Really?" James asked his face lighting up some, "Where did you graduate from?"

"Caseville High School," Virgil replied.

"Wait, so I have two freaking geniuses living with me? Damn I guess I don't have to worry about my grades this semester," Boyd said. Virgil and Damian exchanged glances, and they both rolled their eyes at Boyd. That earned a giggle from Stacey, and a smile from James.

"So, what are you ladies up to tonight?" Boyd asked trying to sound suave and chill.

"I'm not sure," Stacey looked to her friends, "What do you girls feel like doing?"

"Movie night!" one of them said loudly with a laugh.

"We got invited to a Frat party later tonight, if you ladies are interested? We'd love to bring you along," Boyd boasted. "We could all carpool there and back."

"I'm not into drinking," Stacey frowned, "It's not even legal for any of us anyways."

"Well no freaking duh!" Boyd exclaimed. "But people do it anyways. Are you telling me none of you ladies would like to go out to a real college party your first night living at college? None of you girls like to have a good time?" Boyd asked surprise filling his voice.

"You don't need alcohol to have a good time," James responded.

"I don't think we're interested," Stacey and her friends agreed.

"Hmm okay," Boyd responded sounding bored and disinterested. They ate the rest of their food talking casually. James and Stacey talking more to their friends. Virgil could tell that Boyd had rubbed them the wrong way, partying wasn't what these people were about. Boyd, Virgil, and Damian got up to get more food.

As they walked away Boyd said, "So who else thinks that James and his ball and chain are a bunch of Debby Downers?"

"Debby Downers?" Virgil asked raising his eyebrows.

"You're dumb, moving on," Damian retorted with a bored expression.

"Boys we have three things on our agendas tonight," Boyd smirked throwing his arms around them.

"Oh God, I'm scared to hear this," Damian sighed.

"Number one have a good time," Boyd told them, "Number two get shit faced, and number three get some tail." Virgil and Damian laughed. Virgil wasn't sure if he thought Boyd's rude manor was amusing, or tactless.

"James isn't that bad," Virgil said getting some ice cream for himself.

"Man, you are way too nice, you need to loosen up," Boyd barked.

"Yeah, since we've met, I haven't heard you say anything mean," Damian agreed.

"Come on, I can be just as rude as the next jerk, I just," Virgil paused thinking of how best to phrase it, "I don't like hurting people's feelings okay!" he exclaimed.

"Some jerk," Boyd said rolling his eyes at Virgil. "Get your hands out of your pants and man up!" Boyd demanded of Virgil.

Later that night Virgil was driving his two dormmates down the long road that led off from campus, and towards Greek housing. The Greek houses were off the west side of campus, down a road that led deep into the forest. The Greek houses were technically on campus property, with each fraternity and sorority given their own section out in the woods. Private and secluded from the other Greeks, they drove past large gates and sweeping driveways which led up to elaborate mansions looking like they belonged more to millionaires than college kids. As they turned down the small drive towards the Beta's house, the whole car was stunned to silence. The Beta's house wasn't a house at all, rather an immaculate five story mansion, and it looked like the dream party destination for any college student. A sea of cars littered the grass stretching back far from the house.

"Damn this place is packed with babes!" Boyd squealed jumping in his seat next to Virgil. Boyd's excitement was contagious. They were all laughing and grinning as they left the vehicle. There were two guys at a small table by the door making everyone sign their names.

"What's up gentlemen? How's your first day at Bay Valley?" The muscled guy asked them in a deep booming voice.

"Pretty good." "Fine." "Good bro." They replied

"How'd you boys hear about us?" The same guy asked them. He was a rather imposing man with arms as huge as Virgil's calves. His hair was buzzed to a fine prickle. His skin was black as night, and his eyes were so dark they were almost lost in his pupils. His gaze was on Virgil unwavering and steady, the man did not blink once.

Virgil stumbled over his words feeling intimidated by this man. The man gave him a funny look and Virgil quickly gained his composure. "Paul and Jesse helped me move my stuff earlier today, they gave me this," Virgil said getting out the invitation and handing it to the guy who'd spoken.

"Paul had mentioned you earlier. What is your name again?" The other man who was sitting at the table asked speaking up. He had platinum blonde hair that was as fair as his skin. His hair was swept back from his cheeks in a tie, putting the focus primarily on his face. His features were striking, with strong cheekbones, and a small straight nose. He had piercing green eyes whose serious gaze felt unbalanced from his seemingly relaxed demeanor. He stared deep into Virgil's eyes, and Virgil felt something inside of him begin to squirm. While the dark man sitting next to him appeared larger, Virgil knew that this blond-haired man was in charge.

"My name is Virgil Pitcher, it's nice to meet you..." Virgil left off for the man to finish.

"I am Malachi, the President of the Betas, and this is Jamal, our Sergeant at Arms. It is nice to meet you Virgil," he said extending a hand. Malachi had an amethyst colored glyph on his extended hand. What was with these guys and their tattoos? Virgil felt like this was a test. He reluctantly shook Malachi's extended hand with the strange tattoo. The familiar crackle of static like energy tingled along Virgil's arm. A ring with a blue gemstone on Malachi's hand lit up. Their hands parted, and Virgil felt puzzled. He noticed the man next to Malachi also had a tattoo on his hand, but his was a golden brown.

Virgil asked before he lost his nerve, "Why do you have different colored tattoos? And if you're in the same group shouldn't you have the same symbol?"

The two men shared a look. "Bro are you feeling okay?" Boyd asked Virgil. "What tattoos?"

"The ones on their hands," Virgil stated pointing at Malachi's amethyst symbol. "Everyone in their fraternity has one, he has a purple one, and his is like a yellow."

"I don't see anything," Boyd stated.

"Me neither," Damian chimed in.

"You been hitting the booze a little early tonight? Obviously, we don't have tattoos on our hands," Malachi asked holding up his hands with a symbol on it clear as day. The others looked like they truly didn't see anything, Virgil nodded and dropped the subject.

The two men shared a look then Jamal said, "Alright just sign your names and head on in. Oh, and boys, we don't want no trouble this evening. It would piss me off greatly if I had to come inside to personally escort you out." Virgil and the others signed their names and told them that they wouldn't start any trouble.

The party was the most wild and crazy place Virgil had ever been. Rooms were crammed wall to wall with people! The three roommates squeezed through the crowd and began to mingle and drink. Damian and Virgil wandered around for a while starting conversations here and there, flirting with the occasional girl. After a few more cups out of the keg, and Virgil's night started to become a blur.

After leaving Damian and Boyd at the Beer Pong tables, Virgil noticed Paul heading up the staircase to the next floor. Virgil wanted to thank him for the invite, so he quickly followed him, slowed by the mass of bodies. Virgil moved through the people making it up to the second floor, but all the doors were shut and locked. Knowing he saw him walk up the stairs, Virgil walked to the next flight of stairs that led to the third floor. The moment he placed a foot on the steps leading up his stomach ached, and he almost fell to the ground. He doubled over with a sudden urge to puke his guts out, feeling like insects were marching along his skin. He stepped back from the stairs, and the feeling left instantly. He was sure he was going to be sick to his stomach just seconds ago, now he felt completely fine. I'm drunk! He thought to himself, I must have imagined it. He stepped on the stairs again, immediately the feeling of sickness came back. He stepped back, looking around for someone else. Just when he thought of heading back downstairs, he heard a faint scream that was quickly muffled. It sounded like a woman crying out in pain and fear! Fighting the sinking feeling in his gut, and the goose bumps along his arms, he crept up the stairs fearful of what he would find.

Virgil reached the third floor, his legs feeling like rubber and his stomach churning violently, but that mattered little. He knew, he felt deep down, that someone up here needed help, and he was raised to never turn his back on someone in need. The hallway was dark, illuminated only by a small sliver of light coming from the crack of an open door down the hall. Virgil crept closer to the door, "Stop-p-p-p please-e-e-e-e," a low muffled voice begged so low that Virgil could barely hear it.

"Stop toying with her Paul, she's obviously not the Pureblood Nephilim we need," a voice commanded, one Virgil recognized as Malachi's.

"I know that, but you don't have to spoil my fun," Paul's familiar voice said.

Virgil peaked inside. A young woman was leaning against the bed, sitting on the floor. Three men were inside, Paul and Malachi, the president of this fraternity. The other man was someone Virgil did not recognize. He was strikingly handsome, with movie star level looks. The unknown man had long dark hair tied back in a tight braid. His face was flawless and smooth, his eyes dark and cold. The woman leaning against the bed was in pain. Her eyes were squeezed shut and she was shaking. She had a small cut along her hand where a sapphire blue tattoo was glowing on her palm. The man held a jewel attached to a chain like necklace. The jewel was unlike any gem he had known. It was glowing dimly with blood, from the girl's wrists, smeared across its flawless surface.

"The blood of the Nephilim, that can break the seal of the Arch Demon, will react when brought in contact with this magicite," the attractive cold man said to Malachi. "We need the Arch Demon to locate the Goddess' Teardrop. We need to find the right Nephilim, soon."

Virgil wanted to speak out and tell them to leave the woman be, but his voice choked in his throat, and no sounds escaped his shaking lips. He blinked a few times trying to make sense of what he was seeing. Virgil got a death chill when he looked at that man, the one who spoke as if he was above Malachi. Virgil could see a strange glowing symbol on one of the man's hand's as well, his was pitch black in color, in the shape of a giant sword. The group of people standing around the woman, their tattoos seemed to pulse with glowing energy, like they held power.

"A shame she is not capable of breaking the seal," the man spoke putting the jewel pendant away. "You'll have to keep looking."

"She saw the Devil Arms symbol on my hand," Paul explained, "I was taught that only Pureblood Nephilim could see them without being initiated."

"She is not of the caliber we need," the man explained in a bored clip. His voice was cold, powerful, with a tone that commanded obedience. "We need a Nephilim of direct decent from a Seraphim Judge's bloodline in order to break the seal on the Arch Demon."

Arch Demon!? Virgil thought, sweat beginning to form on his forehead. What are they talking about?

"There is a young man that my brothers met earlier. He seemed to be aware of the Devil Arms symbols, yet had none of his own," Malachi stated. "His name is Virgil Pitcher."

Virgil's pulse began to race, and his mouth became dry, he knew he had not been imagining things. Coming up here had been a bad idea though, he needed to leave.

"What are you doing here?" a deep voice demanded from behind Virgil. He spun around to a swift kick in the ribs that sent him flying into the door, crashing into the room.

Virgil coughed hard trying to catch the air that had been knocked out of his lungs.

It was Jamal. He asked the others, "How did this guy make it up here?"

"Speak of the devil, this is the young man I had mentioned," Malachi grinned.

"How did he make it up here? I put up the wards for this floor myself, he couldn't have passed through my spells," Jamal spat, his voice practically dripping venom.

"You think he's a spy for the Omegas?" Paul asked.

"No, he does not yet have a Devil Arms, and he's too naïve to be an Omega," Malachi responded.

I'm dead, deader than dead I'm done, he thought. They aren't going to let me go, not after what I've seen. But what exactly had he seen? His mind couldn't make sense of it.

"Virgil," the cold dark voice said playing the word over his tongue slowly. "He must be powerful to have made it up here." Virgil looked the man in his unyielding eyes. Black pools of endless…hunger. Virgil had expected anger at trespassing, but what he saw was something worse. He saw a strong desire to be used and controlled; he saw need in those eyes. "Test him," the man demanded.

Malachi grabbed Virgil's arm and sliced a small cut with a knife. Malachi handed the knife to the man. The stranger brought the gem to the knife and wiped the blood across, the gem lit up like a light bulb. That couldn't be good.

"This could work," the man said. "It would be best if he doesn't remember this," he suggested.

"I'll handle it Sethos," Malachi offered. He spoke words Virgil did not recognize and traced his fingers through the air. A bright purple flash came out from the amethyst symbol on Malachi's hand, and the world went dark.

Chapter 2
<u>The Tale of David and Goliath</u>

Monday brought the start of the semester. Virgil was taking Bio, Math, English, and History, fourteen credits, anymore and he'd be overwhelmed. His first week at Bay Valley was consumed with studying and spending time with Damian and Boyd. Damian had bonded with the Betas and seemed interested in pledging. Boyd met a few different fraternities he liked as well. After the second week of classes Virgil went home for the weekend to see his mom, Sue. She was in her late fifties, his father died from cancer a few years back. They had a small family, with a few relatives in Florida. Virgil was raised knowing his mom died giving birth to him, and his parents had adopted him as a baby. Sue was a close friend to him, and their relationship had more open communication then most. After dinner and a movie, they were getting ready for bed. Sue came to his room to wish him goodnight.

"Thanks for coming home to visit me Virgil," Sue smiled from the doorway. "I had fun catching up tonight."

"I did too mom," Virgil replied with a smile.

"Are you still being looked after by your guardian angel?" Sue asked Virgil. Virgil's mind drew a blank, wondering if she meant the spirit of his father who had passed away two years ago. Sue walked in and sat on Virgil's bed, "Don't you remember? You went missing for a short time when you were five years old. We were at the park by the beach. I took my eyes off you for a minute, and when I looked back, you were just gone." Virgil's face fell, he saw in his mother's eyes how much it had frightened her. "The police came immediately, but nobody had seen you leave the park. There was nothing they could do to help. Three nights later, I heard something coming from this room, your room, just down the hall. I raced to the door, threw it open, and there you were, sleeping in your bed, the window mysteriously left open. I went to the window and saw something white flying away."

"I just remember coming back home," Virgil replied sadly. Virgil did not remember anything from the time he was gone, so the family did their best to move forward.

After the event Virgil would sometimes wake up to the humming of a sad tune when he was a child, but when he became fully aware it stopped. Virgil never remembered seeing anything outside his window, but the song…its lullaby was an ethereal memory. He couldn't remember how any of it went, if he heard it though, he knew he could hum along with every note.

Sue laughed it off telling her son, "Life works in mysterious ways Virgil. We must be thankful for the blessings we are bestowed. When the Creator sends you a gift, you don't ask why it was sent."

They both went to sleep afterwards, and Virgil returned to campus feeling rejuvenated and ready for another week of college. Monday was the third week of the semester, after his classes Virgil went back to the dorm, Boyd was sitting in the living room watching TV.

"What's up?" Virgil said taking a seat.

"Dude will you come with me to information night?" Boyd asked.

"What's that?" Virgil asked turning from the TV and looking at Boyd.

"This is Rush Week for Greek Life," Boyd explained holding a flyer for the Omega's in his hand. "The first night all of the fraternities have information tables at one joined event. The rest of the days, each fraternity has their own events."

"I don't think I want to join," Virgil sighed.

"Yeah I know, you're a goody-goody, but I can't go by myself," Boyd stressed. "I'll look like a weirdo!" he exclaimed.

And taking me along will change that how? "I guess," Virgil agreed.

"Awesome!" Boyd said jumping up off the couch slightly.

"Easy trigger," Virgil laughed. "When do we go?" he asked.

Damian joined them that night wanting to show interest in the Betas. The student multipurpose room was decorated with a casino night theme. There were blackjack and poker tables, video game tournaments, ping pong, and free stuff everywhere. Brothers from different fraternities were dressed in t-shirts with their respective letters across the chest. Fraternity brothers were taking every opportunity to be cordial and meet new guys. Brothers were dealers at the tables, serving pizza and wings, working brag tables, and overall walking around keeping the event lively. Brag tables, as Boyd had called them, were placed against the walls wrapping around the room with trophies, plaques, pictures, and rush schedules. Brothers stood around them to give more information.

Damian went to see the Betas' table, Boyd and Virgil went over to the Omegas. The Omega table was one of the more impressive, second only to the Tekes. It had huge trophies, plaques, paddles, rush schedules, and similar things spread across it. A silver banner hung from the front with royal blue letters across the front. The guys were as they had been before, friendly, open, and inviting. Virgil felt comfortable and welcomed by the Omegas. They were all dressed in casual jeans with royal blue shirts that had two angels on the back holding a scroll that had the Omega's creed on it. Boyd knew a few and they greeted him warmly, Virgil felt awkward standing there.

"Would you boys like to fill out an information sheet?" Doc, a brother of Omega, asked them. He was of average height with black hair kept buzzed short, and dark eyes.

"Yes sir!" Boyd excitedly took a form.

"No thanks, not interested," Virgil said flatly.

"Okay," Doc said giving him a look.

"Dude! Don't be rude," Boyd said firmly.

"I mean, I guess I can," Virgil sighed. He quickly filled out the page with information on himself, which asked mostly generic questions. The last question was, what does brotherhood mean to you, he liked that one. Virgil handed the completed form back to Doc.

"Thanks bud," Doc smiled, and they shook hands. A golden-brown symbol shaped like an axe was on his skin. Doc's handshake was firm and strong. Virgil noticed a ring on Doc's hand lit up brightly when they came into contact. Boyd seemed to make the rings dimly react, but it was almost unnoticeable.

Virgil was going to ask what was up with the rings when Boyd pulled him away. Boyd asked Virgil, "You want to go to a small party with me?"

"Dude, it's a school night," Virgil whined.

"You worried your parents will ground you?" Boyd asked sarcastically. "Landon said a few guys are going to be getting together at their place. I want to go, and I need a sober driver for the ride home."

"Alright," Virgil sighed not wanting Boyd to attempt to drive drunk.

The Omega's fraternity house was overwhelming and spectacular. The grounds were completely gated in by a large red brick wall worn from time, and two large towering gates stood open at the entrance. A large open yard spotted with trees, led up to Omega manor. Small light fixtures adorned the outside of the cement path to a large circular driveway, with a small fountain in the middle. The mansion was painted in cherry and gray, six stories high. Virgil wondered just how many brothers this place could hold! There was an attached garage off to the right of the house big enough to fit vehicles for everyone who lived there. They walked up the front steps stunned. A man standing outside left the group he was entertaining to greet them.

"You guys look shocked, what's up gentlemen?" the man said with a bright smile extending his hand out to them.

"I'm Virgil and this is my roommate Boyd," he said shaking the man's hand.

"Nice meeting both of you. My name's Gabriel," Gabriel said. He radiated confidence and charisma. To put it plainly Gabriel was *cool*. Certain people are just born special, they have a certain magnetism that calls out to others. Gabriel had a distinguished air of authority about him, Virgil thought even if he wasn't the leader of the Omegas in name, he seemed to be in spirit. Gabriel was tall, dark, and handsome making Virgil think he was of Mediterranean descent, maybe Greek or Italian. He stood 6'2 with honey green eyes, and a strong chin and cheek bones. He seemed relaxed in his posture and was rather built, making Virgil think he was a boxer or a fighter. Even though he seemed like a badass, Virgil sensed a kindness within him. Gabriel had a golden-brown colored tattoo on his right hand.

"Alright boys the party's out back make yourselves at home," Gabriel said genuinely with a smile.

The front door opened into a small area, with two closets that could fit lots of coats and shoes. This small room opened into a large foyer, with double stairs leading up, and paths to take underneath it forward, and to either side. They kept walking forward passing underneath the stairs.

"This place is ridiculous," Boyd said with a grin.

Virgil laughed, "Ridiculous? More like mind blowing. Can you imagine living here?" Virgil marveled in wonder.

They passed a bathroom and came to the dining room. There were doors ahead that opened into the back yard, they walked through them going back outside. The back of the mansion opened onto a large clearing. It gradually sloped down into where the trees grew thicker eventually swallowing all visible sight. Large stone steps were off the porch carved into the sloping path, down to where the ground leveled out, a large circular bonfire pit was in the center. Benches and swings were placed around the fire, and many people crowded around its warmth. Looking around Virgil would have estimated at least a hundred people were at the Omega party, and it was a Monday night!

The Omegas were more fun than the Betas. Everyone Virgil met here seemed friendly, inviting, relaxed. They weren't pushy like the Betas. They seemed interested in just being friends. They never brought up the subject of asking people to join. Virgil found himself being the one to ask those questions because his interest was piqued. Virgil was asked to be someone's partner for beer pong, the man introduced himself as Magnus. Virgil quickly realized Magnus was somebody important. He had a cool calculating intelligence about him, and charisma like Gabriel's. They were playing against two very attractive women who giggled as they assembled their cups.

"So, are you an Omega?" Virgil asked unable to stand the suspense.

Magnus chuckled to himself taking aim with his ping pong ball and sinking it into the front cup, "You could say that," he nodded.

"Yeah?" Virgil asked missing his shot.

"Well I'm kind of like the President currently, so I guess that puts me in charge," he replied with a sarcastic tone and chuckle.

"I'm sorry I didn't mean to-"

"You're good, don't sweat it," Magnus answered unperturbed sinking his next shot. He's the flipping President, nice going Virgil way to start off the conversation.

Magnus stood slightly taller than Virgil, with dirty blonde hair that was buzzed down to his head. He had striking blue eyes that reflected a startling intelligence. Beneath his relaxed posture, sly smile, and witty comebacks, burned a mind that didn't miss a beat. The symbol on his hand was amethyst in color like Malachi's.

"Come on it's your shot," Magnus said his joking demeanor ever present. "You ladies are going to have to take it easy on us, this is my first time playing," he said meekly acting shy.

"No way!" the blonde girl on the left replied, "This can't be your first time."

"Now I'm nervous, it's my first game ever, and you're calling me a liar? Not cool," Magnus scowled. Virgil listened to them banter a little longer until Magnus had them convinced it was his first time, and they apologized for questioning him. Virgil highly doubted it was, Magnus hadn't missed a single shot yet, and they won the game with Virgil making only two of the cups.

"What's your story?" Magnus asked putting the cups back in a triangle.

"I went to school in a small town in the Thumb of Michigan," Virgil replied.

"Really? Same here," Magnus said.

"Cool, where at?" Virgil asked.

"Croswell," Magnus told him sinking his first shot.

"I'm from Caseville," Virgil explained. "I lived there pretty much my whole life, graduated top of my class, came here on a full ride, and I'm here just looking to meet some new people."

"That's impressive," Magnus said.

"How does someone join a fraternity?" Virgil asked.

"We have Rush week, which is happening now, fun events for guys to come out to and get to know us. This week is all about hanging out and getting to know each other. Next week when we give out bids, it's all about guys trying to impress us. We're only looking for a certain type of guy, not just anybody can be an Omega," Magnus said firmly. "But that doesn't mean we can't be friends with the guys who we don't think are right for our organization."

"What do you mean a certain type of guy?" Virgil asked.

"Well this is our family, can't be just anyone allowed to come into that, has to be someone with character someone who represents us all," Magnus said. "Are you thinking of going Greek?" Magnus asked sinking his third cup in a row.

"I'm not sure. I want to be involved in something important, I just don't know what yet," Virgil responded honestly.

After a long week of exams, Virgil spent the weekend catching up on sleep. Sunday night Virgil felt nervous for his first Bio exam. This was going to be the hardest exam of his life so far, and he was drained. Boyd and Damian were visibly nervous. The tension in the dorm heightened the darker it became. Boyd and Damian were both sitting in the living room with the TV on, neither watching it, their legs shaking, hands twitching.

"What has you guys on edge?" Virgil asked concerned when he walked out to the kitchen to get some water.

"The fraternities are deciding on bids tonight," Boyd explained. "They told everyone to be at their dorm Sunday night, that they would be handing out invitations to the guys they wanted."

Virgil could tell this meant a lot to him. "How long do you have to wait?" Virgil asked curious.

"They didn't say," Damian shrugged.

There was a knock at the door, a little over a dozen Betas came into the room, dressed in dark clothes with no writing or markings. They had serious faces on, their eyes alive with a faint twinkle of excitement. They lined up in front of the door Malachi at the lead along with Jamal. They stood there tall, proud, and intimidating, silently staring down the three roommates.

Jamal spoke up, "Men of Beta, welcome Damian and Virgil!"

The men chanted and stomped then went silent. A Beta, Paul, stepped forward. He handed them invitations made of fine stationary, with embossed lettering on the front.

"Let's go," Malachi nodded to them. Virgil watched Damian get up and follow them to the door. Virgil remained where he was seated.

"You have until Wednesday night to think about it," Malachi advised him seriously. "This is not something you want to miss out on Virgil. We think you have a lot of potential." He stepped closer looking Virgil square on, "You belong in the Nephilim world Virgil. The Beta house, 10:30pm, Wednesday night," Malachi offered. Nephilim? Virgil wondered. "Anyone who has a bid is welcome to come at that time to accept it."

The Betas left the room, Damian looked back at Virgil, his eyes urging his friend to join him. Virgil looked down. He had a strange feeling not to trust the Betas, and he had to trust his instincts.

Boyd took a deep breath and said, "Glad those jerks left."

Virgil didn't say anything. He took the bid to his room, putting in the desk drawer. He sat down going back to studying for his test. Boyd came to his open door leaning against the frame.

"Are you thinking of joining?" Boyd asked gathering the courage over several seconds.

"Not really," Virgil admitted. "I don't think it's a bad idea for Damien, and I'll be supportive. But I don't think I would fit in with them."

"I was really hoping the Tekes or Omegas would stop by and give me a bid," Boyd said looking a little downcast. "I went to two Rush events for each group!" he exclaimed. "I definitely showed interest."

"They might still come yet, right?" Virgil said trying to be positive. "You still have a chance Boyd. Why don't you do something to keep yourself busy until then?" he suggested.

"You're still studying? What are you trying to do, write your own textbook?" Boyd asked exasperatedly coming to look over Virgil's sprawling study area.

"I want to ace this exam alright," Virgil said waving him off.

"Good luck!" Boyd said rolling his eyes. "I'm going to play some Playstation."

Virgil shut the door returning to his studies. After a half hour there was a faint knock at the front of the dorm. Virgil heard Boyd answer. A loud chorus of yells exploded through the dorm, like a football team had just come running through the door after a big win. It went quiet, there was a knock at Virgil's bedroom door. He put down his study guide and opened the door. A large round man with two different colored eyes behind small glasses, and a cap on his head answered the door.

"Virgil Pitcher?" he asked.

"Yes?" Virgil answered.

"Come with me for a minute," he said backing up slightly motioning to the hallway. "Grab a sweatshirt," he told Virgil.

"I don't think so," Virgil said rubbing his neck trying to think of a good excuse to send this guy away. "I have a big exam in the morning and I'm kind of tired," Virgil started to say.

"Virgil!" Boyd called out. "Get your bitch ass out here!" he barked.

Virgil sighed putting on a zip up hoodie. Virgil walked into the living room and immediately was lifted off his feet, bodies poured around him shouting at the top of their lungs. They raised him up cheering in celebration. Virgil was laughing from the overwhelming sense of excitement. A rush came over him, adrenaline starting to flood his nervous system. They set Virgil down.

"Men of Omega welcome Virgil and Boyd!" they cried out and Doc stepped forward and presented them with their bids. The men burst into a round of applause. Virgil felt speechless as he stared down at his bid.

"Take good care of those bids boys," Doc cautioned. "We want them kept in the same condition they are in right now; pristine and crisp. That means I don't want to see any jizz stains, or anything else freaky that you guys get your marbles off to." Virgil's mouth dropped open a little.

Virgil laughed nervously red in the face, and read the invitation in his hands, the words were in silver printed writing and read as follows:

This bid is the property of <u>Virgil Pitcher</u> and serves as an invitation to join the elite Fraternity of Omega. If said potential is interested in joining the Brotherhood you are to report to the Bell Tower at 10:15pm on Wednesday night. Bring the bid with you, as it will allow admittance into the pledging process.

"You two grab your shit and let's go, bring your bids and remember what I said," Doc barked, and the brothers piled out through the door. The halls were filled with the sound of rambunctious men running and screaming, some were even doing flips off the walls. Virgil followed the flow of people grinning, his bid held firmly in his left hand. These guys were nuts!

"Where are we going?" Virgil asked a guy walking next to him as they left Living Center North and headed to the old freshmen dorms on the other side of the cafeteria. They were the original dorms of the campus, and therefore had the worst amenities.

"I don't know man. I just got a bid, I'm in the same boat as you," the guy said. He had sandy brown hair, fierce blue eyes, a thin face with a pointed nose, and a narrow chin. Virgil felt like he knew him or had at least met him before.

"My name's Aidan," he said shaking Virgil's hand.

"I'm Boyd, the cool roommate," Boyd said stepping between them, "this is my nerdy roommate Virgil. These guys are pretty bad ass, don't you agree?" he asked. Virgil heard a few people laugh in front of them, he assumed it was at Boyd's comment.

Aidan laughed at Boyd, giving Virgil an inquisitive glance then said, "It's nice to meet both of you. And I would agree with you Boyd, I've been partying with these guys since my junior year of high school. My older brother Vahn joined their Brotherhood. I've been dreaming of this day ever since," he told them with passion.

They came to the bell tower, an ornate and lavish structure, stretching high into the starry night. Behind the bell tower, there was a small stone amphitheater where a few brothers were already waiting for them spread out across its stone steps. The men who had received bids stood in a line at the bottom, while over thirty brothers took their place on the different levels of the stone steps staring down at the new recruits.

Gabriel stepped forward drawing focus, and Virgil felt slightly intimidated staring up at him. Gabriel was dressed in letters like his brothers, his dark hair shaved down to a fine bristle on his head, his dark green eyes held a stern seriousness. Gabriel spoke, his voice strong and confident on the silent night air, "Welcome all twenty-four of you. If you are interested in accepting the bid for membership into the Omegas, be here Wednesday, 10:15pm sharp. At this moment none of you are pledges for Omega. Only upon accepting your bid Wednesday will you be considered a candidate. Rush week was about making you interested in us. Pledging for Omega is a different story. This is a six-week dry process, every day of that process you will be working to prove you deserve to join this Brotherhood. I'm not going to lie, this won't be an easy task," Gabriel said stepping down the steps to walk back and forth in front of them, staring directly into each of their eyes as he spoke. "Being a pledge for Omega is a full-time commitment. This is a dry process, as I mentioned. There will be no drinking or use of illegal substances of any kind, that includes pot." A few groans went off from the crowd. "I'm serious when I say this, we have a zero-tolerance policy for candidates. If we find out you have been cheating you will be removed from the process immediately."

A guy raised his hand Gabriel nodded for him to speak, "This is more of a concern," the man said. He had a pale face with greasy hair. "I'm a freshman, as I'm sure most of the guys here are, and I'm wondering how you expect us to give up six weeks of perhaps the craziest partying days of our lives?" he asked.

"What's your name?" Gabriel asked him.

"Josh," the kid replied.

"Being a Brother of Omega is an honor. We can't have our candidates spending more time partying then focusing on getting to know the brothers. This isn't something you have to do.

If you want to leave, the sidewalk is right there," Gabriel said looking the kid dead on. Josh shut up and stared at the ground.

Magnus spoke up addressing the group, "Listen up people, being a pledge is a privilege, one that you can lose anytime if a brother in our Chapter thinks that you are not showing enough commitment. If not drinking or messing around with drugs for less than two months is too hard for you, then you are looking at the wrong fraternity. We accept only the men that want the best out of themselves. This is a university, a place where the great minds of the generation come together to learn and grow. Education comes first and foremost for every brother in this Chapter, that standard will apply to you."

"What we are offering here is the opportunity of a lifetime," Gabriel spoke from the heart, "To not only join one of the most powerful and oldest orders in existence but," he paused and opened his arms towards his brothers looking at them in turn, "the chance to be a part of our family. The next three days are meant for you to dwell on the decision at hand," Gabriel said ending his speech.

After Gabriel had finished the brothers came down the steps, shaking the hands of all the potentials. Virgil was bombarded with so many new faces, slaps on the back, and handshakes it felt a little disorientating. "Thanks for coming out, I hope to see you Wednesday," Gabriel said to Virgil with a friendly smile shaking his hand.

Virgil stammered out a reply, "Thank you sir." Virgil shook hands with the rest of the brothers present. Gabriel came back around to shake Virgil's hand a second time. "I feel like you need another one," he laughed nervously making Virgil feel special. Do I look that nervous, Virgil wondered? Virgil appreciated Gabriel's effort to make him feel welcome.

Virgil and Boyd walked home together, Boyd could barely breathe he talked so fast. His enthusiasm was pleasant, though Virgil's stomach twisted with anticipation. It rained all day Monday, so Virgil was kept indoors after his classes had ended. He had been given a bid from the Betas and the Omegas. Virgil was envious of the close bond the brothers shared. Something about what Malachi had said was bugging him, what was a Nephilim? Virgil looked it up, the search engine said Nephilim were the offspring of angels and humans. There must be more definitions, Virgil thought not looking much into it.

Virgil had World History, from the beginning of time until 1500 AD, Wednesday nights at 7 pm. The professor Dr. Cullen was focusing primarily on the Greeks, Romans, and Medieval time periods. They took a short quiz before class on the week's reading, then the professor began his lecture. Virgil was wondering about the word Nephilim, when he impulsively raised his hand getting the professor's attention.

"Yes, the young man in the third row you have a question?" he asked.

"I was reading an old book the other day, and I came across a peculiar term that I didn't recognize," Virgil pondered. "What does Nephilim mean?"

The professor had an irritated expression on his face, "That's not on point with the topic we were discussing," the Professor sighed, "What old book were you reading the Bible?"

Virgil's interest spiked, "Why would you say that?" he asked.

"The Bible is one of the most ancient texts that refer to Nephilim. One of the most notorious being the story of David and Goliath."

His memory was a little hazy on the details. "What do Nephilim have to do with that story?" Virgil asked.

The Professor sighed, "Everything," he laughed, "Nephilim according to The Bible were the children resulting from the union between angel and man. There are conflicting accounts on just what they were exactly. Some say the first Nephilim were giants standing over forty feet high, devoid of humanity, with an insatiable hunger for mortal flesh. The most famous account of these creatures is the tale of David and Goliath. It was said Goliath was a Nephilim, a giant. David defeated the Nephilim Goliath and became king." Virgil was perplexed. Instead of clearing up his mind, he was more confused.

After class Virgil and Boyd walked together to meet the Omegas. The night sky was overcast with low hanging clouds blocking out most of the stars and moonlight. The brothers were waiting for them at the bell tower. Fourteen potentials showed up. Once it was time, Gabriel led the group to the amphitheater where the brothers took their place on the steps.

Virgil felt so nervous he could barely stand still, his stomach twisted in knots. One of the brothers wasn't on the stone steps, he had been standing off to the side and came up to the candidates. He was handsome mixed Caucasian with Mexican, with short dark hair, brown eyes, and his face was fixed in a sour grimace. He looked grumpy and deadly serious. He opened up his mouth and his first four words set the first impression for his character, "Heads Down! No Talking!" he barked at them. Virgil quickly put his chin on his chest and stared at the gray cement ground. "Heads Down!" he said to a few people down the line who apparently hadn't done so.

"By coming here, you are showing us that you have a desire to join the Brotherhood. If all of you make it through, we will surely be the strongest fraternity on this campus," Gabriel smiled. "It's time for Bid Inspection. For the remainder of this night you will speak when you are spoken to, and you will begin and end your replies with sir, am I clear gentlemen?"

"Sir, yes sir," Virgil said along with the other candidates.

"Good," Gabriel nodded, "Jagger bring the first candidate forward please." Jagger took the first guy in the line up to the steps where the brothers waited. He was a light skinned African American with a large black afro. He was skinny with a cocky spring in his step.

"Love the hair," Gabriel complimented him, "Please state your name for the brothers."

"Sir, my name is Darius sir," Darius said to Gabriel.

"Let's see your bid," Gabriel extended his hand and took Darius' bid. He had a flashlight, using it to examine the bid closely, the other brothers huddling in close to see. "I'm impressed, very nice work here, the first guy's bid never looks this clean," Gabriel said turning it over. He handed it back to Darius. "You're good," Jagger directed Darius over to the side to stand by himself making him put his head back down. Jagger brought forward the stocky jock with reddish brown hair from the Zoo. Gabriel asked him, "What's your name?"

"Sir, its Dante sir," Dante replied his bid held firmly in his left hand. Gabriel motioned for the bid and Dante handed it to him.

"Looks good on the outside, let's see inside," he opened it up and the people crowded around the bid all cringed back and let out with a loud "Oh!" in exclamation.

"What the hell did you do to this? Jerk off with it every night before you went to sleep?" Gabriel asked with mocked seriousness and a few brothers stifled their laughter.

"Sir, no sir," Dante said his pale white skin flushed bright red, "My idiot roommate spilled water on it," Dante explained with clenched fists.

"That's not good enough for my fraternity, see if you can iron that out or something, go to the back of the line try again," Gabriel ordered handing back his bid. Jagger escorted him back to the candidate line.

They continued the same process for all the candidates. Darius was the only one to pass through inspection on the first go. After twenty minutes the fourteen candidates were lined up.

"Remember the men around you gentlemen. From here on out, the fourteen of you are pledges of Omicron Class, you exist as one. You will all join this fraternity as one Pledge class, or not at all. Look to your left and look to your right, remember the order you were placed in. For every Brotherhood and Education assemble in this order," Gabriel told them.

Troy was the guy in front of Virgil. A short stocky guy, with thick curly black hair and small beady dark eyes. Hector stood behind Virgil. He was in his late 20s, tall with glasses.

"Let's head out," Gabriel called out. The brothers stepped down off the amphitheater walked swiftly westward, candidates following closely. They walked across campus heading in the direction of Greek housing, and the forest that surrounded the small university. Once the paved path at the edge of campus ended, they headed towards the tree line of the woods. They slowed down and came to a stop once they reached the first few trees. Jagger stepped forward with long black strips of cloth handing them out to the pledges. The brothers came down the line testing the candidates making sure the blindfolds were securely in place.

"Don't worry your pretty little heads about being messed with while you have the blindfolds on," Doc barked. "We don't need a reason to fuck with ya," Doc laughed wickedly.

"Enough," Gabriel told the brothers. Then he spoke to Virgil and the others, "Omicron turn and face the candidate who is ahead of you in line and place your right hand on his shoulder," Virgil turned forward and found Troy, he held firmly onto his shoulder. Hector slapped his large meaty arm down on Virgil's back. "From this night on I will be your Hegemon, the new member educator," Gabriel told them. "I will lead you tonight and throughout this process, let MY voice give YOU direction," Gabriel told them. "Communication is key here people. Keep up the pace, don't be the one guy that everyone has to drag through this." Gabriel led the group forward and within seconds Virgil was running to keep up with Troy.

The going was rough, and Virgil could barely hang on. Within the first few minutes, Virgil was gagging for air as Hector almost choked the life out of him. Then they lost contact.

"Stop! I can't find the guy in front of me Vir-Vir-Virgil" Hector stuttered out.

"What is the holdup people?!" Gabriel yelled back at them.

"The group got separated," Virgil called out.

"Fix it then," Gabriel barked.

"Hector, where are you?" Virgil called out into the darkness.

"Over here," Hector replied from somewhere behind him.

"Follow my voice! Come on man, you got this, just keep walking towards me, where are you?" Virgil called out until he felt a hand grab his right shoulder firmly.

"Alright we're good!" Virgil yelled.

They began their journey once more. The woods were slowly getting thicker. Virgil heard the guys in front of him yelling warnings, helping the people behind them make it through.

"There's a small creek up ahead!" he heard one of the candidates ahead of him shout. Seconds later his shoes were soaking wet stumbling through a creek, and his mood was taking a nosedive. How much further is this place? As he was thinking he didn't notice Troy had stopped walking and Virgil walked right into him.

"What in the hell is going on back there?" Gabriel shouted from the front.

"Come on guys let's get our shit together, we're looking like pussies out here! The people who keep messing up need to shape up or ship out," Virgil heard one of the candidates ahead of him say, probably Dante.

"Aidan where are you?" someone ahead of him called out.

"Over here man just follow my voice Luther, over here dude," Aidan responded back.

"We need to slow down," someone behind Virgil called out, sounded like the big Asian.

"That's it!" yelled Gabriel, "We are NOT slowing down! You need to communicate. Teamwork and communication are two key aspects of this Brotherhood. Now grab the guy in front of you and DON'T let go, we aren't making any more stops," Gabriel cut across with no room for any dissension.

The next several minutes were intense, and just when Virgil felt like it was too much, they stopped for good. "You can all take your blindfolds off," Jagger told them. Virgil looked around, his eyes adjusting to the near darkness that made up the night wood. The trees had thinned down and ahead was a clearing deep in the woods.

Gabriel walked to stand in front of the pledges gaining their undivided attention. An excited energy coursed through their veins like a high from a drug. "We're here," Gabriel announced with a grin. "Take these few moments to silently reflect on your decision to join. Jagger our Pylortes, will wait with you."

Gabriel left and it was just Jagger and the candidates waiting on the outskirts of a clearing. The time crawled by at an agonizing pace. He wanted to speak with the guys at his shoulders. Shadows blotted out the moonlight filtering down through the trees above. Virgil and the others looked up, people were flying overhead, with large wings on their backs. What was going on?

"Alright they are ready for you," Jagger said leading them out to the clearing.

Chapter 3
<u>The Oath of the Paladin</u>

Jagger led the candidates out from the cover of the woods. All fourteen candidates gasped as they stared unbelieving. Most of the brothers were standing inside a strange stone temple that lacked a roof, with four elegantly chiseled stone archway entrances. The rest were flying above the candidates' heads, dazzling white wings expanding from their backs. Virgil couldn't believe what he was seeing, beautiful and breathtaking, the wings looked surreal. As they flew sparkling blue dust fell from their feathers streaking through the air behind them, quickly fading into the night.

The men flying through the night sky laughed whole heartedly doing flips, and dancing through the sky with grace. Magnus, the President, dived for the candidates, and they had to break out of their line to avoid getting knocked over. He laughed and beat his white wings ascending back into the air going to the stone temple.

"Show offs," mumbled Jagger.

"What in the hell is going on!?" Louie exclaimed. "Are you guys seeing this!"

"How do they conceal their wings?" Virgil asked.

"Quiet!" Jagger grumbled out to Virgil.

The winged men landed outside the stone temple, entering through the northern entrance. The stone structure radiated an air of ancient power. Virgil could feel the hairs standing up on the back of his neck as he approached. The temple was indented downwards, descending stone steps past dozens of stone benches which outlined the whole structure. At the bottom lay a large open space with a large raised platform in the middle, with a stone archway, and a small table. Most of the brothers had taken seats on the benches towards the bottom. Three brothers stood on the platform in the middle, Magnus, Gabriel and a guy with sandy blonde hair, Tarek Jeter. They wore silver robes, white wings on their backs. Three large basins were on the platform filled with fire that lit up the area.

"This is nuts, this is crazy!" Louie babbled enough for the whole class.

"Louie so help me," Jagger threatened through clenched teeth silencing him.

The candidates walked through the arch in single file, headed down the steps to the bottom, and lined up in front of the raised platform. The stone was withered with age. The ground they stood on felt like the center of a power grid. Various symbols and glyphs glowed faintly in the stone. Of the brothers seated towards the bottom on the benches, less than ten had wings tucked on their backs. Maybe not everyone had them?

The table in the middle of the platform was marble, sanded down until anyone could see their reflection in it. On the table was a ritual book, and a chalice at the head of the marble table. It was silver and filled with a golden fluid that cast rays of light up from the cup. Lastly there were fourteen blue gemstones, attached to chains, the gemstones were about the size of a fist.

"Jagger, will you close the circle?" Gabriel asked. Jagger traced lines through the air creating a strange symbol. CRACK! A loud rumble shook the air and echoed throughout the temple as if someone had shot a gun. Virgil saw a faint white wall of energy enclosing the stone. It seemed to shimmer than it faded into the night.

"Now that the circle is closed, we may speak freely and no one outside of this temple can hear us," said Gabriel his voice becoming more relaxed.

"The history of our fraternity is a tale that takes us to the beginning of time," Magnus began. "There were three great sentient races, the Eldest and first born, the Eidolons, they created the physical manifestation of all the worlds. Judges, referred to as Angels by man, were the second born, created to bring order into the universe. They tamed the worlds the Eidolons had brought into existence and an era of prosperity ensued. The third race was the Fey, or sidhe Fairies, more like gods compared to humans, they were descended from Eidolons."

"With the creation of humans brought conflict to the three great races," Magnus told them. "There was an evil entity that used this conflict to his advantage, he tricked Eidolons, Judges, and Fairies into betraying the Creator and they revolted in the most gruesome battle ever to take place in time. The Battle of the Fallen, is what it came to be known as. Those that lost were cast down into the depths of the Fairies home world, the Ever After. Judges that had betrayed their Creator had their wings ripped from their backs, forever known as Fallen. The worlds were sealed from each other with a great barrier, the Greater Weirding, with a single Tear from the Creator. This is the lost history of our world."

"The forces of Chaos are gathering in the Ever After, led by four powerful Fallen Judges, called God Generals. It is said that when seven prophesized Seraphim Nephilim, called Seraphs, are born unto Earth, they will signal the coming of Ragnarok, the end of our world." Magnus said speaking slowly and methodically as if he was reciting this speech from a text.

"This is where we come into the tale," Gabriel said taking over the story, "The forces of Chaos are made up of the Fallen and legions of demon, but they needed more warriors. They turned to us, their children. Offspring of mortals and Judges, often called Judge Spawn, or halflings, but Nephilim is what we have come to call our own race. The Fallen began to scoop up all the Nephilim in the world turning them over to their side, this was the birth of the Death Dealers. The Death Dealers were united by a powerful warrior, who wielded the legendary Chaos Devil Arms, Soul Reaver. Under his cruel leadership, the Death Dealers became a military force of Nephilim that specializes in killing all innocent life," Gabriel's tone was solemn.

Gabriel continued, "When most Nephilim on Earth had gone over to the enemy's side, the Judges left in the Nirvana realized their mistake. They had neglected their mortal children for too long. A host of Judges came down to Earth, to a small group of Nephilim who had banded together against the Death Dealers. The Judges brought with them a chalice given to these Nephilim as a gift. They formed a covenant with those Nephilim, pledging an alliance and recognizing them as their own race, and protectors of humanity. They were given Dreamstones, powerful gems with magical energy inside, called magicite, to cloak their auras from demons. To seal the newfound covenant the Judges produced the Chalice of Immortals. They slashed their wrists and immortal blood, golden fluid called the golden ichor, filled the cup, which the Nephilim drank and awoke to their newfound powers. The first Paladins were born that day, a force to combat the Death Dealers. The Paladins quickly grew into more than a military force, they became a civilization. It has prospered and exists to this day," Gabriel explained excitedly.

Tarek Jeter spoke next, "This tale continues with the fourteen of you. Tonight, we reenact that ritual that the first Paladins underwent many millennia ago. We offer you the strength of the Judges to reach your full potential as Nephilim, and if you accept you will become fledging Paladins, and pledges in our fraternity. The heritage of Omega is thus, a fraternity belonging to the order of Paladins, an order that has existed thousands of years. All of you have been chosen because each of you carry, however large or small, trace amounts of celestial blood running through your veins," Tarek told them.

The guy sitting next to Virgil, Troy, raised his hand. Gabriel nodded that he could speak. "I don't understand why I'm here, my parents aren't angel warriors or whatever you call it. I think you picked the wrong guy," he said meekly.

"That is the funny thing about Nephilim," Magnus said, "Sometimes they go generations before one of their descendants discovers others of their kind," he explained. "You are all here for your own various reasons but deep within all of you there is potential, more than you've ever known. You have the potential to be more than human, more than mortal," his voice enticing the idea.

Dante raised his hand and spoke next, "How are a group of normal college guys going to fit in to all of this? I thought we were joining a fraternity that was about Brotherhood, and now you tell us this whole other stuff. It's a lot to take in," Dante said crossing his arms over his chest.

Gabriel chuckled locking eyes with Dante, "I understand your disbelief, trust me when I say I know how you feel. Two years ago, I was seated where you are now, listening to the same story, and feeling the same distrust for what I was hearing. Since ancient times Paladins have existed together with humans, creating their own place in this world for themselves. Paladins have worked tirelessly throughout time to recruit Nephilim to their ranks, but it is not always easy to find us. Most Nephilim's powers don't manifest until the age of eighteen. Fraternities were first created by Paladins as a recruitment strategy. Our fraternity along with a handful of others are Paladin organizations, our fraternities all funnel into the same order. Though our fraternity is unique from the others," Gabriel said.

Magnus spoke next, "Fraternities could only be joined if you had money or came from a well-known family. Omega's founding fathers wanted to be part of an organization that didn't judge someone for their wealth, or honor, but on personal merit and character."

Virgil had a question and he was called on next, "What about the Betas? Are they part of the Paladins as well?"

"They are," Gabriel replied looking like he wished they weren't. "The birth of the Greek societies was a chance for Paladins to recruit how they saw best. Beta and Omega are two of ten Greek fraternities and sororities that belong to the Paladins. Each has their own principles and ideals that their founding group felt was important."

"No matter how off the Betas may seem, they stand with us against the Death Dealers. We have an alliance with them and it is best to keep it that way," Gabriel said in a matter of fact tone.

"We have talked long enough," Magnus said at last, "It is time to take the Oath of the Paladin."

They were led to the center stage, and the light from the fires died down. "Candidates you are about to take the Oath of the Paladin, the first step to becoming a brother of Omega," Gabriel said. "Take this moment to reflect on the truths we have told you, let the weight of this knowledge rest in your mind," Gabriel became silent letting each reflect on what they'd been told.

"We are gathered here, fraters of the Upsilon Delta Chapter of the Omegas, to induct fourteen candidates into our Brotherhood," Tarek Jeter spoke loudly his voice booming out to the group, "They come to us as men, but they will leave us… as Paladins. May the blessings of the Judges shine down upon us, as we guide these men into their new lives." Tarek Jeter spoke.

"There are twenty-two symbols that make up the angelic alphabet, all our magic and power flows from the language of Creation formed by these runes," Magnus said. "This rune will bring out your Devil Arms and inner celestial abilities."

"This process will not make you something that you are not. The spell only brings out the full potential that already exists within yourselves." Tarek Jeter explained.

"Please say I, give your full name, and repeat after me," Gabriel commanded.

"I, Virgil Pitcher," Virgil said in chorus with the other candidates.

"Accept the challenge of becoming a pledge for the Upsilon Delta Chapter of the Omegas," Gabriel said, and the candidates repeated. "I promise to strive to develop my abilities and contribute them to the Chapter. To develop as a man, and as a warrior, striving to become the best that I can be."

"These are the triple obligations of every Paladin," Gabriel said, "Repeat after me. I promise to protect humanity, to guide it from self-destruction, and the temptations of Chaos. I promise to fight against the evil that is the Demonic Horde, and all who pledge their allegiance to the Demon King, Diablos. And lastly, I promise to protect our brothers in arms, our fellow Nephilim, recruit them to our cause, and train them in the ways of our people," Gabriel recited, and they repeated.

"It is time for the Big Brother's to take their oaths. Big Brothers say I, state your name and repeat after me," Gabriel said. Brothers had come up on stage and lined up behind the candidates. Virgil heard his Big Brother speak behind him but lost his name in the sea of voices that rang out.

"I accept the responsibility of being your Big Brother," Gabriel read, and they repeated. "I will strive to show you true Brotherhood, and work to assist you in becoming a frater in the bond. Through our relationship I hope to exemplify the characteristics, that you need to develop better morally, mentally, and socially in becoming a true gentleman. My wish is that I can be a true friend to you, and that we may grow together, as fellow fraters in the bond, for life."

"Now for the final part, the Prytanis will administer the mark of the Paladin, and the Hypophetes will bring the chalice for each of you to drink from." Gabriel explained. Magnus picked up the dagger off the table, Tarek picked up the silver cup.

They went down the line. Magnus traced a symbol with the dagger on each of the candidates' primary hands, and when he was done a glowing golden character was left written as if in ink. When he got to Virgil, he gave Magnus his right hand, watching as the dagger was used to lightly trace a symbol on the top of his hand. The rune was about the size of a half dollar and glowed with a gold light. It had bold straight lines and one large sweeping arch connecting it together. When Magnus was finished Virgil's skin felt hot instantly, his throat was dry, he needed a drink. Tarek stepped up once Magnus moved on, offering the cup to Virgil, raising it to his mouth. A golden fluid swirled in the cup, lighting up his whole face with rays of light as he looked down into it. Was this safe to drink? Virgil hesitated but the others in the line had done so, and Tarek was waiting on him.

The moment Virgil swallowed the golden fluid he felt change spread through his whole body. Like he'd spent his life only half awake, and anything he had felt or sensed before was through a hazy veil that had suddenly been ripped off. His senses were sharp, his muscles on fire and ready to spring into action. He was alert, taut like a spring ready to snap. Virgil had never felt more alive or more in tune with his own body. He felt like he'd ran a marathon, and his body was ready for the next one. Once Tarek had taken the chalice to all the candidates Gabriel spoke again coming around with the blue gemstones on long chains. He gave one to each candidate putting them around their necks.

"Keep these with you at all times. No brother is allowed to touch them, except for your Big! They will help conceal your auras and protect you from being seen by unwanted things,"

Gabriel told them. "Through the next six weeks you will learn to work as one, all of you are now Omicron class. Be careful and most importantly look out for the brother standing next to you."

"Candidates, turn around and be welcomed by your Big Brothers!" Magnus shouted.

The candidates turned around and were embraced by their Big Brothers. A chorus of cheers sounded out and the rest of the brothers stormed the platform. Virgil was lost in the sea of new faces as brother after brother shook his hand, gave him rib cracking bear hugs, and welcomed him to the group. The formality of the situation had ended, now the brothers seemed as relaxed as they had been at their party and at Rush. A burst of overzealous enthusiasm spread through the group infecting every man in the temple.

Vahn was Virgil's Big. He threw his arm around Virgil giving him a short hug then let go asking him, "How you feeling Lil Bro?"

"I feel amazing!" Virgil said overwhelmed by everything he was processing. Vahn was one of the few brothers Virgil recognized, he was looking forward to getting to know him.

"What the!" Dante exclaimed. The candidates let out astonished yells of surprise looking down at their hands. Every one of them had gained symbols on their hands. They looked like tribal art tattoos. They were ruby red and golden brown symbols, the Asian guy with the red Mohawk, Louie, had blue symbols on both of his hands! Tarek had a similar colored glyph on his left hand. The symbols were in shapes of weapons, some looked like swords or spears, some weren't so obvious as to what the symbol was supposed to be. Looking around it was clear EVERY man there had a symbol on their hand. Virgil looked down at his own hands. They were devoid of any vibrant colored markings.

"What the hell is going on!?" Louie said getting upset. He started rubbing at the symbols on his hands, but they weren't going anywhere.

"Relax man," a stocky wispy blond-haired man said standing next to him, his Big Brother. "It's a Devil Arms, we all got one."

"What the heck are these for? This doesn't make any sense," Dante's tall dark-haired roommate, Alec, said beside him.

"Dude what part of this night makes any sense at all?" Dante replied with a nervous laugh. "Things just keep getting weirder and no one's doing any explaining, it's really starting to piss me off."

"Everyone calm down," Gabriel told the candidates drawing their attention. "Every one of you is Nephilim, if you didn't have the blood already inside you, those symbols wouldn't have appeared. Nephilim are gifted with the Devil Arms, soul weapons, that are unique to every person. They are a reflection of your spirit, your soul. Devil Arms are aligned to one specific element, you can tell by the color of the symbol. Golden brown for Earth, ruby red for Fire, amethyst for Wind, and aquamarine for Water. Nephilim are also able to use spells, limited in only being able to use spells of the element they are aligned to. In time we'll teach all of you how to use your Devil Arms. They will look something like this," Gabriel raised his right hand, there was a golden brown symbol on it. "LionsHeart!" he yelled and from his symbol light flourished forming into a magnificent long sword, more real and more dazzling then any weapon Virgil had ever seen. Yelps and cries of surprise came from the candidates.

"In time each of you will be able to draw on your own unique weapons, your symbols on your hands are the seat of your powers," Magnus told them. Gabriel swung his sword a couple times, showing off, then it disappeared in a flash of yellow light. Virgil's mouth was still open, Vahn elbowed him with a smirk on his face. Virgil sheepishly closed his mouth.

"I don't have any," Virgil said speaking up. The attention of the group turned to him. Everyone had colored symbols on their hands, except for Virgil.

"Virgil how old are you?" Magnus asked him.

"Seventeen," Virgil said.

"Most Nephilim don't get their Devil Arms until they are eighteen," Magnus suggested, "When's your birthday?"

"Monday," Virgil told them.

"Sunday night at midnight, you should get your Devil Arms bud," Gabriel told him. "Funny coincidence that's our first Education. Don't worry about it till then."

"Question," Nolan, a candidate, said speaking up, "How long have all of you had those symbols on your hands?" he asked. The rest of Omicron class realized every brother had symbols on their hands, something Virgil had seen the whole time.

"We've had these the whole time, don't worry about people seeing your Devil Arms, none of your family or friends will see them, unless they are Nephilim. Normal people can't see past their own auras, and therefore are blind to all this extra stuff going on in the world around them," Gabriel explained. "Now enough of this serious crap for one night!" Gabriel shook his head. "Who wants to get some food!" He shouted out excited. "Come on Lil," Gabriel grabbed Aidan and started to talk privately to his Little Brother.

"Ohh man!" Louie said cracking up, "I'm totally starving dude!" and the men erupted into laughter.

"Let's hit up Denny's!" one brother shouted.

"No B-Dubs!" another argued. "I'm tired of always going to Denny's."

The group made their way out of the stone structure and towards the fraternity house. The brothers leading the way. The brothers with wings retracted them into their backs, the wings disappearing like they never existed.

"What do you like to do for fun man?" Vahn asked Virgil as they walked back.

"I like to hang out with friends, go on random outings and trips, play video games, read, all the usual stuff," Virgil replied.

"That's cool, so you like reading?" Vahn asked him.

"Yeah when I have time for it, which hasn't been lately now that I'm at college," Virgil added.

"I hear you on that. I'm an English major so I'm constantly reading crap I don't care about, and then typing up papers on that same crap. It takes the fun out of it," Vahn shrugged.

The group made their way back to the house and drove out to Denny's in Saginaw. Apparently, it was a tradition to go there after candidate induction. Virgil sat with Vahn and a few other people he didn't know. He had a hard time jumping into conversations because the brothers had such strong rapport. Their conversations always seemed to be about things he knew little about. All the brothers were dying to learn more about the candidates though, so people were constantly asking Virgil questions about himself. He felt a little shy with all the attention.

Boyd came over and sat down next to them for a minute. He gave Virgil a smile then slapped hands with Vahn, "What's up man?" Boyd asked.

"Nothing much, just getting to know my Lil," Vahn said.

"This kid here?" Boyd interjected. "Yeah he's alright once you get past his stubborn attitude, and his whiny ass, every time he doesn't get his own way, attitude."

"Yeah right," Virgil said giving him a shove off the booth.

"What do you think of this fraternity?" Boyd asked cutting to the point. He got up and sat back down.

"Me?" Vahn asked Boyd.

"Yeah," Boyd said, "I have a lot on my mind right now and I want to know how one of its own members feel. If you could do it over again would you? Is all this worth it?"

"Would I do pledging over again? In a heartbeat," Vahn said, "Pledging is one of the hardest, busiest, most hectic, and stressful time of your life while you're at college. I'm not exaggerating that either."

"If it is so bad then why do it?" Boyd asked.

"I didn't say it was bad, I said it was hard," Vahn corrected him. "Nothing worth doing is ever easy guys, you have to earn the right to be called a brother. It is one of the most sacred rights that all the brothers here value. Every day of your life while pledging you will have something to do for us. You literally eat, sleep, study, and hang out with us. There is nothing else. However my memories of that time, are fresh upon my mind, and it was some of the most fun I've ever had. It's when I met my best friends, we went through a lot together but in the end the hard times brought us together and we united as one," he said starring across the table.

Virgil and Boyd stared across the table at Gabriel and Magnus who were busy chatting with their own Little Brothers now that their order was placed.

"Gabriel and Magnus," Virgil said, "Were they your…?"

"Pledge Brothers," Vahn added nodding. "We're Lambda class."

"LAMBDA!" The small guy, Landon, yelled from across the table throwing out an upside down peace sign with his index and middle finger.

"What does that mean?" Virgil asked.

"That's the sign for Lambda, we throw up that sign to signal that we're pledge brothers. You have your own symbol too, you're Omicron class so that's an O or a circle," Vahn said. "It's Greek man."

"So what do we have to do as a pledge?" Virgil asked curious to know more. "Do we have to steal girl's panties or go on scavenger hunts?"

Vahn laughed at that, "What?" he said not able to keep a straight face. "What movies have you been watching? Fraternities aren't like the media portrays them. Most fraternities have upstanding members that later on go to be the leaders in the world. Some Presidents of the United States have been in fraternities. You think we could create leaders just by having you do illegal and juvenile stunts? Fraternities are about values and finding sterling men who possess the same values by which we can live our lives."

Virgil relaxed as they ate and talked, he watched the others, laughing and joking with one another. The atmosphere was fun-loving, humorous and filled with excitement. Virgil laughed as a big African-American brother named Jamal spat out his drink. Brody had poured half a bottle of salt in when he wasn't looking. Reece shot spit-wads at people, trying to get them in to other brothers' drinks. Jamal complained at the end of the table ranting 'That's not cool dude!' his voice so loud Virgil was sure everyone in the restaurant could hear him. Magnus seemed to be making bets with different people around the table discussing sports and the fraternity interchangeably. They debated how well teams were going to do this season of football and things about the Omegas that didn't make much sense to him at the time.

Gabriel started to tease Vahn. "Come on man just admit it. You have a thing for MILF's," Gabriel chided Vahn with a large grin.

"I don't so stop saying that! Point of information I found out she had a kid after we were already sleeping together," Vahn said.

"How old is your son?" Jace, a big guy with glasses, said seated down a little from them.

"I don't have a kid!" He's HER son not mine," Vahn said.

"Are you guys still dating? What's your girlfriend's name?" Virgil asked his Big Brother interested in the conversation.

"Ah!" Vahn exclaimed getting a few chuckles from his friends. "Virgil I DO NOT have a girlfriend. I was seeing this chick over the summer but she broke it off before it went anywhere," he said to Virgil. "And for your information I happened to love that kid, he was freaking adorable," he said to Jace.

Virgil got stuffed fast and the other brothers got their fill as well. Soon everyone was done. Virgil thought the brothers were a pretty rowdy group of guys. Some of them had great senses of humor. They liked to joke around and rag on each other but what they said was never tainted with malicious intent. Everyone seemed to genuinely care about one another.

"You okay?" Vahn asked him.

"Well," Virgil didn't know how to phrase it, "Just watching all of you, it's like you guys have been friends for a long time. But you guys can't have known each other that long, right? Maybe I'm just rambling."

"No your fine man. Don't sweat it, I think I know what you're getting at though," Vahn said, "I've heard it put best as this, 'Looking in you'll never understand, Looking out you'll never be able to explain…welcome to Omega.' I can't describe to you or explain how all of us are as close as we are. It is part of our bond, the bond of this fraternity. It changes people, it brings out the best in people, being your brother's keeper and looking out for his best interests as your own. Doing what we do, you quickly get to know the real people behind the charade that everyone carries, and once you see them, I mean really see them, that is when it just kind of happens," Vahn grinned.

"When what happens" Virgil asked arching an eyebrow?

"Love," Gabriel said interrupting them. Virgil and Vahn both turned to look at Gabriel who was a few places down. "It creeps up on you slowly, day by day, living together, hanging out together, partying together, pledging together, and protecting each other, knowing you have his back and he's got yours. It is an overwhelming feeling that comes with time, wild and reckless, it is an emotion of passion."

"Passion...owowwo" Boyd said, "That sounds kind of gay."

"Not at all," Gabriel said, "How do you think you would feel if you saw a five-ton demon the size of a lion coming at your best friend or maybe your mother? How do you think you would feel? That anger and enragement from the demon trying to take from you is pure passion."

"That makes sense," Virgil said, "Everyone here just seems so...close."

"We are close," Vahn said.

"We are a family. Don't you remember me telling you that Sunday night?" Gabriel said.

"I guess, I didn't realize how serious you were," Virgil replied.

"Alright everyone listen up!" Gabriel's voice rising, everyone went quiet. "Pledges, you are to be at the Omega house on Sunday at ten pm sharp. Make sure you bring your Dreamstones, they aren't to be removed, ever! You got that! I want every one of you to wear those under your inner most shirt. Do not show them to people. Until Sunday you are free to do as you wish. Come Sunday night I will be your Hegemon, and my word will be law for the next six weeks. Bigs take your Lils back to their dorms!"

Chapter 4
<u>Education</u>

Virgil woke in the morning covered in sweat, feeling like he hadn't slept at all. He was

Nephilim, though he hadn't gotten his Devil Arms yet. Virgil always wondered about his

biological parents. Was an Angel or Judge his father? He decided not to dwell on it, or he'd end

up driving himself crazy. He lost himself in his studies that week. Virgil went to Caseville for the

weekend to be with his mom, Sue, because it was his birthday on Monday. They celebrated just

the two of them, going out to dinner, and enjoying each other's company. Virgil didn't tell her

what he'd found out about himself. He didn't know if his mom would believe him. Sunday

evening Virgil started the hour drive back to campus. The pledging process started at 10pm.

Virgil and Boyd rode over to the Omega house together. The property reminded Virgil of a state

building. They hurried into the mansion's large foyer. The other candidates were standing in the

entryway as well.

"Welcome back gentlemen I'm glad you came," Gabriel said coming down the stairs into

the massive foyer. The decorations were elegant but simplistic, trophy cases were scattered

around the house, old guns and knives were displayed, and pictures of brothers filled the walls.

The pictures were of brothers laughing, at the beach, doing community service, and composites

where the whole fraternity was dressed up and placed in one giant photograph. The house was

painted a soft red with a tasteful gold trim.

Gabriel shook each of their hands and led them on a short tour around the fraternity

house. The second floor held the meeting room, the house library and study area, as well as the

pledge dorms, for use by candidates and guests. The third, fourth, and fifth floors were rooms for the brothers and the sixth floor was used by the Chapter Advisors along with a few fancy guest rooms for high ranking guests. They ended the tour coming back down to the second-floor meeting room where Education would be taking place. It was a large room with plenty of long tables and chairs, and a white board at the front of the room. The fourteen candidates took their seats and Gabriel got started.

"This is our Meeting Room. Every Sunday night you are to be in this room by 10pm. I trust you will be able to find your way back," Gabriel said. Gabriel picked up a backpack and briefcase that were leaning against the desk and dumped out an array of things onto the table. He then turned around to face the pledges leaning back against the desk, he had a large grin plastered across his face.

"What's up?" Gabriel said with a chuckle. "Are you guys excited? Scared? Don't piss your pants if you are, it's not going to be that bad. You guys can speak when you have something to say. Educations are just between the Hegemon and candidates, and I want you guys to be comfortable."

Gabriel continued, "First, I'm going to give you a brief overview of what is expected of you as a pledge for the Omegas. Afterwards, we'll put together your pledge manuals. I promise that once we get the manuals completed you can get some sleep, so how soon, or how late you leave is up to all of you."

Gabriel grabbed a stack of white binders distributing them to each of the pledges, then he went to the white board.

"This binder, when we are finished, is your pledge manual. It will ALWAYS stay with you, along with the Dreamstones around your necks. Speaking of which everyone take out your Dreamstones so I can make sure you have them on," Gabriel demanded and Omicron complied.

"It is imperative that you keep them hidden when you are going about your daily business, at Educations and Brotherhoods, you are to wear them outside your clothes," Gabriel explained. "The chains that the Dreamstones rest on have significance, there are twenty-one links in every one of your chains, representing the twenty-one brothers in Alpha class who founded our Chapter."

"What are our pledge binders for?" Dante asked.

"Good question Dante," Gabriel nodded changing topics. "Your pledge binders are your ticket to keeping your sanity these next six weeks, they help keep your lives organized. Inside you will have all the stuff you will need for this pledging process, a copy of your class schedules, and your homework for your classes, so you stay on top on your grades. You can't be an Omega if you're not at college, so keep your grades up guys."

"For the next six weeks I am your judge, jury, and executioner in this fraternity," Gabriel spoke with a stern tone. "I'm in charge of teaching you not only about Omega, and its heritage, but also about the Paladins. If at any time you are overwhelmed, please come to me or your Big Brother, or anyone you feel comfortable around. We are here for you. I'm telling you right now I might seem like a hardass at times, especially tonight. I might become your least favorite brother in this whole fraternity, because I want the best from all of you. Bottom line is, we're all in this together. I am your Hegemon, if any of you need anything I'm a phone call away. I'll be giving you the brothers' phone numbers at the end of the night, and they will have yours, so expect some phone calls Omicron."

"Let's move on. Here are the requirements to be admitted as a brother into Alpha Omega," Gabriel's tone softened, and he went to the board and began writing on it making a list. "You must interview every active brother and take some notes. An interview is something you do in private. It could last from thirty minutes to over an hour, it involves you sitting down with a brother, having a one on one to bond and learn. We pride ourselves on being a close-knit group, and the interviews help us to get to know one another. Secondly, you must come to every Education and every Brotherhood, one hundred percent attendance is mandatory. Educations are on Sunday nights and Brotherhoods are on Tuesday nights. If you miss one mandatory event, you are out, no exceptions."

"You will be required to log study hours with the brothers in this fraternity, so we know that you're not neglecting your schoolwork," Gabriel continued making a list of the requirements on the white board. "Our Hypophetes, Tarek Jeter, holds study sessions on Mondays and Tuesdays from seven to ten pm in the library on the fifth floor. You can go then, or meet up separately with a brother, if you get a signature stating that you studied with them. There are morning runs. We do this to help you guys get into shape. Paladins need to be in top shape for when action hits. You will be required to complete a philanthropy project."

Virgil was busy taking notes quickly feeling overwhelmed.

"Lastly, there will be a final test on week six. I must warn you however, the test is not to be taken lightly. All of you must pass or none of you will get in. All of you are Omicron class," Gabriel said moving his arms across the room motioning to the fourteen candidates. "You will come together as one or fail as individuals."

"Let me break down what an average week of your life is going to entail," Gabriel said writing on the board the seven days of the week starting with Sunday and going to Saturday. He wrote down Education on Sunday night at 10 pm and Brotherhood at 10 pm on Tuesday night. "Monday, Wednesday, and sometimes Friday at 7 am you will all meet outside the Alpha Omega house and go on a two-mile jog," he said adding it to the list.

"You've got to be kidding me!" Louie cried out. Virgil and some of the other pledges looked over at him. Louie was a bigger guy and clearly out of shape, with a gut that hung over his waist, he was Asian with a dark complexion and dark eyes.

"You can't expect us all to run that far, two miles!" Louie exclaimed.

Gabriel turned from the board and looked directly at Louie. "One hundred percent attendance is mandatory. You want to skip one thing, you're out, no discussion." Five minutes later Gabriel's week by week schedule on the white board was packed full. Virgil was getting a headache thinking of how the next week was going to run. He had something to do almost every day!

Louie asked about Brotherhoods, "What goes on exactly?"

"It's a tradition that we get together once a week for family time, run by the Hypophetes," Gabriel said casually. "Doesn't have to be something big, sometimes we play cards or go bowling, as long as we're doing it as a group. But during the Pledging process it is a time to learn the secrets and traditions of our fraternity, so the Hegemon runs Brotherhoods."

"Education should stay your top priority. That is the reason why we're all here, so go to class! Don't be skipping, especially for a brother. They will be calling all of you throughout the week, so answer your phones people!" Gabriel barked. "If they call, I'll expect you to respond, even if it's a text saying, I'm in class can't talk now," Gabriel suggested.

Nolan asked, "What are they going to call us for?"

"Everything and anything man, a brother can ask you to hang out, or go on a random adventure. You get out of this fraternity what you put into it. If you don't put forth the effort and time to be a good brother to others, brothers will not put the time and effort into being good friends with you. Above all else the most important thing to remember is to manage your time wisely," Gabriel explained.

Luther raised his hand.

"Question?" Gabriel asked.

"How are we supposed to find the time to do all this?" Luther asked frustrated.

"That's why your binders are so important," Gabriel stressed. "Time management gentlemen, it's one of the most crucial aspects of any college student."

"This is overwhelming!" Luther cried out throwing his pen down on the table.

"That's why we're here bud," Louie said to Luther, he was sitting in the row in front of Luther and he turned to him. "We are pledge brothers, we are here to support each other," Louie was empathetic and supportive. "I'm overwhelmed too, but we're doing this together! You're not going through this alone."

"Exactly," Gabriel said with enthusiasm, "Your pledge brothers are some of your best resources. Be there for each other, until you join the Omegas you are your own brotherhood. Alright everyone stand up, stretch your legs out," Gabriel sighed looking like he was ready for bed. Virgil and the others stood up cracking some joints and stretching out their cramping muscles. "Now I want all of you to look at the guy on your left," Gabriel said, "then look at the guy on your right." Virgil saw Boyd to his left and Louie to his right.

"Nine times out of ten, the guys standing next to you will be the ones to stand up in your wedding, and someday a long time from now, will be the ones to carry your coffin at your funeral," Gabriel spoke with passion. "Your pledge brothers are typically the brothers you are closest to, I know that is true for me. I'm a Lambda, and be glad you didn't have our Hegemon!

Magnus, Jagger, Vahn, and Landon are honestly the guys I trust most in this fraternity and I would be lost without them."

Gabriel looked at the clock, "Okay making good time, let's get your pledge binders started." The binders were slow and painful. Every time one person messed up, they all ripped out the page they were working on. Gabriel was teaching them unity and demanded that they work as one. After the first couple pages the pledges crowded together, paying more attention to what the guy next to him was doing. The first page had each candidate's name, contact information, and nine goals. Three pledge goals, three fraternal goals, and three personal goals. The second page took even longer than the first, and the third page longer than the second. The second page was a list of the Greek Alphabet, including twenty-four characters, from Alpha to Omega. The third page was the Angelic Alphabet, which threw everyone in the room for a loop. There were twenty-two characters in the Angelic Alphabet starting with a weird U-shaped letter called 'Thes' and ending with a slanted T looking letter called 'Kuff.'

Once both were done Gabriel had them lay down their pens and relax their hands for a minute. "We have a lot of ground to cover, stay with me guys," Gabriel said as they moved on. The next page was the Jeweled Officers, it listed eight Jeweled Officers along with four committee chairs that served on the Executive Board. The Chapter Sweethearts, Ariel and Raven, were listed on the same page as the Chapter advisors. The next part of the binder was making an individual page for every brother in the fraternity, going through the Jeweled Officers first, then from the oldest to the newest brothers. Each brother's page had spots for their information and room to write stuff down for interviews. There were five numbers on each page as well for signatures from the brothers. Everyone in the room turned to see Luther standing up his face flushed with anger as he let out a frustrated scream.

"I can't take this anymore. Do this do that, follow this rule follow that rule, I can't take this!" Luther yelled at the room.

"Calm down buddy," Gabriel gently advised.

"No," Luther said with a snarky tone, "I don't have to listen to you. I don't have to do any of this stuff."

Gabriel's expression became sympathetic, "No you don't."

Luther threw his Dreamstone onto the table and walked out.

"Guys hold tight for a second," Gabriel looked stressed as he chased after him.

It was quiet, for ten seconds, then everyone started talking to the person next to them. Boyd's whispers were more like loud barks, "What do you think Gabriel is going to do to him?"

"I don't know," Virgil replied wanting to keep moving forward.

Boyd spoke to the pledge class drawing in everyone's attention, "Alright if we're all going to be pledge brothers we should start getting to know each other. Obviously we need a leader, no one better suited for that than me," he said proudly standing with one foot on his chair.

Dante smirked letting out a mocking laugh, "You as our leader? I don't think so leprechaun, your brain must be rattled if you think I'd follow you anywhere."

Boyd's face scrunched up in a scowl, "Who are you calling a leprechaun, you aren't much taller than me, ginger!"

"What did you just call me?" Dante asked his voice thick with anger, "Someone shut this kid up before I have to."

At that point Boyd made a move to get up, but Virgil grabbed Boyd while Alec calmed Dante down. "Drop it Dante, he is not worth it," Alec said to his roommate.

"This is stupid," Louie said speaking up, "This is supposed to be a Brotherhood, not who can be the biggest prick. There are no leaders, Gabriel said we are all one," Louie recalled. "We are supposed to be bonding not arguing. One of our pledge brothers just left," Louie looked genuinely concerned.

"You mean that Luther kid? He threw his Dreamstone on the table, he disrespected our letters, our fraternity! And you feel sorry for him?" Dante laughed. "I say good riddance, get rid of any weak links now," he said bluntly crossing his arms and leaning back in his chair.

"Um, first of all, those aren't your letters, we aren't Omegas yet!" Louie responded. "We are trying to get into this fraternity. We are pledges. I want to join this fraternity for Brotherhood and family. What kind of family turns on their own? We are supposed to be pledge brothers, which means we stick together."

"This fraternity is for the elite, only the best get in Louie," Dante sighed as if explaining two plus two to a forty year old. "If this kid wants to quit the very first night how elite is that to you?"

Virgil ignored the new outburst of voices as some agreed with Louie and others defended Dante. He had been trying to ignore the headache that was pounding against his skull, his skin felt on fire ready to burst into flames. He was sweating, and his thoughts were becoming cloudy. Despite the pain in his head he agreed with what Louie said, and felt an immediate kinship towards him. Dante wanted to throw Luther away because he had a moment of weakness. Louie wanted to be forgiving if he came back.

Gabriel came in looking annoyed. "Alright guys listen up," he said to Omicron. "I just talked to Luther and his Big, Zender. Luther's calmed down, and he wants to come back to Education. But this isn't my decision alone. You are Omicron, this is your family. I am leaving the decision to you guys. Either you let Luther back into Omicron, or you don't. I'll give you a few minutes to decide."

Dante stood up addressing the pledge class, "I think I speak for most of us when I say we shouldn't let Luther back in here. He disrespected the fraternity by walking out on us!" He became impassioned, "do you guys want that kind of commitment from him the next six weeks? I want people in this pledge class who care about this."

Louie immediately stood up, "I most certainly do not agree with you Dante, what happened to sticking by family no matter what? We are just starting, and we don't know crap about this fraternity. To say that any of us want this more than the rest is bull. I understand Luther got stressed, to be honest I am too! That is why we need to stick together."

Virgil's headache was moving from painful to unbearable, he regretted not bringing some Tylenol with him. Virgil stood up swaying slightly. "I agree with Louie," Virgil said his voice sounding hoarser than it should have. The guys turned to him listening to what he had to say. "We shouldn't be arguing, we are Omicron. We set the pace for what our group is like for the next six weeks. Will we be known as the class that turned on their own at the first sign of hardships, or will we unite as one?"

"Yeah screw Dante, let's trade him for Luther," Boyd chimed in.

"You little," Dante muttered the rest under his breath.

A few more candidates spoke, it seemed like everyone had reached the same decision, Luther was welcomed back in the group.

"I like what I heard, I will let them know," Gabriel hurried from the room.

Dante spoke up saying, "I hope all of you don't think I hate Luther, I barely know him. I'm just pissed he walked out. We're all stressed out but that's no excuse to quit."

"It is not a good excuse, we aren't perfect, we're only human," Louie pointed out.

"How much of us is human though?" Nolan asked. "The Paladins are Nephilim, part man, part Judge, why do you think they chose us? And that fluid we drank, most likely the blood of a Judge," he told them.

"That ain't even right," Louie said leaning back like he might get sick.

"Are you saying we're not human?" Axel asked, "Because I definitely feel human."

"Guys I think something's wrong with me," Virgil said bile rising in his throat. He felt sick to his stomach, he didn't think he'd be able to keep his dinner down.

"I think we're part human, but to what degree," Nolan asked out loud looking at the amethyst Devil Arms symbol on his right hand that looked like a staff.

Virgil looked at the clock, less than a minute to his birthday! Spasms suddenly rocked his body, pain coursing through his system sending him off his chair to the floor.

"Virgil!" Boyd yelled out coming over to his side.

"Hey guys I think something is wrong with this G," Louie exclaimed pointing to Virgil, sliding away from him. Omicron stopped talking and came to Virgil's side.

"I think we should get Gabriel," Dante suggested.

Alec leaned down next to Virgil, "What's hurting buddy?" he asked.

Virgil's every nerve fiber rippled with a strange burning energy. Louie and Alec helped him to his feet, and his body began to glow a faint gold light like a beacon.

"What's happening to him?" Boyd asked backing away from Virgil's spasming body. Louie and Alec let go, Virgil swayed but did not fall.

"He's Awakening," Nolan said, "Like we did Wednesday night, he's going to get Devil Arms like the rest of us. Virgil was the only one to not have a Devil Arms because he wasn't eighteen."

"What time is it?" Alec asked.

Virgil's phone went off in his pocket, the alarm for his birthday blaring music.

"It's midnight," Nolan said.

White lightning cracked into existence out of the ceiling hitting Virgil square in the chest, lifting him up off the ground in its powerful embrace. Virgil threw back his head as several more bolts of white energy pierced his flesh, letting out the screams that he had struggled to hold. The room and half the mansion became engulfed in blinding light. Virgil's bellowing screams echoed the halls of the Omega house.

Virgil awoke on the floor surrounded by his pledge brothers, Gabriel, and three older men. They were the Chapter Advisors, or Elders as the Paladins called them. "What happened?" he asked disoriented.

"You Awakened into your power Nephilim," one of the three Advisors said. He was an old bald man with a long white beard. He was a professor at the university, friendly, and wise. His name was Professor Ramuh.

"Awakened?" Virgil asked Professor Ramuh.

"It's the term for when a Nephilim's Devil Arms appear," Gabriel added. "Virgil is different from the rest of Omicron, everyone has celestial blood to some degree, but Virgil is a Pureborn Nephilim."

"Pureborn?" Nolan asked, "What does that mean?"

"It means that one of Virgil's biological parents is a Judge," said one of the other Advisors. He had wild red flaming hair that was unkempt with a big moustache. His gaze was not altogether friendly, with dark brown eyes that tore into your thoughts. The room grew rather silent until Virgil felt awkward. He wanted to shrivel up and disappear. The son of an Angel? How is that even possible?

"How do you feel?" The old man with a long white beard and gray eyes like storm clouds asked.

Virgil leaned back, "I feel great actually," surprised at how true his words were. Standing up he realized the burning sensation in his skin has subsided, his skull no longer felt like it would burst. He felt better than normal, the best he'd ever felt.

"Wow look at his hands!" Louie cried out. "He has two symbols like me!"

Virgil put his hands out seeing for the first time his Devil Arms. A black scythe on his left hand, and a white shooting star on his right hand. He was shocked. He'd never seen Devil Arms of these colors among Nephilim at Bay Valley.

"What kind of Devil Arms are those?" Nolan asked.

"Virgil is aligned with Spirit," the third Advisor pointed out. He was handsome, and Gabriel's biological older brother. His name was Ezekiel. He was a young professor at the university. "Spirit is divided into Creation, or light and harmony, and Chaos, or darkness and malevolence. They are two sides of the same power."

"Is it normal to have two different colors?" Virgil asked the Chapter Advisors.

"No," Professor Ramuh admitted. "Sometimes Nephilim are blessed with more than one Devil Arms, but they are always the same alignment. This is a first."

The room was quiet for a moment. "Is the black symbol a bad thing?" Virgil asked what they were all thinking.

"Not necessarily," Professor Ramuh put it politely. "The Devil Arms is wielded by the Nephilim. It is your choice how to use your gifts."

"I recognize the Chaos Devil Arms," Professor Ifrit said. "It's," and then he mouthed the name, but it was silent to Virgil's ears.

"What?" Virgil asked, "I couldn't hear you."

"Until you can learn the name of your weapons for yourselves, even if someone tries to tell you, you won't be able to hear it," Professor Ramuh explained. "Your Hegemon will give you Devil Arms training. Each of you will learn your Devil Arms names in time then you will be able to call them to your side."

"Really?" Gabriel asked Professor Ifrit. "Did someone wield this weapon before him?"

Professor Ifrit laughed, "The most infamous Death Dealer of all time, the founding member, Loiken. He killed thousands of humans and Nephilim alike. Loiken was recruited by the God Generals, to create a military order under their dominion, with him as the Commander. They called them Death Dealers, because Loiken's Devil Arms could burn through people's auras. It was a fearsome weapon of death. Loiken was stopped by the founder of the Paladins, Lady Diamond. She was one of the five Nephilim who were given the Chalice of Immortals by the Judges. Lady Diamond wielded one of the most powerful Devil Arms in history, a staff called Divine Light. She was able to subdue Loiken in a fierce battle to the death, putting an end to his blight upon the land." Professor Ifrit finished with, "You should know Virgil, Loiken was the son of Lucifer, the Commander of the God Generals."

The room got quiet. Am I the son of Lucifer? Virgil thought frantically. Is that why they are all looking at me like I'm dangerous?

"Settle down," Gabriel called the room to order. "Everyone has questions about their Devil Arms, and Paladin stuff right at the beginning. It is too overwhelming to jump in all at once," he said simply. "Tuesday night is our first Devil Arms practice. Everyone will get some basic training, and some of you might get to use them for the first time. Gentlemen thank you for coming," Gabriel dismissed the Chapter Advisors.

"Good luck little brother," Ezekiel said in a baby tone that made Gabriel flush with embarrassment.

The Elders made their exit and the late night winded down to a conclusion. They had to be at the house by 7 am for their first morning run. They headed down the hall to the large sleeping area, a room in the Omega manor set aside for pledges. It was a large open room with rows of bunk beds, and a small living room. A large bathroom that could accommodate the whole group was through a door at the back. Virgil choose a bunk towards the middle preferring the bottom closest to the floor, Boyd got the spot above him. The guys quickly passed out after Education. Everyone had been blown away by the amount of responsibility it was going to take to get through the next thirty-nine days of being a candidate. Virgil stared at the new symbols on his hands until he fell asleep, wondering what kind of weapons his soul would reflect.

Chapter 5
Hooters and Demons

Virgil awoke to a chorus of annoying alarms from everyone's cell phones. The guys shuffled slowly around the room, grunting to one another like zombies, too tired to talk. They'd only been asleep for a few hours, and were about to go on a run, not the best Birthday so far, Virgil thought lacing up his running shoes with a large yawn. He had on some sweatpants with a white t-shirt under a hoodie, the Dreamstone around his neck. The fourteen groggy men made their way from the room and down the hall to the grand staircase in the foyer of the Omega mansion. Gabriel was waiting for them outside. The look around his eyes betrayed his weariness, though he only displayed drive and enthusiasm to his men.

Gabriel talked to them as they stretched. "Being a Paladin, and a brother of this fraternity, sometimes you get put in situations where you have to have strength or speed. Building muscle and stamina is rewarding but it takes a lot of hard work, dedication, and most of all…perseverance. I will set the pace for the runs. We will push harder as the weeks go by, and I expect you guys to keep up. Understood?"

"Sir, yes, sir!" Omicron responded.

"Let's go," Gabriel started jogging for the backyard. They crossed the grounds of the fraternity and came to the forest behind the house, taking the well-worn trail. Gabriel led them on a jog to the clearing with the stone temple. They circled the clearing heading back to the house, the run was around two miles. No one could keep up with Gabriel. He'd speed up if they approached, more machine than man. They weren't sprinting, but Gabriel was making them haul ass. Louie V and Hector were trailing behind.

"Pick up the pace, we're almost there!" Gabriel called back annoyed.

Virgil was at the head of the pack with Alec, Aidan, Dante and Darius, he'd always been one of the fastest runners. Virgil dropped back, running alongside Louie. "Come on Louie you can do this," Virgil encouraged him. "We're almost there, just push through it the rest of the way Louie! The faster you make it to the house, the sooner you can stop for good," Virgil said between breaths.

Louie was drenched with sweat, and pain was clearly etched across his face, "I'm not made for this shit man!" his exasperated tone indicating he was tired. They reached the Omega house panting and gasping for air.

"Thanks a lot guys. I appreciate your effort this morning," Gabriel spoke just as winded. "Everyone get something to drink, and get your days started. Go to class, and hit up the brothers for interviews," Gabriel dismissed them.

Virgil drudged through his classes, then went back to his dorm to relax. He looked through his pledge binder, and the Omega guide, a guide to the fraternity and the Paladins. He flipped through it for a few minutes, it was well over three hundred pages, and had an overwhelming wealth of information. It talked a lot in the beginning about what the fraternity Omega stood for, its history, and had a list of famous alumni.

The Omega binder brought back memories from last night. He looked through the pages coming to the brothers' section. The oldest members were closer to the front while the newest classes were at the back. The class right before Omicron was Xi. They had only three members, and it had been Gabriel's first pledge class, initiated in April. The candidates were expected to integrate themselves into the brotherhood, which meant bonding with the brothers.

Virgil called Doc from Nu class, it was easy striking up a conversation with him. Virgil went to the gym meeting up with the loud and colorful Gareth, aka Doc. He was a Caucasian man with a shaved head, dark eyes, and a soul patch on his chin. They hit the weight room, spending an hour at the gym. They began to get comfortable with one another. Doc told him small things about himself as they got through their reps, like how he grew up in Macomb County. He loved it there, bigger and busier than Bay City, more to do, more to see. Doc was nineteen years old and had several younger siblings, who lived with their single mother.

"My mom had raised me and made me the man I am. I have a lot of respect for her," Doc said. He didn't talk much about his dad, just something about him being a Nephilim. The Omega's saw him for what he was with the Dreamstone rings they wore.

After they were finished at the gym Virgil was sweaty, so he parted ways with Doc to head back to his dorm to shower and change back into warmer clothes. He got a call on his short drive to the Omega house.

His mother's enthusiastic voice rang out, "Happy Birthday!" Virgil laughed.

"It is great to hear from you!" Virgil told her feeling appreciated. They talked for a few minutes, briefly catching up. He got off the phone when he arrived at the Omega house. He held onto the steering wheel after shutting off the blazer.

It was hard for Virgil not to stare at the white and black symbols on his hands, as real as any tattoo, but more permanent. The Devil Arms that he had gained at midnight were still very out of place for him. The brothers had only one symbol on their hands, except Louie. Nephilim are almost never born with two. The black symbol on his left hand frightened him. It was like finding out a deep ugly truth about yourself, a daunting task to face. Nephilim with black Devil Arms almost always go bad they say, the allure of power all corrupting. A black sickle shape on his left hand, and a white shooting star on his right hand. He didn't know either of their names, which was something he was supposed to figure out on his own.

Virgil walked inside, going to Doc's room on the third floor.

"Tell me Doc, why did you join the Omegas?" Virgil asked once they were comfortable.

"Listen up and write this down, the questions you should ask every brother: Why the Omegas? What does Brotherhood mean to you? And lastly, but most important, what is your Devil Arms? Those three questions will tell you a lot about a brother's personality, and who they are as a person," Doc said.

Virgil quickly wrote all of them down. "Alright then," Virgil asked, "Why the Omegas?" he asked again.

"In high school I was really big into sports, football, basketball, and all that jazz," Doc talked with a relaxed demeanor explaining his past. "When I came to college, I wanted that same kind of feeling, that closeness you have with your best buds. I kind of stumbled upon the Greek system, and something about the Omegas just seemed to click with me. I pledged and became a brother, and the rest is all good from there."

"What does Brotherhood mean to you?" Virgil asked.

"Brotherhood is something more than some cheap talk that a 'frat' guy uses to explain his group," Doc explained with passion. "To me Brotherhood is knowing that no matter what the situation, normal or all hells crazy, your brother is standing right beside you. He won't leave your side, not until his very last breath. I would do anything for one of my brothers, they are my family. Becoming a part of this fraternity, the Omegas, it is like finding your place in the world that you'd always knew was out there but until then, had never known," Doc spoke from the heart. His eyes grew misty and for the first time since they'd talked Virgil could see something besides the big tool that he masqueraded as, something very raw and real. He respected the man he saw in that moment. "This fraternity made me into the man I am today," Doc shrugged. "It gave me more than I could ever give back."

"You've been in the fraternity for a whole year, right? I'm sure you've seen some demons," Virgil asked switching gears, "or maybe you've gotten into some battles, what are they like?"

Doc was silent for a few moments. Virgil remained mute respecting the quiet between the two men. Doc's face was very still, his eyes staring at something off in the distance before he spoke, "I've seen a lot of things in the past year, some things I wish I hadn't. And yeah, I have seen demons, lots of them, that's what we do in this fraternity. We patrol the streets at night taking down the rogue ones, monitoring their progress, and making tactical strikes on large groups."

Virgil looked at Doc's golden-brown Devil Arms a few times, he'd been meaning to ask and now felt like the right time. "What is your Devil Arms?" he asked pointing to Doc's hand.

Doc smiled a big grin, he was proud. "My Devil Arms is an axe. It is small and easy to throw, aligned with Earth, which you can tell by the color," he said pointing to his hand. "Its name is Jagged Edge," he told Virgil and the symbol lit up slightly at the sound of its name.

They talked for over an hour more, and once they'd finished Virgil left his room heading back to his car. He bumped into a tall, large man on the way to the stairs.

"Yo what's up small fry!" Lamar said to him in a booming voice. "What are you doing here?"

"Just got done with an interview with Doc," Virgil told him.

"Doc's my pledge brother, good guy," Lamar nodded. "Where you headed to?" he asked.

"Back to campus," Virgil said.

"No, no, no," Lamar said draping his arm around Virgil, turning him around back down the hall. "Let's get our interview done while you're here," Lamar told him, not taking no for an answer.

Lamar was tall, with a large belly, a rectangular face, and small dark eyes. He had dark curly hair he kept short. Lamar was a friendly guy, who loved to laugh. He had a booming voice, recognizable a house away. Lamar was very much into sports and he talked about that for a while. Lamar had a golden-brown Devil Arms symbol. He told Virgil his Devil Arms was a large hammer.

"What does Brotherhood mean to you?" Virgil asked, once he had the opportunity.

"I like that question. To me brotherhood is calling up your bro going over to his house and shooting the shit with him, drinking a beer, watching TV, just hanging out," Lamar said. "There are a bunch of guys that I could just list off that I could call anytime, anywhere, and in a heartbeat he would be there for me even if it was to just hang out and see how I'd been doing. Being able to just be friends with people, true and honest friendship, that's what brotherhood is."

After they were finished Virgil and Lamar headed toward the first floor, when they got to the grand staircase a crowd of people shouted,

"SURPRISE!"

At least half the fraternity was present along with most of Virgil's pledge brothers.

"Happy Birthday!" brothers called out to him. Virgil and Lamar came down to the first floor, Virgil was shocked. Boyd and Louie came over and gave him a welcoming pat on the back.

"We've been waiting down here for over a half an hour!" Vahn said coming up to Virgil. "You guys took forever," he said with a small laugh.

"Your Lil has the longest interview ever dude," Lamar said with a sigh. "We were talking for over two hours."

"Alright everybody listen up!" Vahn said and the room went quiet. "We're heading out to Hooters now, grab a ride." The room of thirty some men hurried out the door loading up into the cars.

"You're riding with me bud," Vahn called out and Virgil followed him to his vehicle. Landon and his Lil Axel also got into Vahn's red jeep.

"So are you excited? Surprised?" Vahn asked Virgil as they pulled out of Omega's estate.

"I'm really surprised, I didn't expect this!" Virgil laughed excited.

"Good, I'm glad you didn't find out. The brothers have a hard time keeping secrets to themselves," Vahn rolled his eyes.

"I love Hooters," Axel grinned. "But not for their food," he said wiggling his eyebrows.

They arrived and inside their rowdy friends had already garnished several sections of seating. Virgil got a grin on his face the moment he entered, happy to relax for at least a little while in the company of his newfound friends. A football game was on that most brothers were focused on. Virgil was sitting at a table with Alec, Dante, Louie, Boyd, and Nolan. They were talking about what they had done that day.

"Alec and I hung out with Gabriel and Magnus today," Dante said triumphantly. "Gabriel's freaking hilarious, he was cracking my shit up like no other."

"I got ten signatures today," Nolan said in an offhand kind of way.

"Ten?!" Louie said, "I only got one," he said laughing, "You trying to show us up bro?"

"Not at all," Nolan said, "I'm just, trying to do my best, it has no impact on how you should act. I'm a perfectionist, that's just how I like to work."

Virgil sighed, he had a lot of work to do to catch up to Nolan. Boyd wanted to talk to Virgil and he nagged him till he listened to what he had to say.

"What?" Virgil asked turning to focus on his rambunctious little friend.

"Like I was saying, our roommates haven't seen Damian since Wednesday night," Boyd told him with a worried tone.

"It's not a big deal Boyd, he's pledging like we are. He's going to be gone a lot."

"Don't you think it's a little weird. We're pledges, but we are allowed to still walk around campus, and talk to who we want? I don't see Damian having that option," Boyd said.

"I'm sure he does Boyd. I'm just not sure he wants to spend his time talking to Omega pledges," Virgil suggested with a shrug.

"Doesn't that bother you?" Boyd asked. "You guys were getting close, he's your friend," he pointed out.

"Damian's doing what he wants. I still like him, and I'm sure he feels the same way. Stop worrying so much okay?" Virgil suggested.

After the game, Virgil walked to the parking lot with his pledge brothers. Dante was talking about the waitress who'd been helping them, Axel had gotten her number, and everyone cheered for him. They were almost to the cars when Virgil felt the hair on the back of his neck stand up. He stopped walking and looked around. A very unsettling feeling came over him.

"Guys hold up," Virgil said to the group.

"What's up Lil?" Vahn called back turning to face Virgil.

"I think that-" Virgil tried to speak but his words were drowned by a deafening roar that bellowed out into the night. It was profound, like a lion, but... it sounded deeper, more ferocious.

A red sphere of energy rocketed to the ground near the group and exploded on impact, flames spreading out like wildfire, knocking most of the men near it off their feet.

"Demons!" Vahn shouted.

Landon yelled, "Create a perimeter around the pledges!"

Everything got crazy, fast, the parking lot morphing into a battle zone. Explosions blasted throughout the night, cars were flipped over or set on fire. The Omegas reacted instantly, the brothers summoned spectacular weapons from their Devil Arms into their hands. Vahn brought a flaming short sword to his hand, Gabriel had a longsword, and Tarek wielded a dangerous looking lance that was a marriage of ice and metal. The creatures that came down from the sky had lanky frames, suspended by leathery wet wings. The creatures had red eyes and dark skin, they were shorter than an adult, but their small bodies beguiled their enormous strength. One such creature flew down in a dive and slammed into a brother Virgil didn't know. He was flung off his feet sailing yards across the parking lot, skidding across the pavement with sickening force.

The brothers using mainly their Devil Arms a mix of swords, pole arms, and axes, fought back against the airborne demons. They worked hard on creating a perimeter around the candidates, to shield them from the demons' attacks. A beast slammed to the ground just yards from Virgil, it stared down the pledges, its blood red eyes filled with malice. It looked like a bat, given a humanoid form. It opened its mouth filled with razor teeth bellowing a mighty roar. Louie screamed out of fear in response, almost fainting. He slumped backwards against Dante.

"Get your shit together man!" Dante shouted shoving Louie back to his feet. Vahn stood in front of Virgil, shielding him with his own body. Vahn shifted his sword to his non-Devil Arms hand, his palm with his Devil Arms symbol stretched towards the monster.

"Beam!" Vahn shouted. A cylinder-shaped beam of fire erupted from Vahn's hand blasting through the approaching fiend's middle, it fell to the ground, disintegrating into black ash.

"Get some cars in here, we need to get these candidates secured now!" Gabriel commanded.

"Magnus is on his way, he has a few brothers coming as well!" Landon shouted back, a staff cradled in his grasp, his free hand typing furiously away at his cell phone.

One of the fiends in the air shot a sphere of red energy from his maw, right in front of Vahn, the brothers who had been standing in front of the pledges were lifted off their feet. The creatures descended on the brothers still standing, barreling into them with the momentum of their bodies, tearing at them with claws, and teeth. Vahn was on the ground, not far from Virgil, clearly in pain suffering from visible burns, but thankfully he was alive. Virgil was pissed! Anger began to pump through his blood like liquid fire. He hadn't known them long, but these men had treated him like family, and every fiber of his being screamed with rage!

"NO!" Virgil bellowed into the night his hands clenching into fists.

"Virgil's right we can't just stand here. We gotta do something guys, or we all gonna be dead," Louie talked with a lot of hand motion, his eyes filled with fear.

"How do we help them? I don't know how to fight something like that," Hector barely stuttered out, fear evident in his voice and etched upon his face.

"Use a spell or something homie!" Louie shouted.

"I think we would've already done that if we KNEW HOW!" Dante shouted back.

Another demon landed in front of the candidates, its attention firmly on the unarmed men. It looked at them with obvious disgust, a low growl hummed along its sick lips, a black tongue darted out wetting them. The demon's claws were slicked red with fresh blood from the brothers. It took a step towards the group, enjoying the recoil that it garnered from some.

Virgil's initial response to the demons was shock and fear of the unknown. Now anger was his only thought. Virgil's left hand began to burn. Virgil let his frustration and anger consume him, rage licked at his mind, threatening to consume him. His anger acted as a catalyst, sparking something inside. The black brand on his left palm and backhand blazed to life, to Virgil's ears it sounded like it was screaming, demanding to be heard. Virgil felt an instant connection, deep and permanent. He could almost hear the weapon's voice in his mind, fuzzy at first, but coming into focus. Raising his hand towards the night sky Virgil yelled two simple words. Words that defined a part of him, a part that was pure rage, malice, and power.

"SOUL REAVER!" Virgil screamed into the night.

Virgil's palm burst with dark light as black flames consumed his skin, licking the black symbol that now beamed like an unholy star. A sleek black scythe snaked into reality from the smoky fire. The handle and head had an exquisite and intricate design of black onyx. The blade shone with a sharp gleam that was unlike anything he had seen. The silver blade was alive…and hungry. The scythe floated before his hand, just within reach, waiting for his command.

The demon gave a fierce and determined roar, bringing Virgil back to reality. The demon beat its fists against the ground and bounded towards Virgil. The demon's claws stretched towards him, its teeth barred and ready to sink into flesh. Virgil gripped the length of the scythe and the weapon became ablaze with black flames that spread up his hand to his shoulder. Virgil cocked his arm back and threw the scythe with as much force as he could muster. The scythe whirled through the air, slicing cleanly through the beast in a singing arc of flame and metal, stopping the creature mid gallop, turning it into black ash that fell to the ground. The blade came

flying back on an arc towards Virgil.

Stop! He shouted out in his thoughts fearful the scythe would slice through him as well.

The scythe came to a halt, hovering just within his reach. Surprised, the blade responded to his

thoughts, he grabbed the scythe. His black Devil Arms symbol, Soul Reaver, shined fiercely and

when the scythe entered his grasp once more, black flames flowed up his arm to his shoulder

again.

"Wow!" Virgil heard the surprised shock of his fellow candidates behind him.

Tarek Jeter, Gabriel, and Landon were quickly getting the chaos under control. There

were only a few demons left. A few cars came racing into the parking lot. The doors opened and

brothers joined the battle.

"Get them out of here!" Gabriel shouted to his men; his mighty longsword grasped firmly

in his hands.

"Let's go!" Tarek Jeter said seemingly materializing at Virgil's side, his stunning lance in

his left hand, glowing with a blue light like the symbol on his hand, it looked to be made of ice

and metal.

"Virgil shut your Devil Arms off!" Tarek Jeter commanded.

"How?" Virgil asked looking at the large flaming scythe in his left hand.

"Let it go, close off that part of your mind, WILL it to return to its dormant state, until

you are in need of it again," Tarek Jeter stated.

Virgil stared at the scythe, it looked so foreign in his hands, yet holding it now felt

so…good. There was a very dominant part of Virgil's mind that did not want to let it go, that

liked the power it gave to him. Virgil closed his eyes and took a deep breath. Thank you for saving me, please go back Soul Reaver, he thought. The scythe disappeared in a blaze of smoke and flame. Then the black symbol on Virgil's hand went back to its normal state. The pledges were being herded into the three vehicles that were waiting.

Virgil was pushed into a van, and it sped off. Magnus was driving, Tarek Jeter was riding shotgun. Magnus drove like a mad man. In the van were Dante, Louie V, Alec, Nolan, Boyd, Axel and Virgil. They were cramped and Axel and Boyd were on the floor.

"Who is hurt?" Tarek Jeter asked.

"Pretty much, all of us G," Louie said from the back with an over dramatic expression across his face.

"Shut up, Louie, you barely have a scratch on ya," Dante barked. "Dumb ass over here got the brunt of it," Dante said motioning to his roommate, Alec. His gruff tone hiding the concern on his face.

Virgil realized that most of his pledge brothers looked a little beat, the worst being Alec and Axel, neither seemed fully conscious. Tarek Jeter focused in concentration for a moment, the blue symbol on his hand glowing, then spoke, "Ply!" A pale blue light spread from his Devil Arms, then moved to surround and envelope Alec. He seemed to respond immediately, opening his eyes fully and sitting up straighter, cuts on his face from hitting the ground, seemed to be growing smaller before everyone's eyes before disappearing all together.

"What the deuce?" Louie V expressed his mouth falling open.

"Ply!" Tarek Jeter said again, this time the light spread to Axel, having the same effect on him.

"It's a healing spell, unique to Paladins aligned to water. Through prayer and meditation, it can heal wounds by rapidly increasing cellular regeneration." Magnus stated.

"WOW!" Virgil and a few others exclaimed. Alec and Axel were now fully recovered and impressed that they had not a scratch on them.

"Not many of our brothers can use restoration magic. It's an art form that is difficult to master, and an invaluable gift," Magnus said.

"Aww thanks man, next you're going to ask to hold my hand, and wipe my ass?" Tarek Jeter asked Magnus sweetly.

Magnus chuckled at his jest. "Not even if you had double D's my friend," Magnus responded.

"I appreciate it bro," Tarek Jeter said to Magnus.

"But seriously, we'd be screwed without a few brothers or sweethearts who can do that for us," Magnus told the candidates.

"Is that normal for y'all? Just go get some wing from Hooter, and be munchy and crunchy afterward for the local demon?" Louie said missing plurals from his speech making it hard to understand him.

"Uhh…what?" Magnus asked not understanding Louie as his speech lacked plurals, more so when he was nervous.

"I think what the MTV brain washed Asian is trying to say is, how often does this…demons popping up out of nowhere crap happen," Dante translated.

"Well, we more or less are responsible for cleaning up the demon activity in our city." Magnus responded. "More often than you think, but not that much once you get the feel for it. Not everyone is cut out for this kind of lifestyle," he added with a shrug.

"The local vampires, lycans, and witches, look to us for protection from the demons, but the true enemies are Death Dealers and the Fallen," Tarek Jeter said. "They are the ones leading the demons."

"We're more than a match for the demons that pop up, but normally it is us that hunt them," Magnus stated.

"So Virgil, that was crazy back there how you called your Devil Arms, huh?" Tarek Jeter said breaking the tension. "Not many pledges are able to use their Devil Arms without proper instruction."

"I'm not even sure how I did it really," Virgil remarked.

"How did you use it?" Boyd asked Virgil with a curious stare.

"I just felt anger inside, rage. I felt something come over me, calling to me, I only needed to think about it, and it was, there," Virgil said. "It's weird, I don't know where the name came from. One moment I was utterly oblivious and the next, it was like, the Devil Arms told me what its name was."

"Summoning your Devil Arms is all about understanding yourself really," Magnus commented. "It's about knowing what your strengths are, what your limits are. Calling out your soul weapon's name, that kind of self-awareness is empowering. But learning those inner truths can sometimes be frightening. People learn of things lurking inside their souls, that they never knew were there," Magnus looked in the rearview mirror staring Virgil down as he said that. Virgil felt his face grow red and looked down at his hands. "Don't worry though Omicron," Magnus said to the van. "Your Devil Arms will come to you when you are ready for it. Your Devil Arms symbol is the source of all our powers. Mastering its use is every Paladin's first task."

The candidates got back to the house and gathered in the living room. Gabriel wanted to have a talk before they went back to their homes. "Sorry to keep you gentlemen waiting," Gabriel said walking in not long after. "It seems we had a little incident tonight, one of the Omicron rules to live by was broken. If all candidates could please present their Dreamstones," he asked calmly.

Omicron class quickly got out their drawstring bags and put their Dreamstones on their necks. It was annoying to keep them on 24/7 and the big chains could be noticeable to regular people. Everyone was looking around and one Omicron pledge didn't have his chain on, Brady the guy at the very back of the line.

Gabriel walked up to him and said, "Brady, where are your chain and stone?"

Brady replied, "I don't know."

"You don't know. Frater Jace, could you step forward," Gabriel asked.

Frater Jace, a bigger guy who often wore a baseball cap with small glasses over eyes of two different colors, stepped up. "I had an interview with Brady today. He left this at my place," he produced Brady's Dreamstone and Pledge Binder. "Didn't even come looking for it." Jace stated clearly not happy.

"Candidate Brady what is the first and most important of Omicron rules to live by?" Gabriel asked.

"Always carry your Dreamstone," Brady sighed.

"Exactly, because you weren't wearing this you gave away our position to any demons in the area. You must keep this jewel on your person, everywhere you go. When you don't your aura is visible for all to see. Even initiated brothers take these things with us wherever we go," Gabriel said tapping the ring on his finger. "Is that understood?" Gabriel asked.

"Sir, Yes, Sir!" Omicron said in unison.

"Alright, you guys have Brotherhood tomorrow night, be here on time!" Gabriel said. "Brady and his Big Brother, stay behind."

Omicron class quickly dispersed. The group headed outside to their cars parked in front of the parking garage. They huddled together for a quick meeting, Louie speaking up first.

"So tonight was kinda whack, not gonna lie. But that was just one day, we got a long way to go if we are ever gonna join these guys," Louie ended with a serious tone.

"We need to come to Brotherhood as a unit, where do you all want to meet?" Nolan asked them.

"Why don't we meet at the Bell Tower and head out from there?" Alec added.

"Everyone be there by 9:45 pm SHARP tomorrow, we're going to get shit from Gabriel if we don't step up our game," Dante stated.

"You mean our Hegemon?" Nolan said in a correcting tone.

"Uh, his name is Gabriel, the guys that he's cool with can call him that. I'm not saying you should, Hegemon's just fine," Dante retorted.

"Guys this isn't a contest of who the brothers think sucks the best dick," Hector added stuttering on the sucks part. "We've got to get our signatures and interviews to show the brothers we care about the fraternity."

"There are only twenty-three active brothers," Nolan stated. "I got two interviews done today, two tomorrow, three more over the weekend."

"Shieet!" Louie V said, "I'm screwed!" he laughed.

"People, get interviews and signatures, it is not hard!" Dante crossed his arms. "Reach out to the brothers! They are dying to get to know us, you'd be surprised with what they can teach us."

"Thank you, Pledge Master," Alec said to his roommate.

"So help me," Dante said raising his hand as if to give his roommate a backhanded slap.

"What do you guys think is gonna happen to Brady inside?" Louie asked, tension in his voice. "Do you think he could get kicked out for that?"

"Maybe," Nolan said. "He is the reason our group got attacked tonight. Our Hegemon wasn't kidding when he said Dreamstones need to remain on our person. We've woken up to the world, and now the world can see us for what we are too."

"Serves him right if he gets kicked out, we don't need any weak links," Devin, one of the pledges, stated speaking up.

"It was just an honest mistake," Louie sighed, "Anyone of us could have done the same thing."

"When one of us fucks up, it makes the whole group look like shit," Dante stated.

"If they don't kick him out, he will be a part of this group when he comes back. Let's stay focused on the bigger picture," Virgil added hoping to take the focus off their pledge brother.

Chapter 6
<u>Brotherhood</u>

The news coverage reported on the 'natural disaster' at Hooters the next day. It was speculation by the press that a tornado had touched down briefly in the parking lot. Virgil went to the food court next to the library after his classes were over. Some of his pledge brothers Boyd, Dante, Alec, and Hector were sitting with brothers, Doc, Lamar, Jace, Zender, Tarek, Landon and a guy everyone called "Mu." Virgil waved at them then got in a line for some food. He joined Nolan sitting at a table, that was pulled next to the booth with the brothers. Nolan was organizing his schedule for the week and studying for a class. Virgil asked Nolan how he could do so much.

"Just make a lot of lists. Organization is the key to success. People who have goals written down and see them every day, achieve them. More so over those who don't."

"I'm worried about these next six weeks. I don't know if we're all going to make it," Virgil said discreetly voicing inner concerns to Nolan.

"We need to prove ourselves to them. That's why they are acting like this pledging process is so important to us getting in, or getting the boot," Nolan said rolling his eyes. "But in reality, they NEED us. They are getting lower in number, only twenty-three active brothers, and of those only fifteen or sixteen regularly come around. They need our help to make their Chapter bigger and stronger as a unit. Aidan, you, and me are the only ones in the group on a full ride scholarship. They need some intelligent guys in the Chapter. Our class is going to lead this fraternity someday," Nolan explained confidently, surprising Virgil.

"Leading? Easy bro, we're on day two of pledging here," Virgil pointed out.

"Just saying what I see," Nolan said looking down. "Can't you tell who the important pledges are to them?"

"What?! That's not a nice thing to say," Virgil said furrowing his brow at Nolan, surprised by such a judgmental remark from a nice quiet guy like him.

"Virgil don't be naïve. I was there last night. Don't pretend that you didn't see those things," Nolan said his eyes still on the floor. "They scared most of us, some of the guys are still pretty shaken up. They need guys who aren't afraid to stand against those things. They need leaders."

The demons, Virgil thought, were terrifying abominations, powerful, and destructive. It had not been the high point of his birthday. Truthfully, he hadn't had any trouble sleeping. When faced with the demon last night, his flight or fight basic instincts had kicked in, and with the resolve to fight came a calming confidence.

"The pledges closest to being Purebloods are most important in fighting those things," Nolan said. "They are the strongest warriors in the long run. And the brothers with the most 'Judge' running through their veins are always stronger. Don't worry much about what I said," Nolan smiled wide looking goofy, changing the subject. "I just wanted you to know that you don't have to worry too much, everyone just needs to be themselves, work hard, and we'll be good."

Virgil could hear Boyd being loud and obnoxious, causing some disgruntled looks from a few different Sorority girls nearby. They didn't appreciate the crass language.

"Being ourselves isn't always a good thing," Virgil quipped with a sigh.

"In some places we might need a little work," Nolan agreed.

Doc barked at the next table over, "I was just telling a bomb ass story about this crazy hot chick that was digging on me the other night."

"He's excited because this is the first time a woman looked at him like he wasn't a total dumpster fire," Jace added.

"Hey now," Doc admonished defensively, "My face is the money maker, ladies give no complaints."

After he had finished eating Virgil spoke with the brothers called 'Mu' and Jace, two guys he didn't know much about. Mu was very tall, with long legs, short black hair, and glasses. Jace was slightly shorter with a bigger belly, with short legs, and a longer upper body. He had short brown hair, with a baseball cap on. One of Jace's eyes weas brown while the other was green. They sat next to each other. Mu was Jace's Big Brother, as well as Dante's.

"So Mu why do they call you Mu?" Virgil asked him.

"Aww yes, I was wondering when one of ya was going to ask," Mu smiled enjoying the spotlight. "I'm Mu because I'm the only guy that was in Mu Class."

Virgil asked a little surprised, "That happens?"

"Well the winter pledge classes are always smaller than the fall ones, cause we usually Rush most of the potential Nephilim. I transferred here from Delta College in the winter, and came out to Rush because I wanted something to do. I wanted to meet some new guys, and get some drinking buddies," Mu said earning cheers from Jace and Lamar.

"They gave out a few bids that semester but only two guys showed up on bid acceptance night, me and another guy and he was older than me!" Mu laughed.

"How old are you Mu?" Nolan asked.

"I'm twenty-nine damn it, and proud of it," Mu said sternly but with a smile. "The other guy was in his thirties. Mu class just attracts old guys I guess," he said with a shrug. "He dropped out after the second week."

"What's your real name?" Virgil asked him.

"Ehh you don't need to call me anything but Mu… its Justin though," Mu said.

"Who the hell is that?" Landon asked in a joking manner from the next table over.

"Yeah really, Justin? Who is that guy?" Mu joked getting a few laughs from his brothers.

"How was it pledging by yourself?" Boyd asked. "I imagine it must have been hard having all the brothers calling just one pledge."

"It sucked," Mu admitted. "It was frustrating, having nineteen-year old kids bossing me around. This is a brotherhood though, and it's all in good fun. They also treated me like gold, not all the brothers razz you during the process and some of the older ones were looking out for me. But guys listen," Mu said to the pledges, motioning with his hands for them to lean in and pay attention.

Dante, Alec, Nolan, Boyd, Hector, and Virgil leaned in towards Mu.

"The Omegas are a family. You may get some shit as a pledge, or even after you've become a brother, but every one of us has each other's backs. We hang out together, we laugh together, and we love each other," Mu said putting his arm around Jace who rolled his eyes and tried scooting away as he did. "It is worth it," Mu spoke with resolute belief.

"Agreed," Doc nodded.

"Yeah, it's the best decision I ever made," Landon added.

Virgil enjoyed visiting with the brothers, and soon it was time for him to get to his class. Dante and Alec were talking about setting up some interview times with Mu. Boyd, Nolan, and Hector were doing the same with other brothers.

"Do you mind if I could join in your guys' interview?" Virgil asked.

"Works better for me, means I have to tell the same stories less times," Mu laughed.

"We were going to grab some dinner and just casually talk while we ate," Dante said.

"We're going to B-dubs. You can catch a ride with us," Alec offered.

"Wait, off campus?" Virgil asked. "Is that safe?"

"Of course, it's safe!" Mu said in an exasperated tone. "You'll have ol' reliable Mu taking care of you, so don't get your pretty head in a tizzy over nothing."

"But what about last night?" Virgil asked speaking softly looking around.

"Keep your Dreamstone on you at all times!" Tarek said, "It isn't rocket science. We don't have you carry them for nothing. You have those things on you, demons can't see you...basically."

"Really?" Virgil asked, "It's that simple?"

"Not at all, but no use confusing you now. Just take our advice and don't be an idiot," Tarek advised.

"The only reason last night happened was Brady messed up," Dante said. "None of the pledges or brothers have seen him since."

"I heard Gabriel ripped him a new one after we left," Alec said.

"Cause you were messing with him!" Boyd stated to Jace.

"Hey don't blame his mistake on me!" Jace said defensively. "Pledges are responsible for themselves. He left his pledge materials at my place and didn't come back looking for them. If that's the kind of attitude he is going to have I don't want him as my brother."

"I'm sure he'll do better, it is only the second day," Virgil said coming to his defense. Virgil didn't know Brady. They'd never even talked, but defending others was something ingrained in his very being.

"We'll see," Jace remarked. "How important you treat this process is reflective of how you will treat this brotherhood. That kid needs to shape up."

Dante and Alec had class too, so Virgil left with them going to the science building which was attached to the food court.

"Watch out for Jace," Dante commented as he walked. "He's a part of Xi class, they just got initiated last semester, so we're their first pledge class."

"Is Jace giving pledges a hard time?" Virgil asked them.

"Ehh it's all part of the process," Alec remarked, "Don't take things too personally, it's all in good fun."

"I'm Jace's Twin so he hasn't been giving me a hard time, but he has been hassling a few pledges, Alec here included," Dante stated.

"Yup, called me at 1 am, asking for chips and a pop. I had just gotten to bed," Alec said with a big dorky grin.

"And you're smiling about that?" Virgil asked. "That sounds awful to me."

"Like I said it's all in good fun. How I perceive it is, the more the guys call you and ask you to do things, the more you get to know them and be friends with them. They wouldn't call if they weren't interested in getting to know me, so I take it as a compliment," Alec said optimistically. Virgil liked his attitude.

"I guess this is all about perspective, your mind set on how you approach this can make or break you," Virgil commented. "Wait, Dante you said Jace is your Twin?" Virgil asked. "What does that mean?"

"It means we have the same Big Brother. You have a twin too I think, Vahn had a little brother last year," Dante said. "Though I wouldn't recommend bringing it up to him until you guys get to know each other better."

"Why what happened?" Virgil asked as they rounded the corner coming to the main entrance to the next building. Alec and Dante were headed in a different direction from him and they waved goodbye to one another.

"Just take my advice bro," Dante said as they parted ways.

After bio lab, Virgil walked over to the food court. There weren't many brothers there anymore, Virgil sat next to Hector.

"Hi ya Vir- Vir-Virgil," Hector greeted him. He lived off campus and stayed at the food court throughout the day.

"Virgil, I got a proposition for you," Zender said to Virgil coming over to their table. Zender slid into the booth next to Hector, across from Virgil. Zender was of average male height, with dark hair cut short and spiked at the front, pale blue eyes behind glasses, a small straight nose, and a muscular frame, with a mischievous grin written across his face. He was handsome and intelligent but had an attitude problem.

"What's up Zender?" Virgil asked him.

"We would like your help to prank Vahn's room," Zender grinned.

"That sounds like something bad," Virgil said softly thinking it over, "I don't know if I want to mess with my Big like that."

"Listen kid, it's not a big deal. Jace and I will both give you some merits and our signatures if you do what we ask," Zender explained gently.

"We just need you to lure Vahn out of his room, so we can go in to flip everything upside down," Jace explained.

"Flip it upside down?" Virgil asked.

"You go into a brother's room and mess it up. It's hilarious when they go in and see their shit's been messed with," Jace said.

"Why do you guys want to mess with Vahn?" Virgil asked defensively.

"It's what we do!" Zender exclaimed as if it explained everything. "What is life without a little harmless fun between friends?" he asked. "We're not going to destroy any of his things. It's a simple prank Virgil, and we're asking you to help us out."

Virgil bit his lip, "I'm not sure," he said after a few moments, "Can I think about it?"

"You have until tonight at Brotherhood," Zender said curtly, "I'll be expecting a favorable response." Virgil felt slightly intimidated by Zender. He seemed very serious, not the type of guy you wanted to mess with. Virgil nodded to Zender that he got the message.

"This shouldn't be that hard, so he's your Big, big deal!" Lamar said speaking up on the topic. "We all prank one another. He won't care if you help them, so man up and do it already."

"Well it was nice running into you guys," Virgil said getting up, not wanting to be pressured anymore. "I have some homework I should try to get done." Virgil said goodbye to the brothers, and Hector, going back to his dorm room. Time crept by slowly, Virgil's cell phone started buzzing and he quickly answered it.

"Hello?"

"Virgil, Alec and I are waiting for you outside," Dante said in an excited tone.

Dante and Alec were in Dante's small white car in the small employee lot behind the freshmen dorms.

"Thanks for letting me come along guys," Virgil said getting in. Dante grunted in response and Alec turned to him with a smile.

"It's not a big deal bro," Alec smirked.

Dante drove down the main road that ran through campus, State Park Drive, and headed into Bay City.

"Aren't you guys worried about leaving campus?" Virgil asked them.

"Why?" Dante asked like it was a dumb question. "Dude, you can't live life worrying about the what if's," Dante spoke with confidence. "We've lived our whole lives without knowing or worrying about the stuff that was going on around us and we made it this far. Gabriel assured us that we should be okay, as long as we keep our Dreamstones on us, demons should see us as normal people."

"I thought that's what we were," Virgil said softly.

"Not even close," Alec chuckled from the front. "Anyone who can make a flaming scythe appear out of thin air is *not* normal bro."

"Normal is all I ever really wanted to be," Virgil responded.

"Normal is an overrated fairy tale, pedaled to the general populace in a glamorized package by society to control how we think. As if we should all push to attain something so mundane," Dante quipped. "There is no normal, be grateful for who you are, and embrace it."

The restaurant was mostly empty. The trio spotted Mu sitting at a tall table with a beer, he waved to the pledges and they joined him.

"Hey guys," Mu greeted them enthusiastically, "take a seat, let's chill."

The server took their orders and they got comfortable.

"This is my interview and I'm telling you, you don't have to take notes," Mu told them. "For me this should be a casual thing, just a couple of buds sitting around talking about life. I don't like formal stuff, ask what you want."

"Sounds good Big," Dante said with a nod.

The group ordered some food and quickly got into the interview. Alec, Dante, and Virgil took turns asking Mu questions about himself, his life, his interests, and his dreams. Mu was a friendly, fun-loving guy. Mu told them he had been adopted as a baby by his parents, he didn't know much of his birth family only that they were from Texas. Mu's Devil Arms was a giant club aligned with earth. He laughed stating he was disappointed as some guys got swords and he just got a "big stick." Mu was the Grammateus, or Secretary of the fraternity. He explained the job was mostly taking notes during the meeting, reserving meeting rooms, and keeping correspondence with Internationals at the Paladin Capital.

"Internationals?" Virgil asked.

"Yeah. you know, the head of our fraternity," Mu said. "Omega is a part of the Paladins, which is an international organization that has members in most countries around the world. Our headquarters are located where all Paladin Greek Organizations are located, in the Nephilim Capital, the city of Alexandros."

"Where is that exactly?" Alec asked. "I've never heard of it."

"No one's told you about that yet?" Mu asked. Seeing the puzzled looks on their faces Mu cracked a smile. "Alexandros was founded thousands of years ago. The city is on a piece of land, about the size of the State of Rhode Island, which floats above Lake Michigan."

"Wait what?" Virgil asked not sure he heard Mu right.

"Yeah, floats!" Mu cried out. "It sounds crazy right? But there is a giant floating island that rests high in the clouds over Lake Michigan. It has been there for a long time."

"If a giant floating landmass is over Lake Michigan, wouldn't it be visible from Chicago, or wouldn't people have seen it?" Alec asked.

"You would think, but like so much of the stuff you've been learning about recently, it's a secret from humans, one hidden right in front of them," Mu said. "The landmass is filled with old ancient magic, powerful ley lines, which makes it impossible to be seen by an ordinary person."

"That still doesn't make sense though, what about planes, wouldn't they have crashed into it? And how does an island that big hover?" Virgil wondered.

"You guys are still really new to this whole Nephilim thing," Mu sighed. "Trust me when I say this isn't going to be the craziest thing you'll learn. A powerful source of magic keeps the land afloat. People say that the land is an Eidolon grave yard. Eidolons, sometimes referred to as gods by different civilizations, are essentially powerful spirits. Because of the magic in the land, humans can't see it. It also disorients human made devices, like air planes that come near it keeping them above or below it safely, albeit unknowingly," Mu explained.

They thanked Mu for his time and went back to campus. Later that night Virgil met his pledge brothers at the bell tower. Dante and Alec were already there along with Nolan and Troy.

"How was your day?" Nolan asked Virgil.

"I got an interview done," Virgil answered proudly. "What about you?"

"I had a productive day, should have eight of my interviews done by Sunday," Nolan stated.

"Eight!?" Boyd responded. "Dude, you need to chill out, take a second to relax, admire the babes."

"No time to relax, got too much to do," Nolan responded.

Slowly the rest of the pledges trickled in, though Brady didn't show.

"Where the heck is this guy?" Louie asked.

"We should head over there, we don't want to be late," Darius told the group.

"We need to show up as a group," Dante said firmly, "Its better we be late than show up on time missing one guy."

"He's not coming," Aidan explained to the group. "I hung out with my Big Brother, Gabriel, today and he said that Brady quit."

"Quit?" A few of the pledges asked at once.

"He told Gabriel he was too overwhelmed with everything and just wanted to go back to being a normal college student," Aidan stated.

"Screw him," Dante said, "We don't need him weighing us down."

Louie became irritated with Dante, "That was our pledge brother. We should reach out to him."

"I wonder what happens when you quit," Virgil said thinking out loud. "I mean we're supposed to be completely changed after the Oath of the Pledge. How do they expect him to just jump back into the real world after going through all of this?"

The group was silent for a moment, Aidan was the first to speak up. "I've heard it isn't uncommon for at least a few pledges to drop out of each class. They do something that is painless and helps you forget, only if you want them to though."

The pledges arrived at the Omega manor a few minutes ahead of schedule. Jagger was waiting for them in the foyer, quiet, serious, and stern faced as usual. He gruffly told them to file into their correct order. The pledges quickly arranged themselves as they had been on bid acceptance night. They stood in the entrance of the fraternity house. They could hear some brothers laughing and talking with one another further inside.

"Sir, what are we doing," the pledge Devin attempted to ask.

"Keep quiet! Heads down, no talking!" Jagger said his arms crossed over his chest.

"You guys made it on time," Gabriel commented coming into the foyer moments later.

"I can take it from here Jagger, thanks," Gabriel told him. Jagger nodded and left.

"Alright boys, tonight is your first Brotherhood. After you become brothers, we will bond and do different fun stuff on Brotherhood nights. During the candidate process it's a time to teach you about the fraternity," Gabriel explained seriously. "We're going to the back yard, follow me."

Gabriel walked through the Omega's home heading towards the back porch. The brothers had all moved to the bottom of the area where there was an open grassy area. The sky was lit up that night with thousands of stars, helping to give them plenty of light to see. The pledges followed Gabriel back through the yard to the open area just near the edge of the forest that surrounded the Omega's land. Gabriel came to a few paces away from the group of brothers. The candidates turned and faced the brothers.

"I'd like to say, before we get started, that candidate Brady will not be moving forward with the process. He came to me and told me that this is too much for him. I don't want anyone to hassle him if you run into him on campus. Joining this fraternity requires a big-time commitment, and it isn't for everyone. Brady met with Professor Ramuh shortly thereafter who performed the Oath of Depledging. It makes one unaware of the things they learned about Nephilim, with a slight reworking of some of his memories. Brady will not remember his time with this fraternity. All he remembers is that he had fun, but it was too stressful," Gabriel offered reassuring the group.

The announcement that Brady was gone wasn't news to anyone, but the erasing of his memories made more than a few pledges stand a little straighter. "Please don't be alarmed. Brady was unharmed in the process. It was just as much to protect him as it was us," Gabriel said his voice powerful, confident, and filled with charisma. "It's standard procedure to alter the memories of any candidate who quits so they do not remember anything of Paladins, Devil Arms, or demons. Now moving forward, tonight is your first brotherhood. We have two short exercises for you to complete, then the second half will be dedicated to Devil Arms instruction. Let's begin!"

Gabriel came over to Darius, "You stay here, the rest follow me," Gabriel had the candidates follow him a short distance then had Nolan, the next guy in line stop, while the rest followed. The group quickly became spread out in a large circle, with Devin, the last guy in line closer to Darius, at the starting point.

"This exercise is called Telephone. I am going to relay a message to Darius, and he in turn will run as fast as he can to Nolan, and so on. You will carry the message until the last guy,

Devin receives it. Devin will tell the brothers what he heard. You must whisper it to the next guy, got it!?" Gabriel asked.

"Sir, yes sir!" the candidates replied in unison.

Gabriel nodded and went to Darius to relay the message. Afterwards Darius shot off like an arrow, sprinting towards Nolan. Nolan listened for a few seconds, then ran to Aidan, to relay what he had heard. Virgil stood between Troy and Hector. He watched his pledge brothers, nervous, knowing his turn was approaching. The brothers heckled the candidates shouting comments like 'hurry up!' and 'my grandma can run faster than that!' Dante ran over to Troy and whispered quickly to him, then Troy turned and made his way to Virgil.

"Lamar's grandmother bad gas, stank up the house," Troy whispered to Virgil.

"What?" Virgil asked not sure he heard it right.

"I don't know, that's what Dante said. He thought it got messed up already," Troy quickly said.

"What's the hold up!?" they heard the brothers shout at them.

"Go!" Troy told him and Virgil turned and ran to Hector.

"Lamar's grandmother bad gas, stank up the house," Virgil told him.

"W-wh-wh-what?" Hector asked him. Virgil repeated his words with more pronunciation for Hector. The brothers started to yell and shout, so Hector moved on. Virgil didn't feel confident that they were doing well.

Axel relayed the message to Devin, who ran before the brothers.

"Well?" Gabriel asked.

"Lamar's bad gas, stank up the house," he said nervously.

The brothers erupted into a chorus of laughter, and Lamar told the brothers to shove it where the sun doesn't shine.

"That is not the message I gave Darius," Gabriel said. "Darius, what did I tell you to tell your fellow pledge brothers?"

"Lamar's grandmother's bad gas stank up the house so much we had to rewallpaper," Darius said earning a few more chuckles from the group.

"It was not that bad!" Lamar shouted out defensively to the group.

"Omicron!" Gabriel shouted to the group. "Is this the best you have to offer? What if that message was of vital importance on a mission? You can endanger the group if you don't relay things carefully. This is not how Omega's do things Omicron! If you want to be a part of this family, you have got to work as a team! Alright, these guys don't know what they're doing, brothers let's show 'em how it's done."

The candidates moved to where the brothers were standing, and a group of the brothers quickly spread out, excited and shouting out as they ran, full of energy.

"Alright now Tarek, I'm going to give you the message and I want all of you to show Omicron Class how it's done. Ready?" Gabriel asked.

"Ready!" replied a chorus of voices from the brotherhood.

Gabriel went to Tarek and whispered the message into his ear. After he was done, Tarek pivoted on his foot as if to spring into action, but then turned and remained still, putting his hands in front of him calmly. The brothers and pledges shouted to Tarek to run but he stayed still. Virgil and the pledges were confused.

"Frater Tarek why aren't you relaying the message to your fellow brothers?" Gabriel asked him.

"Because I don't spread rumors about Omega," Tarek responded.

The pledges let out groans of frustration. They had been set up from the beginning. As much as the brothers were pushing them to go faster, the real way to complete their game was not to participate.

"This fraternity is only as strong as its weakest link. What is said here, what is done here, does not leave this group. It is imperative that you don't reveal fraternity secrets to those not privileged to hear them; that is how rumors are started. Look what happened with just the thirteen of you, how garbled the messages got. When you tell someone outside of this organization things about us, they can get twisted and damage us. Reputation is everything people. Alright candidates line up please."

Virgil and the others did as they were told.

"Now the Paladins, and by association our fraternity, are a military force. One that patrols the world, doing our best to maintain peace by exterminating demons and those they serve. Humans, our friends and family, are unaware of this war going on around them. This military force is made up of thousands of Nephilim squadrons, just like this one here. When men are on the battlefield, when WE are on the battlefield, you must be focused, be vigilant. At any moment we could be attacked, or ambushed. It is your job to protect your brothers, your friends standing around you," Gabriel said to them walking back and forth in front of them.

"Let's say this pop can is actually a grenade. What are you going to do?" Gabriel asked them and threw it in front of the pledges.

Nolan quickly jumped out of line landing on the pop can curling his body around it. None of the other pledges had even moved. Virgil had just failed, his face flushed from embarrassment.

"Pathetic!" Gabriel shouted. "Thank you, candidate Nolan, you can get up now," he spoke to Nolan with reverence and respect.

"Out of all of you, only Nolan is willing to sacrifice himself to protect the rest of you? You're letting your smartest pledge brother take the fall just like that?" Gabriel asked them. "Does that sound like a smart decision for Omicron?"

"That's my Little!" Magnus called out with his hands cupped around his mouth. A big grin plastered across Nolan's face.

Gabriel turned to Magnus who didn't say anything else but wore a smile with pride.

"We are a unit, a family, it is our job to look out for one another, to protect one another. That can be as simple as squashing a rumor you hear people talking about, interrupt them and correct them, stop it at its source. It can be as dangerous as taking a bullet for your fellow brothers. This is the fraternity for life, and we mean that. Look at the men around you, these men will be the best men at your wedding, the godfathers to your children, and the ones to carry your coffin," Gabriel's voice got thick with emotion. "Take what you've learned here to heart gentlemen," He paused, and everyone was silent. The tone of the night shifted. "Moving forward, for the last part of the evening, some Devil Arms instruction," Gabriel announced, and the brothers cheered.

Chapter 7
Devil Arms

"The Devil Arms symbols on each of your hands are your most important resource as a Paladin," Gabriel explained to Omicron's thirteen candidates. "There are two aspects of every Nephilim's power, Might and Will. Might, in the form of the soul weapons each Nephilim is gifted with, Devil Arms we call them. Devil Arms are the unique symbols on your hands. Will, the ability to shape the element one is aligned with and use it in the form of spells. Will is complicated and takes years more practice and training to use than Might. Every Nephilim can train with their weapons and become skilled warriors. Not everyone can become skilled casters. You must will your weapons into being with your mind, and spells work the same way. Concentrating on the name of your weapon can be enough, some people have an easier time if they just say the name of their Devil Arms."

Gabriel raised his right hand up like he was giving someone a high five. His symbol was golden brown, aligned with Earth, it came alive suddenly glowing. "LionsHeart!" Gabriel yelled. Light poured out from his symbol forming a long blade, which materialized into a weapon whose beauty was breathtaking to behold. The candidates all let out sounds of envy. They had seen the brothers in action last night, but the moment had been so chaotic there had not been time to really take in their Devil Arms. The sword's blade gleamed silver, with a golden handle and yellow topaz in the center of the pummel. The sword had a long blade that was made for powerful swings and looked heavy and hard to wield. Gabriel gripped the sword firmly in his hand, turning his gaze to the candidates, most of whom wore expressions of awe and wonder.

"Each Nephilim has a unique Devil Arms that is all their own, no two weapons are the same," Gabriel told them. "The Devil Arms picks the Nephilim, your unique personality, and characteristics, are matched to one weapon, your soul weapon, a reflection of who you are as a being. Much can be said about who someone is, just by the weapon they carry. My weapon is the longsword, LionsHeart. As you can see from the color of my Devil Arms symbol, I'm only able to use the element earth in casting. The color of your Devil Arms tells you what element your weapon is aligned with."

"We'll give you guys a little demonstration, and then we'll break you off into pairs with your Bigs, to try and summon the corporeal forms of your weapons to your hands. Tarek, you care to help me with the demonstration?" Gabriel turned to his brother.

Tarek stepped forward a cocky smile on his face.

Gabriel said to the candidates, "Tarek is our Hypophetes, or Chaplin, the spiritual leader. They are head of brotherhoods when we don't have pledges, and third in command of the Chapter. He's the only brother we currently have who is aligned with the element water. Tarek could you show them your Devil Arms please?"

"You got it boss," Tarek told Gabriel giving him a mock salute. Tarek's Devil Arms was on his left hand, a turquoise colored symbol.

"Stiria's Lance!" Tarek called out and blue light flowed from the symbol into a long lance, whose shaft was slightly blue leading up to a sharp silver blade. Tarek started spinning the lance around, ending in a small flip, bringing the lance crashing down into the grass. Where the blade struck the ground, ice spread out slightly coating a small area of grass. Tarek stood back up, his lance firmly in his left hand.

"Learning how to properly use your Devil Arms is the most important thing you will be doing in this pledging process," Gabriel said. "Bonding with the brothers is a very close second," he added. "Until you have firm control of your weapon, and are able to wield it with some skill, you will not be allowed to engage in fraternity missions."

"There are six elements; a Nephilim is generally born to one specific group, earth, like me, water like Tarek, fire like Vahn, wind like Magnus, then the last two, creation and chaos, are two separate forms of spirit. But Nephilim aligned to spirit are a rare breed," Gabriel said.

Virgil felt his face warm as more than a few gazes landed on him, he clenched his fists, wishing he could hide his hands marked with a white and black Devil Arms.

"Learning to gain some measure of control over your aligned element will take time. Let's move on with the demonstration," Gabriel stretched readying his sword. He turned to Tarek and the two squared off, everyone else backed up to give them space.

"It's important when practicing to properly guard your weapon as to not cause undo harm to your sparring partner," Gabriel told them. Each brother said 'Dull' and a faint barrier of light outlined their weapons, and the symbols on their hands.

The two brothers stared each other down, their bodies poised, eyes focused. Gabriel stomped the grass with his left foot, a large block of earth rose up from the ground to hover before him.

"Scatter Shot!" Gabriel called out and the block of earth broke into dozens of sharp dagger like pieces, and flung themselves at Tarek.

"Look out!" Virgil called to him.

Tarek spun his lance in a circle in front of him, moving the weapon so fast it started to blur and make a faint whistling sound. The rock shards slammed into the spinning lance and were destroyed. Tarek stopped spinning the lance.

"My turn," Tarek said moving his lance to his right hand as he stretched his left out towards Gabriel. "Blizzard!" He yelled and from his symbol burst a gust of ice and snow. Gabriel parried his blade across his face, the ice shards pelted him creating small cuts along his skin, pushing him back slightly across the grass by the sheer force of the ice.

"Only by utilizing both your Devil Arms and timed bursts of Will, can you effectively subdue a Nephilim opponent," Gabriel strained voice came out as he protected his face from the spell. The icy burst subsided, Gabriel stood tall, and charged Tarek. Tarek ran to meet him, both yelling as their weapons collided, sparks flying from their blades, as they pushed against each other clashed in a test of strength and skill. Gabriel was swift, and his sword was powerful, Tarek was barely able to catch the blows with his lance. Gabriel was nimble and quick footed, using his sword he drove Tarek back, Tarek struggling to keep up with him. Gabriel slashed his sword at Tarek, Tarek parried the blow with the length of his lance, and spun it quickly in retaliation, hitting Gabriel square on the chest with the butt of the lance, knocking Gabriel off balance.

Tarek twirled his lance, "Deluge!" he cried. A torrent of water exploded into existence slamming into Gabriel and sweeping him back off his feet. Gabriel spurted struggling to keep water out of his lungs as he was thrown yards back from the force of the spell, landing onto his back on the ground. The water dissipated, Gabriel got to his feet looking pissed.

"Enough!" Gabriel called out, anger thick in his voice. He slammed his fist with his Devil Arms into the ground saying, "Quake!"

The ground shook violently, and then large chucks of rock and earth shot up around Tarek knocking him down and throwing him around.

Tarek yelled and a flash of light came from him. Two large white wings burst from his back, Tarek shot into the air, he was fast. Tarek dived towards Gabriel jabbing at him with his lance, Gabriel attempted to parry Tarek's lance, but Tarek got in more than one strike on Gabriel. If it weren't for the barrier spell around Tarek's weapon, the lance would have gored Gabriel.

Gabriel winced as a strike from Tarek's lance caught him in the ribs. Gabriel grabbed onto Tarek's lance with his left hand, Tarek struggled to pull it from his grasp, Gabriel let out a loud bellow and swung his sword at Tarek. It connected with his body, knocking him out of the air onto the ground. Gabriel quickly rounded on the momentarily dazed Tarek, readying his sword once more. Tarek placed his hand on the ground and ice spread like a river, washing over Gabriel's legs, locking him in place. Tarek used the time to get back up. Gabriel looked annoyed, he stabbed the ice with his blade, and the ground shot up into spikes, breaking the ice, and heading towards Tarek. Tarek spread his wings once more and took to the air. The candidate's eyes were glued on the two men, Virgil was taking in every movement like it was the greatest action movie he'd ever seen.

"Your earth spells don't do you much good against an aerial opponent," Tarek taunted Gabriel. Gabriel's brow furrowed, he stomped the ground, and a chunk of earth shot up to float in front of him he punched the rock and it catapulted towards Tarek. Tarek lazily dodged the incoming projectile. Gabriel again stomped the ground, sending another chunk of rock up, Tarek dodged it as easily.

"Is that the best our Hegemon can do?!" Tarek yelled enjoying taunting Gabriel.

"Damn it!" Gabriel cried. He took his sword and traced a circle around himself and stabbed the blade firmly in the ground. The ground erupted around him and a giant human shaped hand, made of earth rose forth, as Gabriel imitated with his own hand. Gabriel reached up towards Tarek with his hand, and the large hand made of earth copied him. Tarek beat his wings to gain altitude, but the large hand shot towards him with startling speed, closing its fingers firmly around him, pulling him towards the ground. The hand was swallowed into the ground like a drop of water landing into a lake, the ground smoothed back out, looking untouched, with Tarek wedged firmly in it. Tarek's head and shoulders were above ground, the rest, hidden from view under the earth.

There were whoops and cheering from the brothers, along with a few disappointed groans, and a few of them exchanged money. Gabriel picked his sword back up and went to Tarek, leveling the point at his throat but not making contact, Gabriel and Tarek locked eyes.

"Do you yield frater Tarek?" Gabriel asked him.

"I yield Gabriel," Tarek said to him, "Can you release me now?"

Gabriel's sword disappeared in a flash of yellow light, then he placed his hands on the ground. The ground came alive, flowing like water rather than land, slowly Tarek rose out of the earth until he stood once more on solid ground. Tarek's left wing looked crooked. Tarek and Gabriel shared a hard look, then let out a shared laugh, and embraced. Tarek's wings disappeared into his back, and with a flash of light he was back to his normal self, his shirt forever ruined with slits running down the back. Both men had some minor cuts and scrapes on them.

"Ply," Tarek commanded. Gabriel was bathed in a warm blue light, his skin seeming to close over his wounds, until one couldn't tell where there had been cuts.

"Ply," Tarek said again, the same light washing over him, healing his wounds.

"Alright demonstration is over, Bigs break off with your Lils, the rest of the brothers are dismissed to the house," Gabriel called out.

"Aww," Doc let out a groan. "Can't we stay and watch the little guys struggle?"

"If you're being a nuisance, you WILL head back into the house," Gabriel commanded. Most brothers stayed to watch, the Bigs separated across the yard to have space with their Lils.

Once Vahn and Virgil had some privacy, Vahn started talking, "The first few practices we're just trying to get you used to summoning the physical form of your weapon. Then get some practice swinging it around a little."

Virgil looked at Vahn's ruby Devil Arms glyph, he asked his Big, "What's your Devil Arms?"

"Furybrand," Vahn boasted with pride. His Devil Arms symbol came alive at hearing its name, light shining through the symbol. Virgil stared at Vahn's Devil Arms with awe.

"Come forth Furybrand," Vahn said. Red light flowed from the glyph, quickly forming into a sword. Vahn's sword was very different from Gabriel's. Gabriel's sword had been very long, Vahn's was much shorter with a thicker blade, classified as a "shortsword." The blade was silver like most Devil Arms, with a more pronounced cross guard that looked like red flames. A ruby was encrusted in the pummel. The shorter length granted it more agility at delivering strikes than Gabriel's.

"Sweet," Virgil stared wide eyed.

"Yeah it's a pretty cool sword," Vahn commented staring at the blade in his hands. "Got me out of a few sticky situations," he joked, but then his face clouded in thought, dark memories came to him.

"You okay?" Virgil asked putting his hand on Vahn's shoulder.

"I'm fine bro," Vahn said shrugging him off. "Tonight's not about my Devil Arms training, we need to work on you." Vahn's sword disappeared in a flash of flames, his symbol going back to its dormant state.

"I'm not sure what to do," Virgil said honestly looking around at his fellow candidates who were each engrossed in conversation with their respective Bigs. None of them had produced a weapon from their Devil Arms symbols yet.

"The first few times you use your Devil Arms can be difficult, but once you start to get the hang of it, it becomes second nature. You have to envision in your mind, your weapon, what it looks like, and then let it be reality," Vahn explained. "I saw you use your scythe at the restaurant last night, it was impressive."

"Thanks," Virgil nodded. "But I'd rather use this one," he said lifting his right hand, the white Devil Arms glyph sat on the back of his hand and palm. "I don't want to wield the other one, if it's bad."

"Virgil, it's the warrior who wields them that decides their fate," Vahn said.

"Yeah but, this is a chaos Devil Arms, I'd prefer to wield a creation based one," Virgil said.

"Well most people aren't lucky enough to be born with more than one bud, the fact that you were shows that there is something special about you, if it warrants a Creation Devil Arms. If you want, let's try out the one on your right hand, concentrate on the symbol, close your mind and envision it in your mind, what does it feel like to you?" Vahn asked him.

Virgil looked down at the white glyph memorizing its shape and form, then closed his eyes picturing it. The symbol was elegant, graceful, and somehow…powerful. Virgil could feel the power in the Devil Arms, more so than the scythe. Virgil felt a gentle warmth begin to grow inside. The white Devil Arms exuded light, happiness, and hope. Virgil could feel that it was something big, something great, his lips moved, the name of it almost on the tip of his tongue, what are you called, he wondered. Virgil felt like he was onto something, then his mind drew a blank, the warmth fading from him as quickly as it had come. He opened his eyes and stared at Vahn, disappointed.

"Hey don't beat yourself up, sometimes it can take weeks to first summon your Devil Arms, it will come to you," Vahn encouraged him.

"Gaia's Wrath!" Dante shouted out from across the grass.

Virgil and Vahn turned watching as a large double-bladed axe materialized into Dante's hands. The axe was larger than Vahn's sword, it looked heavy, with the same silver metal. Dante was excited, screaming as he gave his axe a few swings.

"Easy killer," Mu cautioned his Little Brother.

A few brothers cheered for Dante and a few nearby pledges congratulated him on his success. Dante looked at Virgil and smiled holding up the mighty axe in triumph.

Virgil turned his attention back to Vahn. "I'm not really sure how I summoned this one," he said showing of his left hand, the black glyph on his hand like a dark stain.

"Devil Arms reflect your soul Virgil, your inner most self, learning how to use it, is a process of self-discovery. There isn't a set answer on how to find yourself, you have to look inside," Vahn said placing a finger over Virgil's heart.

"What if, what if I don't like what I see in there?" he asked Vahn hesitantly.

Vahn laughed a little. "We all have the capacity for good and evil, Virgil. Trust me when I say we all have a little bit of darkness and light within us. Life is about choices, everyday each of us is given the opportunity to do what's right, or to do what is wrong. These choices over time begin to shape the man you are to be. I know we don't know each other well but I'm good at people, and I can tell you this, you're not bad Virgil," Vahn told him.

"But I wouldn't have this Chaos Devil Arms if there wasn't something dark inside me. You said that the Devil Arms reflects our souls? If that is the case, this symbol, it means that there is darkness within mine," Virgil said, his words landing like bricks upon his back, the truth of his words ringing clear throughout his mind.

"There is darkness within us all my friend," Vahn said. "You can wallow in the darkness and let it control you, or you can accept that you have the capacity for evil and choose to rise above it."

"I will never let it control me," Virgil spoke his words steel.

"Then don't," Vahn said, "Now accept yourself Virgil, accept your Devil Arms, and call it to your side!" He yelled.

Virgil looked down at his left hand, once so familiar to him, now seemed like a foreign stranger upon his arm. Virgil took a deep breath, he concentrated on the symbol of his hand. Feelings of anger and rage welled up, bubbling within him like a beaker ready to burst. This Devil Arms was wilder than the other, more savage, and more blood thirsty. Virgil knew its name, having spoken it once already.

"Soul Reaver!" Virgil called out the black glyph blazing to life. Dark smoke gushed from his hand quickly sizzling into black flames. A scythe snaked out from the flames, the weapon's shaft came into his hand, he gripped it firmly, black flames danced along the weapon then climbed up his hand, to cover most of his arm. The flames did not burn Virgil, but he could feel their heat, he knew that they would scorch any who touched them. Virgil stared at the long black shaft of the scythe, taking in its dark beauty, leading up to the sickle shaped silver blade.

He looked up and noticed the entire group staring at him, most were looks of concern, some envy, and others contempt. Virgil felt embarrassed of the scythe, it was a weapon aligned with Chaos, a weapon of evil.

"Hey, don't be concerned with what they're thinking," Vahn waved off his concerns. "I'm proud of you Virgil." He said clapping his hand on his right shoulder, avoiding the left side with the black flames. "The Nephilim makes the weapon, not the other way around."

"Thanks, Vahn."

"What are Big Brothers for?" Vahn asked with a smile.

"Now what?" Virgil asked him, feeling weird holding the flaming weapon.

"Practice getting used to your scythe," Vahn suggested. "Walk a little further away from the group, I saw how much range that thing has last night."

The weapon was long and heavy, Virgil found it was difficult to wield with just one hand. Holding it with two hands, he was better able to swing the blade. He practiced slashing in front of him at invisible targets. A few minutes passed by of him swinging the scythe around, he wasn't sure what more to do.

"You're not going to become a pro overnight. Next practice we'll let you practice more with your scythe, and I can give you some instruction on proper stances and foot placement. We won't start sparring for a little bit yet, and Magnus will be giving you guys a lesson on spell casting eventually," Vahn told Virgil.

"Last time I was able to stop it with a thought," Virgil added. Vahn's eyebrows raised up slightly. "Is that not normal?" Virgil asked.

"Well," Vahn paused scratching the back of his neck. "It's not typical. Let's see," Vahn encouraged him.

Virgil readied the weapon and stepped forward into the throw, the flames along his arm disappeared when it left his grip. The scythe still ablaze whirled through the air, it was intimidating to watch. Virgil concentrated on the scythe, go left, he commanded, and the scythe instantly veered left. He wanted it to go higher and it instantly went up.

"Damn, are you doing that?" Vahn asked him.

"I think I am," Virgil responded. Come back to me, the scythe turned, and made its way back to Virgil. Stop! The scythe came to a halt before him, he grabbed its handle, the flames once more coated his arm.

"That is scary," Vahn's eyebrows were raised, his face somber, putting emphasis on scary and drawing out the word. "I think that's enough training for tonight bud," Vahn smiled. "Why don't you turn off those flames and put your Devil Arms away?"

"How?" Virgil asked.

"Just tell your weapon to lose its physical form," Vahn suggested.

Virgil stared at the black glyph, thank you, he told Soul Reaver, you can rest now. The scythe melted into black smoke that flowed back into his hand, and it was gone. Vahn put his arm around Virgil, and they walked back to the group.

"You're a natural," he told him messing up Virgil's hair.

"Hey!" Virgil said irritated trying to get out from his arm, "Don't mess with the hair!"

"Sensitive about your hair?" Vahn teased him.

"Yes!" Virgil exclaimed fixing it with his hands.

The pledges were mostly frustrated, only Nolan, Aidan, Dante, Alec, and Louie had managed to summon their Devil Arms to their hands. Nolan was holding a staff about the same height as himself with a rather disappointed look. Aidan was wielding a sword like Vahn's, his blade was thinner and longer though. Dante had a triumphant look upon his face, his double-bladed axe proudly held in his hands. Alec was holding a lance, it was slightly longer than Tarek's had been, with a large blade at the end. Lastly, Louie's weapon was the most different, in his right hand he held a bow, looked to have been carved from ice, its surface glistening.

"Wow!" Virgil exclaimed looking at his fellow pledge brothers. "That's awesome!" he told them running up to the pledges who were moving towards one another.

"Yeah well you know," Louie said dusting off his shoulders.

"It's alright," Nolan said to Virgil shrugging his shoulders at his staff. "Your scythe is pretty sweet looking."

"Thanks Nolan," Virgil said, feeling slightly better about Soul Reaver.

"Look at this!" Alec said giving his lance a little spin, "Isn't this freaking awesome!" he exclaimed with excitement. He brought the lance down to the ground and inadvertently a small jolt of electricity shot from the end, zapping Louie in the butt.

"Shit yo!" Louie yelled dropping his bow and grabbing his behind. "You dumbass be careful with that thing," he yelled at Alec.

"Fucking Birdy," Dante murmured under his breath.

"What?!" Virgil laughed. "Birdy, what's that mean?"

"Just a little nick name I came up with for dumbass," Dante said. "Alec's last name is Birdman, whenever he does something stupid, I call him Birdy, cause he's such an airhead. I end up calling him Birdy most of the day," Dante said with a smirk.

"Birdy, that's kind of funny," Virgil liked the nickname.

"Alright kiddies put those things away before you poke an eye out," Gabriel joked. "Let's go back up to the house. Candidates if you need to set up interviews with brothers, now is a good time to ask."

The candidates and brothers walked back to the Omega house. Most were caught up in excited conversation, the ones who hadn't been able to produce their Devil Arms were less lively. Virgil pulled his Big Brother aside.

"Vahn I wanted to tell you something quick," Virgil quickly and quietly told him.

"What's up?" Vahn asked him.

"Earlier at the food court, Zender and Jace asked me to help pull a prank on you. They want to mess with your room, and asked me to distract you," Virgil said sheepishly feeling awkward having to bring up something so juvenile after what they had just done.

"Really? Zender, he's the one behind this I guarantee it," Vahn laughed a little.

"What's so funny?" Virgil asked.

"Zender and I were dormmates our freshmen year, he's smart, like stupid smart, guy has more brains than he knows what to do with. I pledged Omega my freshmen year and was in Lambda class, he ended up not pledging until the following fall, and was in Nu class. We've always had this little friendly feud going on, he likes to start shit with me," Vahn sighed. "I'm going to get him back for this though, let me think of something and I'll let you in on it, thanks for the warning bud," Vahn smiled a real genuine smile at Virgil, and the two shared a moment.

"I'm glad you're my Big," Virgil blurted out.

"Me too," Vahn agreed with a nod and a smile.

The pledges got out their pledge binders, asking brothers to set up interview times and asking others for signatures. Most brothers were cooperative, others…not so much.

"If anyone has a signature from Abe, I won't be signing your book for the rest of the week," Jace told them telling a few pledges to get lost.

"Hey man, why you gotta dis a brother like that?" Abe said coming up to Jace. Abe was a guy of average height, thinning dirty blonde hair, with blue eyes, a long bulbous nose, big round cheeks, and trimmed goatee.

"Because I don't like you," Jace replied coldly without the hint of humor.

"Come on Jace that was a long time ago," Abe said.

"Get lost," Jace told him.

Meanwhile Zender had Dante, Alec, and Nolan gathered round him, they were asking him about interviews.

"I will be placing a signup sheet on my door tomorrow, to earn an interview with me, you must find a time slot. When you come to the interview you will bring me dinner and something to drink, if I am not pleased with your interview, after I've finished eating what you've brought me, we will call it quits, and you can sign up for another try," Zender told them, his face stern. Dante wore an annoyed expression at hearing this, Nolan wasn't even phased.

"I'll be here sometime round noon will the posting be up by then?" Nolan asked Zender.

"I'll make sure it's up by then," Zender replied happy to hear compliance with his demands.

Virgil felt slightly nervous to go near Zender, especially after overhearing what he had to say to the others. Virgil decided to talk with someone he hadn't yet. One of the brothers he spotted was a Latino guy that was a little older looking then the rest of the group. He seemed more quiet and withdrawn than what Virgil was used to of an Omega. Virgil went over to him.

"Sir? My name is Virgil, I was hoping I could get a signature from you, sir?" Virgil asked the man.

"What's my name?" he asked. Virgil drew a blank standing in front of the man. "I'm one of the lowest scrolls on your signature page, scroll #74," he told Virgil. Virgil was quiet still not sure of his name.

"It's Thiago, don't forget it or I'll give you some demerits," he sighed taking Virgil's book and signing it.

Thiago had a dark complexion, with short black hair unkempt that grew straight out from his scalp. He had a large nose and big puffy lips. Thiago had small dark eyes with big lazy eyelids that drooped over, giving him a permanent expression of boredom or contempt.

"The lowest scroll, which means you're the active brother who has been in Omega the longest right?" Virgil asked him.

"Yup, Theta class, Buck, Benson, and I are the only actives left from that pledge class," Thiago told him. His speech was slightly rapid with a lisp.

"It's nice to meet you, sir, hopefully we can schedule an interview sometime?" Virgil asked.

"Ehh I don't have time for that right now, ask me again in a few weeks," Thiago said handing Virgil's pledge binder back to him.

Virgil made his way over to another brother who he hadn't had much contact with yet. Louie was standing next to him engrossed in a humorous conversation that had them both smiling and laughing.

"Sir? Sorry to interrupt, could I bother you for a signature," Virgil said.

"Oh shit! You're famous Big, everyone here be wanting your signature," Louie joked.

"I guess," Louie's Big said with a shrug.

"Wait, what's my name first?" he asked. Virgil drew a blank. "It's Benson, scroll #88, make sure you remember that for next time," Benson told Virgil taking the binder.

"I will sir," Virgil thanked him as Benson signed his pledge binder. Benson was a tall, broad shouldered guy, built like a football player. Benson had wispy blond hair with a receding hairline, lively blue eyes, with big rosy cheeks. He had a laidback, friendly disposition.

Zender spotted Virgil and came over. "What the hell man? I gave you a simple task and you went and blabbed to your Big? Give me your pledge binder," Zender ordered him. Virgil handed him his pledge binder.

Zender flipped to his personal page within Virgil's pledge binder.

"Recite the Greek Alphabet for me," Zender commanded.

"I don't know it sir," Virgil said.

"Alright then recite the Angelic Alphabet," Zender commanded.

"I don't know that either sir," Virgil said.

"Such a pity," Zender said scribbling something down on his brother page. "You're on my shit list Pitcher," Zender told him handing him back the pledge binder.

Virgil looked down at Zender's page, under the Merit/Demerit section Zender had given him -25 Demerits for not being able to be trusted with a secret, and -50 for not being able to recite either Alphabet when asked. Virgil's heart sank to the floor, it was the first time he'd been given merits or demerits, and he was starting out -75 in the hole, great!

"Omicron class listen up!" Gabriel called out to the group ending brother's conversations. "Tomorrow morning you will be at Omega House for our morning run. Feel free to spend the night. See all of you in seven hours!"

Chapter 8
<u>Homecoming</u>

Thursday night the candidates had Devil Arms practice at the Omega house. Practice lasted over an hour. Virgil spent his time with Vahn, summoning Soul Reaver from its black symbol, and becoming comfortable with the scythe. Vahn made Virgil send the weapon away, then summon its corporeal form again several times. Virgil was getting more comfortable with the long and unusual weapon. He was enjoying slashing and spinning the scythe at invisible targets. The other candidates were working on getting used to handling their respective weapons. By the end of practice, only Luther and Devin couldn't produce the physical manifestation of their Devil Arms. Vahn told Virgil they'd begin sparring against one another soon, as only so much could be learned without an opponent to practice against.

Sunday night, the thirteen pledges found themselves at the Omega meeting room. Gabriel was lecturing on the history of the fraternity. Omega was started by a group of Nephilim at University of Michigan, who didn't quite fit in with any of the other fraternities. They forged their own brotherhood, with a more accepting outlook on recruitment standards. Other Nephilim fraternities were only recruiting Purebloods, or half-human half-judge, whereas most students were only a quarter judge or often less even. Gabriel explained that The Declaration of Principles was a document written by one of the most important men in Omega's history. The frater had written out a guideline of what Omega's stood for, and what they wanted their fraternity to be about. The Omega's were a brotherhood for life, a family of men working under the Paladins to protect all mankind. The Omega's triple principles were honor, valor, and brotherhood.

Gabriel then talked about how fraternities were started back in the 1700s. One of the earliest organizations was called the Flat Hat Club, because of the hats the members wore, though historians do not know the organizations real name. Some of the Founding Fathers of the US had belonged to the organization. Gabriel told Omicron Class fraternities were started by Paladins as a means of recruiting Nephilim to their order. Gabriel explained that many Nephilim are unaware of their heritage, and the Paladins work to find and educate people of their race, empowering them.

"Brotherhood is Tuesday night, be here, we'll be working on float building," Gabriel said as their education was winding down. "Which brings us to the topic of Homecoming. This week you need to help the brothers out with the Homecoming events as much as possible, here's what's going on each day," Gabriel said going over to the other half of the board.

The events were window decorating, basketball, pool volleyball, variety show, a community service event, powder puff football, and most importantly the float on Saturday's parade for the football game. Most of the events were competitions with points awarded to the top three, but some were just participation, meaning you just needed to have guys there to get points. The organization with the most points by Saturday won the Homecoming trophy. The candidates wrote down the events and grouped together to start a discussion on who could help.

No one talked much afterwards, they went to the pledge dorms just down the hall on the second floor and passed out. The following day was long and rough. Virgil was tired and his Biology professor told them they had an exam next week, and a Biology paper due in a few weeks. Math was as boring as ever, the professor doing little to help prep them for the exam on Wednesday.

On Tuesday, after getting through his classes, Virgil bumped into Frater Abe who suggested they do an interview. Abe was nineteen, a man of average height, with thinning dirty blonde hair. Abe was loud, enthusiastic, and dedicated. Abe told of how his father had been a

Paladin before him, dying in the line of duty. Abe was aligned with wind, an amethyst Devil Arms symbol on his hand. Abe's pledge brothers were Tarek, Zender, Doc, and Lamar, the ones that were still active he told Virgil. Of the three others, one couldn't take the stress of being a Paladin and left school, the other failed out of college, and the last one…Abe got quiet for a moment.

"What happened to the other guy?" Virgil asked.

"Scroll #112, he was your Twin," Abe said sadly. "He was a great guy."

"Oh," Virgil said suddenly making sense of what he was saying. Vahn's first Little Brother…had died. "How, how did it happen?" Virgil asked.

"Big Mission we had in the summer, operation was the cumulative effort of all Paladin fraternities and sororities in Michigan. There was a large demon assault on the city of Detroit in the summer, and it was an all-out battle waged in the streets against the demons," Abe explained. "Demons have been getting bolder lately, more numerous, it's getting harder to keep their numbers down without alerting regular people. Hooper, he…didn't make it through."

"That's awful," Virgil said feeling the weight of Abe's words. The loss and devastation of his friend was reflected within Abe's eyes, shining a light on the inner well spring of hurt within him.

"He was one of my best friends," Abe said tears rolling down his face. "Vahn was our Prytanis at the time, he stepped down right before the Fall semester started. Magnus who had been the Hypophetes stepped up to the position for the Chapter."

"Wait a minute, wouldn't the Vice President, the Epiprytanis step in first?" Virgil asked.

"Buck had been the Prytanis and Vahn the Epiprytanis, but Buck stepped down after a few months into the winter semester, forcing Vahn to step into the position. It's been a very rocky year for our Chapter, way too much turnover, but we're hoping things start to get better with you guys," Abe said encouragingly.

Virgil had been talking with Abe for over three hours, they were both starving, so they parted ways and Virgil went to eat dinner and relax until Brotherhood. Virgil walked with Boyd to meet the others. Virgil listened to Boyd boast about all the hot women he had met from the sororities.

"Dude there are some HOT Nephilim chicks that go here," Boyd squealed with delight.

"Really?" Virgil asked turning to Boyd, his brow arching in genuine interest.

Boyd let out a masculine chuckle, "I thought that'd get your attention. The Alphas, they are the only female Nephilim group on campus. I met a dozen of them at the events, all of them have Devil Arms, most of 'em are pretty good looking too. They have some cool pledges this semester, I heard one of them is Landon's little sister," Boyd said excitedly.

At the Omega house Gabriel was waiting for Omicron, "Tonight is going to be informal," he said earning some relieved looks. "We invited the Sweethearts over, we have to get the float built, and a big part of that is making the skirts for the trailer. One side will say Omega, the other BVSU," Gabriel told them. "Frater Vahn is in charge of building the damn thing, half of you work on the skirts, half work on getting the construction going, the float is in the garage with most of the brothers."

Virgil decided to join the skirt making, not knowing much about building things. In the living room making the skirts were two women talking with Landon and Jace. Virgil, Alec, Troy, Nolan, and Louie went into the living room to help with the skirt making.

"Well hello boys!" The ladies welcomed them warmly.

"Gentlemen for those of you who haven't been properly introduced, these are the lovely Sweethearts," Gabriel said. "We have Sweetheart #2, Ariel on the left, and Sweetheart #4, Raven on the right."

"Take a seat, we're happy to have you here," Ariel welcomed them warmly. Ariel was rather short, even for a girl. She had auburn red hair, with honey brown eyes that dazzled with life and warmth. Ariel had a heart shaped face with a small nose and rosy cheeks. Ariel was fun, zany, outgoing, and not afraid to say what she thought. Ariel was like that cool older sister you could always go to for advice, and never feel judged for what you had to say. Ariel had an aquamarine Devil Arms symbol on her right hand. She caught Virgil staring at it and gave him a bright smile, her eyes seeming to grow bigger and twinkle.

"Easy boy," Gabriel said jokingly but seriously telling him she was off limits.

"Oh Gabriel, leave the poor guy alone," Ariel said shoving Gabriel a little.

"I'm Raven," Raven said introducing herself. "I don't think I've met any of you yet." Raven was slightly taller than Ariel, with dark brown hair in a short pixie cut. Raven had bright blue eyes, with a small and graceful figure. Raven was like one of the guys, she was witty, sassy, flirty, and bossy. Raven was fiery and didn't take crap from people, she had a bad girl kind of vibe, but was very sweet and loving to the brothers. Raven was dressed very stylish; she had a taste for fashion. On her left hand was a golden-brown Devil Arms symbol.

Both Sweethearts were more than attractive, they were the epitome of everything a guy could want in a woman, smart, fun, loving. Virgil was guessing it was hard picking out Sweethearts for the fraternity. The bar was set high as far as quality was concerned.

The pledges quickly introduced themselves, then set to work, each on a section of the long wire, using plastic strips of white and blue, to tie onto it to spell out the letters. The pledges talked with the Sweethearts asking and answering questions, getting to know one another. Each pledge was saying a little about themselves, which took some time to get through everyone. A half hour quickly passed, and they slowly began to make progress on the skirt. When a Sweetheart would ask him a question, Virgil would get red in the face, and feel slightly nervous. They found it adorable, he felt utterly mortified.

"I grew up in Caseville, Michigan," he told them. "Small town but beautiful up there. How long have you been Sweethearts?" he asked.

"Oh gosh four years ago now," Ariel answered first. "We'd been a Chapter for one year and a colony for two years when I got asked to be a Sweetheart, they'd had one Sweetheart before me, Dawn. She later married a brother."

"I became a Sweetheart two years ago, as of this upcoming winter semester," Raven told them.

"How do you become a Sweetheart anyways?" Boyd asked.

"A Sweetheart is a woman who embodies the Omega spirit, one who is there for the brothers in thought, word, and deed," Ariel said passionately. "A Sweetheart is a friend, confidante, and advocate for the brothers, here to support all of you, as you in turn are a friend to us."

"A Sweetheart is one of the boys," Raven added in with a slight flip of her short hair. "When picking a new one, it is important to pick someone who is visible, someone who comes around and is dedicated to the Chapter. A Sweetheart is essentially a female honorary member of a fraternity, since most fraternities don't allow women to join. As long as it's a girl that all the brothers feel is already like one of the group, the fraternity can make her a Sweetheart, then she becomes an Omega."

"A Sweetheart isn't the girl every Brother sleeps with," Ariel affirmed clearly to the pledges repeating it once more. "A Sweetheart is a classy woman YOU want representing your letters out there, a woman that wears your letters represents who you are to the community."

The pledges continued to work with the Brothers and Sweethearts. After a while Aidan, Darius, and Axel came in from float building to switch up jobs and introduce themselves to the Sweethearts. They all fawned over Aidan, being Vahn's actual little brother.

Jace turned to Alec sitting next to Virgil and told him, "Candidate Birdy, could you go get me a drink please?" Dante's nickname for Alec had caught on quick and everyone referred to Alec as Birdy now.

"Sure," he said getting up and going to the kitchen. Birdy left his drawstring backpack sitting next to Virgil with all his pledge materials. Jace quickly scooped it up, set it underneath the couch cushion, and sat back down. Birdy came back, unaware his bag was no longer with him. Louie had also noticed what Jace was doing. Virgil and Louie shared a look. The candidates started to ask the Sweethearts for signatures and to set up interview times. Birdy jumped into action, the tall 6'4 lanky framed man suddenly started to tear through the area in a panic, looking for something…

"What's going on Birdy?" Jace asked him.

"Uhh…nothing. Just looking for something," Birdy said nervously his face red.

"You've been doing a great job Birdy, I want to reward you for helping us out, let me see your pledge binder," Jace said to him whole heartedly, with a devilish gleam in his eye.

"Sure thing, just give me a minute," Birdy said looking underneath the couch he was sitting on, moving things around when it wasn't there, gaining more attention from the room.

"Dude what's going on what are you looking for?" Axel asked him.

"I can't find my pledge binder," he said meekly.

"WHAT?!" Jace shouted. "What the hell man, you've got to keep better track of your shit."

"I had it here just a minute ago," Birdy said in his defense.

"You lose that on campus, someone gets a hold of it, and has access to our fraternity's secrets!" Jace yelled at him.

"Knock it off Jace! You big bully," Ariel said to Jace.

"Stay out of this Ariel," he quipped with a laugh.

"I remember a certain candidate last semester who was getting a lot of gruff from the Brothers, and came to us often upset and cry-" Raven started to say to the group when Jace cut in.

"Alright, Alright!" Jace exclaimed. "Gosh Birdy, I have your pledge bag."

"What?" Birdy asked still seeming to not get what was going on.

"Dang it Birdy!" Louie said starting to laugh, "He is messing with you man."

"Jace, give me back my bag," Birdy asked with a little sass.

"Ask nicely," Jace said taking out the bag and dangling it in front of Birdy.

Birdy reached out and snatched the bag from Jace's fingers.

"Hey!" Jace said in surprise. "I wasn't done yet."

"Fuck off," Birdy said with a scowl going back to his work.

"Excuse me?" Jace asked Birdy, all pretense of horsing around gone from his demeanor and tone.

Birdy didn't respond, he knew he was in trouble.

"Did you just tell a brother to fuck off! Give me your binder," he demanded.

"No," Birdy said laughing nervously.

"This isn't funny, I am a brother, and I am ordering you to give me that bag candidate," Jace said firmly.

Virgil scooted a little further down the couch away from Birdy's spot and closer to Louie, as the other candidates went quiet watching Jace and Birdy. Jace took his binder out and gave him a hundred demerits for messing up.

"Never openly disrespect a brother like that again," Jace said to him sternly.

"Yes, sir," Birdy said gloomily.

Virgil was getting tired of sitting, so he went for a walk to the garage. The garage was a spacious parking complex, capable of fitting dozens of vehicles. One half was being kept empty with a large trailer being used as the base to build the float. The brothers had decided on the three little pigs as the theme for the float. They were working on building three houses, but construction didn't seem to be progressing.

"Hey Vahn," Virgil greeted his big brother.

"Virge! How's it going buddy?" Vahn called back to him waving a drill in one hand.

"Virge?" Virgil asked with a raised eyebrow leaning against the trailer next to him. There were eight brothers and a few pledges, though only a few were building something.

"It's something I'm working on, a nickname for you," Vahn said cryptically.

"Virge?" Virgil asked again.

"Well there's more to it than that, but the guys wanted to call you Virgin Virgil, I said no," Vahn said. Virge wasn't so bad, Virgil thought.

"So what's happening here?" Virgil asked gesturing to the mostly empty, unbuilt float.

"No idea," he said with a deep laugh.

"What?" Virgil asked in a disbelieving tone.

"We're trying to build three collapsible houses that we can have fall down, and easily be set back up. Have three candidates in each one as one of the three little pigs. We'll have two brothers on the trailer, one being SVSU's Cardinal as the big bad wolf, and the other will be our BVSU Falcon who saves the day," Vahn painted a picture for him.

"That's different for a float, sounds more like a skit," Virgil remarked.

"Dude, that's the shit that the judges eat up," Vahn said to him. "This is my third homecoming, third float. The judges like floats that are more than just a display, if we can build the set for us to play out the thirty second skit, it'll be enough wow factor to get us first."

"That sounds pretty good," Virgil nodded in agreement.

"I'm sorry I haven't been around too much for you so far," Vahn said to Virgil taking a nervous swig of his drink. "I've been busy with school and Omega stuff, I haven't had a lot of free time."

"Dude, it's cool. I've seen you, and I've been busy too, I have a lot of people to get to know," Virgil said rolling his shoulders and laughing.

"We need to hang out after the stress of all this Homecoming rivalry nonsense is over," Vahn said. "What day works for you?"

"Let's see," Virgil thought, as he did a chorus of shouts and screams engulfed the room. A dozen girls had raided the garage, throwing water balloons, using silly string, and shooting Omega's with squirt guns. The guys jumped into defense mode, some ducking for cover, others chasing after a few of them.

Virgil and Vahn hurried outside where the group of Alpha sorority sisters were playfully attacking the Omega's. The Sweethearts, Ariel and Raven, hurried outside the Omega Manor to the porch carrying a cooler full of water balloons.

"I thought you ladies would be showing up," Ariel said mischievously pulling out a squirt gun from seemingly nowhere catching a sorority sister off guard, square in the face. "Think you got the drop on us?" Ariel shouted with a wide grin on her face grabbing a balloon with the other hand and whipping it at a passing sister.

"You don't mess with the Omegas!" Raven shouted grabbing a balloon in each hand and joining the water fight. Raven was currently a pledge for the sorority sisters, though she'd been an Omega Sweetheart for a year and a half.

Virgil and Vahn ran to the water balloons grabbing a few. Virgil saw a woman with dyed blond, with embroidered letters across her chest run past him. He threw a balloon at her, she turned to lock eyes with Virgil just as it hit her head, drenching water down her face.

"You!" She yelled. "It's on boy!" She ran at Virgil, who started to run away, but was tackled to the ground before he made it far. She took out a can of silly string and started to spray Virgil, while wrestling with him to keep him subdued.

"Alright I give, I give!" Virgil shouted in defeat to the rather tough woman who had him pinned down.

"That's what I thought pretty boy!" the woman triumphantly told Virgil as she let him up, grabbing his hand and helping him to his feet.

"This is kind of fun!" Virgil laughed. "I didn't expect this."

"The sisters said that we have a long history of pranking you boys," she told Virgil. "A group of us were working on our float, got bored and thought it'd be fun to take a break, so we came over to check on your float."

"I'm Virgil by the way, Virgil Pitcher, nice to meet you," Virgil said extending his hand.

"I'm Blair, Blair Neadeau," Blair said with a bright smile. Blair's shoulder length dyed blond hair was wet from the water balloon, her eye makeup slightly running. Blair was 5'6, with honey brown eyes, and a permanent mischievous grin on her face. Blair was a wild one, full of energy, sass, and confidence. She wasn't your typical stuck up pretty college girl. Virgil noticed she had a ruby colored Devil Arms glyph on her left hand.

"You're in the Nephilim sorority I take it?" Virgil asked motioning to her Devil Arms.

"Well I'm still a pledge actually," Blair shrugged, "Although the ladies don't allow us to use the term 'pledge' because they say that's hazing."

"Awesome I'm a pledge too!" Virgil laughed.

"Yeah, I can tell," Blair said with a laugh. "You got this doe eyed innocence about you," she told him jokingly.

Blair's sorority sisters were rounding up, quickly getting into their cars to head back to their own Greek house.

"I should probably go with my girls," Blair said sadly, like she wanted to stay and talk. "It was nice meeting you Virgil, hope to see you around," she called to him heading over to one of the running vehicles. Tarek and Lamar were waiting by the vehicles with water balloons to get the stragglers before they left.

"Listen here dicks!" Blair told the guys putting her hands on her hips. "I'm not afraid to kick all your asses, so just hold onto those balloons if you know what's good for you," she threatened them. Tarek and Lamar shared a look, then nodded and let her get in the car.

A tall skinny dirty blond girl was close behind Blair, also trying to get into the car.

"Guys please don't!" she asked nicely of them. Tarek and Lamar shared a look, then threw their balloons at her. She shrieked and ran to the vehicle dripping wet.

"Hey!" Landon called out, "That's my sister!" he admonished them. "Sorry Helene!" Landon called to his sister.

"Bye Landon!" Helene called out the window to her brother as the cars took off, taking the rowdy chaotic energy with them.

The guys and their Sweethearts quickly cleaned up, everyone in a great mood.

"That was awesome!" Virgil said to Vahn helping to clean up the yard.

"Yeah those sorority sisters are fun," Vahn agreed. "We always do fun stuff together, it's nice having a close relationship with a cool sorority."

"Blair said they were coming to check on our float," Virgil said to him.

"Blair?" Vahn asked whistling at Virgil, "Found a cute girl you like?" Vahn teased him.

"Come on now, we barely spoke," Virgil said in his own defense.

"I'm just hassling you bro," Vahn said giving Virgil's arm a soft punch. Virgil and Vahn made plans to hang out together next week, Thursday, after they were both done with classes.

Saturday morning Virgil stood shivering in the student parking lot with his fellow pledge brothers, guarding the float to make sure it wasn't being tampered with. The sun was just starting to come up on the day, Vahn and Zender along with Abe, Jace, Reece and Brody milled around their precious cargo, created from long hours of many sleepless nights. The float had turned out to be impressive, much to Vahn and Zender's credit. Though it had obviously cost them. Vahn looked a little worn down and tired, with heavy bags under his eyes. The setup was as Vahn had described, a scene straight from the Three Little Pigs, with the big bad wolf played by the Saginaw Valley Cardinal, and the Bay Valley Falcon kicking his butt and saving the little pigs. The judges ate up the short performance, of the Cardinal blowing down the houses, made to be collapsible through a lot of trial and error, hinges and screws, tears and beers. The Omegas won first place for the float, which put them at first place in the homecoming competition, winning a chorus of cheers from all the brothers.

Before the football game started, the student body tailgated in the parking lot next to the football stadium. The Omegas partied like they had just won the lottery. Soon the students were being corralled into the football game, as campus police were telling everyone they could go to the game or leave. Virgil and the rest of the group gathered together in the football stadium to watch the game between the two schools.

Halftime brought about the announcement of the Homecoming champions and the Homecoming queen. The Homecoming queen was announced to cheers and Virgil was surprised to see the stunning beauty waving to the crowd was Selene, Brody's girlfriend. She was a lady of elegant class and fierce intelligence. Her long curly black hair was intricately done up, with a dazzling forest green dress that accented her mixed Caucasian and Native American complexion. Virgil didn't miss the ruby red Devil Arms on her hand either. When the announcer called out Omega as the winners, the brothers erupted into screams, Vahn and Zender took the field to accept the trophy on behalf of their fraternity.

Virgil was tapped on the shoulder by Gabriel. He leaned in over the loud crowd to say, "I need you to take your Big Brother back to the house. He's looking pretty toasty, and needs someone to look out for him," Gabriel had a genuine look of concern. "And I mean, he is your Big, so he's kind of your responsibility," he added with a shrug

"Great!" Virgil replied sarcastically. "You can count on me sir," Virgil nodded in response.

"I know I can," Gabriel said patting his shoulder and giving him a big grin.

"Sir, um, if you don't mind me asking, who is taking care of you?" Virgil asked noticing his unsteady gait.

"That would be me!" said a gorgeous beauty that quickly came to his side, wrapping her arm around him and giving him a kiss. "I'm TK," she said extending her hand out to Virgil.

"Nice to meet you!" Virgil said shaking her hand and giving her a smile to match her own. TK was just as striking as Selene, even in casual jeans and sandals with a purple hoodie. TK looked short standing next to Gabriel, though she was of average height for a woman. She had black hair which was tied up in a bun. She had a thin frame, with skinny arms and legs. She had an elegant looking face, with breath taking green eyes that sparkled with a fire. Gabriel and TK looked great together, basking in a glow of their affection for one another.

"Virgil, I want to introduce you to my lovely girlfriend. TK is the Vice President of the Alphas, she's kind of a big deal," Gabriel said with a boastful grin on his face, one arm wrapped possessively around her side.

"I'm honored to meet my Hegemon's lady," Virgil said slightly bowing his head. "You're very pretty."

"Hey!" Gabriel snapped. "Watch it buddy."

"Aww you're so adorable! I'm taking you home," TK said to Virgil giving him a one-armed hug.

"Absolutely not!" Gabriel said playing along.

"Why not, he could be my new bestie," TK rounded on Gabriel. "I met a few of your new guys today," TK sighed, "I wasn't impressed with that Dante fellow, he's arrogant, loud, and a little full of himself."

Virgil laughed at TK's summation of Dante, which wasn't too far off.

"Dante's my boy!" Gabriel said, "That kid's cool as shit!"

TK and Virgil hit it off immediately, sharing a look and an eye roll at Gabriel's enthusiasm over Dante. TK was a third-year college student, like Gabriel, majoring in social work. She'd joined her sorority freshmen year. TK was all over the place in conversation, full of energy, loving, and genuinely funny! Virgil felt a connection with her, a sense of mutual respect, they had the kind of friendship that is almost instantaneous.

"Hey," Gabriel called to Virgil giving him a slight push with his finger. "I gave you a job, remember? Get your Big home safely and stop hogging my woman!"

"Who is your Big?" TK asked with a curious expression biting her lip.

"Vahn," Virgil replied.

"I love Vahn!" TK exclaimed, "That is a great match for you, Vahn's one of the best guys in Omega," TK assured him.

"Hey!" Gabriel rounded. "We are all good guys," he argued proudly.

"Is he a good Hegemon?" TK asked Virgil whispering but loud enough that Gabriel could still hear. "You can tell me if he's ever being mean to you, I'll kick his butt for ya," she said to Virgil with a wink and a cute laugh.

"No!" Virgil hurriedly said catching a sharp look from Gabriel. "He's the best!"

"Virgil go take care of your Big, now!" Gabriel told him a little gruffly, TK easily making him jealous.

"Yes sir!" Virgil agreed taking his arm back from TK and moving away to find Vahn.

"I meant what I said buddy," TK called after him, "Let me know if you're getting too much flak from this guy."

"Bye guys!" Virgil called back to them.

Then the two acted like they were the only people in the world, gazing into each other's eyes, everything else falling away. Virgil couldn't decide who was luckier of the two of them…probably Gabriel.

Virgil searched through the drunken crowd of brothers, strangers, and friends of the brothers. He saw Louie chatting up Troy, none of them had slept last night, staying up with the float, helping in any way they could to get it completed.

"Virge in the house!" Louie called out to him.

Virgil narrowed his eyes at Louie, "Don't call me that," he retorted. Virgil asked them if they had seen his Big.

"Yeah, he was stumbling around the concession stand area," Louie recalled. "We're all being recruited to drive home brothers, but dude…I'm so tired!" He whined.

"I'm going to fall asleep standing up," Troy agreed his dark curly mop of hair sticking up in all directions with bloodshot eyes.

"Get your people back, then you can pass out," Virgil encouraged them. "I'm going to grab Vahn, then crash in the pledge dorms at the house."

"Same here," Louie yawned, "I don't have the energy to drive back to campus."

Virgil walked towards the concessions and caught sight of Vahn and Doc, eating some nachos at a table.

Virgil laughed at them, "You guys ready to head back to the house?" he asked.

"Yes!" they both agreed. "I'm so tired bro," Doc said, "I need to take a power nap before campus comes over to celebrate."

"I can't even think of drinking," Vahn hiccupped, "more right now."

"You okay there champ?" Virgil asked Vahn.

"Shut," Vahn hiccupped, "Up! Shut up Lil! Don't be standing there judging your Big for acting a fool," he said waving a nacho chip in the air, a big glob of cheese flinging off and landing on Doc's tailgating shirt.

Doc and Vahn looked down at the forming stain, then up at each other. "Bro!" Doc exclaimed.

Virgil gave Vahn a look that said 'really?' and Vahn laughed. "So I'm a little," Vahn hiccupped, "drunk. Whatever. Let's go back to the house Lil, lead the way."

Abe wondered up to them as Virgil managed to get them both moving towards the exit and parking lot beyond. "Guys!" Abe yelled out to them stumbling along.

"We got a ride man, you can come with us," Doc volunteered.

"Oh thank God!" Abe exclaimed at an obnoxiously drunk volume.

They walked towards the parking lot and Abe praised Virgil for being the sober driver.

"Bro, dude, I think you're awesome man," Abe said throwing an arm around Virgil's shoulders. "I really appreciate you, I'm glad you're joining our fraternity."

"Thanks Abe that's really nice of you to say," Virgil said warmly to Abe. Though he was a little sloppy, he was being heartfelt and sincere, Virgil felt humbled by his praise.

"Duh, you're not telling me anything I don't already know," Vahn replied with a snarky tone.

"Hey! I wasn't asking for you to chime in Sprinkles!" Abe retorted to Vahn.

"Don't call me that!" Vahn barked angrily Abe hitting a nerve.

"Why, that's your name, Sprinkles," Abe chided him.

"Vahn, what's he talking about?" Virgil asked his Big.

"My stupid nickname in the fraternity is Sprinkles, your Big Brother picks it. Mine was a dumbass," Vahn said suddenly seeming sober, and a little angry.

Virgil regretted asking, "I hadn't heard."

"Its fine buddy," Vahn said with a sloppy smile, "He's not important, and that nickname doesn't mean anything, people only call me that as a joke, I don't go by that."

"We call you that all the time!" Abe said with a hearty laugh.

"People who MATTER don't," Vahn said coolly.

They got to the Omegas fraternity house and the brothers shuffled in to their respective rooms to pass out. Virgil went to the pledge dorm on the second floor to do the same. A few of his pledge brothers, Troy and Louie were already there passed out in their usual spots. Virgil kicked off his shoes next to the bottom bunk of the bed he had been using, crawled into the bed, and drifted off before he had time to think.

Chapter 9
<u>The Seven Seraphs</u>

Sunday after they had taken quizzes over last week's lesson, Gabriel's lecture started with the core principles of the fraternity. Omega was founded on Brotherhood, Valor, and Respect. As Omegas it was their job to protect mankind and fight against all who sought to destroy them. Omegas were meant to be leaders, in their community, in their cities, in their nations, in the world. Gabriel explained the structure of the Omegas and Internationals. Individual Omega groups, at separate colleges, were called Chapters, and the Chapters across the US were organized into four regions. Gabriel stated that although Omega was its own organization, they belonged and answered to a higher organization, the Paladins.

Upon graduating from college all Omega's became Alumni, they were given the title of Delta Class Paladins. All Paladins were organized into four classes, with the Delta being the lowest and Alpha being the highest. Once men of Omega graduated from college, they could choose to lead regular lives in the world. They retained their rank in the Paladins, serving as a reserve member of the larger fighting force. Or they could officially join the Paladins active ranks. All active Paladins were moved to Gamma class as a starting rank, all inactive Paladins not currently serving in the active military were Delta class. It was a choice all Omega's had to make upon graduating.

Gabriel explained that together the eight Grand Jeweled Officers were the main governing body of Alexandros, and the Paladin world across all countries and continents. Gabriel added the headquarters of the Paladins was in Alexandros, a floating landmass the size of Rhode Island, which hovered high above the center of Lake Michigan. The city had been founded before the pyramids were built, serving as the main Nephilim city in the world for thousands of years. Over the years the Paladins had protected mankind from countless catastrophes, unbeknownst to humanity. The Death Dealers, the Nephilim that served the Fallen, were becoming more aggressive over the years, a sign that things were moving towards something…

"Have any of the brothers told you of the prophecy of the Seven Seraphim Nephilim?" Gabriel asked Omicron. "They are called the Seven Seraphs as well."

Nolan eagerly raised his hand. "Don't you ever get sick of being a know-it-all?" Dante murmured under his breath earning a few laughs from some of the pledges. Gabriel gave Dante a look that silenced him.

"The prophecy was supposedly given by the Creator after the Battle of the Fallen. The Demon King Diablos led a third of the heavenly host against the Creator, in a battle for dominion of the world. The humans believe Lucifer, a Fallen Judge, was the leader of the rebellion. In truth it was the first demon, Diablos," Nolan explained.

"We try not to use the Demon King's name, names have power, and especially that name…it calls to things… in the dark," Gabriel warned. "Luckily the Demon King and Lucifer lost. All the Judges who allied with them, had their white wings cut, and they were cast out. The Creator then sealed the countless realms of the world off from one another, supposedly crying a single teardrop that held the barrier in place. The seal is called the Greater Weirding, and it was meant to keep the evil creatures, who had revolted against the creator, trapped in the realm of the Ever After."

"Ragnorak is in many legends, and has two meanings," Gabriel told them. "First, it is the name for the Apocalypse, or end of days. Secondly, Ragnorak is the name of the Holy Blade, the most powerful weapon in all of existence. Ragnorak was once wielded by the Judge Raphael, he betrayed his order, and joined Lucifer and the Demon King in their rebellion. The Holy Blade was taken from him for turning his back on the Light. It is said to be the only thing in this world capable of truly defeating the Demon King."

"The Creator told the host of Judges that seven Seraphim Nephilim, the Seven Seraphs, would herald the coming of Ragnorak. These seven will be powerful Nephilim," Gabriel almost whispered. "The Nephilim were given titles by the Creator, and each would be given special gifts. In order of birth they are the Avatar, the Oracle, the Doppelganger, the Harbinger, the Gatekeeper, the Redeemer, and the Chosen. Once the seven appeared in this world, it would be a sign to all the war of Ragnorak was at hand," Gabriel told them. "We already know of two of the Seven Seraphs, they our Grand Officers in are fraternity! Rasler Daedra is the Doppelganger. He is the Grand Pylortes of the Paladins. The King of Alexandros, Aseril Diamond, is the Grand Prytanis of the Paladins. He is the Oracle, or the Second Seraph. Aseril is a direct descendant of Lady Diamond, the legendary Nephilim who defeated the founder of the Death Dealers, Lokien. Lady Diamond is credited with founding Alexandros, her family has ruled over Alexandros for most of its history."

"Wait what?!" Louie said interrupting Gabriel's long speech. "What was the point of all that?"

Gabriel sighed his patience thin, "I'm saying Louie, that the end of days is quickly approaching. No one knows for sure when exactly, it will happen within our lifetimes. The signs are all there, human society is on a collision course for destruction, and the demons and Death Dealers are becoming bolder. The greatest indicator that Ragnoark is approaching is that the Seraphs have made their appearance. King Aseril revealed himself to Nephilim society seventeen years ago, giving a proclamation that he was the Second Seraph, the Oracle. If Ragnorak truly is

on the horizon, this world will need warriors, ready to defend humanity in the coming war,"
Gabriel told them solemnly.

"Wait a minute, I wanted to be in a fraternity, not some doomsday warrior troupe,"
Luther said speaking up. "I didn't sign up for this, I'm not ready for the end of the world," he
said his voice rising, his demeanor clearly saying he was upset.

"None of us want this, we all want to live the normal lives we always have, but facts are
facts," Gabriel said plainly. "The people you love, the people you know, are in danger. Humanity
can sense the impending doom, the coming of something…disastrous. You can sit around blind
to it, or you can choose to do something about it. I don't want to lie to you, that's why I'm
telling you all this. Every Nephilim should be aware of what is going on in our world," Gabriel
said spreading his arms out. "As Omegas we need to be prepared for this, and this process is
going to reflect that. The first few weeks have mostly been about getting to know us, and us
getting to know you. Now that you've been candidates for a few weeks, it's time for the real
process to start. From here on out, we will be focusing more on training, training you all to be
warriors. Playtime is over kiddies."

The room was quiet, Virgil looked at Luther, he was visibly shaking, and a little pale.
Devin, whom Virgil hadn't had much interaction with rolled his eyes at Gabriel, it was clear he
didn't believe any of what Gabriel was saying. Most of the candidates were stern faced, lost in
deep thought at the information Gabriel had told them.

"I know this information is a lot to take in, I don't expect you all to believe me at face
value. With time you'll come to learn what I have told you is the truth. Now let's talk about your
progress on getting to know the brothers," Gabriel grabbed their pledge binders and dropped
them in front of their respectful owners.

"Some of you are doing great, but others are quickly falling behind. You guys are doing awful on your merits and demerits, let's face it you guys suck at making good stats," Gabriel said knocking them down as if they weren't there. "Let's not focus on that. The whole point of this is for you to hang out with us and for us to get to know you. Which is why the interviews are essential to this process. The other key components, besides getting to know each other, are mastering of your individual skills, and learning to use them as part of a team. Working as a unit and on communication is vital to success, for this process and the brotherhood of our fraternity.

"Luther, you have three interviews total," Gabriel said calling out Luther. "This is a Brotherhood, first and foremost. We're a family, and you can't be a part of this family if you don't know any of us. I've talked with brothers, and they don't feel like you're making any effort whatsoever."

"I've been busy!" Luther exclaimed. "I'm in Band, plus my classes and this, it is too much for me! This mark on my hand," he said looking down at his ruby Devil Arms, "Ever since its appeared that first night we accepted our bids, everything has changed, and I don't like it. I want everything to go back to the way it was, I don't want any of this!" he screamed standing up and slamming his hands down on the desk. "I've tried to be okay with all this weird Nephilim crap, but it is too much, it's just too much!" he yelled.

"You are not being forced to do this," Gabriel told him calmly. "If you want to stop that is your choice."

Luther took off the Dreamstone from around his neck, placed it once more on the desk, as he had their first Education, and left the room.

"Sit tight guys," Gabriel said leaving after him.

"What did I tell ya?" Dante said to the group. "We should have kicked his whiny ass out the first time he bailed on us."

"Knock it off," Louie told Dante. "He's stressed out, we all are. You can't blame him for quitting, it is not for everyone."

Gabriel was gone for some time before he came back to the meeting room. "Hey guys sorry about that, I had to contact Master Ramuh to come and perform the Oath of Depledging," Gabriel told them.

"I have a question," Virgil asked his Hegemon.

"Shoot," Gabriel said looking tired.

"You said that if we took the Dreamstones off and left campus that it would be dangerous. I'm worried about Luther, is he going to be okay without it?" Virgil asked.

"Good question. Listen, most Nephilim aren't Pureblood or Pureborn," Gabriel explained to the group. "They need the Oath of the Paladin ceremony to bring out their inner power, like their Devil Arms and the ability to use spells. When a Nephilim who has gone through the ceremony that brings out a Nephilim's inner powers, their aura becomes like a walking firework display. But if anyone decides to leave the fraternity, we make sure to protect them by placing powerful spells on them. Basically these powerful spells, dampen the previous benefits that were originally bestowed upon that Nephilim, turning them, for all sense and purpose, back into a normal human. We also remove most of their memories of the fraternity and the Nephilim world. Luther will remember being a pledge for us, but he won't remember much of what he learned. He'll be just like a regular person out in the world, and won't be any more appealing to a demon, than a normal person."

"So, his Devil Arms, it'll be gone as well?" Virgil asked.

"No," Gabriel told Virgil. "No one should be able to see it, but it will still be there. Devil Arms don't disappear once they awaken. The best we can do for those Nephilim is erase their knowledge of the true world, and place powerful illusion spells over their Devil Arms so other Nephilim won't recognize them for what they are. Now is a good time to speak up, if you think this is too much."

Omicron class stayed quiet, they looked at one another, waiting for the next person who would be the one to say this wasn't for him. But none of them did.

"At our Chapter meeting, one of Omicron was brought up for removal," Gabriel sighed.

"Who?" Louie V asked worry etched on his face.

"Axel," Gabriel said looking Axel straight on. "A brother brought you up for removal tonight. He said that he thinks you're half assin' this process, not putting your all into this, and not taking it seriously," Gabriel said sternly staring straight at him. Virgil was glad Gabriel wasn't staring him down with that harsh and daunting gaze.

Axel shrugged, "So am I out?" he asked not appearing to be very worked up.

"No," Gabriel replied tartly. "We voted and it was decided that you should be allowed to continue this process. But this should be a warning to all of you, at any time, if the brothers feel you aren't making a strong effort to join this family, you can be brought up for removal," he warned them.

Monday night the group was behind the Omega's home near the woods. Virgil was practicing with Vahn, he called out, "Soul Reaver!" A cloud of black smoke erupted from his hand, the scythe hovering just out of reach. Virgil grabbed it, feeling its power pulse through him. Vahn and Virgil worked on footing. Vahn explained that it wasn't enough to swing it wildly. It was about becoming one with the weapon, being able to move fluidly, to be mindful of how and where you're attacks hit, and parry incoming blows. Combat had a rhythm to it, and being a good warrior involved learning this rhythm, how to predict an opponent's moves, without revealing your own.

Vahn noted that though in his first encounter with a demon, merely throwing his scythe at the enemy had worked, against more intelligent foes, it could leave him exposed to a lethal counter attack. Unless he was wielding his other Devil Arms, the white symbol on his right hand. Vahn suggested that Virgil not stress out mastering that one. Vahn didn't wield a scythe, so he wasn't an expert on how to utilize one, but he did know how to use a sword in combat. Together he and Virgil helped to work on developing moves he could do with the scythe, getting used to his positioning, how he had to stand to set up different attacks. The weapon was rather bulky and clunky, not as graceful as a sword or a spear. Virgil's blade seemed to have a deadly mind of its own. The scythe whirled around rather quickly with little force from Virgil, its silver curved blade seemingly thirsting for action. As much control as he seemed to have over it, Virgil became very aware that it had a will of its own.

Gabriel came over to Virgil and Vahn after a half hour of practice.

"Good job Virgil, you're seeming to catch on quick," Gabriel complimented him.

"He can control the blade with his mind," Vahn said to Gabriel.

"Show me," Gabriel said placing both hands behind his back.

Virgil brought his body to the starting fighting stance Vahn had instructed him, his right foot forward and his left back. Vahn stepped forward, utilizing the momentum of his body Virgil swung the scythe. Virgil released his scythe at the end of his strong swing, sending it arching into the air. Virgil was one with its movement, it sailed through the air a good distance, flying back at an incredible speed, coming to a gentle hover as it approached his hand.

"You're a natural," Gabriel said stone faced unmoving. "You need to practice against an actual opponent however, so you can start to gain some skill. Starting Wednesday, you guys will begin sparring," Gabriel smiled moving on.

"Alright," Virgil said a little uneasy, grabbing the scythe from the air. He didn't like the idea of trying to hurt his Big.

Tuesday, Virgil came back to his dorm after class was finished. Damian's door was cracked slightly, and his light was on. It was the first time Virgil could recall Damian being home since they had started pledging their fraternities. Virgil knocked lightly on the door, "Damian can I come in?" he asked. He didn't hear a response and decided to push open the door a little. Damien appeared to be working on his studies at his desk, books and notebooks laying open. His clothes were strewn about the room. A bag was open on his bed, with a few pieces of clothing folded up and placed inside.

"Hey bro, haven't seen you around lately, how you been?" Virgil asked with a smile on his face trying his hardest to be friendly.

Damian turned to Virgil removing the earbuds from his ears, music blaring loudly from them, he hadn't heard Virgil come in.

"Don't you knock?" Damian asked in a short tone.

"I'm sorry I did knock, you must have not heard it," Virgil said in an apologetic tone. "I was wondering how you were doing. I haven't seen you lately and I've been worried about you," Virgil said looking Damien in the eyes trying to convey his sincerity.

"What's it to you?" Damien asked.

"Dude, all I want is to be your friend. We got along great before this whole fraternity thing came up. I don't care if we are joining different groups, I want to be your friend regardless of any petty rivalry," Virgil told him in frustration.

"I appreciate you trying to be nice to me, you're a good guy Virgil," Damian said more warmly looking a little sad. "But the Betas, they don't want their pledges associating with Omegas. Nothing personal, I have to listen to them, just like you have to listen to the Omegas. That's why I've been staying away, makes things easier on all of us," Damian told Virgil, his tone more neutral, less hostile.

"How are you holding up? This pledging thing is stressful as hell," Virgil said leaning against the door frame.

"I'm hanging in there, it's almost half way over thank goodness. I've barely been able to keep up with my classes. It is definitely one of the most stressful things I've ever done," Damian told Virgil.

"Have you guys started training in Devil Arms yet?" Virgil asked him.

Damian noticeably cringed at that and looked away from Virgil. "I'm not allowed to divulge fraternity secrets Virgil, so don't try to get anything out of me for your Omega buddies," he retorted sourly.

"Dude what the hell! I could care less about learning your fraternity's secrets, you're my friend, and I care about you! I was just asking, this whole situation is overwhelming, and it can't hurt to have a friendly ear to vent to occasionally," Virgil shrugged.

"Virgil, the Betas hate the Omegas, HATE them!" Damian's voice rose. "I don't think you realize how strong their rivalry is, no matter what you say or do, the guys in my fraternity will continue to feel that way. I don't feel that way, especially about you, I know you're a good guy. But I want this, I want to be a part of this group, so I fall in line, or get out. I'd appreciate it if you wouldn't make this harder than it has to be," Damian said sadly not looking Virgil in the eyes.

"Are you saying you don't want to be friends anymore? That's stupid! Both our fraternities have Nephilim members, they both belong to the Paladins. We should be coming together and uniting as a stronger unit, not bickering over whose bigger and better," Virgil's voice rising not wanting to lose his friendship.

"I agree, but it is what it is," Damian said shrugging his shoulders. "I have a lot of stuff to get done, it was nice seeing you Virgil," Damian put his earbuds in, and went back to homework and music. Virgil left Damian's room closing the door behind him.

That night everyone but Aidan showed up at the Omega house, Gabriel and Jagger were waiting for them in the front foyer. Gabriel led them to the back, most of the brothers were already outside waiting for them along with the Sweethearts, Ariel and Raven. The girls waved warmly to the candidates and Virgil smiled brightly, things always seemed to be a little more fun when they graced the men with their presence. Once they were situated Gabriel asked them to put on their Dreamstones. The candidates did so, and one of them let out a cryptic 'Uh Oh.' Louie looked up from his bag, his face etched in panic.

"Umm I forgot my Dreamstone back at my dorm," Louie said softly.

"What!?" Gabriel said with a groan. "Damn it Louie V, you're a pain in my ass," he said letting out a frustrated growl. "Go back and get it," he told him.

"I didn't drive here," Louie V said looking down at the ground as he did.

"I-I-I'll take him," Hector stuttered out.

"Go," Gabriel instructed, and they left in a hurry.

Nolan raised his hand and Gabriel replied, "What is it?"

"Aidan didn't show up when we met to come here, I was wondering if you guys had heard anything," Nolan asked.

"Aidan decided to stop pledging today," Gabriel said with flat affect. "He's here on a Presidential scholarship and isn't doing well in his classes. He stopped to focus on his studies. He wanted me to tell everyone that he's sorry he had to leave, and he plans to pledge again." Gabriel was clearly disappointed and didn't want to talk about it.

Omicron was quiet, they were down to eleven guys, and Virgil had thought Aidan was one of the stronger members of their group. He was Vahn's blood brother after all, and he was intelligent, losing him was certainly a blow to the pledge class. Twenty minutes later Louie and Hector came back.

"Now that everyone is here, we can finally begin," Gabriel said to them. "I want all of you to drop down, give me twenty push-ups. You wasted my time and the brothers' time by making us wait for you."

Omicron got down and started doing their push-ups.

"I want you to count them out as a group!" Gabriel commanded, and Omicron shouted out the number they were on together.

"Don't waste our time people, when I say I want you here on time I mean it! This shit will not be tolerated, if it continues you will all be made to pay the consequences. One of you fails, you all fail. If you guys want to be doing push-ups every day of this process, fine by me," Gabriel barked clearly not okay with it.

Louie struggled to get down all the way and was doing half-assed push-ups.

"Louie, get your stomach to the ground mister those are NOT push-ups. Everyone starts over!" Gabriel barked at him. Louie pushed himself harder, with some obvious strain.

"Keep going big man!" Birdy called out from beside Louie. "You're doing good man, almost there." With Omicron giving each other encouragement, they finished.

"Let's get started with Brotherhood. Darius you stay out here, Jagger, take the rest inside and we'll send for the next one when we're ready," Gabriel instructed. Jagger led Virgil and the others back inside. After a few minutes, Landon came in escorting them one at a time outside.

Virgil followed Landon outside when it was his turn, the candidates who had gone before Virgil were watching intently. The brothers were gathered around with keen focus. What drew Virgil's attention though was Gabriel, he was elevated in the air fourteen feet high, standing on a large rocky platform made of dark earth. Virgil assumed Gabriel had raised it from the ground, Virgil's senses started to get sharper, adrenaline flooding his brain preparing him for the task ahead.

"Virgil, your objective is simple, get to your Hegemon, by any means necessary!" Gabriel shouted clearly.

Virgil ran forward, his feet pounding against the ground, he started to pick up momentum and leapt into the air at the wall of rock and dirt. He hit the wall about half way up, gripping into the dirt with his fingers, desperately trying to gain some traction in his feet. He skidded down hitting the ground. Frustrated he jumped up and tried to climb again, there weren't any places for him to grab onto though. Virgil took a step back, staring at the puzzle, looking up at Gabriel, this was a test of some kind. It wasn't meant to be climbed, Virgil thought, so how am I supposed to get up there?

"We're waiting Virgil!" Gabriel called out, "Get to your Hegemon, now!"

Virgil looked down at the symbols on his hands. Perhaps the wall wasn't meant to be climbed, maybe it was meant to be conquered. Virgil channeled thoughts of rage and anger, the black symbol on his left-hand blazing to life.

"Soul Reaver!" he called out and in a blaze of black flames, the scythe came into being. A few brothers, Sweethearts, and candidates let out cries of surprise.

Virgil grabbed onto it and charged at the wall, striking at the earth again, and again. Screaming as he attempted to destroy the barrier in front of him. After a few swings Virgil took a step back, the spots where he had gouged long deep rivets, were flowing back together, like water. Damn it! He cried out in his mind, not knowing what he was supposed to do.

"Virgil, get to your HEGEMON!" Gabriel shouted.

Virgil charged the wall again, this time jumping at the wall and stabbing his scythe into it. Using the scythe as a pick, he dug it in deep, and used it as leverage to start climbing. He started to make some progress, moving up the wall slowly. Suddenly the wall surged at him, in the shape of a fist, punching him off the wall. He landed on his back, the wind getting knocked out of him, his scythe landing next to him in the grass. Virgil wheezed slowly standing struggling to regain his composure.

"Frater Landon, please take Virgil to stand with the rest of Omicron," Gabriel asked. Virgil closed his left hand, willing the scythe to return to the darkness and flame from which it came. Virgil stood next to Troy feeling defeated. The rest of the candidates came, one by one, to attempt the same test. None of them succeeded.

"Brothers, Omicron has failed this test, would one among you like to try?" Gabriel asked them.

"I'll do it!" Magnus said volunteering. He walked up to the wall, took a few paces back and charged the wall, as many of the candidates had. Magnus stopped within feet of the wall and turned to his brothers.

"Brothers! Will you please help me?" Magnus asked the fraternity.

The whole of the group eagerly came forward, and as a group they were able to bring down the walls with ease. The earth that had risen up, eased back into the ground, and the platform Gabriel stood on sank till he was on the ground, and Magnus walked across to shake his hand.

Gabriel stepped forward to the candidates, "Not every obstacle in life can be overcome with brute force. Sometimes there will be obstacles that you can't take on by yourself. Use Your Resources," Gabriel said putting emphasis on each of those three words. "The Brothers in this fraternity are your resources. If you are needing help with something, turn to one of us. We have among us practically every major offered at this university, you need help with a class, or you're having girl trouble, come to us. Whatever it is, we will help. You can't get through life on your own, attempting to do everything by yourself. When we work as a team, and rely on each other's strengths, we can overcome any obstacle. Do you understand this lesson?" he asked Omicron class.

Omicron gave a few nods, some people said yes, sir. "I can't hear you!" Gabriel yelled.

"SIR, YES SIR!" Omicron shouted in unison.

"That's better. I want to talk with you guys about unity for a minute. There are eleven guys in Omicron now. You guys are a decent group of people, individually you're pretty good. We don't want good, Omegas are great. Brothers are seeing effort from some of you, but we have eleven different individuals trying to get through this process on their own. We don't need eleven individuals trying to go in eleven separate directions, we need Omicron class. Some of you are bonding, but it is not enough! Before you can be a part of our family, you need to make your OWN. I am in Lambda class, those guys are some of the closest friends I have. How many of you can say the same thing about the guy standing next to you? How many of you can say that, raise your hand!" Gabriel demanded.

Virgil looked to the guy ahead of him, Troy, and the guy in line behind him, Hector, he couldn't raise his hand. None of Omicron raised their hands.

"Exactly," Gabriel said in a knowing but disappointed voice. "None of you. How can you expect us to accept you guys as our brothers, when you can't even accept each other? This class needs to come together, NOW! I'm tired of seeing each member of Omicron doing everything on their own, from now on, I had better see you guys walking in packs. You are a pledge class and you need to start acting like it. Have you had a group interview yet?" Gabriel asked them.

"Sir, no sir," Omicron responded in unison.

"I want to see some unity out of you guys. You're Omicron, get your shit together people," Gabriel sighed irritated with them. "Dismissed."

The candidates were left by themselves as most of the brothers and the Sweethearts had already headed inside, not wanting to stick around to listen to Gabriel admonish them. Omicron turned towards one another, now the only people left outside.

"When do you guys want to do this?" Nolan asked taking out his planner, which looked like anyone's worst night.

"No, we don't schedule this for later, we do it now," Dante said stomping a foot. "Gabriel's right, we haven't been coming together as a group. We need to fix that, I say we go up to the pledge dorms, sit down as a whole and talk," Dante said getting worked up as he did.

"Dude, I'm so tired, can't we do it a night we don't have Omega stuff beforehand?" Louie asked with a yawn stretching out his arms.

"No Louie, we can't! Wake up, you big sleepy panda, we got shit to do," Dante snapped.

Louie looked a little peeved at Dante but didn't say anything back. "Let's just get it over with," Axel sighed patting his roommate Louie on the back.

"This isn't something we have to 'get over' and be done with," Dante chided, mocking Axel with and exaggerated emphasis on get over. "We need to come together as a group. I'm guilty of it, I barely know any of you guys, and we've been together for weeks now. Gabriel was telling me that his class, Lambda, did EVERYTHING together. By the time they were initiated they were inseparable. That's what they want of us, they want us to stop just being pledges in the same class, and start being friends. That's only going to happen if we're all on board, and everyone is putting in effort. This group needs an intervention, not this week, not tomorrow, tonight!" Dante was passionate.

Virgil had always found Dante to be a little abrasive and domineering, in that moment he saw in Dante a leader. The morale of the group was low, but Virgil saw a new drive that hadn't been there before. Tonight's Brotherhood had lit a fire under some of them, including Virgil. He felt a little differently about this process than he had before. Whether it was the message that Gabriel had taught them with the actual Brotherhood, or what he had said after. Virgil felt excited about it, like a new energy had been breathed into him. The more he experienced and learned, the more he wanted to know and do. The group was quickly in agreement with Dante. They went inside the Omega manor, raided the fridge for some drinks and snacks, and went to the pledge dorms for Omicron bonding time.

Chapter 10
<u>Omicron</u>

Omicron was full of laughter, crude jokes, and stories shared about past experiences. The eleven guys were on the bunks, floor, chairs, and clothing chests at the end of the bunk beds in the pledge dorms. They were introducing themselves, saying where they were from, their interests, and why they'd decided to join Omega. Devin and Axel had gone first. Alec or Birdy, as he was now called, volunteered to go next.

"I'm Alec," he said raising his hand to the group.

"Who?" Louie asked earning a few laughs.

"Or Birdy, whichever you prefer," Birdy nodded acknowledging his nickname. Birdy was a tall, lanky guy with dark hair, bright eyes, a dopey smile, big ears, and a gentle disposition.

"We prefer Birdy," Dante said seated near his roommate.

"I'm eighteen, from Macomb, came to BVSU because I liked the dorms, dual major in Criminal Justice and Social Work," Birdy described himself. "I like basketball and baseball. I also like video games every now and then. I am a mama's boy," he added earning a few sarcastic 'awws' from the group. "Seriously my family is very important to me. Something interesting about me, I was born with only twenty percent of my hearing capacity. Had to learn sign language when I was younger, still know some of it. I have hearing aids, and most people don't notice," Alec told the group. "I saw some posters when I came through for my tour, emailed the rush chair Doc, and kept in touch with him over the summer," Alec concluded.

"What's up y'all I'm Louie V," Louie beamed brightly. Louie was Asian with a dark complexion, he was a bigger guy, small dark eyes, a big wide nose, and a round plump face.

"Everyone knows who you are Louie," Dante sighed.

"I'm eighteen years young, come from Sterling Heights," Louie continued unabated. "I'm half Vietnamese, with some Chinese and a little Caucasian. I love football, video games, and art. Everyone on campus knows me. Folks know me as that big loveable Asian whose down for a good time. Something interesting about me, my dad was offered over three thousand dollars for a painting I did when I was ten. My dad turned him down, cause he said it was priceless to him," Louie said getting a little emotional. Virgil's eyebrows raised at the number. "I wanted to major in Art, my parents won't let me, so I'm currently majoring in Communication, plan to change it to something else, not sure yet. I joined Omega because I thought it would be fun, and my dad is a Paladin, so he told me to join as well."

Boyd went next, Virgil knew the most about him out of the group. Hector didn't have much to say, then Dante spoke. "Hey guys I'm Dante," Dante said confidently. Dante was the second shortest member of the group, slightly taller than Boyd. He had reddish auburn hair, with brown eyes and a pale white complexion. "I'm eighteen, from Clio. I played football for four years and was the captain my senior year. I love most sports, I love to work out, and have fun. I'm a Biology major, not sure what I want to do yet. Something interesting about me is I am a male cheerleader, with Hector over there. I saw a bunch of girls on the cheer squad working out and I was hooked. I actually had a threesome with one of the girls on the cheer team who lives above me with her and her friend," he boasted earning him cheers and congratulations from around the room.

"Oh-h-h-h shit man which one?" Hector asked.

"Ashley," Dante said proudly getting a jealous response from Hector. "I joined the Omegas because I was looking for that family away from home, missed the comradery that I had with the guys on the football team."

"I'm Nolan," Nolan said introducing himself. Nolan had light brown hair that stuck up all over from multiple cowlicks oddly positioned on his head, making it impossible for it to lie down straight. Nolan had dark brown eyes, and a strong square jaw, coated in an eternal five o'clock shadow. Nolan's voice was deep and gravelly. Despite his overly masculine appearance, he was one of the most well-mannered of the group. "I'm eighteen, from Deerfield Michigan," he told the group. "I like anime, video games, and learning. I love school, came to BVSU on a Presidential scholarship. Something interesting about me, I was a dual enrolled high school student and transferred enough credits into this university, that I'm already considered a sophomore credit wise. I'm an Accounting major, I'm going to make lots of money, and help my family. I joined the Omegas because I want to be more outgoing, and I need help getting a girlfriend."

"What do you mean you need help getting a girlfriend?" Dante asked Nolan.

"I've never been with a woman, and I have a hard time talking to girls. I need some help learning how to talk with them. I'm hoping to get a girlfriend soon, I don't want to stay a virgin," he admitted his face growing red.

"Ohh shit!" Louie V said in a high-pitched voice. "Little Nolan wants to get his dick wet!" Louie said laughing hard.

"I'll help you out bud," Dante told him. "We'll get you laid, no problem."

"I don't want to sleep with some random chick, I'd like to lose my virginity to a girl I'm dating," Nolan asserted.

"Girlfriend or drunk party chick with low standards, either way we'll make it happen," Dante assured him with confidence.

"I'll go next," Virgil said. "I like soccer and baseball, reading, playing video games like most of us sounds like. I'm a Pre-med major, came to BVSU on a Presidential scholarship. Something interesting about me, I was interviewed and given my scholarship by an Omega, one of the older brothers who work in the admissions office. I met an Omega before I even knew what it was," Virgil told his pledge brothers.

"That happened to me too," Nolan said to Virgil. "I got interviewed by Vic Taylor, scroll #1, aka The Godfather of this Chapter." Nolan told Virgil.

"I'm Troy from Saginaw," Troy said meekly the last in the group to talk. Troy was an average height guy, with thick black curly hair. Like Nolan he had constant stubble on his face. Troy had a small face with a little nose, round cheeks, and brown squinty eyes. "I like baseball, sports, watching TV, and hanging out with the guys. I'm an Accounting major like Nolan. Something interesting about me, my dad is a Paladin, and he told me about my lineage and to join the Omegas. I joined because I was hoping to find the group that I belonged with." Virgil instantly liked Troy. He was genuine, honest, and kind, not something common among young adult men especially in their generation.

Once the group had taken turns introducing themselves, they quickly jumped into sharing stories of their youth, times they almost got caught doing crazy shenanigans with their buddies in high school, babes they chased and or got with, and things that they felt were important or funny. It was the first time any of them had sat down as a group to talk.

"We should have done this sooner," Louie pointed out to Virgil and the others after they had been 'bro-ing out' for an hour.

"I'm glad we did this," Birdy added, "thanks for making us," he said clapping Dante on the back.

"We need to work on being together more, and we have to work on communication," Dante said to the group.

"We will," Virgil said feeling confident that they had taken a big first step in becoming a more solidified unit.

"We need to text each other more," Nolan said to the group, "Let each other know when one of us is headed to the cafeteria, or the library, or the gym. Chances are at least one of us is sitting around looking for someone to go do these things with as well."

"Tomorrow is going to be a whole new process," Dante said. "A whole new Omicron, we need to show the brothers that we're serious about this and we're dedicated to each other and this fraternity."

"We still need to talk about getting our Philanthropy project set up," Nolan reminded them. Virgil and the others let out a groan. "Luckily I took the liberty of getting something arranged," Noland said reassuringly. The group let out a collective sigh of relief.

"God bless that big beautiful brain of yours," Louie said passionately. "What's the plan?"

"I did some research, St. Jude's Children's Hospital is an organization our fraternity donates to and supports regularly. I figured we could raise some money to donate from Upsilon Delta Chapter," Nolan offered. "I contacted Bennigan's in Saginaw, we're going to have a day there in a few weeks where anyone who brings in a coupon, made up by us, will have twenty percent of their bill donated to St. Jude's Hospital on our behalf. I figured we could make up some posters, put up some flyers with the coupons, get the word out," he explained.

"What would we do without you?" Boyd asked.

Nolan shrugged his shoulders. "I figured we'd have some trouble with the time crunch, so I took the liberty of handling it, couldn't have it hanging over my head, making me stress out," he tried to make it sound nonchalant, but he'd done a great thing.

"We should get some sleep," Louie V said yawing.

"I'm too excited to sleep!" Dante exclaimed, "We should do something as a group."

"Like what?" Virgil asked.

"Let's go mess with someone! Come on we're pledges in a fraternity, we need to get a little wild!" Dante shouted and laughed.

"I'm down," Darius agreed, "Who are we messing with?"

"Jace," Birdy said instantly.

"Jace," agreed Louie nodding his head.

"Screw that guy!" Axel said, "He's been running me ragged!"

"Jace it is," Dante said a devilish grin coming over his face.

Omicron class went as a group and bought flour, and plastic wrap. They went to the Omegas parking garage to mess with Jace's truck, completely wrapping it up, and covering it in flour. Once the truck had been thoroughly messed with, the group retired to the pledge dorms to get some rest before the next day. Virgil and the others were starting to feel more like a unified group for the first time.

Virgil's cell phone kept going off the next day. A text from Dante inviting everyone to the gym in a half hour. A text from Louie V, he was headed to the cafeteria and he'd enjoy some company. Virgil managed to join up with a big group of them after five in the evening for dinner. Louie, Alec, Dante, Nolan, Troy and Virgil were seated together in the cafeteria, talking about what they'd done that day, and their plans for the weekend. Dante was suggesting an Omicron field trip to the casino.

"It's a great idea, we all ride down to Mt. Pleasant together, stop by the casino, plenty of time for making memories," Dante told them in between shoveling lasagna into his mouth.

"That could be fun," Nolan told him, "we'll talk it over as a group. I think that's a good idea for us all to take a trip together. Besides we need to get our paddles ordered for our Bigs anyway, Mt Pleasant has a place that the brothers go to, we could all go there as a group."

"Did you hear Jace is on a warpath looking for the pledge responsible for messing with his truck? He said it took him forever to get inside the dang thing let alone get it cleaned up," Louie laughed.

"Does he know it was all of us?" Virgil whispered.

"Hell no!" Louie laughed. "He thinks it was Axel, me and a few others, but he doesn't know we ALL did it!" Louie grinned. "He's threatening to make our lives all hell if we don't fess up to who is responsible."

"Damned if we do, damned if we don't," Virgil shrugged. "We're not going to tell him anything."

"Omicron man," Louie said elbowing Virgil, a large grin on his face.

After dinner they went their separate ways. Virgil had History from seven till ten. They were learning about Ancient Greek history now, Virgil found it very interesting, and the professor was passionate about the subject which always made lectures more stimulating.

After class Virgil hurried to the Bell Tower to meet up with the guys, Dante and Louie gave him an enthusiastic greeting.

"How was class?" Louie asked him.

"Good, went by fast," Virgil told him. "We all here yet?"

"Yup we were waiting on you," Dante said kindly. "Alright guys move out!" He called to Omicron. The candidates broke up into smaller groups as usual and made their way to the Omega house for Devil Arms training.

Dante was driving, Birdy rode shotgun, Louie and Virgil were in the back. Louie was catching everyone up on what the different members of Omicron had been up to. Louie had taken it upon himself to text each one of them throughout the day, keeping up on what they were doing, and who they were hanging out with. Birdy was talking with Virgil more, they'd started to bond. Virgil had went with him to the store last night and they'd had fun talking. Birdy was kind of goofy and absent minded, and very friendly. Dante was being friendlier to Virgil as well, being the one who'd invited Virgil to ride with them. Whereas before, Dante had seemed arrogant and bossy, Virgil was starting to see a different side to him, Dante was funny, something Virgil hadn't noticed. Louie always seemed nice, but now he was going the extra mile with everyone, doing his part to make Omicron a better pledge class.

"I know it has only been a day, but I feel like we were better today, more unified, or at least trying to be," Virgil remarked.

"We were better, but friendships don't form overnight," Dante said in response to Virgil. "You can't force friendships either, some people click well together, and others just don't. The best we can do is be friendly and try to spend time together. The more you get to know someone, the more you learn about them, and the more they grow on you. I'm glad we started talking more, I didn't really care for you at first," Dante spoke truthfully staring Virgil down in the rearview mirror being upfront with his feeling.

"Dante," Birdy chided him telling his roommate with his eyes to 'play nice.' Virgil and Louie exchanged a look, and Louie shrugged putting his hands up in the air as if to say, it was the first he was hearing of it. Virgil felt embarrassed and didn't know what to say in response.

"I guess if we're being honest, I didn't like you all that much either," Virgil said racking his brain for a good response knowing that wasn't it.

"Not that I had anything against you in particular, it's just you were always with Boyd, so I assumed you were just like him," Dante said trying to lessen the blow of what he'd said.

"Sorry, I've kind of noticed you guys don't get along so well...," Virgil said biting his lip.

"Boyd's just cocky, and full of himself, always has to be right, uhhh!" Dante growled in frustration. "He drives me crazy!" Virgil let out a hearty laugh. Dante looked back at him in the rearview mirror, "What's so funny?" he asked a serious scowl on his face.

"It's just, how you described him; is exactly how I would have described you. I think one of the reasons you guys butt heads so much is, you have some things in common," Virgil explained to Dante.

"Virgil has a point Dante," Louie said in agreement with Virgil. "You are pretty cocky."

"Oh please! I'm just confident, me and that little dwarf have NOTHING in common," Dante said getting a little worked up, fidgeting in his seat.

Birdy cracked a grin on his face, "You do always think you're right about things too," he added.

"Enough!" Dante asserted curtly making Alec, Louie, and Virgil share a laugh. "We're getting off track here," Dante said his face slightly flushed with anger. "Virgil I was trying to give you a compliment, you are a cool guy, and I'm glad I had a chance to change my mind."

"Thanks Dante," Virgil replied glad he was riding with Louie, Birdy and Dante. "I feel the same. I think I had this preconceived notion about who all of you were, without getting to know you guys first. I'm glad last night happened. I feel more comfortable around everyone now."

"I do too," Birdy nodded. "This whole time we've been kind of doing our own thing, and not working as a group. I'm glad Gabriel said something to light a fire underneath us."

"But Virgil, back to what I was saying earlier," Dante cut in. "Most of us didn't really have a good feel for you, we all kind of thought you were a douche bag like Boyd."

"Does nobody like Boyd?" Virgil asked looking around at their expressions. No one really wanted to meet his gaze, looking outside the window had gained a sudden appeal.

"Is it really that big of a shock to you?" Dante asked him. "Most of the brothers can't stand him either. But they don't really want to cut him from the group because they were worried, you'd quit if he did. Honestly dude it kind of seems to me like he uses you. He needs you a lot more than you need him."

"How do you know that?" Virgil asked his brows furrowing together. "Who told you the brothers were thinking of cutting him?"

"Gabriel," Dante said plainly. "We talk quite a bit. I've been going to the gym with him regularly, he wanted some pointers on working out," Dante grinned proudly, and Birdy rolled his eyes. Dante continued, "I'm surprised you didn't realize it sooner," Dante told Virgil, "You're a smart guy, you should've picked up on it."

"Why doesn't anyone like him?" Virgil asked again, feeling sad for his friend.

"Well," Louie said speaking up, "It isn't that I don't like him, it's just that he is annoying," Louie said shyly, uncharacteristic for him.

"I've eaten with him a few times," Birdy jumped in from the passenger seat. "You can't get a word in, and when you do get to talk he always has to one-up you're story, even if it sounds like he's making stuff up."

"He's not all bad," Virgil said defending him.

"We're not saying he is," Louie agreed.

"I know he can be kind of a turd sometimes, but he isn't a bad guy," Virgil protested.

"I wasn't trying to upset you," Dante said sounding genuinely sorry. "The point I was trying to make was, I didn't really know you. After last night, I'm looking forward to hanging out more. You're a nice guy, a little green around the edges, but we can corrupt ya," Dante winked at him.

"Dante you got Virgil all sad over here," Louie chided Dante looking over at Virgil.

"Hey buddy, I'm sorry for what I said, can we get a smile?" Dante asked Virgil. "Come on show us a smile," Dante said in baby talk to Virgil, which made him smile as it was ridiculous coming from Dante. "Hey, listen man," Dante said, getting serious, making eye contact with Virgil through the mirror. "If you say that there is good stuff to Boyd, maybe I was wrong about him, and I can give him another chance," Dante offered with a polite smile.

Virgil was impressed by the depth of character in Dante at that moment. Virgil let a genuine smile come over him, "Thanks Dante," Virgil nodded.

"Yeah," Dante said smiling for real now, "Regardless of how annoying the little guy is, he's still one of us, and if you say he's cool, I can try harder."

"He's not much shorter than you," Louie whispered more to the car than anyone. Birdy and Virgil shared a look with Louie, they looked out their windows trying to hold in their laughs.

"Louie, how does walking the rest of the way sound?" Dante asked.

"I appreciate what you said," Virgil said, and Dante nodded.

They arrived at the Omega house and headed to the back yard. Their Big Brothers and Gabriel were already there. The group broke up into pairs with their Big's, spreading out across the yard, and got to work.

"How have you been?" Vahn asked Virgil.

"I've been good, had a pretty busy day with classes, feeling a little tired, just a side effect of pledging," Virgil told him. "How have you been?" Virgil asked Vahn.

"Been better, this whole semester has just been stressful," Vahn said with a shrug.

"You want to talk about it?" Virgil asked. Vahn had a lot on his mind.

"No, I'll be fine, let's focus on your training," Vahn asserted. Virgil nodded, not wanting to push the subject. Virgil remembered what Abe had told him about Vahn, that he'd lost his first Little Brother this year, he decided he'd ask him more about it later.

Vahn snapped his fingers and brought his fire sword, Furybrand, into its corporeal form. The sword blazed into life, its silver blade stretching out, a small fire danced along the sharp edges. When Vahn swung his sword, flames trailed behind it. Vahn's sword was impressive, Virgil would rather have that over his scythe any day.

"Alright Virgil, you're turn," Vahn stood ready.

Virgil looked down at his Devil Arms, black for Chaos, white for Creation. "Soul Reaver," Virgil commanded the black flames spreading out to consume his arm when he grabbed the weapon.

"Good," Vahn nodded. "I'm going to teach you an important spell. This is a spell that has been used by Nephilim for thousands of years. It places a protective barrier around the weapon so if it does hit someone, it won't cut through them. Important for when training with a friend or ally."

Vahn came over to Virgil he raised his right hand, the one with Furybrand's symbol and said, "Dull." A faint blue light traced around the black symbol that was Soul Reaver. As it completed tracing the symbol, the same blue light traced around the actual scythe. When it was finished Virgil's weapon had a faint blue light that hung around the edges of the scythe like a barrier, staying in place even as Virgil moved the scythe.

"That was it?" Virgil asked. "That seemed rather…simple."

"Spells don't have to be complex to work, some of the most intricate spells have the simplest incantations. It's not just about the words that you say, it is about thinking in your mind what you want the spell to do, and willing it so," Vahn told him. "There are numerous ways to go about casting the same or similar spells. The words are merely the catalyst, the ingredients are what you have in your mind, what you're *willing* the words to do."

"So, I just have to think it to make it happen?" Virgil asked. "That seems too easy."

"Careful though, that line of thinking can lead you to trouble. Never use a spell that requires too much of your energy. Spells take their energy from us. The bigger the spell, the more energy needed. Use a spell that requires a tremendous amount of energy, and it could literally burn up your aura's power, ending your life. Many Nephilim have died over exerting themselves with 'easy' spells," Vahn warned. "Let's practice with your scythe now, it has a protective barrier over it to stop it from killing me." Vahn took a few paces away from Virgil placing the Dull spell on his sword.

Vahn lunged forward taking a slash at Virgil with his sword. Instinct took over, Virgil swung his scythe forward catching Vahn's blade against his own. The force of Vahn's lunge nearly knocked Virgil off his feet and the scythe out of his hands. Virgil struggled against him trying to regain his balance. Vahn pushed his blade against the scythe, overpowering Virgil and shoving him to the ground.

"Positioning and technique are important, in combat you can't afford to take your time with it. You need to practice so it becomes second nature, like walking," Vahn advised standing over him. He reached down and helped Virgil to his feet.

"We'll take turns, I'll start off on defense," Vahn offered.

They took a few paces away from each other. Virgil balanced his footing, took a breath, and lunged at Vahn, swinging his scythe, carrying it forward through his step, and exhaling his breath all at once, as Vahn had showed him during last practice. Vahn was quick, he parried the blow with his sword, his arm only trembling slightly beneath the force Virgil exerted against him.

"Good follow through, that was a powerful swing," Vahn nodded. "You were a dead giveaway where you were aiming at though, you gave me plenty of time to react."

Virgil continued to practice with Soul Reaver. A scythe wasn't the most graceful weapon, Virgil learned its bulky movements made him open to counter strikes. He realized that it would take a lot practice before he'd be able to use it in real combat. After being on the offensive, Vahn made him switch to blocking incoming attacks. This was much harder for Virgil. He caught some swings from Vahn's sword on the long shaft of the scythe, but it came dangerously close to his hands often. Vahn pointed out it would be easy for someone to slide their weapon down, slicing off his fingers in the process. Virgil failed consistently to catch Vahn's attacks, Vahn lightly rapping him with his sword on the ribs or legs. Virgil began to feel sore from all the blows Vahn was landing, feelings of frustration began to build.

Virgil barely noticed the flames along his scythe and arm grow, like an angry fire searching for more fuel. Vahn came at Virgil again, Virgil side stepped left just as his sword swung down, Virgil lashed out in an arc with his own weapon. The sickle of the blade caught Vahn across the waist, knocking him down.

Vahn cried silent tears whispering, "My aura, it was…drained."

Tarek hurried over to them, kneeling next to Vahn, "Ply," he commanded. A pale blue light shone from his hand covering Vahn's wound. The skin along his side began to knit itself back to normal, leaving a bright pink spot of new flesh, the burn was no more.

"What happened?" Tarek asked looking up at Virgil.

"I hit him with Soul Reaver," Virgil felt ashamed.

Tarek looked at Soul Reaver intently for several seconds, before helping Vahn to his feet. The other brothers and candidates had stopped, Magnus and Gabriel came over.

"Is everyone okay?" Magnus asked his gaze piercing.

"I'm fine," Vahn said confidently.

"Virgil, you need to be careful Soul Reaver does not make contact with any of the brothers," Gabriel told him firmly.

"It was strange," Vahn acknowledged.

"What was strange?" Gabriel asked his friend.

"When that fire touched me, I could feel my energy, my aura being drained from me. It wasn't a lot, but if it hit me a couple more times, I doubt I'd be able to cast the simplest of spells," Vahn said softly, carefully avoiding Virgil's gaze.

The brothers were silent. Magnus stared intently at Vahn, he said "His aura does seem to have been damaged, nothing a good night's rest won't fix." Magnus and Gabriel then shared a look that spoke volumes.

"Alright guys get back to practice, we still have a half hour left," Gabriel barked. The brothers and their Lil's spread back out, but they were whispering quietly to one another, Virgil felt himself grow warm.

"Virgil you don't have anything to be embarrassed about," Gabriel said encouragingly. "You didn't know what your scythe would do when it made contact with someone."

"What happened exactly?" Virgil asked.

Magnus spoke purposefully and carefully, "Soul Reaver has the ability to damage our spirits. Vahn felt his aura being drained when the fire touched him. Every human and Nephilim are surrounded by a spiritual circumference of energy, we call that an aura. Everyone's auras are different, some are bigger with more energy, and we use our auras to power spells. Once too much has been used, the aura begins to shrink in size eventually retreating inside the person when weakened. Use more than that amount, and you risk death. Our Will is our spiritual energy, which fuels our mortal bodies. Nephilim can tap into this, to manipulate the world around them. Soul Reaver's black fire burns the spiritual energy of anything it touches, a cruel and deadly weapon," Magnus remarked with one hand cupping his chin, his brows furrowed in thought.

"Anyone who trains with Virgil needs to have more protective spells on them," Gabriel remarked.

"The spell Protect should suffice," Magnus nodded. "Virgil just be careful when training with someone. Luckily Tarek can heal us. If you hit someone enough with that thing however, you could burn away their aura completely, killing them in the process" he warned. Virgil stared aghast at the scythe.

Vahn shrugged, "We'll be more careful from now on, he needs to train."

"We'll take turns working with him," Gabriel agreed, "Virgil won't harm us."

Vahn and Virgil resumed practicing. Vahn cast a spell on himself before they started, Protect, a white barrier broken into many smaller squares came around him, before fading out of sight. Vahn assured Virgil that the spell was active. Vahn told Virgil it was a spell that lowered physical forces impact on the body, even stopping arrows or bullets in their tracks.

The last few minutes Virgil spent watching his fellow candidates practice. Dante, Birdy, Louie V, and Nolan seemed to be the ones that stood out the most. Dante was a natural warrior wielding his earth axe with impunity. He was sparring with Gabriel at the end of practice, able to keep up with him with ease, and more than a few times, was able to knock Gabriel off his balance. Alec wielded an electrified lance, though he was often clumsy and air headed, with his weapon in hand, he exuded an air of control and grace. Louie wielded an ice bow, he was spending his time with target practice, and demonstrated good aim. Nolan wielded a staff, the same as Magnus, he looked to be practicing spells, the only one of the group who had been instructed on how that worked. Virgil watched with interest as he created a small wind funnel in his hand and sent it at Magnus, who easily deflected it, dissipating it back into nothingness.

Chapter 11
<u>Big & Lil Time</u>

After Thursday classes Virgil met up with Louie, Troy, and Nolan for a late lunch. They talked about classes, the pledging process, and girls. Only Darius, Hector, and Devin weren't freshmen, for the rest of Omicron this was their first semester of college, and transitioning required a lot of work. Virgil was doing well in most of his classes, averaging about a 'C' in his Math class. He was too busy with everything and something had to give.

"I can't wait to just be brothers," Louie sighed. "I need help in classes."

"Which classes?" Nolan asked.

"English and Math," Louie said a worried look on his face. "My parents are paying for my tuition, if I fail a bunch of classes, they may drop their financial support from me. I don't know if I can keep going here if that happens." Louie seemed dejected at the idea of leaving.

"I can help you with English," Virgil volunteered with a cheerful smile. "I've gotten A's on my papers. I'll be happy to help revise your next one and polish it up."

"Yes!" Louie cried out ecstatically. "I need all the help I can get homie."

"If Virgil can take care of the English class, I'd be happy to tutor you in Math," Nolan offered. "I'm already tutoring several students through the University and getting paid for it."

"We want you to stick around," Virgil said encouragingly. "Omicron wouldn't be the same without you Louie, you're the guy that keeps us all together," Virgil complimented him. "Hit me up sometime and we'll get your paper fixed up," Virgil told Louie.

Virgil went to the Omegas after, stopping by the large living room to the right of the foyer. A group of brothers and candidates gathered together, some watching TV, others playing cards. Virgil said hello then walked to the fourth floor where the upper classmen of the fraternity lived.

Virgil walked into Vahn's small cozy room reflecting his personality. The walls were covered with Omega decorations, pictures of him and various brothers, along with some family. The room had a small bed in the corner next to a desk. There was a small TV and a sofa, along with a small table and chairs near the entrance. Vahn and Dante were watching a movie sitting on the sofa laughing together.

"What's up Lil?" Vahn called to Virgil.

"Vahn and I just had an interview," Dante bragged. "You're lucky he's your Big."

"I haven't had an interview with him yet," Virgil remarked.

"I wanted you to interview most of the brothers before we had our talk. You're my Lil, we already share a special bond. Anyways," Vahn said changing topics. "You guys ready?"

"Ready for what?" Virgil asked surprised.

"We're going on a road trip," Vahn declared, "Come on."

"Dante's coming with us?" Virgil asked.

"Yeah, I invited him along, he's a riot!" Vahn laughed. "It'll be fun hanging out the three of us!"

They piled into Vahn's Jeep and jammed out to some music as they hit the road. They drove out of Bay City, heading west on US-10.

"Where are we headed?" Virgil asked.

"It's a surprise," Dante replied brashly.

"I wasn't asking you," Virgil retorted to Dante.

"Relax Lil, we're going to Freeland, not too far now," Vahn smiled.

Vahn and Dante had such easy chemistry, the conversation flowing between them, Virgil felt a little envious. They arrived at an apple orchard just outside Freeland.

"What are we doing here?" Virgil asked as they walked up.

"I thought it'd be fun to come check this place out," Vahn shrugged. "I've never been here before. They make all kinds of products, ciders, pies, doughnuts, and since it is close to Halloween, I figured we could carve pumpkins."

They walked through the apple orchard enjoying the autumn afternoon. Fall was a beautiful time in Michigan, the leaves on all the trees changing color. They looked around inside the main shop, and each of them bought a hot apple cider, and an apple cinnamon donut. They went outside and sat down at a picnic table to enjoy their snack.

"This is so good!" Dante exclaimed enjoying the sweet sugary taste of the donut. "I'm having fun," Dante said. "This place is pretty cool."

"I agree," Vahn said with a smile.

"I am too," Virgil said. "Honestly I don't care what we do, hanging out with you guys is a lot of fun."

"Oh! Look at those," Dante exclaimed. There were wooden stand ups with holes cut in the faces, there were ones with a farmer and his animals, and a family with adults and kids.

"We should take some pictures of us acting stupid," Dante joked.

"Let's do it," Vahn laughed in agreement.

The three of them took turns jumping into various funny poses and snapping pictures. Dante made them all burst into laughter as he did various ridiculous antics, sticking out his tongue, and sticking his bum through the hole instead of his face. Once they had taken enough pictures, they each bought a pumpkin, and drove back to the Omega house.

Vahn gathered some old newspaper, some knives, and they got to work cleaning them out. Dante was telling them about cheerleading practice, how it was more work than he had originally thought. Dante admitted he was quitting soon, as it wasn't much fun, and he was more interested in being active in the fraternity.

"How is your Big doing Dante?" Virgil asked him.

"Mu is good," Dante said nonchalantly.

"I haven't seen him around much lately," Virgil said.

"Yeah, he got a new girlfriend recently and he's been spending a lot of his time with her," Dante sighed. "I haven't seen him much either."

"That happens, guys get a new girl and they disappear. Mu will come back around, he loves this fraternity," Vahn said encouragingly to Dante.

"Yeah," Dante said clearly wanting to talk about something else.

They carved their pumpkins once they had finished cleaning them, Vahn's turned out the best, he was very artistic. Dante's was the most humorous, going for more of a silly face. Virgil sighed in frustration when he revealed his and they laughed.

"What is it supposed to be?" Dante asked.

"A scary face, with fangs," Virgil said in defense of his pumpkin. "I'm not very artistic."

"It looks fine, don't be so hard on yourself all the time. No one's perfect," Vahn said.

Afterwards they sat around talking. "You know what would have gone good with that apple cider?" Vahn asked them.

"What?" Virgil and Dante asked together.

"Some Captain Morgan spiced rum," Vahn said with a big grin. "Nothing tastes better on a chilly autumn day than apple cider and Captain. I like to have some at tailgating," he told them.

"My favorite drink is So Co and Coke," Dante told them. They looked at Virgil for his response.

"Umm," Virgil wasn't sure what to say. "I haven't had experience with drinking really," Virgil told them. "I drank only a few times before we pledged Omega."

"That's okay, it's not legal for you anyways, you have plenty of time to find out what you like," Vahn suggested.

Dante and Vahn were similar in a lot of ways, very talkative, humorous, and fun to be around. Virgil wanted to be more like them. Vahn yawned and stretched telling them he was thinking of taking a nap before their Devil Arms practice that night. Vahn left the room to use the bathroom.

"I had fun spending time with you Virgil, take care man," Dante said leaving the room. Virgil was a little grumpy. He'd been upet with them at first, but he'd enjoyed having Dante around. Virgil started to leave when Vahn came back to the room.

"You taking off?" Vahn asked.

"Yeah, I'll probably text some of my pledge brothers, see if anyone wants to hang out for a little bit before training," Virgil nodded.

"I'm not taking a nap, I just said that so Dante would leave," Vahn told him taking a seat at the little table.

"Oh," Virgil said in surprise, not sure what that meant.

"Come on bud, take a seat," Vahn said shoving out a chair for him with his foot. "Dude, I know you feel awkward sometimes, and I can tell you're a little uncomfortable in social situations, but you're still young. You're fresh out of high school, and contrary to what kids think, after graduation you're just finding yourself. It takes people years to learn who they really are, some people their whole lives, heck I'm still finding myself," Vahn joked.

"You?" Virgil asked, "You seem so confident though, and sure of yourself, like you got it all together."

Vahn laughed heartily, "Is that how you see me?" he asked Virgil with humor laced in his words.

"Well yeah," Virgil shrugged. "You're awesome!" he laughed with a smile. It sounded dumb to say out loud.

"We all have insecurities Virgil. I'm just a guy trying to find his way in a shit world, like everyone else," Vahn said sounding kind of sad.

"You don't really know me, and I don't really know you, not yet anyway. How about we do our interview?" Vahn suggested.

"Right now?" Virgil asked excited.

"Yeah, why not? Let's get to know each other better," Vahn smiled. "An easy, albeit forced way, is to just sit down and talk about ourselves. That's the whole point of the interviews, to quickly get everyone acquainted."

"That sounds good," Virgil beamed.

"Alright, let's start off with your childhood," Virgil asked opening his pledge binder. "A wise man once said to know where a man is headed, you need to know where he came from."

Vahn gave Virgil a look that said 'really?' though he didn't mock him. "I grew up in Ithaca, Michigan. Tiny little town in the middle of nowhere. I have four younger brothers, I'm the oldest of five. You met Aidan, he's the second oldest. He had to stop pledging cause his grades were going down the drain. He's going to come back. Anyways," Vahn said waving his hand, "Back to my story. We grew up in the country outside of town, on a farm. We helped my dad with the work, which was always hard because there was more to do then we had time for. I kind of had a rough time, my dad was a Paladin, leaving on secret missions without being able to tell my mom or us. Living the double life style takes its toll. My dad turned to booze, and quickly became a mean drunk. My mom left him, she got remarried to a douche bag who hated her first three boys. They had two sons together, which were treated better than us older boys. We never resented them for it, we're brothers first and foremost. I was the eldest, so I was always expected to do the most for both my parents, which got old quick."

"I wasn't popular in school, though I had some friends. I played soccer for most of school, loved it. Gave me an escape from home. All my brothers except Aidan play soccer, he's the only one who played football. Had a serious girlfriend in high school, we dated for a few years, even tried to make it work when I went to college, it almost never does. I got a full ride scholarship here for grades, lost it after the first year between pledging, going home often to see my girl, and juggling a job. Now I'm taking out loans like the rest of America, with no idea how I'm going to pay them back either," Vahn said with a laugh that was half joking half serious.

"What's your major?" Virgil asked next.

"Education," Vahn said. "I want to be an English teacher."

"A teacher?" Virgil asked surprised. "Why that?"

"I've always wanted to be a teacher. I love to teach people new things, it's fun for me. And now that I'm a Paladin, it has made that dream even stronger," Vahn asserted.

"Well what happens after graduation, being a Nephilim warrior and all, I guess I don't really understand how that works," Virgil asked.

"Well there are a few options," Vahn said his tone taking that of a lecturer. "Quit the Paladins all together and try to resume a normal human lifestyle; or stay on part time as a Paladin, helping here or there when demonic activity spikes in the area. In the meantime, living as anyone would after college. Most Paladins go into a job where they can interact with people, and search out other Nephilim, like teachers, social workers, nurses, lawyers, police officers. Being a Paladin is voluntary, they aren't about forcing people into their ranks."

"Okay, I guess that makes sense. Just seems so weird, living among everyone else, but knowing about all this extra stuff going on," Virgil commented.

"It is challenging to say the least," Vahn agreed. "It takes its toll, living the double life style. There is a third option, and that is joining the Paladins ranks full time, foregoing the human lifestyle. There are Paladin cities all over the world with only people like us living there, no humans," Vahn explained excitedly.

"WOW!" Virgil said getting excited. "What are they like?" he asked with enthusiasm.

"I've only been to one. Alexandros is the biggest Nephilim city in the world, I'm sure you've heard if it?" Vahn asked and Virgil nodded.

"Mu said it is this floating land mass the size of Rhode Island that is centered over Lake Michigan," Virgil remembered.

"You won't believe it until you see it," Vahn's eyes became glossy. "It's breathtaking, humbling, and an enlightening experience," Vahn said wistfully, fondly pondering memories.

"So why join Omega?" Virgil asked Vahn.

"That's a great question, two questions you should ask every brother, why Omega, and what does Brotherhood mean to you," Vahn told him. "I joined Omega completely by accident,"

Vahn joked. "I was walking down the hall, there were some brothers at a recruitment table, I walked up, signed my name with some information and I got a bid."

"Why do you think they gave you a bid?" Virgil asked.

"They probably noticed the Devil Arms symbol on my hand," Vahn remarked. "When I turned eighteen my Nephilim powers came 'on-line' so to speak. My dad explained why a red glowing tattoo had suddenly appeared on my hand, also telling me about the Paladins. By that point my dad had been retired for several years, he encouraged me to seek out the Paladins. Honestly, I fell into this amazing organization by complete accident, and I thank God every day. Joining this fraternity was the best decision I ever made. I met my best friends and have grown more as a person than I ever thought possible," Vahn's voice thick with passion.

"What was pledging like for you?" Virgil asked.

"Pledging was hell," Vahn said plainly shaking his head. "I was in Lambda class though, and we became a close class rather quickly. We did everything as a group, we were inseparable. It also helped that many of our pledge brothers were legacies," Vahn bragged.

"I've heard that a few times, what is a legacy exactly?" Virgil asked confused.

"It means that a member of your family was also in the same fraternity. Gabriel and Magnus' older brothers were in our Chapter, and still going to school here. Jagger's older brother was an Omega at another school. Everyone in our class was very talented in combat, each of us had our own strengths, together we worked as a single cohesive unit. We were one of the best pledge classes to come along in years. Every one of the brothers told us we'd be leading this fraternity someday. We had a dick of a Hegemon though, not lucky like you guys," Vahn rolled his eyes.

"I've never heard of Lambda's Hegemon," Virgil remarked.

"He was hard on us, the brothers are divided on him, half love him, half can't stand him. We eventually made it through, and everyday thereafter has been amazing."

"Who was your Big Brother, my Grand Big?" Virgil asked.

"Tim was a member of Kappa class, he'd gotten into the fraternity in the Winter semester, right before Lambda class. Normally brothers aren't given Littles until after they'd been in for a year, so they can be a better mentor. Tim was the worst Big you could possibly be, he just drank all the time, made fun of me a little too much to be joking, never was there for me or tried to get to know me. I struggled a lot during the pledge process, almost quit a dozen times because it was too stressful. I stuck in it for my pledge brothers. That's how Landon and I became best friends, he was always there for me. When I got initiated, I got Tim a paddle, like all Lils. The Bigs are supposed to get their Lils a shirt or hoodie with our Greek Letters sewed on the front. Tim didn't get me anything because he 'didn't have the money.' Though he did have the money to drink that night. I was the only one in my pledge class who didn't get a set of Letters from their Big. My Grand Big, Crowbar, felt bad and eventually bought me a pair," Vahn said. He spoke quickly his face getting red with anger from the memories of which he regaled.

"I'm sorry," Virgil said to his Big.

"It's fine dude, I don't let it bother me. This fraternity isn't about just being close to your Big. I think too many people have this misconception that your Big Brother is supposed to be your best friend. A Big is supposed to guide their Lil's through the process of the fraternity and be a role model for them. Best friend isn't in the job description," Vahn explained. "We're supposed to be great friends with everyone, not just one particular brother."

"After you got in the fraternity what did you do?" Virgil asked.

"Slept A LOT!" Vahn joked and they shared a laugh.

"Yeah I could use a three-day long nap after this is all over," Virgil nodded.

Vahn sighed, then said with fondness and regret, "Our fraternity has changed a lot since I was a pledge. It has only been two years since I got in, and a lot changed very quickly."

"What do you mean?" Virgil asked curiously.

"When I was a pledge, we still had a lot of brothers in the fraternity from when we were first founded. This Chapter is only six years old, relatively young, when I was a freshman it was only four years old. The fraternity was focused on being a Paladin organization first, and a fraternity second. We trained what felt like non-stop on how to use our Nephilim abilities while pledging. We were very focused on being good Paladins, good warriors. The fraternity was old school back then, and everyone was so close," Vahn reminisced fondly.

"What changed?" Virgil asked not getting the point.

"We got a few bad pledge classes, the fraternity changes as new members come in, the fraternity IS the brothers. When the fraternity was first founded here, the brothers were all very powerful Nephilim, most were Purebloods, or half human, half Judge. As time went on, more and more people who joined, had less and less angel blood. The newer brothers wanted it to be more about being a regular fraternity, not so much a Nephilim fraternity, which isn't really a bad thing. It led to conflict between the older brothers and the newer ones. Long story short the fraternity is nothing like it was when I first joined. A big difference from when I was a pledge, we had over fifty active brothers, now we barely have over twenty," Vahn said sadly.

"Fifty!" Virgil whistled. "That's a big difference."

"Yup," Vahn agreed with a dejected look. "Right now, we're hurting for numbers, we had too many brothers graduate, fail out of college, or worse, and not enough to replace them. The brothers and Gabriel may be hard on Omicron, realistically we NEED you guys. Without

Omicron, we won't be doing well. Brothers are the lifeblood of any fraternity. I can see Omicron being like Lambda, you have a lot of leaders in your class, you guys will probably take over once Lambda steps down."

"Have you ever been a Jeweled Officer of the fraternity?" Virgil asked next.

"Of course!" Vahn said as if that was the silliest thing he'd ever been asked. "Elections for the Jeweled Officers take place at the end of the Fall semester in December, and their term lasts two semesters until the following December. I was given the advertising chairman position the winter after I got initiated. The following election last year Buck got Prytanis, I got Epiprytanis, Magnus got Hypophetes," Vahn explained to Virgil.

"Wait," Virgil said getting confused. He flipped open his pledge binder going to the second page, which listed the active E-Board of the fraternity, it was very different from what Vahn had said. "I don't get it, if the terms are one year, shouldn't you still be Epiprytanis? And why is Magnus the Prytanis instead of the Hypophetes?" Virgil wondered.

"I'm getting to that Virgil," Vahn told him moving his palm up and down telling Virgil to settle down. "Half way into the winter, Buck came to me one day and said, 'Well I hope you're ready to lead the Chapter,' and handed me the gavel. He was overwhelmed with school, and his relationship was failing due to spending too much time on Omega stuff. I was elected the Epiprytanis, that's the position I wanted, I never wanted to lead the fraternity as Prytanis. Landon had to step up to Epiprytanis to replace me, and Mu took over Grammatues to replace Landon. Buck was one of the oldest and most experienced active fraters we had, no one wanted a second-year student like me to lead the fraternity. The older Alumni of our Chapter were pissed. I didn't have a choice. It's the Vice President's job to step up when the President steps down," Vahn grumbled irritated.

"What happened next?" Virgil wondered why Vahn was no longer Prytanis.

"This past summer, there was a large demonic outbreak in Detroit. The demon population was swelling, they feed on human auras and emotion, causing people to go berserk. It was chaos, you probably remember hearing about it on the news. They called it gang violence reaching an all-time high. It was demons driving the people to madness, humans were attacking one another without provocation, resulting in countless deaths. A large-scale Paladin operation was planned, to go in and clean up the city, coordinated by Paladins from Alexandros. Our Chapter is young, and it was the biggest tactical operation we'd ever taken part in. Long story short, it was a blood bath. We were successful, the violence and rioting ending the same night we eradicated the demonic presence in the city, but our victory came at a price. Our Chapter suffered the loss of brothers for the first time in battle. It is a part of being a Paladin, men die in the line of duty, it was something our Chapter hadn't gone through yet. We lost over a dozen men, my first Lil Brother, being one of the causalities," Vahn spoke, his voice thick with emotion, eyes misting over.

"Vahn, I," Virgil didn't know what to say.

"He was young and cocky; thought he was too good to be taken down. The Alumni were furious with me, many of them had taken part in the operation. They looked to me to arrange the funerals, organize the brothers, they told me I was doing a shitty job as Prytanis," Vahn spoke still marred from the loss and pain.

"It wasn't your fault that those men died!" Virgil yelled causing Vahn to look up at him.

"The Alumni were just hurting. It was too much though, a week before this semester started, I knew that I couldn't handle being Prytanis. I had a talk with Magnus and asked him to step into the role of our Chapter's leader. Tarek Jeter stepped up into Hypophetes to replace him.

It's the most turn over in an E-Board our Chapter's ever had, and everyone blames me for it," Vahn said bitterly looking down.

"They shouldn't, this fraternity is made up of individuals, not just one man. We EACH have a part to play in the outcome of this fraternity, and I think you're one of the greatest men this Chapter has," Virgil said with confidence his words steel.

Vahn gave Virgil a weak smile. "You want to know the worst part of it?" Vahn asked him, "I don't care that I lost my Jeweled Officer positions, I wanted to be a leader to help this fraternity not for the esteem the position gives. I would have given anything to have my Lil back," Vahn almost choked on the word 'Lil.' "We were best friends, inseparable, he was one of the greatest guys I've ever known." Two tears trembled down Vahn's face as he hung his head.

They sat in silence, Virgil respecting Vahn's story with revered stillness. Vahn wiped his face and laughed. "To be honest buddy, I didn't want another Lil. I was still beaten up inside from this summer, sick of the fraternity in a way, and just wanting to do my own thing as much as possible."

Virgil's face fell a little and Vahn noticed the change in his demeanor. "I'm glad Gabriel talked me into it. He told me everyone could feel I was pulling away. He said that there was this kid that they didn't know too much about, that he was smart like me, a little shy, who could use a good Big to help get him through. I told him no at first, Gabriel insisted that no one else fit you like I did. Gabriel wanted to be Aidan's Big, since Gabriel and I are best friends. He said that if I wouldn't take you, he'd have to, and then Aidan would get saddled with someone else, someone not as good. Gabriel told me that I was a big part of this fraternity, and that the guys needed me back, the real me, not the ghost I'd become. He told me being a Big again, would make me appreciate this fraternity once more and reaffirm my love for it. I decided at the last minute to do it, and it is helping me, like he said it would," Vahn met Virgil's eyes. "I'm proud to be your Big Virgil, and I wouldn't want to be anyone else's."

"Thank you," Virgil said feeling humbled and overwhelmed by Vahn's honesty.

"I know we don't know each other well yet, but we will be great friends, I can tell," Vahn told him smiling and wiping his face.

"I'm honored to have such an amazing Big," Virgil said fighting back the tears that had welled up in his eyes.

Vahn got up and Virgil followed, they shared a hug. Vahn patted him on the back and they parted. They sat down keeping the mood less serious. They took turns telling what their favorites were, going down the list of everything from music, food, to movies. Vahn asked Virgil about his life. Hours went by and soon it was getting close to Devil Arms training.

"Last question," Virgil promised. "What does brotherhood mean to you?"

"Glad you asked," Vahn nodded. "Brotherhood to me in one word means family. The guys you spend your days with, the guys you eat with, the guys you fight with. Brotherhood is about being there for one another through the good times and the bad. I'd die for anyone of these guys in an instant if needed. These guys are my best friends, they'll one day stand up in my wedding, be Godfathers to my children, and God willing someday far in the future, be the ones to carry my coffin when I pass on."

Chapter 12
<u>Road Trip</u>

Friday Omicron was going on a road trip to Mt. Pleasant to get their paddles ordered for their Bigs. Virgil walked over to Louie's place in the Zoo. It was more crowded than Virgil's dorm, eight men had to share a living space half the size of his own. Virgil knocked, and Louie answered the door as enthusiastic as ever.

"How you doin homie?" Louie called embracing him in a bear hug.

"Good Louie," Virgil gasped for air. "Just starving."

They walked to Dante and Birdy's dorm. Virgil hadn't hung out at their place before. Louie walked right in without knocking and headed over to their bedroom. Their dorm was set up like Louie's. Louie rapped on their door before throwing it open.

"Hand check!" Louie shouted. "Get your hands off your wang, and let's go grab some lunch," Louie jested.

"Hey guys," Dante greeted them, not taking his eyes off his laptop at the long desk by the door that he shared with Birdy. He was engrossed in an online video game, earbuds in blaring with music, which held his attention firmly. Birdy was at his desk, working on his studies.

"You guys hungry?" Louie asked sitting down on the bottom bed of their bunk bed, making himself at home.

"Yeah, I could go for some food," Birdy replied putting his pen down, rubbing his eyes.

"I'm so sore from all this practice," Louie complained to them laying back on the bed, his feet on the floor.

"How?" Dante quipped. "You have a bow for a weapon Louie, you're not getting beat up as you practice with your Devil Arms."

"My hands and arms get swore," Louie whined, "You know how hard it is to use a bow for a long period of time without a break?"

"I guess," Dante said rolling his eyes making Virgil chuckle. Virgil and Dante shared a look and a grin that said, oh Louie. Virgil leaned against their closet.

"What's up bitches?" a familiar voice called from the doorway.

The four of them turned their heads to see Gabriel and Brody, standing in the doorway.

"Hey guys!" Dante greeted them enthusiastically taking his earbuds out.

"Oh! Look at little Dante over there, brothers come in and his little tongue and tail start wagging!" Louie joked sitting up in the bed laughing himself silly.

"Shut up Louie," Dante said flatty not bothering to turn around and look at him.

"What are you guys doing?" Gabriel asked them in a long drawn out way, like an adult speaking to a five-year-old who was coloring.

"We were about to grab some lunch, before we head to Mt Pleasant for our paddles," Virgil replied.

"Good, you guys are getting that done today," Gabriel said nodding his head. "Make sure everyone wears their Dreamstone so you don't have a problem with demons," he warned. "The reason we came here though is Jace's room is unlocked, and unguarded," Gabriel said a mischievous grin spreading across his face.

"What?" Birdy said looking up from his laptop his interest piqued.

"We just came from the Omega house and Jace left his room open, must have left for class in a hurry. I hear he's been giving some of you a rough time these past few weeks," Gabriel said innocently with a sly fox like smile.

"And he is still pissed about his truck!" Brody laughed.

"He called me a few nights ago, to go get him McDonalds at three in the morning!" Birdy yelled obviously holding a small grudge against him.

"He had me deliver a pop to him while he was in class one day," Dante said non-chantingly like it wasn't too big a deal. "He's my twin so he hasn't been too bad to me."

"He's been running me ragged," Louie sighed. "I've made three deliveries to him this past week alone, bringing toilet paper and trash bags, since freshmen get them free."

"Seems like a perfect opportunity to get some revenge," Brody suggested. "He's my pledge brother, but the guy can be a dick to people. You guys should mess his room!"

"How do we do that?" Virgil asked.

"You trash it," Gabriel said simply. "Lots of ways to do it, my favorite is turning everything upside down. He'd be really pissed. Brody and I are keeping our mouths shut on this. If you go, we won't tell him who did it. You may get away with it completely if you don't tell anyone else," Gabriel suggested slyly.

Dante and Birdy turned around in their chairs and Louie and Virgil stepped closer to them. The four of them shared a look.

"Should we go?" Birdy asked.

"Hell yeah!" Louie said.

"Screw him," Dante laughed.

"I'm in," Virgil nodded.

"Better get going, Jace's class only lasts till one," Brody told them.

Virgil and the others hurried out the door, Dante and Birdy didn't bother locking their room, as they rushed to the parking lot.

"I'll drive!" Birdy shouted.

"Shotgun!" Dante called out.

"How in the hell do you expect a big guy like me to crawl back in there?" Louie asked incredulously.

"You'll figure it out big man," Dante said holding the seat back for Virgil and Louie to climb in. The car had very little leg room, and Louie complained a few times making sure everyone in the car knew about it. Birdy threw his car into motion and they flew to the Omega house. Virgil was immediately made uncomfortable by the speed and overall absentminded attitude with which Birdy seemed to drive. Twice they almost hit another vehicle, and Dante would just mutter under his breath every time they almost crashed. They made it to Omega's fraternity house in record time, running inside to get to Jace's room.

They arrived at Jace's room on the third floor, and all of them let out sounds of confusion. His room was destroyed. The floor was littered with books, papers, clothes, blankets, it looked like someone had already beaten them to it.

"What the deuce?" Louie cried out.

"Who got his room?" Birdy asked out loud.

"Why would Gabriel and Brody send us here if it was already messed with?" Dante wondered.

"Guys, we left them alone at your room," Virgil said thinking out loud. "We left in such a hurry we didn't walk them out, you don't think…" Virgil didn't finish his sentence letting the group think about it themselves.

"Back to our room!" Dante shouted. The four of them turned and ran back to Birdy's sportscar. They sped back to campus practically jumping over one another to get back to Dante and Birdy's dorm to see what had happened. Birdy was the first one inside, followed closely by

Dante, with Virgil right on his heels. They all heard Birdy let out a loud groan of discontent from his room, they crossed the small living room to looking inside. The whole room was an even worse mess than Jace's had been.

"Those bastards!" Dante said clenching his fist and pounding it on his desk. "They tricked us!"

"You guys want some help?" Louie asked.

"Yeah, might as well," Birdy said with a heavy sigh.

The four friends quickly got the room back in order, grumbling about Gabriel and Brody. Once they had finished, everyone was ready for some food. They saw Gabriel and Brody sitting at a table in the cafeteria, waving at them with shit eating grins plastered across their faces. The four of them walked over to them.

"How'd it go?" Gabriel asked. "Get the job done right?"

"No," Louie replied with a snarky attitude, "Someone already messed with the room."

"And when we got back to our room it was TRASHED!" Birdy yelled.

Gabriel and Brody shared a look then burst out laughing. "You've got to be smarter than that," Gabriel warned. "Next time don't leave your room wide open like an invitation."

"Yeah, yeah. You got us, big deal," Dante said with a shrug. "Let's get some food."

Once they had all gotten some lunch they sat with the brothers.

"Selene and I have a date later tonight," Brody told them. "She's been so busy lately I haven't seen her much. We're going to cook dinner together at her place, then watch a movie and cuddle on her couch."

"Isn't that the chick who won Homecoming Queen?" Birdy asked.

"Yup," Brody said proudly. "That's my girlfriend."

"You guys are official now?" Louie asked.

"Yeah we have been for about a week now," Brody said. "I asked her the night of the Homecoming party."

"TK and I are going out to the movies later," Gabriel added in. "I've been so swamped with classes and being Hegemon, it has been a few weeks since we've had a date night."

"I like her," Virgil said jumping in. "She's really cool and funny too."

"All the guys seem to like her," Gabriel said flatly giving Virgil a strange and hard look.

"I didn't mean anything by it, I just had fun talking with her," Virgil said defensively.

"It's okay bud, I was just messing with you," Gabriel said his once serious gaze now softened up.

"I heard from Vahn and Reece, you give a pretty good interview," Brody complimented Virgil.

"What?" Virgil asked surprised.

"They said you ask a lot of good questions, and talked their ears off, but they said it was one of the best interviews they've had," Brody spoke with food in his mouth.

"Thanks," Virgil said a little embarrassed and not sure what else to say.

"If you got time, I wouldn't mind doing our interview after we're done eating," Brody said.

"Sure, we have a little time before we head to Mt. Pleasant that sounds good to me," Virgil nodded.

Brody led Virgil to one of the small rooms in the building, which were made of all glass, so you could look outside and see people walking by. Brody was a second year, studying communications with a business minor. Brody was turning nineteen in November, making him less than a year older than Virgil. He had dark brown eyes, with a round nose, big plump cheeks, and a big toothy smile that he wore most often. Brody had sandy brown hair spiked at the front, which was receding, giving him a large forehead. Brody had a class clown type of personality, always joking around, making funny voices, and noises.

Brody grew up in Wayne, Michigan, the youngest of three kids. Brody had a very positive attitude, he was passionate about life and people, and was one of those guys who never seemed to get down about anything. Brody stated he was on the swim team in high school. He joked their school's mascot was a rock, funny as they had one of the best swim teams in the state, and rocks generally just sink.

Brody had gotten a bid for the Omega's in the fall semester, when Nu class had pledged the previous year. Because he struggled academically, he decided to wait until winter semester when he had some time to adjust to college classes. Brody had a small halberd Devil Arms aligned with earth. An alarm went off on Virgil's phone, letting him know he had to meet up with Omicron.

"Has it been over two hours already?" Virgil asked with surprise.

"Time flies when you're having a good conversation," Brody remarked.

"Thanks for the interview," Virgil said, "I really appreciate it. I had a lot of fun getting to know you better."

"Me too," Brody laughed with his ever-present goofy grin. "I'm looking forward to having you join our Brotherhood."

Virgil offered him his hand for a bro shake. "Get that shit outta here," Brody barked swiping his hand away, opening his arms for a big bear hug. "I'm a hugger," he demanded grabbing Virgil tightly.

"Brody you're crushing me," Virgil strained with forced effort. Brody let him go and gave him a strong pat on the back.

"You're alright Pitcher," Brody told him. "Let's hang out sometime, I think we'd have fun together."

"I'd like that Brody," Virgil nodded. "Later man," Virgil hurried to Dante's room. Louie had messaged him: *Hey ninja, we are meeting up at Birdtweed's room, get your bitch ass over here!* Virgil assumed he meant Birdy, Louie's text messages didn't always use proper English or make sense. Omicron walked to the parking lot once the group had gathered. Darius, Nolan, Troy, and Axel were in Darius' car. Dante, Birdy, Louie, Virgil, and Boyd were riding in Dante's car. Hector and Devin canceled last minute and were going another day by themselves.

"You guys have the address?" Nolan asked them.

"We're good!" Dante said holding his hand up as he walked away from the others leading the way to his car. The five of them piled in.

"You're riding in the middle Boyd," Virgil told him.

"No way!" Boyd said, "Have Birdy do it."

"I'm the tallest with the longest legs!" Birdy protested, "You sit in the middle."

"Virgil will you ride bitch?" Boyd asked him sweetly.

"No," Virgil replied. "You're the smallest, you're riding in the middle."

"Boyd get your ass in the middle or ride with Darius," Dante commanded from the driver's seat, his tone leaving no room for further discussion.

Grumbling Boyd got in the middle and they were off. The drive from Bay City to Mt. Pleasant took an hour. They got on US-10 driving to Midland, and from there getting on M-20 continuing west for a half hour. The drive was fun. Virgil had started to build a good rapport with the others, and everyone spoke with ease. Virgil tried to include Boyd in the conversation.

Amid an interesting retelling of Dante's interview with Landon, Louie let out an epic fart that

seemed to rumble the whole car. "Louie!" everyone shouted in unison. Suddenly a rotten foul

odor permeated the air, causing all of them to gag.

"What the hell did you eat!" Dante said as all the windows in the car went down.

"Sorry, sorry," Louie let out a sigh of relief another rumble escaped causing everyone to

groan in terror. "Stir fry goes right through me," Louie chuckled patting his belly.

The stench that had rotted so pungently slowly dissipated. They passed the city's most

infamous attraction on the way in, Soaring Eagle Casino and Resort. The city was on the small

side, more of a college town for Central Michigan. It didn't have any malls but had a few

superstores. The casino brought in people from towns and cities from hours away, making Mt.

Pleasant a frequent destination for many.

They found the small engraving store ten minutes from the casino. The shop was small,

filled with displays of various work they could do. Everything from plaques, wooden signs,

picture frames, lawn decorations, to Greek organization things like paddles. There were two

ladies working, and it took some time to get all their orders done. Virgil was helped by the

worker to create an outline of what his paddle would look like, then paid the sixty-three dollars

to place the order. Virgil waited for the others to finish, looking around at the myriad of

interesting displays in the store.

Dante came over to stand by him. "What do you feel like doing after this?" he asked

Virgil.

"Maybe we could all eat dinner together?" Virgil suggested.

"We can do that any day on campus, I was thinking we should all hit up the casino while we're in Mt. Pleasant," Dante replied.

"That sounds fun!" Louie said coming up behind them throwing his arms around both their shoulders. "I could go for some Black Jack."

"Alright sounds like a plan," Dante nodded with a big smile on his face. "Let's win some money!"

"I'm not a fan of gambling," Nolan said walking up to them. "Just a waste of money. I'd rather do something else, like laser tag or putt putt."

"This isn't a date Nolan," Dante said rolling his eyes. "Laser tag sounds alright, but the casino sounds better."

"I got shit to do tonight," Darius said walking over to them. "My car is headed back to Bay City."

Once everyone had finished the guys left the shop and said their goodbyes, parting ways. Darius' group was headed back to Bay City, while Dante's car was headed to the casino.

"Dude can I borrow some money from you?" Boyd asked Virgil softly. "The paddle tapped me out."

"Boyd you shouldn't be gambling if you don't have any money," Virgil admonished him.

"Yeah yeah, can I borrow some money or not?" Boyd asked him.

"Virgil don't borrow him any money," Dante said from the front. "He won't pay you back."

"Yes I will!" Boyd said getting defensive. "I'm good for my word."

"Alright what about the twenty bucks you still owe me from poker at the Omega house last week?" Dante asked in a condescending tone.

"I'll get it to you," Boyd said sheepishly.

"I'm not going to be spending a lot of money on myself there, let alone you Boyd," Virgil affirmed. "If you can't afford to gamble then don't."

"I'll spot you forty bucks," Louie said turning around from the passenger seat. "You just have to pay me back soon, or else my parents will get angry, they monitor my account. They'll want to know where my money went."

"Thanks Louie I appreciate it," Boyd beamed with sincerity. "Besides, I'll win enough money, I'll triple what you give me! Then I'll pay you back, plus have enough to take home a nice little wad of dough," Boyd said rubbing his hands together with glee.

They arrived at Soaring Eagle Casino, which was owned by Saginaw Chippewa Tribal Nation. The casino brought in big name entertainment once or twice a month in the form of standup comedians and bands. Virgil had never been to a casino before, he was excited to see what it was like. The building didn't seem too big from far away, but as the five of them walked up to it the size of it loomed before them. Inside the ceiling seemed to stretch endlessly, lights and sounds from every direction vying for Virgil's attention.

"What should we do first?" Virgil asked.

"I'm going to the Black Jack table," Dante told them.

"Right behind ya bud," Louie told him.

Boyd followed Louie. Birdy turned to Virgil who was feeling sensory overload from all the stimulation around him. "Why don't you stick with me while you get your feet wet," Birdy offered Virgil.

It was noisy and hard for Birdy to hear anyone over all the sounds with his hearing aids, so the two sat next to each other at some slot machines to pass the time. Virgil used twenty dollars, then he'd had enough. After Birdy finished, they walked around. After a few hours the group was ready to leave, they cashed out, making the long trek back to the parking lot.

"Dude, we're so coming back here," Dante was excited talking to Birdy. "I won two hundred dollars!"

"Good for you!" Birdy smiled. "You buying dinner?" Birdy asked nicely.

"Buy your own damn dinner," Dante said gruffly.

"I'll pay you the money back when I get the chance," Boyd told Louie rubbing his neck.

"We're cool, I made a good amount, so I'm not worried," Louie assured him. "You guys make anything?" Louie asked Birdy and Virgil.

Darkness had descended, the night sky lit up with stars, there wasn't a moon visible. The October nights were cold in Michigan. The guys walked briskly to Dante's car, anxious to be out of the chilly breeze. A wail followed by a painful moan pierced the night. Virgil pivoted on his heel, taking the attack stance Vahn had taught him, Soul Reaver's symbol on his hand blazing to life.

"What was that!" Louie asked, a note of fear hanging upon his words.

"Let's check it out," Virgil answered, walking in the direction of the noise.

"Are you crazy?" Louie squealed, in a hushed voice. "Let's get to Dante's car and get the hell out of here! It could be a mugger or worse!" he cried out, his voice rising nervously.

"If it is worse, than we should do something about it," Virgil said moving away from the group and towards the noise.

"Can't we just go home?" Louie whined.

Another scream, from a woman, rang out causing Louie to scream a little in response. Dante slugged Louie in the shoulder, "Man up!" he said, a scowl on his face.

"Ow!" Louie clutched his arm, "I'm scared!" Louie complained looking around like a deer caught in headlights.

"I got you Virgil," Birdy said moving up next to Virgil following him to the noise.

"Same here," Dante said right on their heels.

"You guys want me to get the car running?" Louie asked, having not moved an inch.

"Louie get your big fat Asian ass over here, NOW!" Dante demanded.

"Oh God, we're going to get killed!" Louie cried, stomping his feet and following the group at a distance.

Virgil rounded a section of the parking lot coming to a wide-open lane, it was lit by tall lights pushing the complete darkness of night at bay. Halfway down the row of cars was a woman laying on her back, on the cold cement ground. Hunched over her were three grotesque figures, their deformed bodies twisted and revolting. Their mouths were gaping holes, missing lips, with large sharp dagger like teeth. They seemed to be feeding on the woman, they weren't devouring her flesh, their mouths sucked at her aura, feeding off her spiritual energy.

"What the hell are those?" Louie gasped.

The three dark figures heads snapped towards Virgil and the others. Their eyes were large empty sockets. The creatures hissed at them, rising up to stand on two legs. They stood about four feet tall, with lanky limbs, and putrid flesh hanging from their bodies. Their hands were claws, sharp and with flecks of blood coating them.

"Demons," Birdy whispered.

"What are we supposed to do?" Louie said, fear rising within him.

"Get your shit together!" Virgil barked. "Get your bow out and take them down!" Virgil commanded. Virgil turned and looked at Louie, he was shaking, sweat beading on his forehead.

"Be brave Louie," Virgil encouraged him. "You're one of the best guys I've ever known! This woman needs us," Virgil emphasized.

The demons got down on all fours and began to crawl with alarming speed.

"Soul Reaver!" Virgil yelled out. The symbol blazed with flame, his weapon taking physical form. Virgil grabbed the scythe and charged forward letting out a loud battle cry.

"Gaia's Wrath!" Dante yelled, his double-bladed earth axe materializing into his hands.

"Ixion's Glaive!" Birdy shouted, his lightning lance taking form.

"Golem's Hatchet!" Boyd yelled out, his small, one-handed, earth throwing axe coming into his hand.

"Shiva's Bow!" Louie yelled, his ice bow gently snaking into existence as if a goddess had delicately carved it from a winter breeze.

Virgil charged at the demons almost upon him. He pivoted on his heel and spun to the left, bringing his scythe spinning around with him. The demon in the lead leaped into the air at Virgil. Virgil came full circle, slashing with his blade, catching the demon in mid leap across its middle. The demon didn't have time to scream, it disintegrated into ash to the ground. The demons behind it leapt at Virgil letting out snarls. They each latched onto an arm, their force knocking Virgil off balance, he fell onto his back with a demon clinging to each side. The demon that had jumped on his left arm howled in aguish, the black flames that ran along his arm from Soul Reaver, burning it. It fell off Virgil meekly, writhing in pain on the pavement next to him.

Virgil pushed against the demon as it clawed at him, biting down on his arm taking swipes at his face, fresh cuts stinging along his cheekbone from its claws. Pain shot through his arm, it felt like sharp needles were being shoved into his flesh, tearing around in circles, trying to cut deeper.

"Get off him!" Louie yelled. An ice arrow flew straight into the demon's skull. It disintegrated into ash.

Dante let out a battle cry and brought his axe down onto the demon lying next to Virgil. It dissolved into ash around Dante's axe.

"Are you okay?" Birdy asked Virgil grabbing his right hand and helping him up.

"Ahh! Easy," Virgil said the wound painful to the touch and Birdy let go.
"I think so," Virgil said looking at his right forearm. His wounds looked sickly, his arm had about a dozen puncture wounds, blood slowly running from the small but deep cuts.

"Wow," Boyd said looking at his wound. "That's going to need some attention."

"No kidding," Dante said irritated. "Louie could you help us out over here."

"Uhh what do you mean?" Louie asked confused.

"Patch him up," Dante said motioning to Virgil's arm. "Use a healing spell like Tarek does."

"I don't know how to do that!" Louie exclaimed. "I'm still kind of learning."

"Great," Dante sighed. "We need to get him back to the Omega house and get someone to heal his wounds."

"What about her?" Virgil asked more concerned for the stranger. The woman on the ground was stirring, which was a good sign, she didn't seem too badly injured.

"If we can't help treat our own, we're not much good for her either," Dante sighed.

Virgil noticed a car near, where she was, had its door open, keys were still in the door.
"Let's get her inside her own car at least and lock the doors. When she comes to, hopefully she drives herself home, or calls 911," Virgil thought out loud.

"We got it," Birdy told Virgil as he tried to go near her. "It'd be a bad idea if she woke up with any blood on her, might freak her out."

Everyone put their weapons away. Birdy and Dante helped get the woman back in her own car, put her keys next to her, and locked and shut the doors. They said she was breathing fine and appeared to be okay.

"Let's get out of here!" Louie said to them. The five of them made their way back to Dante's car. They drove mostly in silence, Dante speeding heavily to get them home. Dante asked Virgil to not get any blood on his seats. He had an old towel in the car, which Virgil and Louie used to put around his wounds to stem the flow of blood. The pain in his wrist was moderate more of a stinging achy feeling, but Virgil tried to concentrate on other things to keep his mind off it.

Dante dialed up Tarek on his phone once they were pulling into campus. "Hey Tarek Jeter, was wondering if you were around by chance," Dante asked.

"Yeah I'm at the house, why whats up?" Tarek asked him.

"Umm not too much, a group of us are stopping by, Virgil is with us. He got a little scrape on his arm he needs you to look at," Dante said relaxed as if it was the most normal thing in the world.

Tarek was quiet for a minute, then said, "What happened?"

"Not much, not much, Virgil does need to see you though," Dante said firmly.

"What happened?" Tarek asked again louder this time. There was some hushed talking on the other line then Gabriel's voice came through, clear and in command.

"Dante cut the shit right now, what happened to your pledge brother?" Gabriel demanded.

"A demon bit him a little and he has a few claw marks on his face, but he's conscious and they are superficial cat scratches really," Dante said, waving his left hand off.

"How close are you?" Gabriel asked, not happy.

"Coming down State Park Drive right now," Dante told him.

"We'll be waiting," Gabriel barked, then hung up.

They pulled through the open gate to the Omega yard, and quickly parked the car. The five Omicron candidates headed inside. There was a small group of brothers waiting for them in the first floor living room, Landon, Vahn, Tarek, Gabriel and Magnus.

Tarek had a stained towel on the floor and Virgil went and sat down next to him. Tarek quickly took Virgil's makeshift bandages off to see the wound underneath. The cuts still looked sickly, and trickled blood.

"Cat scratches?" Gabriel asked Dante. "What kind of cat was it, a Puma?"

"We ran into some demons at the casino," Dante said awkwardly. "It was an accident really. We didn't mean for it to happen."

"We all heard this lady scream and Virgil charged ahead," Louie recalled. "I was the voice of reason, suggesting we get to safety, but he wanted to make sure she was all right."

The brothers looked at Virgil and his face got red. He decided looking at his wrist was better than taking in their gazes.

"Ply," Tarek said. A warm soft blue light flowed from Tarek's blue Devil Arms symbol, over to Virgil's skin. The wound began to knit itself back together, the cellular regrowth exponentially heightened by Tarek's spell. After maintaining the spell for several seconds, the wounds were almost gone, replaced with pink new flesh.

"Good thing you guys got here, Virgil was likely going to pass out soon from blood loss if this was left untreated," Tarek commented, with a worried expression. "You'll be fine," he assured Virgil, ending the spell.

Virgil tightened his right hand into a fist then let go. "Thank you," Virgil said to Tarek, getting up. "You don't know how grateful I am to you."

"You're welcome," Tarek said, rolling up the towel.

"How many were there?" Magnus asked.

"Three," Dante told him.

"You guys took them down?" Magnus asked.

"Virgil got one, Louie another, and I took the last one," Dante explained.

"We're glad you're all alright, but it isn't a good idea to be traveling all over after dark without a brother. Demons can't manifest in this world while the sun is out, at least the weak ones can't. Until you guys get a better handle on your abilities, don't take unnecessary risks," Gabriel reprimanded.

Chapter 13
<u>Tradition</u>

Sunday night Omicron was at the meeting room for Education. Virgil spent the rest of his free time with Louie, Birdy, and Dante. The four of them had started hanging out as a group every day. He had a Math test on Monday, a rough draft for his next paper due Tuesday, and a History test on Wednesday. Virgil had a Biology exam the following week, but he was too busy with his other stuff to get a head start on studying. He used his planner like a map, organizing his assignments, Omega activities, and plotting out study time.

Gabriel was somber at their Education, something was wrong. "At our Chapter meeting, two of Omicron were brought up for removal," Gabriel announced sadly. The room went silent. "Devin," Gabriel said looking him in the eyes. "I am sorry, you are no longer a candidate in this process."

Devin was completely taken back, a shocked expression on his face as he gathered up his things from the desk and handed in his things. He stared up at Gabriel, a questioning look with some hurt.

"Sit tight people," Gabriel clapped Devin on the shoulder, and they left.

"Who do you think the other guy was?" Dante asked out loud.

"I can't believe they kicked Devin out!" Louie exclaimed.

"If we were going to lose anyone it was most likely him," Nolan sighed as if it was the most obvious thing in the world. "He is the only one who hasn't bonded with many brothers or pledge brothers. He's also struggling with Devil Arms training."

"Really?" Dante asked. He didn't know, no one really did, Devin was the pledge brother who stood out the least.

"The first time I was able to summon my spear was just two practices ago. This shit isn't easy, it doesn't come naturally for all of us." Axel pointed out. "I'm better with computers than people."

"And that's fine," Louie said sticking up for his roommate, "we need a variety of strengths, that is what makes us stronger as a whole."

Gabriel was gone for fifteen minutes before he came back to the room. "Sorry about that," he said as he came in and leaned against the front desk. "I know some of you may have questions, losing a pledge brother can be upsetting. None of you are in right now, okay? You're not brothers, though you may be privileged to come into our home and be a part of our world, we are still deciding if we want to keep you around. This brotherhood is a family, first and foremost. If we don't feel like you're a part of it, any brother at any time, has the right to bring someone up for removal. A vote is called after discussion, and the majority decides the outcome," Gabriel said.

"So, you can kick any of us out at any time and we're not allowed to speak in our defense?" Louie asked not happy.

"This is OUR fraternity, not yours, not yet. Pledges do not get to make decisions about recruitment," Gabriel said shortly. "I'm the Hegemon, I run this candidate process. But when it comes to deciding if you should be a fellow frater, every brother's voice and vote is equal. Trust me when I say, I'm always fighting for you guys," Gabriel said standing up to pace slowly in front of them. "Every Chapter meeting, I am talking you guys up, but you HAVE to show effort. Devin was removed because the brothers felt he didn't care. In the past three weeks he'd gotten four interviews. He has done poorly on the quizzes I give, and he told Tarek that he is failing two of his classes. A lot of brothers still do not know him, going into the fourth week that is not acceptable. We're a close-knit group, and every new member that comes in changes us, we want to change for the better." Gabriel finished what he had to say and went quiet, he looked down cast, the expression so foreign on his confident face.

Louie shook his head mumbling unhappily to himself. Dante raised his hand and Gabriel nodded to him. "Who was the second guy?"

Gabriel nodded, replying casually, "The second Omicron brought up for removal, was Axel." Axel's eyebrows went up. "The Chapter vote was close, more of us wanted you here though," Gabriel said. "But you NEED to show the brothers some real effort these next few days," Gabriel warned. "Tradition is Tuesday, and brothers like to weed out the guys who aren't fitting in before then," Gabriel said not wanting to talk about the subject any longer.

Education was a focus on how individual Chapters of Omega were structured. There were eight Jeweled Officers which ran the Chapter. The Prytanis, or President, presided over the Chapter meetings and served as the chief administrator. The Epiprytanis, or Vice President, was the head of all the committees, and the parliamentarian. The Hypophetes, or Chaplain, was third in command, the brotherhood chair who handled the Chapter's scholarship affairs.

The Pylortes, or Risk Management Officer's, job was to protect the fraternity from itself and others. The Hegemon, or Chapter Educator, was the officer in charge of the candidates for membership from the time of induction until their initiation. There was also the Grammateus or Secretary, Histor or Historian, and lastly the Crysophlos or Treasurer.

Chapter Retreats, Gabriel told them were twice a year, during the breaks between semesters. Retreat was a two to three-day event where the brothers went away to relax, bond, and plan out the agenda for next semester: make goals, go over Rush, and refocus as a group. Gabriel also added that they had a lot of fun, some of the best times in the fraternity; brothers got rowdy and hilarious stories came out of every venture.

"Who is the most important member of Omega?" Gabriel asked Omicron class next.

Nolan raised his hand eagerly. "Someone besides Nolan," Gabriel said flatly looking at the other candidates.

Louie looked around then raised his hand hesitantly. Gabriel nodded for him to respond. "We are?" he answered uncertainly.

"Well yes and no. The answer is, the next member you recruit, they are the most important member. We are only as strong as the members we have, the more brothers, the more we can accomplish. Rush is NOT just the responsibility of the Rush Chair, it is everyone's responsibility," Gabriel emphasized.

"Let's talk a little about proper Rush techniques," Gabriel said. "When Rushing a potential member, it is important to introduce yourself with a firm handshake. Ask them questions about themselves, get to know the person, it is easier to recruit a friend you know than a stranger you don't. Make the conversation about him, don't bombard him with information about the fraternity; they know you're with Omega, they don't need it shoved down their throats. They'll start to ask questions about Omega once their curiosity is peaked."

"Something else to add, we are a Paladin fraternity, we're looking for Nephilim, no matter what degree their bloodline. It can be hard to spot them if they don't have a Devil Arms on their hands, which is more often the case in people who are a few generations from a Pureblood Nephilim. That is where the Dreamstones come into play," Gabriel said, holding up his hand. All the brothers wore the same fraternity ring, with a small Dreamstone embedded in it.

"The Dreamstones we have you carry around, are magicite, powerful stones containing high amounts of concentrated energy or spiritual power. They help conceal our auras, or spiritual energy, from demons and other entities. Their second purpose is to act as a magic detector, they respond to the presence of another Nephilim. If you shake a potential's hand with a Dreamstone on, it will react to them if they are of Nephilim bloodline," Gabriel said.

"Question," Virgil threw out. "If your small ring does the same thing as our heavy chains and big stone, why'd don't we all just use rings?"

Gabriel looked at Virgil, giving him a stern commanding statement. "Because then you wouldn't learn the importance of always carrying it on you," Gabriel barked. "With as much hassle as those are to carry, some of you still forget the importance of carrying them," Gabriel jabbed at them, a truth that they couldn't deny. "When you become brothers, you are given your own ring. A symbol of acceptance into the brotherhood of Paladins," Gabriel said. "The amount of Dreamstone isn't important, it achieves the same thing. That concludes Education for tonight guys," Gabriel said, directing their attention to the second half of the board. "Monday night we will have Devil Arms training, Tuesday night is Tradition one of the most sacred nights of our brotherhood," Gabriel stressed. "Wednesday night we will be having a Mixer with the Alpha sisters."

This earned some cheers and excited hollering from Omicron class. "Easy fellas," Gabriel said with a grin on his face. "We'll be meeting at the girls' sorority house down the road. I want everyone to be on their best behavior. Thursday and Friday night, we'll be having Devil Arms practice, the rest of the weekend is yours. I suggest that this week you fellas concentrate on studying and grades, and try to get ahead," Gabriel advised. "We're having a Halloween party next weekend, and then Omicron's Initiation party the following weekend. After Tradition it is all downhill," Gabriel spoke with enthusiasm and obvious delight. "I know you guys have been stressed out, this process takes a lot out of you. Hang in there with me guys," Gabriel pleaded.

"One final thing before I let you go for the night," Gabriel said quickly, Omicron going silent. "Tradition is our most sacred Brotherhood. We don't like to let just anyone see it," Gabriel said seriously, speaking from the heart. "The next forty-eight hours are crucial in showing the brothers you want this, that you're dedicated to the fraternity," he warned cryptically.

Monday, Virgil got an interview with Thiago completed. He was Hispanic, a real quiet brother who liked having fun, and flirting with chicks. Thiago lived off campus not far down the road, choosing to get his own apartment over living at the Omega house. Thiago liked his space and privacy and was introverted. He was close to a group of older brothers that Virgil had seen around but didn't know very well.

Tuesday, Virgil was racked with anxiety, like the rest of Omicron, this brotherhood was going to be different. The group arrived at the Omega house dressed in hoodies, long sleeved shirts, hats, gloves, and coats. Next week was Halloween and by late October the nights were very cold in Michigan. The ten of them had grown close over the past few weeks. They took a minute of silence outside, to pray for a successful night. Omicron then went inside, placed their hands in front of them, and hung their heads looking at the ground. Jagger seemed to be happy as he let out a grunt of appreciation, he didn't have to ask them this time.

Gabriel appeared at last from the large staircase, "Let's get this show on the road. Omicron, our Chapter called an emergency meeting, candidates were brought up for removal from this process. After an hour of debate and voting, it has been decided that candidate Axel will no longer be a part of Omicron class. Axel please remove your pledging materials and give them to frater Jagger."

"Don't we have a say in this?" Louie argued.

"The brothers get to decide which candidates they want in their fraternity," Gabriel said flatly staring at Louie.

Professor Ramuh came into the room. "If you would follow me please," he asked of Axel. Axel wore a bored expression as he followed the Chapter Advisor upstairs. Louie seemed the most upset out of Omicron, Axel being his roommate. They were down to nine pledges. Gabriel told them to hang tight and went with Professor Ramuh. Gabriel was back in minutes, "Follow me," he commanded, the candidates followed him to the edge of their property where the brick square wall that surrounded their property met the forest. The candidates' Bigs were there each holding a blindfold in their hands, everyone present except the Sweethearts.

"Omicron, tonight is Tradition," Gabriel said standing before them. "None of you are to talk about, or share with, anyone outside of this circle of people, what you witness. Omicron is down two guys from where you started this week. In my opinion you're stronger without them. The nine of you are Omicron, this is the pledge class we're looking for. We want to see how well you work as one, show all of us, what Omicron's got. Brothers, the blindfolds." Vahn tied a bandana on Virgil's eyes, pulling it tight making sure he couldn't see.

"These are to stay on at all times, you are only allowed to take them off, when we say," Gabriel instructed. "Tonight, I am in charge, listen to MY voice. Candidates reach out with your right hand, place it on the shoulder of your pledge brother. Hold onto him tight. If you lose the person in front of, or behind you, make sure you yell STOP! Make sure you know who is in front of and behind you," Gabriel told them.

Virgil's hand firmly grabbed onto Troy's backpack, hanging on his right shoulder. Hector was behind Virgil holding onto his right shoulder. The candidates went through and talked to one another. Louie was now the end of the line, Darius in the lead as he'd been since the beginning.

"Move out!" Gabriel shouted, and they started running. The brothers crashed into the forest ahead, whooping and hollering, Gabriel was in front of Darius, Darius moving as fast as he could to keep up. The world was dark to Virgil, the blindfold kept his vision obscured. The sound of leaves and sticks breaking underfoot filled the night, his sense of hearing was his most important resource.

The guys in front of him started making frustrated noises as things crashed around them, Virgil soon found out why as a branch hit him in the face. Shortly thereafter he almost tripped over a log that was on the ground.

"You're not communicating!" Gabriel yelled back. "Darius you're in front let your pledge brothers know what's going on."

"Branch, low branch duck, duck!" he yelled back.

"Branch, duck low!" Boyd yelled out next as they moved forward.

Omicron started talking to one another, yelling out what obstacle was next as they started to get more plentiful, and harder to miss. Brothers were moving all around the candidates, sometimes yelling out warnings that weren't there. It was disorienting at first as Birdy and Louie would end up listening to the wrong person, causing them to hit obstacles. Hector was practically choking Virgil as the group behind him was clearly lagging, Virgil desperately tried to keep pace with Troy.

"Slow down, slow down!" Hector called giving a forceful yank on Virgil's hoodie choking him in the process. "You are losing us."

"We will NOT BE SLOWING DOWN!" Gabriel yelled out in an angry voice. "Pick up the pace, keep up with the guy in front of you."

They sped up instead of slowing down. Gabriel had a fraternity chant they practiced as they marched through the night woods, stumbling and crashing their way to a destination unseen and unknown. It rhymed and was the typical lewd and crude things one would expect from a fraternity, but that's what made it so much fun to sing out into the night. Virgil's own voice mingling with the thirty others around him, blind to the world yet exhilarated by the unknown. The candidates did their best to stay as a group, getting broken up occasionally, having to stop to regroup. Finally, Gabriel brought Omicron to a stop. The nine candidates swayed with ragged breathing.

"Darius this way," Gabriel said at the head of the group. One by one, the candidates were led away from the chain of Omicron brothers. When it was Virgil's turn a brother led him away from where he stood, after several paces he let go of Virgil. Virgil stood for the first time in this Brotherhood, alone. Virgil had no idea where they were, his sense of direction disoriented from the brisk hike.

Several minutes passed, the cold of the night air seeping into Virgil. Now that he had been standing still, he quickly lost the heat he'd generated from running, his breathing returning to normal. He couldn't hear anyone, though it felt like someone or others were nearby.

"OMICRON!" Gabriel's voice rang out, in the distance. His voice was muffled by the cold wind, he sounded far off...

"Get back in formation!" Gabriel commanded.

"Troy!" Dante called out around him.

"Birdy!" Louie whistled and called trying to evoke some laughter and response.

"Troy! Hector!" Virgil called out into the night around him.

The night erupted into a frenzy of voices, noise and chaos. The once quiet and empty feeling around him, was replaced with signals from twenty directions. "Virgil! Virgil!" Someone called out to him. Virgil turned towards the voice.

"I'm right here!" Virgil said walking to the voice, his right hand outstretched.

"Virgil! Virgil!" Other voices called out. Virgil reached the guy, who he'd first heard.

"Hector? Troy?" Virgil asked. He heard laughter. "Who is this?" The man didn't respond. Virgil walked away from the brother, knowing it wasn't one of Omicron.

"Troy!" Virgil called out.

"Over here bud!" Troy called out.

"Follow OUR voices!" Dante called to Virgil and the others.

Virgil followed Dante and Troy's voices, ignoring the buzz of the other people calling out. Virgil ran into a tree, then made a habit of keeping his hands out. He tripped over something, catching himself on his hands. Virgil got back up and kept following Dante's loud booming voice calling out. Virgil's hand finally found Troy, and he got behind him, placing his right hand firmly on his shoulder.

"Who do we got?" Virgil asked.

"Just us, right now," Dante answered. "OMICRON!" Dante shouted out. "Follow my voice! The brothers are trying to trick us, only follow Omicron brothers!"

"Dante!" Birdy yelled from some ways off.

"This way Birdy!" Dante yelled back.

"Virgil!" Hector yelled.

"This way Hector!" Virgil yelled back.

The rest of Omicron found each other within minutes, and they were back in their order.

"Impressive," Gabriel commended them. "That's the fastest time of any pledge class. Now onto the rest of Brotherhood."

Gabriel led the group through the forest. They were moving at a steady pace, everyone had an easier time keeping up. They came to a stop, Gabriel walked them slowly forward, and the forest below their feet gave way to stone. They walked down a series of steps, and then were led up a few more steps. Virgil guessed they were at the stone temple.

"You can take your blindfolds off now," Gabriel told them.

Virgil removed his blindfold, seeing they were on the raised platform in the middle standing in front of the stone archway that was in the center. The brothers surrounded the middle platform, a few of them had white wings protruding from their backs.

"Where we are going, is a Chapter Tradition started during the first pledge class. None of you are to ever tell anyone about this trip, even to other Omegas from different Chapters and other Paladins. We could get in a lot of trouble for where we're about to go, maybe even get shut down as a Chapter. I need all of you to swear to me you will never tell anyone outside of this Brotherhood what you see and learn tonight," Gabriel spoke harshly. He was more serious then Virgil had ever seen him.

"Sir, we swear, sir!" Omicron replied to Gabriel.

Magnus raised his staff to the arch way muttering softly to himself. He touched the archway at three points, tracing a triangle in the air with his staff. He kept chanting and inscribing symbols on the stone, whatever spell he was using was complicated. The air between the stone pillars in the arch wavered, then began to swirl with a clockwise circle. Black dark clouds filled the arch way, spinning into a vortex.

"This dais can be used as transporter, it is possible to create portals from one location to another, moving around the world in an instant. This type of magic is very complicated, portals can only be formed near powerful ley lines that run beneath the ground. Bigs pair off with your Lils and lead them through," Gabriel commanded.

Tarek and Darius approached the archway first. They walked forward into the black swirling cloud, disappearing the instant they walked through. Vahn walked up to Virgil when it was their turn, and walked side by side into the black vortex.

Virgil felt like the wind had been knocked out of him, pressure from every direction pushed hard against him, and Virgil began to suffocate as there was no air to breathe in. Then in an instant, Virgil and Vahn came out of the darkness, their feet walking on hard rocky ground.

"WOW!" Virgil exclaimed in awe, falling off balance and landing on his butt, disoriented from the portal. The view before them was unlike anything Virgil had ever known. The sky an endless mass of ebony stormy clouds, marred only by the occasional lightning bolt with a booming clap of thunder. A sickly red sun drifted across the horizon, giving little light, barely visible in the dark sky. They stood on a flat patch of rock, high up in a large mountain chain. Mountains loomed all around them going on for miles beyond visible range of sight, dark spires of earth stretching up to meld with the blanketing black clouds. Virgil looked out at what was below the mountains. The land was withered, the ground barren and devoid of any growth, no animals or other creatures could be seen, bones were the only decoration…lots of them. The world around Virgil was a twisted macabre horror unlike anything they had on Earth.

Virgil looked up at the unrecognizable dying sun, "Where are we?" Virgil whispered.

"The Ever After," Vahn replied standing next to him, looking out at the scarred and sickly land spreading before them.

The other candidates arrived, and Gabriel gathered the group together, close to the edge of the cliff. Gabriel wore white wings on his back, making him seem even more regal than normal. Magnus walked around the perimeter of where they stood tracing his staff through the air, leaving faint golden ruins floating where he had drawn them. The symbols lasted a moment before they faded into nothingness. Magnus was casting a barrier around where they stood. Virgil could feel deep down that this was a dangerous place, a sense of foreboding and darkness lingered close.

"This is the Ever After gentlemen," Gabriel spoke low. "A dimension distinctly different from our own yet irrevocably linked to us. This was once the home world of the Fey, the race of Fairies."

Boyd stifled a laughter to which Gabriel gave him a hard-cold stare that sufficiently silenced him.

"After the Battle of the Fallen, the demons, Eidolons, and Fallen who rose against the Light, were cast out of Nirvana and landed here with their crippled and defeated Master. They drove out the Fey from their homeland, corrupting this once beautiful world into a desolate and empty shell. This is now the realm of the demons, the Fallen, and the Death Dealers. All demons who enter our world come from this place. If they have it their way, they will wash over our lands consuming everything in their path. This is what we are fighting for gentlemen," Gabriel said turning to face the dying world around them. The demons will do whatever it takes to end the race of men and destroy everything that is good in the universe. We are fighting for nothing less than the soul of our world," Gabriel whispered to them.

"It is illegal for ANY Paladin to enter the Ever After, unless it is a mission sanctified by the Grand Council at Internationals," Magnus told Omicron taking their attention from Gabriel.

He was one of the few brothers with large white wings on his back. "This is a dangerous, and evil place. We wanted to show it to you, to sink home the reality of the situation. A war is brewing. Judges with black hearts and dark wings, these things exist, and are lurking just beyond sight," Magnus said coldly, a chill running down Virgil's spine making him want to look behind him.

"Take a look around you, let this place sink into your memories. This is what will come to pass if we do not take a stand," Gabriel believed his words, and so did Virgil.

Virgil stared out across the dark landscape, its eerie and haunting visage clawing into his mind. He doubted he'd be able to forget this place. A large wyvern-like creature could be seen in the distance flying in the air, a bellowing roar rent from its maw, making Virgil's stomach queasy. Omicron was suddenly gripped with fear, all eyes glued to the massive winged creature that glided through the dark sky.

"It shouldn't be able to see us," Magnus assured the group. "I put up warding spells around us, making us invisible to those outside the circle."

"Nevertheless, we should return quickly," Gabriel advised. "There are worse things than powerful demons in the Ever After." There were no complaints. The group turned back towards the swirling black vortex that had led them there. It had stayed in the same spot since they arrived, slowly swirling around.

"A few brothers stayed behind to keep it open for us," Vahn explained to Virgil. "A portal doesn't last long once the person who cast it goes through, unless someone holds it open. If someone wasn't holding it for us, we'd all have been stranded on these mountains in the Ever After, until Magnus conjured up another one."

The candidates walked back through the black spiraling gateway, the brothers who had come through watching the skies around them cautiously. Virgil felt sick to his stomach he was so scared, this place was *very* unsafe, the brothers were eager to leave. Virgil walked through the portal with Vahn, immense pressure bombarding him from all directions, and the air ripped from his lungs. The sensation was overwhelming and just as it threatened to approach intolerable their feet found the stone of the temple. Virgil took a deep breath, relieved they were no longer in the Ever After.

Once they had all gotten back through safely, Magnus went up to the archway and spoke to the stone moving his hand across as if washing something away. The black vortex dissipated as quickly as it had appeared.

"We're heading back to the Omega house," Gabriel looked relieved to be back, "Never let what you have seen here tonight fade from your memory. That world is as real as this one, and can very well become our own, unless men like you stand against that crap when it tries to get into ours."

Chapter 14
Mixer

Wednesday night, Virgil met up with Dante, Birdy, and Louie. Dante drove them over to the Alpha's sorority house, for the Mixer. The sorority house was bigger than the Omegas, with more aesthetic landscaping, and a large pond with a fountain in front of the house. The inside of their home was feminine, elegantly decorated with vibrant colors, curtains, plants, and pictures. They followed the laughter and noise coming from a large dining hall where dozens of ladies were mingling with a dozen brothers, and the Omicron pledge class. Virgil didn't know any of them.

"Listen up!" Lamar called the room to attention. "I have in this bowl pieces of paper with our candidates' names on them. Pick out a name, and that will be their partner for this activity. We bought some pumpkins for you guys to carve. While all of you are busy with that, the brothers and ladies will be playing some games, and visiting in the other room."

Virgil stood around with the rest of the guys awkwardly waiting for his partner to pick his name. After a few members of Omicron had been picked, a girl called out, "Virgil Pitcher?" Virgil walked forward and recognized Blair, the sorority sister he had water ballooned at Homecoming. Blair had dyed blonde hair, brown eyes, a small nose, and a pointy chin. Her eyes blazed with a mischievous fire.

"Blair?" Virgil asked extending his hand to her.

"Yup," she said with a big smile shaking Virgil's hand with a strong, firm grip. "You're my partner huh? Well pal let's get this show on the road," she said, leading Virgil over to the table where a pumpkin was waiting for them.

"You know what you're doing pretty boy?" Blair asked him, hands on her hips as Virgil cut a large hole out of the top.

"I just did this with my Big last week," Virgil replied confidently. "Though I'm not good at carving the face," he added less so.

"No worries, if it looks a little stupid, we'll just steal someone else's and give them ours," she joked with a devilish grin.

"What's your sorority like?" Virgil asked with interest.

"The sisters are pretty awesome, we have forty-nine active sisters here," Blair boasted.

"That's a lot," Virgil said not realizing how much bigger they were than Omega.

"The sorority was founded on the ideals of women being classy, upstanding members of their community. Our sorority is focused on helping women empower themselves, get educated, and be successful. We do A LOT of community service, we have fun too," Blair giggled remembering something.

"What are the ladies like?" Virgil asked.

"Well there are a lot of bad ass bitches in our sorority," she said confidently with a smirk. "We also have some uptight sisters who are really strict. I wish we were a little more like you guys. I hear stories about some of things you guys get to do, makes me a little jealous," Blair remarked.

"What do you mean?" Virgil asked her, confused.

"Well for starters, we are a Nephilim sorority. We were the first Greek organization founded at this school, and the first Paladin organization here. Yet over the years, the girls have become less focused on the Paladin side of things, we aren't trained in how to use them," Blair rolled her eyes.

"What?!" Virgil asked surprised. "Our Devil Arms training is mandatory! We skip one we're kicked out."

Blair laughed, "Exactly! I think we should do the same thing, we're a Paladin sorority, we should be training our girls how to fight!"

"You can't make it mandatory?" Virgil asked.

"We can't make any of our new member education stuff mandatory," Blair sighed.

"That's dumb," Virgil shook his head. "How are your new members supposed to know anything about your organization if they don't have to attend any of the Educations!?" Virgil asked a little angry.

"Our sorority has different rules," Blair shrugged. "Forcing new members to attend mandatory educations is seen as hazing."

"We have a no hazing policy as well," Virgil argued.

Blair arched an eyebrow at Virgil, like he'd just said his mom had a golden car. "Well we do," Virgil said sheepishly. "I've never been hazed. I'd have no problem leaving if it was like that."

"It's just all about perception, rules, red tape, yada yada," Blair grumbled. "Beneath it all this is a good organization, and a great group of women. The older sisters that lead our sorority are really fun, and I've seen them practice with their Devil Arms. They're *good*."

"You think they could take on the brothers of Omega?" Virgil asked incredulously.

"Listen here you little shit, our girls could lay the smack down on your boys any day!" Blair said with sass. They shared a hard look, each refusing to back down, then their stern faces began to crack, and they shared a laugh. Blair had a very outspoken personality, saying what she thought when she wanted, to who she wanted. She was sassy, confident, and very funny. Virgil thought she was outrageous, and easily the coolest chick he'd met. He noticed she had a ruby red Devil Arms symbol on her left hand.

"What kind of weapon do you have?" Virgil asked.

"You've been staring at it for the past ten minutes, I was wondering when you'd ask," Blair smirked. "It is called Flametongue. It's a shortsword, aligned with fire. I'm still not too good with it, but I'm getting better."

"Yeah right!" the girl sitting across the table from them said. Virgil recognized her as Helene, Landon's little sister. She had been at the Omega house with Blair. "Blair is the best fighter in our class! TK said Blair has real talent and could be one of the best Paladins she has ever seen," Helene complimented her.

"Hey lips," Blair said to Helene, "Why don't you stay focused on what you're doing over there and butt out of our conversation."

"I was just saying," Helen said exasperated.

"Yeah, yeah, that's enough from the peanut gallery," Blair said, waving her off with one hand.

"Whatever, you're mean," Helene said laughing, a little red in the face as she rolled her eyes at Blair. Helene was seated with Dante, who appeared to be crushing on her. Helene was a pretty girl, she looked a lot like Landon, small frame, blue eyes, thin long blond hair, with the same nose and facial structure. She seemed sweet, a little naive, but well-meaning and polite.

"Is that how you always talk to her?" Virgil asked, looking up at Blair.

"No," Blair said, cutting into the pumpkin. "I've known Helene and her brother, Landon, since we were kids, we're best friends and roommates. I was just giving her a hard time," Blair said, looking at Helene fondly. Friends have an interesting way of hassling each other, that could be interpreted as being mean from outsiders. "What's your Devil Arms?" Blair asked motioning

to Virgil's hands. "I've never seen someone with two, let alone those colors."

"The black one is Soul Reaver," Virgil said, showing her the scythe symbol on his left

hand. "It is a flaming scythe, aligned with Chaos."

"Awesome!" Blair said looking at it with genuine interest. "What about that one?" She

asked, pointing to his right hand, the shooting star that always drew everyone's attention.

"Well, I'm not sure what that one is called. I haven't been able to use it yet," Virgil

admitted. "I feel like a freak though."

"Why do you feel that way?" Blair asked Virgil, a concerned look on her face. She

stopped what she was doing to turn her full attention to him.

"I mean we're all Nephilim, so we're different and definitely *not* normal right? I just feel

like a super freak in a sea of freaks," Virgil said, throwing up his hands and leaning back in his

chair.

"Because of your Devil Arms?" Blair asked, arching an eyebrow.

"Yes," Virgil sighed.

"Dude, you're lucky to have such unique Devil Arms," Blair spoke passionately. "Our

Devil Arms are a look at our innermost selves, that's what TK told me. Devil Arms like these, it

must mean that you are somebody special," Blair put her hand on his arm. "I think you're Devil

Arms are some of the more interesting symbols I've seen."

"Thanks," Virgil said shyly.

"No problem," Blair told him. "And besides we're not freaks, we're just special. I don't

see what's so great about 'normal'. I'm proud that we're different, we're warriors! We should

practice together sometime," Blair suggested.

"Really?" Virgil asked, wondering if she was serious.

"Yeah!" Blair exclaimed getting excited. "It would be nice to get more practice, and really let go, not have to be careful like I am with the girls," she rolled her eyes. Then whispered, "Most of them are a bunch of whiny little bitches. Can't take a punch or a few raps from Flametongue without crying."

"A few raps! I have bruises all over my ribs from the other day you bully!" Helene called out to her from across the table.

Blair started chuckling, "Aww shut up you whiner!" she told her friend.

Their pumpkin was done, everyone was having a good time, Virgil was happy their groups could be good friends.

"What are you guys doing after this?" Dante asked Blair and Virgil from across the table.

"Not shit," Blair said. "You want to hang out?" she asked him.

"Heck ya, let's go play some video games or something," Dante suggested.

"I have the newest console back at my place," Blair told them. "We could play some games or watch a movie."

"I'm down, mind if I bring Birdy?" Dante asked.

"What's a Birdy?" Blair asked with a confused look.

"My roommate, he's a dumbass, but a nice guy," Dante said, pointing to Birdy a few people down the table.

"Sure, Helene and I don't mind. The more the merrier!" Blair declared.

"Blair, I have an exam tomorrow," Helene whined. "I wanted to get some studying done after the Mixer."

"Oh meerr," Blair said making a funny sound that made no sense. "Then stay here and study, we're going to go have some fun," Blair said, shrugging her off.

"No, I want to come too," Helene complained.

"You dick!" Blair joked. "Make up your mind." A big smile spread across Helene's face.

"I can study while you guys play your games," Helene said with a shrug.

They milled about visiting with the other groups as they finished. They took turns introducing themselves, the girls had only six candidates, so the boys had to double up a little. The group of candidates wandered into the other room where the brothers and sisters were hanging out. Virgil recognized TK, she was one of the most attractive women in their group, and she was charismatic. She had a charm about her, an easy going and friendly demeanor that made people feel like they could trust her. TK saw Virgil and she walked over giving him a big hug.

"Hey cutie!" TK said embracing him.

"Hey TK!" Virgil greeted her with enthusiasm.

"Are you having fun?" TK asked him.

"Yeah, it has been really nice meeting your sorority sisters," Virgil told her.

Blair was standing next to him and TK greeted her warmly. "You guys get a chance to talk?" She asked.

"Yeah, I picked him for the pumpkin carving, he's a cool kid," Blair said.

"Aww I'm glad you guys like each other, Blair is one of the best sisters we have," TK told Virgil. "Just stay on your toes around her, this girl is wild!"

"Whatever TK, we all know you're the craziest bitch here!" Blair joked giving TK a little shove.

The brothers decided it was time to leave as well, everyone shared handshakes, hugs, and heartfelt goodbyes. The atmosphere at the Mixer had been friendly and inviting, it was the most fun Virgil had had in a while.

"I should probably get going too," Gabriel said walking up to TK and giving her a side hug and a kiss. "I got a paper due tomorrow I need to finish tonight."

"Alright babe, text me!" TK said to Gabriel and they shared a kiss.

Blair and Virgil shared a look and tried to hide their smiles. Virgil left with Blair, Helene, Dante, and Birdy.

"Yo yo!" Louie called out to them. "Where you ladies and douche bags headed?"

"Our place," Blair told Louie, "Games and movies, you want to join?"

"Heck ya!" Louie said, walking over to them.

There was a small group of guys standing in front of the cars, Virgil recognized them instantly as Betas. Malachi, Beta's President, was standing at the head of the group. Malachi's platinum blond hair was pulled back, he was dressed in jeans and a shirt with his fraternity's letters on it, under a winter coat. Jamal, the powerful dark-skinned Beta, was standing closely at his side. Virgil saw Damian was among the group.

"Evening Omega pledges," Malachi said coldly to them.

Virgil and the others stopped dead in their tracks. No one really knew what to say, the Betas standing there was unexpected. Blair was the first to speak, her fiery spirit not hampered by the Betas act of intimidation. "Nice of you all to drop by, we're on our way out, if you would excuse us," Blair told them taking a few steps forward. The men did not budge, Malachi towered over her, he stared down at her, and if looks could kill she would have been vaporized on the spot.

"Is there a problem here gentlemen?" Gabriel asked, coming outside and quickly walking over to them.

"Having fun with the Alpha ladies?" Malachi asked in a snatchy tone. "Playing dress up and giving each other makeovers?" he mocked earning a few chuckles from the guys.

"We were just having a Mixer Malachi, we're leaving now, could you move aside so my friends here can head home?" Gabriel asked nicely.

"Make me," Malachi spat at Gabriel.

"Grow up," Gabriel told him. "We're on the same side. We aren't interested in this petty rivalry, and it would be better if our fraternities could get along."

"We will never be friends," Malachi's words were heated. "You think you can steal my girl and act like a friend to me! You are NOTHING Gabriel, your day is coming," Malachi angrily gritted his teeth and clenched his hands at his side.

"Hey what's your deal!" TK shouted, out coming up to the group with a few of her sorority sisters. "Malachi what are you doing here?" she asked with a sharp tone. The kind and loving girl was gone, this strong and confident woman was a warrior, and she stood her ground.

"We came to have a word with the Omegas," Malachi said, not meeting her gaze.

"This is our property Malachi. We were having a get together with our friends, if you are here to start a fight, get out," TK said firmly.

"We won't be having any male pissing contests here!" a woman with short blond hair said walking up to the conversation. She had the letters of her sorority on her shirt, president was written underneath the letters in cursive.

"We meant no disrespect Peoples," Malachi said to the blond woman.

"Yes, you did. These boys are our guests, and any guest in our home will not be bullied or harassed. If you came here to start something, turn around and leave, unless you want to be permanently banned from our house. Is that what you guys are looking for? To be on bad terms with the only female Paladins at this University?" Peoples asked Malachi incredulously. She had an amethyst Devil Arms that looked like a sword with lightning wrapping around it.

"Who is she?" Virgil whispered to Blair.

"That's Terra Peoples, our sorority's President. If there is one chick you don't mess with in our group," Blair trailed off.

"We were just leaving mam," Jamal said to Peoples.

"Good to know," Peoples said tartly.

"Gabriel," Malachi called out looking at Virgil's Hegemon with distain. "We challenge your pledges, to do battle with our pledges. Winner gets bragging rights…and the Homecoming Trophy," Malachi said, snatching everyone's firm attention.

"That is hazing!" Peoples said getting offended. "Those candidates could get hurt or worse trying to beat each other up for your enjoyment!"

"We can take 'em," Dante said speaking up. "We're not afraid of their pledges."

"Dante!" Gabriel chided.

"We challenge your candidates to a friendly skirmish with our own, what do you say?" Malachi asked Gabriel.

Gabriel and Magnus shared a long look, a silent conversation passing between the two friends. Gabriel was the first to break eye contact and he looked back at the members of Omicron, they looked at their Hegemon, fierce determination etched in their faces.

"We accept your challenge," Magnus told Malachi.

"This is unacceptable," Peoples told them, "I won't stand for your two fraternities hazing your pledges by making them beat the crap out of each other, its wrong!" She said, stomping her foot.

"We could wait until the candidates are initiated brothers. Once they are brothers, they have the right to not participate," Magnus said in a gentle and diplomatic tone.

"Agreed," Malachi nodded.

They sealed the agreement with a handshake. Malachi took one last look at TK then the group of Betas left heading back to their own fraternity house.

"Omicron! Practice at the Omega house tomorrow night!" Gabriel called out to them.

"Sir, yes sir!" Omicron responded back.

Virgil went with Blair, Helene, Dante, Birdy, and Louie to the girls' dorm room. They spent the night joking and laughing with one another. It was nice to enjoy the normalcy of doing average college kid stuff.

"So, what was up with the whole Malachi, Gabriel situation?" Birdy wondered out loud an hour into them hanging out.

"Didn't you know?" Helene said in an exaggerated tone that seemed genuine. "TK is Malachi's old girlfriend."

"What?" The guys said in response.

"Yup," Blair grinned. "Apparently after she met Gabriel, she called it off with Malachi to be with him," she said with a bright smile. "Who can blame the poor girl?"

"Gabriel is a sexy!" Helene sighed and nodded in agreement, they had dazed looks on their faces.

After a few hours of being at Blair's dorm, everyone was getting tired so they decided to call it a night. Virgil had a strong connection with Blair, talking with her felt so…easy. It was like they'd been friends for a long time. They exchanged numbers and agreed to hang out again soon, sharing a hug goodbye.

The next day after his classes were done, Virgil ran into a familiar face as he was walking across campus back to his dorm. "Hey, aren't you a Sweetheart?" Virgil asked the woman. She had a long-sleeved shirt on under a hoodie, the letters of the fraternity were across the chest of her shirt, just barely readable as the hoodie was mostly zipped up.

She laughed and flipped her short brown hair, "My name is Raven, we've met a couple times," she added as if to say, duh I'm a Sweetheart.

"I'm sorry, Raven, that's right. It is nice to see you, I haven't had a chance to talk with you much," Virgil said, moving his back-pack strap on his shoulder out of nervousness.

"I was just heading home to get some food. Want to join me?" Raven offered.

"Yeah!" Virgil said a little too quickly causing Raven to laugh at him.

They walked together heading back to Raven's dorm exchanging small talk along the way. Raven lived in the upperclassmen dorms, which were town house style apartments.

"So what year are you?" Virgil asked Raven.

"I'm a third year," Raven told him. "I got made a Sweetheart winter semester my freshmen year, when Mu was pledging still."

Arriving at Raven's empty dorm, they headed upstairs to have their interview in her room where they could speak freely. Virgil got out his pledge binder and started his interview with Raven. Raven was a sassy woman, with a lot of attitude. Virgil also found her to be loving, especially to the guys in Omega. An unspoken bond was shared between her and all the guys, she was their Sweetheart, their friend. Raven told Virgil that she grew up in southern Michigan. She showed him a picture of her from senior year, she was dressed in a cheerleading uniform with long dark hair that hung down to her legs.

"Wow!" Virgil said slightly blushing.

"What?" Raven asked defensively.

"It's just, you look so different," Virgil said not able to take his eyes off the picture.

"No, I don't!" Raven protested. "My hair was longer, that's about it."

"You look breathtaking in that picture," Virgil said handing it back to her.

"Are you saying I don't look good now?" Raven asked a little edge to her voice, putting it back in her box.

"NO!" Virgil shouted. "You're a very lovely lady," he told her.

"Uh huh," Raven said, with her eyes slightly narrowed like she didn't believe him.

"Honest! You are beautiful Raven, I just think that the long hair really complimented you, that's all," Virgil told her.

"You think I really looked that good with long hair?" Raven asked, taking the picture back out and giving it a hard look.

"Well you look great either way. I have a thing for long hair on women, that's all," Virgil shrugged.

"Maybe I should grow it out again," Raven mused. "It is just so much work having long hair."

"I need my hair cut," Virgil said running his fingers through his hair. It had quickly turned into a messy mop, with no real style or design. Virgil had become so busy with the pledging process he hadn't even really thought about it, until one day he noticed it was wild and overgrown.

"I could cut it for you," Raven offered.

"Really?" Virgil asked.

"Yeah, I have my cosmetology license, I work at one of the best beauty shops in Bay City, Scissor Wizards on Old Kawkawlin Rd, owned by this lovely lady Pam, a doll to work for. But I cut most of the boys hair for them here or at the Omega house," Raven said.

"Awesome! Sounds good to me," Virgil said.

They went down stairs and Raven got out her kit, with the scissors, razors, and electric shavers. Virgil sat in a chair and Raven put a black cover over him to keep most of the hair off his clothes.

"I like a three guard on the sides and keep it short on the top so I can spike up my bangs," Virgil told her.

Raven cut his hair while they continued talking. Raven told him that joining the fraternity had been a life changing experience.

"I didn't know anything about the Paladins before the Omegas," Raven said. "I still remember the night the boys initiated me as their Sweetheart, they invited me over to the house, told me there was a party going on. But when I got there, no one but brothers were there. They were all dressed up, got down on one knee and sung the Sweetheart Song to me. Gave me a big bouquet of flowers, and my first pair of letters. Told me that they wanted me to be a part of their family. It was one of the happiest nights of my life," Raven recalled getting a little teary eyed.

"That sounds really special," Virgil said with a smile imagining Raven standing at the Omega house with all the guys kneeling and serenading her.

"It was. They had a huge party afterwards to celebrate, they'd invited me a little early before the other guests arrived. All the other girls who came were so jealous when they found out I was picked," Raven told him.

"Why?" Virgil asked.

"Oh, because that's just how girls are," Raven sighed. "Most women who get to know the boys, want into their group, because you guys are awesome. Once freshmen girls find out about the Sweetheart position, they start sucking up to the boys, trying to do anything they can to win 'em over. Some even try to sleep their way in," Raven said, wrinkling her nose in disgust.

"What?!" Virgil asked surprised. "But Gabriel said the Sweetheart was a position of great honor. That the Sweetheart was supposed to be a classy lady that represented the fraternity."

"Exactly," Raven said nodding. "They are an honorary member, one of the guys. It isn't a position you suck up for, it is something that happens naturally, because she is such a strong part of the group already."

As Raven worked on Virgil's hair, he noticed the golden-brown Devil Arms glyph on her right hand.

"What's your Devil Arms?" Virgil asked.

"Oh, that," Raven said, suddenly getting uncharacteristically shy and quiet.

"I'm sorry, you don't have to tell me if you don't want to," Virgil told her, wanting to make her comfortable again.

"It's okay, I don't mind telling you," Raven said. "Honestly, I love the guys and Omega, but this part of the fraternity is my least favorite," she said rubbing her other hand over the symbol of her Devil Arms.

"The Nephilim part?" Virgil asked.

Raven nodded. "I had no idea I had Nephilim blood in me. I have a normal family, had a normal life before I became a Sweetheart. Once they initiated me, this symbol came onto my hand, and my life has changed ever since. I don't enjoy fighting. I've seen demons on a few occasions, and they terrify me.

"All of this exists whether you know about it or not," Virgil interjected. "Just because you didn't see it doesn't mean that it wasn't there. It is better to be aware of it and be able to protect the people you care about."

"I guess," Raven nodded. "It's just…it can be overwhelming."

"Yeah it can be," Virgil agreed.

"A dagger," Raven said.

"Huh?" Virgil asked.

"My Devil Arms is a dagger," Raven told him.

"Cool, you are the first person I know of to have a weapon like that," Virgil said.

"It is rather beautiful," Raven said, looking down at her Devil Arms. "I don't use it much, but it does make me feel safe sometimes, knowing it is there if I need it."

"Wow! Nice job," Virgil said once Raven finished. It was one of the best haircuts he'd ever had.

"I'm starving!" Raven exclaimed as she cleaned up. "Let's make dinner."

Chapter 15
Gabriel's Interview

"Through our veins flows the blood of Judges, this gives us the ability to manipulate the matter of the world around us. Each of you is aligned with an element, identifiable by the color of your Devil Arms," Magnus explained. It was Thursday, they were in the clearing with the stone temple used for Paladin rituals. "Each of us is limited by our aligned elements, I'm a wind adept," Magnus said raising his amethyst colored staff Devil Arms on his hand. "I can only manipulate wind and electricity-based energy. Learning the incantations is the easy part, our blood wills our words into reality, with proper focus. The difficult part of casting is cost, it's basic chemistry, you can't make something from nothing, and energy is never lost it is simply redirected. Our spells are fueled by our auras, the spiritual energy that powers our bodies emanates from each of us. The average Nephilim can only cast a few spells before their auras are drained. The first step is centering one's self, calming one's mind, and focusing on sensing one's aura and the spiritual world around us," Magnus instructed.

Omicron was spread out so they could stretch their arms and not touch one another. "Close your eyes and take in a deep breath," Magnus spoke softly. "Feel the power surrounding you." Virgil concentrated hard; he felt as if a small wind was circling around him. Virgil opened his eyes and could see a sphere of gold light surrounding him, he almost fell backwards.

"Wow!" Louie said looking over at Virgil. "Virgil's is HUGE!" Louie said.

A small sphere of light was emanating from all of them, each the same light as their Devil Arms symbol. Most of their spheres were rather small, Nolan had the second biggest out of the group, and Louie's was bigger than average as well. Virgil looked at his own, which was by far the largest of anyone present, even the older brothers. Virgil's aura was colored with gold light, unique from everyone present. He let go of his concentration and everyone's auras vanished from his vision going back to being unseen.

"There are six schools of magic, Alteration, Conjuration, Destruction, Enchanting, Illusion, and Restoration," Magnus explained. "Destruction is easy to learn the basics, and it is what we use primarily in the field. You can only use spells if your aura is strong enough to handle the cost. Casting takes its energy directly from your aura, draining it in the process. A Judge's aura can be overpowering for any mortal, which is why they are so dangerous."

The candidates broke off with their Bigs. Vahn told Virgil that he was aligned with spirit. Since Soul Reaver was both a darkness and fire weapon, however, it was possible Virgil may be able to manipulate fire.

"Spells are broken into four categories, or tiers," Vahn said, "Basic, Complex, Master, and Ultimate. Let's try a Basic spell. Concentrate in your mind, imagine the heat of fire, WILL it into existence. See with your mind the spell taking place, and make it happen," Vahn instructed. "Watch me." Vahn extended his hand out, took a deep breath then said, "Fire!" His ruby Devil Arms glowed, and a burst of flames erupted several feet in front of them.

"Wow!" Virgil said, the heat from the fire warming his skin. The fire lasted a few seconds then died out.

"The most basic element spell of Fire has higher forms," Vahn told Virgil. "Fire, Fira, Firaga, and Firaja which is the Ultimate spell of Fire. But spells aren't limited to the basics, anything you can imagine in your mind you can manipulate the element to perform. Here's another Basic spell, that's more powerful than Fire, Fire Lance!" Vahn said. From his Devil Arms erupted two large arrows that were made of fire, that shot forward crashing into the ground and scorching the earth.

"Fire Lance is more destructive than Fire and takes more energy to cast. Using spells in tandem with your Devil Arms in combat is key to success. You try one," Vahn suggested

"I just say the same thing you said?" Virgil asked.

"The words aren't enough. You have to concentrate with your mind, see with your thoughts the spell taking form, and as you imagine it, it will be," Vahn said.

Virgil imagined fire coming from his hand and rushing forth in the form of a large arrow like he'd just seen. "Fire Lance!" Virgil shouted. Two large arrows of fire came out from Soul Reaver's black symbol rushing forth and burning the ground. The instant he said the words, Virgil felt the energy being pulled from his aura. It made his legs shaky, and his headache. "Uh," Virgil put a hand to his head, vertigo suddenly coming over him. Vahn put a hand on his shoulder to steady him.

"Easy," Vahn said. "It takes some getting used to. The cost of using magic, is instantaneous, your aura has shrunk some."

"Really?" Virgil asked. He closed his eyes and centered himself once more like Magnus had instructed, opening his eyes he saw his aura. The golden sphere that extended out from him had shrank, but it was still larger than the others. Virgil was starting to feel normal again, the aftereffects of using the spell dissipating.

"Why is my aura so much bigger than everyone else's?" Virgil asked his Big.

"Probably because you're a Pureborn?" Vahn guessed. "I'm not sure really, every Nephilim's different. Don't worry too much about it," he suggested. After three spells Virgil felt queasy, his aura having shrank dramatically. Vahn assured him his energy would heal gradually with time. Vahn also told Virgil the more he practiced using his aura to fuel spells, eventually his aura would be able to handle more. Like any muscle it needed to be used frequently to build it up. Virgil's friends had all been practicing; most guys were done after one or two spells. Their auras had become so dim they barely extended off their bodies. Nolan was the only one among them who seemed a natural.

"He's good," Virgil commented to Vahn.

"It's because of his staff," Vahn pointed out, "Nephilim who have staffs for Devil Arms are natural spell casters. They aren't as deadly outright as an axe or spear, but they make using magic much easier. Holding onto their staffs lowers the cost that each spell takes on their aura."

Sunday was the start of their fifth week of pledging, the nine Omicron pledge brothers sat in the meeting room with Gabriel. This week's class Gabriel was lecturing on character, the foundation of the Omegas. Gabriel explained that perception is everything in society, "How people perceive you to be, regardless if it is truth or slander, becomes reality to that person." Gabriel told them that they had to work hard to build up their reputations as honorable and virtuous men, it took years to build a good name, and one story or bad deed to destroy it. Gabriel stated that men of Omega were polite and respectful to women, out in public and in their personal lives. Gabriel said that how oneself, treated others, was a direct reflection of who that person was. Men of Omega were leaders, leadership is about doing, about acting and creating solutions, not over talking about the problems.

Gabriel quoted from the Omega guide, "Character stands for men, men who have the courage to stand up for their convictions and are humble enough to respect the viewpoint of others." Gabriel said that sterling character is *THE* necessary qualification for membership and all other characteristics, though desirable, are secondary to this.

"Now about ladies and etiquette, the Brotherhood for this week will be Etiquette Dinner. You will have to prepare a dinner for yourselves, the Sweethearts, and me of course. It is up to you guys what you make," Gabriel said ending education.

"This week we have something else going on as well," Nolan stood up. "Sunday there will be an Omicron presents Omega fundraiser for St. Jude hospital. Everyone who brings in a coupon that has our name on it to Bennigan's, will have twenty percent of their bill donated to St. Jude's Children hospital. I figured we could all pass them out to everyone around campus and hopefully get a nice turnout," Nolan said, passing around flyers with a coupon portion printed on the bottom.

"That will work nicely!" Gabriel was proud. "We're having a party here Saturday night, and we can give those flyers away to people then as well."

"There's a party Saturday?" Louie asked getting excited. "It has been far too long! Louie V needs to cut lose and have some fun son!" Louie exclaimed.

"Keep your pants on Louie, we can't drink," Dante said rolling his eyes.

"We can still have fun!" Louie said not missing a beat.

"Since Halloween is the night before, we are having a Halloween themed party. We're having you candidates dress up as well," Gabriel said.

"Booyah!" Birdy said, clapping his hands and doing a little dance in his chair. "I got the perfect costume."

"Oh, you don't need to worry about that," Gabriel reassured him. "We already have you're costumes picked out."

"Noooo!" Louie exclaimed. "Please tell me we don't have to wear dresses to the party!"

"Of course not! I'm not that awful of a Hegemon," Gabriel sighed. "You guys get to pick your costumes. We made a list at the meeting, and who has the most interviews, signatures and merits, will decide the order you get to choose."

There were several choices including a trash can, a baby, a tree, a pimp, and a sperm. Most of them were things Virgil would not want to be seen in. He felt mortified imagining himself showing up to the Omega mansion, dressed as a sperm. He looked at the list and prayed for something halfway decent.

"Nolan gets first pick as he is the star pledge of Omicron so far," Gabriel said, looking at his sheet of Omicron's stats. Nolan picked the rock star, one of the few fun costumes. Birdy was next. Virgil was pleasantly surprised Birdy was doing so well in the group, he had quickly become one of Virgil's best friends. Birdy chose the pimp costume. Virgil was next, he picked the tree, seeing it as simple and not embarrassing. Once the candidates had all picked their costumes, Virgil was most looking forward to seeing Louie as a baby and Dante as a sperm, Gabriel went back to business.

"Twelve days left as of today gentlemen," Gabriel said checking the clock. "I know all of you are stressed out, this process takes a lot out of you. Hang in there guys, we're almost done. If you're feeling overwhelmed or need someone to talk to, my phone is always on. I will make time for any of you, if you need me," Gabriel offered.

"I'm ready to call you my brothers, but not all the brothers feel the same," Gabriel warned them. "They don't see you as much as I do, they don't see how bad all of you want this. I challenge each of you, put yourselves out there, show the brothers you want to be a part of this family," Gabriel said, using his hands as he spoke.

The candidates went to sleep in the candidate dorm as usual after Education, they'd grown close in a few short weeks, everyone changing bunks to be closer together. Virgil still shared a bunk with Boyd. The next day Virgil was in Louie's dorm helping to revise his paper.

"This is awesome!" Louie said with excitement, after they had been working on it for a while. "I'll get a B at least with this," Louie said. "Thank you so much, it really means a lot to me," he said, giving Virgil a quick hug and pat on the back.

"My pleasure, I like having you around buddy, can't have you flunking out of college," Virgil winked. "I don't mind helping you with future papers. Just have your paper typed out already, like you had this time, so I can help with the revising and making it better," Virgil asked of him.

"I can do that," Louie nodded. "I'm starvin'!" Louie declared, making Virgil laugh as he rubbed his belly. "Want to get some food?" he asked.

"Heck yeah," Virgil replied. "I'll text Blair and ask if she wants to come."

"Awww lil' Virgil got a crush?" Louie crooned in a joking manner.

"No!" Virgil firmly asserted. "We're friends Louie, that's all."

"Whatever you say man," Louie said with a shrug grabbing his coat. "I'll text Birdy and Dante, see if they want to join."

Blair messaged Virgil that she would meet them there with her roommate. Virgil and Louie met Dante and Birdy at the cafeteria, they were already sitting with Blair and Helene.

"So how were your exams?" Blair asked Virgil. Her dyed blonde hair up in its usual messy ponytail.

"They were alright, I'm glad they are over now," Virgil sighed.

"I'm looking forward to the party this weekend!" Blair laughed "I have a cool costume already picked out."

"You're lucky you can drink," Louie pouted. "I'll be glad when this pledging process is over."

"We only have twelve days!" Birdy said, patting Louie on the back.

"What are you guys up to tonight?" Dante asked them.

"Some of the girls are getting together to watch movies and play games," Blair shrugged.

"We got practice again tonight," Dante said, rolling his eyes. "It'll be nice when we're brothers and get a day to ourselves."

"I think you are lucky you guys train so much," Helene said in a matter of fact tone. "We don't do much Paladin stuff at all. I've only gotten to use my Devil Arms a few times."

"It isn't all that great," Louie said with a shrug. "It'll be nice when we can just be brothers and don't have to jump through all these hoops."

"I like that your pledging stuff is mandatory, that is how a process should be run," Blair said thoughtfully. "If I was in charge of New Member Ed, all the girls would be required to come to Educations, and we would be training our new girls how to fight!"

"The girls would never go for that," Helene said rolling her eyes.

"How many candidates do you ladies have?" Dante asked.

"There are six of us," Helene told him.

"But Helene and I are the only ones who show up for Educations half the time," Blair said with an annoyed huff.

"Your girls don't have to go to Education?" Birdy asked in disbelief. "But how do they learn about your Sorority?" he wondered. "Are you saying a girl could accept a bid to join your group, then never come around to anything and still get in?"

"Pretty much," Blair nodded. "It's ridiculous! We don't get dedicated girls that way, and they don't gain an appreciation for the sorority, like you boys do for your fraternity. People appreciate things they have to work hard for, way more than things that are just given to them," Blair said making a strong point.

"Your Sorority is really different than our Fraternity," Virgil remarked.

"It is what it is," Blair said with a shrug. "When I'm in charge things will be run differently," she said confidently.

"You'd make a good Hegemon," Virgil told Blair. "I could see you whipping that Sorority into shape."

"Thanks," Blair smiled.

"Aww look at Virgil hitting on Blair," Louie joked elbowing Dante.

"Louie, I swear to God, if you don't knock that crap off!" Virgil said with clenched teeth.

"Look at how red he's getting!" Louie teased.

"Louie!" Virgil snapped at his friend, giving him a swift kick in the shin from across the table.

"Ow!" Louie cried out. "Anger issues watch out for this one Blair," Louie said with a wink.

"The thing of it is, the girls don't want our Sorority to change," Helene explained. "We pride ourselves in not forcing our members to do anything they don't want to do. Our girls prefer to do as little as fighting as possible," Helene said with a shrug. "It is just their stance, we fight

when we have to, but prefer to avoid it."

"Let us do the heavy lifting huh?" Birdy teased.

Helene made a face and Blair responded, "Not this girl. If trouble hits, I'm sneaking off

with you guys. I'm not going to sit around while you boys save the day, taking all the glory for

yourselves," Blair said with confidence.

"If shit hits the fan, we will take you with us Blair," Dante said with a nod and a small

grin, admiring her spirit.

"I'm serious!" Blair said, "I'm there if you guys need me."

They finished eating and went their separate ways. Virgil had an interview with Gabriel,

he drove to the Omega house, and went inside without knocking, feeling comfortable enough to

do so. Tarek, Gabriel, Magnus, and Vahn were in the living room playing video games.

"Virgil!" Vahn greeted his Lil Brother enthusiastically. "Take a seat bud, loser gives up

sticks." Virgil sat down on one of the couches, watching the guys playing Mario Kart. The

competition was fierce, and the guys did a lot of trash talking.

"What's up dude?" Tarek asked Virgil once they had finished the race, Tarek handing his

controller to Virgil.

"He came here for an interview with me," Gabriel told them. "You want to head

upstairs?" He asked Virgil.

They said goodbye to the group and went to the fourth floor. Gabriel's room had pictures

and trophies, a hockey stick in the corner, along with a picture of him in hockey gear. He looked

younger, probably from when he was in high school. There were a few sentimental things, Virgil guessed they were from TK, there was a picture of the two of them near Gabriel's desk. They sat down, Gabriel sitting on a little sofa, Virgil pulling up Gabriel's rolling desk chair.

"So, what do you got for me bud?" Gabriel asked, clapping him on the knee.

"Let's start from the beginning," Virgil said, "Tell me about your childhood, your family, what growing up was like."

Gabriel told Virgil that he'd grown up in West Branch, the youngest of four brothers. His dad's family were Italian, from a long line of Pureblood Nephilim. His mother was a Pureblood Nephilim as well, she was a free-spirited woman. Gabriel had a great childhood, full of love and family. Gabriel's parents were mostly inactive Paladins, so they could live among regular Americans and raise families.

The family business, G's Pizzeria which served a wide variety of foods mostly Italian, was started by Gabriel's grandparents. They were restaurants that excelled in quality, atmosphere, and hospitality. Gabriel had been working at a young age juggling school, the restaurant, and hockey. His parents drove him all over the state for his traveling hockey league, and he was good…really good. He wasn't super popular, but the girls always liked him for his good looks, and everyone knew his older brothers, so people treated him pretty well. Life happens, Gabriel's folks couldn't stay together, and Gabriel looked to college and his older brothers. Gabriel's brother Ezekiel had come to Bay Valley. Gabriel hung out with many of the guys years before he was even in college. Gabriel turned eighteen in high school and gained his Devil Arms that night.

"I hear a lot about Lambda class from everyone, and you guys are the leaders in the fraternity," Virgil told Gabriel. "How did you guys come together so quick?"

"Well I had an older brother in Omega and Magnus does too, they were pledge brothers in Epsilon class," Gabriel said.

"Sweet," Virgil grinned.

"Jagger had a brother in Omega at Northern in the Upper Peninsula, so we had three legacies. And we just clicked, everyone liked spending time together, we did everything as a group," Gabriel remembered. "I became best friends with Magnus, Vahn, and Landon quickly but we all were close. We're one of the closest pledge classes," Gabriel bragged.

"Omicron's pretty close," Virgil said confident.

"Ehh you guys aren't as close, not like we were, we went everywhere together. But not because we had to, because we wanted to," Gabriel proclaimed. "You have some good connections, but not everyone is united. You guys still have some work to do," he smiled.

"What was pledging like for you?" Virgil asked. "Everyone has such different experiences," he observed.

"Pledging was hell for Lambda class," Gabriel said bluntly. "We had a shitty Hegemon. The brothers should never have put him in that position. He's gotten better with age, and I don't have problems with him anymore, but some people don't like him," he shrugged.

"Why was pledging so bad for you?" Virgil asked.

"He drove us hard," Gabriel sighed explaining to Virgil, "Expected everything and gave us nothing type of deal. Devil Arms practice night and day, very old school mentality but for all the wrong reasons. One Brotherhood he'd pushed us too far," Gabriel admitted to Virgil. "And I stood up to him."

"Whatttt?" Virgil asked, getting excited. "What the heck happened?!"

"My Hegemon tore me apart," Gabriel's speech growing rapid, tense, the story even now holding strong emotion for him. "Belittled me in front of all my pledge brothers, basically told me I was nothing and would never be anything, then he ripped my Dreamstone off my chest," Gabriel sighed. "That's when I snapped. I told that bastard I wanted to be an Omega, but I WOULD NOT be spoken to like I was nothing. I respected myself and my pledge brothers, Lambda, too much to stand by and watch as the men that I cared about be treated like pieces of shit," Gabriel's words heated with anger.

"Wow," Virgil said. "That's crazy. How did you not get kicked out?" he laughed nervously.

"I quit," Gabriel said.

"What?" Virgil was surprised. "That doesn't sound like you."

"I couldn't take it anymore and just left. I walked out of the Omega manor, my face red, my heart racing, feeling sick to my stomach. Wondering if I was making the biggest mistake of my life," Gabriel had a haunted expression. "But then, the door opened behind me," Gabriel smiled, his eyes misty. "You know who was there?"

"Your older brother or your Big?" Virgil guessed.

"No, it was Lambda class, all of them," Gabriel said, a genuine smile on his face, lighting up his dark green eyes. "My brothers stood by me. The moment I'd left the room, all of them took off their Dreamstones in unison, and handed them in. Then without saying a word, they followed me out the door. They suggested we start own fraternity."

"This is crazy! I've never heard any of this!" Virgil said, not expecting this from his Hegemon, so dedicated to the Omegas.

"It's one of Lambda's stories, and my story," Gabriel owned. "The brothers had no choice but to chase us down, they apologized and asked us to come back to the fraternity. The power had instantly shifted. We agreed to come back, if we were treated with respect. We got initiated two weeks later, and our class have been leaders ever since," Gabriel acknowledged.

"That's impressive, that all your pledge brothers were willing to follow you like that," Virgil remarked.

"It was," Gabriel agreed, "But they had all felt the same as I had, we are a close group, and I was only voicing what we had all been thinking."

That was important Virgil felt, Gabriel considered himself an equal to his peers. A leader is someone who voices the needs of his people, even if he is afraid to do so, Virgil thought. "What made you want to be the Hegemon?" Virgil asked Gabriel.

"It was one of my pledge goals, always wanted to shape the young minds, and show them MY fraternity. And it has been very rewarding, it is a pain in the ass, especially when you fuckers mess up and make me look bad," Gabriel pointed a finger at Virgil and laughed as he said it.

"I like being Hegemon, but it was honestly better for me with Xi class," Gabriel admitted.

"Aww how come?" Virgil asked disappointed.

"There was only three of them," Gabriel exclaimed, pointing out the obvious. "It was easy for me to get to know them and get close to them. Brody and I are really close now. He's probably one of my best friends," he owned. "And with Omicron there are nine of you, it is much harder to spend time with each of you, and you're all so different. But a part of it is, I'm just burned out too, I'm ready for you guys to be brothers," Gabriel chuckled, admitting to Virgil and himself.

"I think you're a good Hegemon," Virgil assured him. "I really feel like you care, and you're stern when you need to be, but I feel respected by you. I respect you man," Virgil said, wanting Gabriel to know how he really felt. "You're a leader, naturally some people are just born that way. Some people just have that magnetism, that draw that pulls others to them. Omicron believes in you. We'd follow you anywhere."

"You've always been so respectful of me," Gabriel said looking down. "Sometimes I just feel I don't deserve it, you know?"

"It's good to stay humble," Virgil offered.

"You're a good guy, Virgil," Gabriel said, reaching forward and placing his hand on Virgil's shoulder. "I'm glad you came out to the Omegas, you're going to be a great brother," Gabriel took his hand back and the two were quiet, respecting the moment.

"The first time I saw you was at bid night," Virgil told Gabriel. "I really didn't want to be there. I thought about sneaking back to my room I was so nervous. But when we came to that amphitheater near the bell tower, and all the brothers went on the steps above us, and you came out and spoke to us," Virgil recalled. "I was moved. I was impressed by you guys. Afterwards you guys were coming through and shaking our hands, and you came back around to shake mine," Virgil smiled. "And that stuck with me."

"I remember that," Gabriel laughed. "You looked like a deer staring into a headlight, I wanted to make sure that I reached out to you, and I'm glad I did! Look where it brought us," he said spreading his arms out.

"I'm glad I pledged," Virgil admitted, "This whole experience has changed me, for the better." Gabriel wanted to know more about Virgil, Virgil told Gabriel his life story and a while later they were relaxed, joking easily with one another. Virgil asked Gabriel about TK, and their relationship.

"She's the love of my life," Gabriel admitted, "What can I say about her? I'm crazy about her, she's beautiful, intelligent, funny as hell, and so cool. Everyone who meets her just adores her, guys are always chasing her like crazy."

"You think she's the one?" Virgil asked.

"I love TK but thinking about spending the rest of my life with one person," Gabriel looked scared. "It is a lot to take," was all he said. "Things didn't work out with my parents. I don't want to go through something like that."

"You guys are great together," Virgil offered.

"Thanks," Gabriel smiled. "There are some couples that go everywhere together, and you rarely see them apart. We don't want to be like that. I try to make time for my friends and so does she. That's something I really like about our relationship, she's really something special," Gabriel admitted.

Their interview was winding down after over three hours. "You're the longest interview I've ever had!" Gabriel joked.

Virgil felt bad, "Sorry," he told Gabriel.

"It's okay bud, you just have a lot to ask and say!" Gabriel pointed out.

"Everyone says I talk a lot," Virgil sighed. "Sometimes I can't help myself and I don't realize I'm doing it."

"I'm not complaining," Gabriel shrugged, "Honestly Virgil, this was the best interview I've ever had. You're a great guy, I'm glad we're friends."

Chapter 16
<u>Etiquette Dinner</u>

Tuesday was Etiquette Dinner with the Sweethearts. Virgil met up with Lamar, Doc, and Troy, after class, at the gym. Virgil stopped by Birdy's after, Dante was gone so Virgil sat in his chair. Birdy was quieter than Dante and Louie, and he was a great listener.... when you could get his attention. Birdy was absentminded, to put it lightly, he spent a lot of time in his own little world, wrapped up in his phone. Besides Louie, Birdy was the person Virgil felt the closest to.

"You got your costume figured out?" Birdy asked him. "What are you going as again?"

"A tree," Virgil answered happily, thankful it was something plain.

"I can't wait to be a pimp!" Birdy said doing a silly dance in his chair. "I'm going to head to the Salvation Army and Goodwill, see if I can find something that works."

"I have a brown long-sleeved shirt, I figured I'd gather some leaves off the ground, tape them to my shirt, stick a few branches in my sleeves, and down my back, and call it good!" Virgil laughed.

Birdy shook his head at Virgil, "Why'd you choose the tree?" he asked arching an eyebrow.

"I don't want to go to a four hundred people plus party dressed as something embarrassing!" Virgil exclaimed, throwing up his hands.

"Whatever," Birdy said shaking his head. "I've got a date for Saturday," Birdy grinned.

"Are you seeing somebody?" Virgil asked interested.

"Maybe," Birdy said bobbing his head side to side.

"What's her name?" Virgil hadn't heard of her.

"Tara," he told Virgil. "We've hung out a couple times, she goes here just lives with her parents in Bay City. I've had her over one night already," he said, wiggling his eyebrows.

Virgil rolled his eyes, "Good for you bro."

"Now we got to find you a girl," Birdy told him.

"Not interested right now," Virgil said wanting to change the subject.

"Why not?" Birdy asked.

"Cause I'm too busy for a woman," Virgil said, "I can barely keep up with my studies and the fraternity, let alone a girlfriend, and I can't lose my scholarship. I'm not sure how I'll pay for school if that happens!" Virgil said getting frustrated.

"Dude you're pretty wound up, we need to get you laid," Birdy said laughing.

"Shut up!" Virgil yelled.

"No really, life isn't all about work, you have to take time to relax and enjoy the finer things in life sometimes, like a horny eighteen-year-old chick whose looking for a young stallion," Birdy said, elbowing Virgil with a wink. "You want to get some food?" Birdy asked. "I need to eat before I go costume shopping."

Afterwards, Virgil ran into Tarek walking on campus.

"Hey Tarek Jeter!" Virgil called out obnoxiously. "What are you up to?"

"Just getting out of class, headed back to the Omega house," Tarek called back walking over. "What about you?"

"I was headed back to my dorm, thinking of relaxing, maybe catching a nap before Brotherhood," Virgil admitted sheepishly.

"What!" Tarek cried getting over animated. "Screw that; you're coming with me!" He told Virgil holding onto his shoulder and steering him as they walked away.

"Where are we going?" Virgil asked Tarek.

"We're going to hang out," Tarek declared. "Gabriel told me you gave an awesome interview."

"Really?" Virgil asked, smiling with pride. "That's a generous offer, I am feeling a little tired….," Virgil said, letting his words trail off hoping Tarek would take the hint.

"Nonsense you can sleep later," Tarek said ignoring Virgil's hint.

"I need to change quickly for the dinner tonight," Virgil sighed in defeat.

"I'll bring my car around to your dorm," Tarek said nodding.

Virgil got changed for Brotherhood, putting on black dress pants, a blue dress shirt with a silver tie. He went outside to where Tarek was waiting hopping into his car. Tarek was considered by many to be one of the most humorous, fun, and brotherly guys in the fraternity. They headed back to the house, going to Tarek's room on the fourth floor, the same layout as Vahn's and Gabriel's. Tarek's room was more Virgil's style, he had a large flat screen TV complete with the newest Playstation, tons of video games, and a movie collection of great taste. The room had a laid-back feel to it, a Bob Marley poster, matching the owner's demeanor.

Tarek took a seat on a comfy looking chair, Virgil sat on the small loveseat. Virgil looked through his games and movies, commenting on the ones he liked, which was most of them, as Tarek's collection was massive.

"I have a shit ton more in totes," Tarek pointed to the closet. "You can borrow something sometime if you want, I have a sign out sheet that you can fill out if you do," Tarek offered.

"A sign out sheet?" Virgil said, trying not to laugh.

"Yeah, you borrow enough stuff to guys in this fraternity, without getting it back, you get a little more cautious about lending everything," Tarek said shaking his head. "I don't care if you borrow stuff, just return it in the same condition I gave it to you." Seemed more than reasonable, Virgil agreed.

They talked about video games and movies, Tarek had varied taste, and Virgil found he was easy to talk with. Tarek went on to tell Virgil about his life before the Omegas. Tarek had grown up in Alexandros, the floating city of the Nephilim, command center of the Paladins. Tarek explained that growing up in a city of only Nephilim, was like being anywhere else really. Tarek had gone to school, had friends, and did most things that brothers have done in their lives in America. To everyone there, it was normal, most young people were born and raised, and seldom left. Tarek told Virgil his father had been killed by Death Dealers when he was still young. Tarek's mother was a legendary Paladin, known to most in Alexandros.

Tarek told Virgil, after he'd graduated from regular school at age eighteen, he'd gone on to the "college" of the Paladins, simply called the Academy. Only the strongest and smartest Nephilim were accepted, Nephilim came from countries all over the world to learn and train at the Academy. Graduates of the Academy went on to become high ranking Paladins in the military. Tarek told Virgil he'd went for a year and did not like it. The Academy was all about power and rank, the strongest men and women with the best family names were treated better than others. Tarek quit and returned home. His mother pushed him to go out into the world and find his own place, that is how he came to be at BVSU. Tarek told Virgil he'd only been to the surface world a few times before. He was curious to see more of the planet that lay beneath Alexandros. He'd received a scholarship to BVSU, with help from his mother, and had started last fall. He joined the Omegas first chance he got, and he loved every minute. The Omegas were a family, and Tarek enjoyed being a part of them.

Tarek never made Virgil feel less than, he had a way about him of validating others. There was never a dull moment with him. Tarek was above all else, entertaining and interesting, he loved to make people laugh. They started to play a video game Virgil had heard about and been dying to try. Soon it was time for Virgil to help with the Etiquette Dinner.

"Thanks for taking the time to talk with me Tarek, I wish I didn't have to go," Virgil could chill with Tarek for hours, he was one of his new favorite brothers.

"The pleasure was all mine dude, let's do something soon," Tarek smiled warmly.

"Definitely!" Virgil nodded with enthusiasm.

Virgil headed to the kitchen Nolan and Troy were already working, they were having spaghetti venison for dinner, with salad and a variety of fruit. Nolan was working on making lots of cheesecake for desert. Virgil helped doing what Nolan asked of him when he needed something. The rest of their pledge class trickled in, Louie jumping in next to Virgil. Gabriel showed up noticing that some of Omicron were milling about. He gave them cleaning supplies and asked that they clean the bathrooms, dining room, and living room. Dinner progressed at a steady pace, Nolan was a perfectionist, he worked diligently to make sure things went according to plan. The dining room had a nice table cloth laid down, plates and silverware set for the nine candidates, their Hegemon, the two Sweethearts, and TK.

Ariel and Raven showed up within minutes, wearing formal women's wear that accented their natural beauty, TK along with them. The ladies and Gabriel took their seats at the head of the table, the candidates pulling out the chairs for the ladies, Virgil getting TK's chair. Gabriel gave Virgil a firm and unfriendly stare while he did. The candidates served the four of them first, making sure they had everything they wanted before making their own plates. Everything was delicious, Nolan did a great job, and everyone visited and enjoyed eating together.

Once dessert had finished, the candidates cleared the table. Virgil loved the Sweethearts and TK, they were great ladies, classy and fun. It was easy to see why people loved being around them. Gabriel told the candidates that this was the part of the dinner where they could ask the Sweethearts advice about women, dating, or whatever came to mind. The Sweethearts were there to support the brothers. Women were somewhat of a conundrum for men, to put it mildly, and the Sweethearts were available to help the Omegas understand the inner workings of the fairer sex.

"I have a question," Nolan said, kicking things off.

Ariel smiled kindly at him taking a loose red curl of hair and placing it behind her ear, "Alright, let's hear it," she said in a welcoming tone.

"How do you know if a girl is interested in you?" Nolan asked, his deep voice sounding mumbled, having to cough and start over once.

"Good question!" Raven said with a laugh and a flip of her short dark hair. "Ladies?" she asked, turning to the other two women.

"Well, I would say that she is probably paying a lot of attention to you," Ariel said confidently looking at Nolan. "Trying to start conversations, asking you questions about your interests, what you did over the weekend, women that like you want to get to know you better."

"I would have to disagree with that," Raven shook her head. "I'm shy and when I like a guy, I have an awful time talking to him. I get nervous, and don't know what to say, so I end up ignoring them."

"So basically, you never know?" Nolan asked, nodding in defeat.

"If someone likes you, most of the time she will try to flirt a little," TK offered. "So, if you notice a woman is making an effort to talk with you, it might be she likes you."

"Thanks," Nolan told them.

"That was a good question," Ariel said, "Who is next?"

Louie raised his hand, "I'll go next," he said. "What would you consider to be a good first date?"

"Not the movies!" Ariel said adamantly. "It is dark, and quiet, and you spend the whole time watching the movie and not getting to know each other. A good first date is somewhere that you can talk with her and get acquainted."

"I agree with Ariel," TK said, "Movies are a terrible first date. Take her out on a walk, or to dinner, or do something that is fun and out of the ordinary. First dates are about seeing how your interests and personalities intersect. If you're having a hard time with conversation it might not be a good fit," she shrugged. "It can be hard to find someone you connect with."

"Got it, thanks ladies," Louie said.

"I got one," Birdy said, raising his hand. "What about when you piss a lady off? What's a good gift to get her over it?" he asked.

"What?!" Raven asked, her jaw dropping in surprise.

"Having trouble with horse face?" Dante quipped.

"Shut up!" Birdy retorted.

"Umm, how about you start off by apologizing?" Raven told him, looking at the other ladies in disbelief.

"How in the world are you able to get a girl to go on a date with you?" Ariel asked Birdy.

"I got it going on!" Birdy said, bobbing his head in cocky confidence.

All three girls burst out laughing.

Gabriel raised his hand, "Ladies might I jump in?" he asked.

"Please do," Raven said, with an exasperated look on her face.

"The woman is always right; you are always wrong. Apologize, get over it, and move on," Gabriel told them.

"But what if they were in the wrong?" Louie protested.

"Doesn't matter," Gabriel said waving him off.

"But-" Louie tried to say, and Gabriel cut him off.

"Doesn't matter man, you want a girlfriend, or do you want to be alone? They are right, even if they really aren't," Gabriel said. TK was staring Gabriel down, he looked next to him and noticed her intense glare, and he smiled brightly and said, "Love you babe." TK nodded with a grimace on her face as if saying 'Uh huh.'

TK spoke up adding in, "The woman is not always right. Relationships are about communication. If you have an argument or a fight, lavishing your girl with expensive gifts is not the solution. You need to talk out the situation, addressing why you had a fight to begin with. An important part of fights between couples though isn't about how you fight. Some of the most successful couples and relationships fight all the time. The most important part is how you make up," TK explained.

"Yes, it is," Gabriel said, wiggling his eyebrows.

"You pig!" TK said, punching her boyfriend in the shoulder. "Guys please don't take dating advice from this man; he does NOT know what he is doing!" TK proclaimed fiercely.

"Oww!" Everyone in the room said at the same time and burst out into laughter.

"Burn!" Louie said laughing. Gabriel gave him a stern look, shutting him up instantly.

"Now what I was trying to say," TK said starting up again, giving a side look at Gabriel daring him to interrupt. "A healthy relationship involves discussing the issue, but then moving past it. Once you've talked out the issue, you can't bring it back up in other fights as ammunition, this is antagonistic behavior. Once you forgive and make up, you must leave past issues in the past. Couples who don't, won't last. Four signs a relationship will fail, or is failing, are lack of communication, lack of trust, lack of intimacy, and lack of reciprocity," TK told them.

"She's a social work major," Gabriel explained.

"Hey! This is important stuff," TK told him.

"I know, I know," Gabriel said in an unfamiliar submissive tone.

"What does reciprocity mean?" Louie asked TK.

"Glad you asked," TK said with a happy toss of her hair. "Reciprocity is exchanging things with others for mutual benefit. If one person gives time, money, energy, love into the relationship, either platonic or romantic, it is important they feel they are getting an equal amount of those things back. When someone doesn't feel they have reciprocity, and one person is doing most of the work, or giving more than the other, this creates resentment. Eventually lack of reciprocity leads to fights and ultimately breakups," TK explained.

"I got one," Dante said, speaking up once TK was done. "How many dates before it is appropriate to try and seal the deal?"

The three girls got quiet their faces flushing slightly, they exchanged a look and they shared a nervous giggle.

"Um," Raven said spinning around in her chair.

"That's a good question," TK said, fidgeting in her seat.

"I think that is something that is decided by each couple, different girls have different rules," Ariel told Dante, nervously twirling a piece of red hair around her finger. "If we are talking kids in high school, they should be dating for years and be over sixteen," Ariel said adamantly. "Now if we're talking college kids in their twenties, maybe a few months, several dates, its different for everyone. Some will sleep with you on a first date, but those aren't necessarily the kind of women you want to be going after. There are still some women out there who are reserving themselves for marriage as well, so it really depends on their views towards sex. I personally like to wait until I feel that the guy cares about me, and just isn't dating me for that reason," Ariel said softly. "Once I feel that he respects me and wants to stick around, I'm open to a more physical relationship, whether that be five dates or several months, it depends on the guy and how mature and romantic he is," Ariel finished red in the face.

"I agree with Ariel," TK said. "Don't ever rush or pressure a girl into doing something."

Raven got a pissed off look on her face, her tone was harsh and firm. "If I find out any of you boys are whoring around, demanding girls to put out, I will show up at your door, summon my dagger to my hand, and you will regret it."

"Got it," Dante nodded.

"After a couple dates, bring up the subject and get her opinion, if it isn't something that fits what you are looking for then be honest, and move on if you need to," Gabriel told them.

"Hey!" TK said hitting Gabriel in the shoulder again.

"I got one, going off of Dante's question," Darius said.

"Oh no," Ariel said a nervous smile spreading across her face.

"What are your favorite positions?" Darius asked with a big grin.

"What?!" TK asked in astonishment.

"Um," Raven started spinning around in her chair laughing.

Gabriel had a small smile on his face as well, looking to the ladies for an answer.

"Missionary," Ariel admitted, her fair complexion growing flaming red. "I'm boring as hell, let's leave it at that." She put her head on the table to hide her face for a moment.

"Umm after you Raven," TK said with a laugh. Virgil thought TK had the prettiest laugh, she was stunning in her green dress, the Sweethearts had chosen pantsuits as women weren't forced to wear dresses. TK's dress matched her eyes, her hair done up, make up on to accentuate her features. Gabriel was a lucky guy.

"What!?" Raven asked, stopping spinning to stare at TK.

"Hey, I'm your Big and these are your brothers dude, you go first!" TK asserted causing both girls to burst into laughter.

"Alright," Raven said looking up at the ceiling. "Gosh you boys need to stop asking these hard questions!" she sighed.

"No way, this is fun!" Darius said, sharing in the laughter, his grin prominently displayed on his face.

"I guess if I had to choose, I would say cowgirl, because I like to be on top," Raven said, still looking up at the ceiling refusing to make eye contact with anyone.

"And I like it doggie style," TK said confidently, earning a chorus of cheers from the guys. TK rolled her eyes, laughing and smiling. Gabriel's face got a little red as well, laughing nervously.

The night continued with the candidates asking the ladies different questions about women, dating, love, and life. Everyone enjoyed themselves laughing for hours. The time passed, soon it was after one in the morning, and they had to call it a night. Looking around Virgil felt lucky to be there, his life had changed drastically over the past four weeks, and nights like this reinforced in his mind how amazing it was to be a part of the fraternity. He imagined what he would have been doing if he wasn't pledging for the Omegas. He thought he'd probably be at his dorm, playing video games or watching TV, same old thing different night.

Virgil and the others cleaned up from the meal then headed back to their dorms. Virgil had a busy week ahead. The candidates were getting closer to becoming brothers, and the Omegas were stepping up their game. Virgil's phone never seemed to stop ringing and beeping with texts, brothers asking for favors and to hang out. Virgil spent most of his time in the company of brothers and his fellow candidates. They had started out as strangers, yet over the course of five weeks, had developed strong friendships, and were welcomed into their social circle as one of their own.

They had two more Devil Arms training that week. Virgil's pledge brothers had grown in skill, and each had developed a strong sense of pride in their own abilities. Virgil practiced with a few spells each practice Vahn had taught him, it took a lot of energy to use them, but Vahn insisted the more he did, the less of a toll they'd take on his aura. Virgil often stared at the white shooting star on his right hand, no matter what he said or did, the symbol wouldn't react for him. He wanted to wield the weapon, and develop his skill even more, but it was no use. He couldn't think of its name, and no amount of concentration was making the symbol light up.

Virgil started going over to the Omega house without a specific plan to meet anyone, just to be around friends. There was always someone who was studying, or watching a movie or TV, playing board games or cards, jamming on some video games, heading into town to look around. For anyone who hadn't been a part of a fraternity, they wouldn't understand. It was like having thirty best friends, who were always willing to hang out. Virgil's dorm mates had made friends as well, but their social circles usually consisted of a handful of people. The Omegas had strong ties with a few different organizations on campus, like the girls over at the Paladin sorority, along with the Rugby club team who were a bunch of rowdy people, and the community service co-ed fraternity, that Brody's girlfriend, Selene was in. Being a part of the Omegas opened friendly communications with literally hundreds of other students around campus. It provided a strong sense of community among everyone. Wherever Virgil went he ran into people he knew. The loneliness that some college students developed from being away from their families and established social circles of childhood, was lost on Virgil and the others.

Virgil ended up doing an interview with Landon on Thursday. They had run into each other after class and decided to have lunch and do an interview. They found a small student room that was empty not far from the food court. Landon was one of the smaller guys in Omega, not the 'typical' looking frat guy. He had a baby face, perpetually stuck looking like a prepubescent teenager with smooth skin, unable to grow much facial hair. Landon was twenty years old, yet he looked sixteen. Landon had sandy brown hair with bright blue eyes. He looked a lot like his little sister, Helene, their family resemblance obvious in their faces.

Landon grew up in Ortonville, same as Blair, a small village in Michigan in North Oakland County. Landon told Virgil he had a regular family with a mom and dad, older sister, and younger sister, Helene, two years younger than him, and a much younger brother, Neal, who was only eight. Landon told Virgil that his father was Nephilim and had passed on the abilities to his children. Landon told Virgil his dad hadn't known who or what he was, not going to college he had slipped through the cracks and never met up with others of his kind. Landon told Virgil the story of when he first went to tell his father about the Paladins, and the fraternity he was joining, the Omegas, his father had wept tears of joy at his story. All his life, Landon's father had thought himself an oddity, a freak in the world, not knowing what the amethyst symbol, the same color as his children, on his hand had meant. His father had never even invoked his Devil Arms into a corporeal form. Landon and his father spent days practicing until his dad discovered the name of his Devil Arms, calling it into its physical form. Landon's father wielded a staff, just like his son. It had been a special day for them both, one that would never have happened without the Omegas.

"People often say about fraternities, that we are buying our friends," Landon said with disdain. "I think that is complete trash but whatever, let people think what they want," he shrugged. "If I am buying my friends, I'm buying the best damn friends money can buy."

Landon was very big into the fraternity, he was a diehard Omega, and told Virgil he planned to always stay active no matter where life took him. There were Chapters of Omega all over the world. Landon was going to be a teacher like Vahn and Tarek. Landon shared funny stories about experiences in the fraternity that made them both laugh, he was one of the nicer guys to be around.

One of Landon's favorite parts about the fraternity were the Retreats. Landon told Virgil that twice a year the brothers went on Retreat, going for three to four days, to a rented house or cabin somewhere in Michigan to relax, have fun, and bond as group. The purpose was to plan out the goals and agenda for the following semester, and after the business, came the all-day bonding party. Everyone was at their best, cutting loose and getting wild. The best memories and stories were almost always linked to Retreat somehow. They finished their interview and shook hands, Virgil feeling much closer to another brother.

Virgil kept his promise to spend some time with Boyd. Friday night, Virgil and Boyd turned their dorm living room into a mini hockey arena, with small nets, playing on their knees with mini sticks. Boyd's Big Brother Buck came by joining in the fray. Birdy, Louie, and Nolan stopped in not long after and they had a solid game going. Playing on their knees to deal with the small area, slowed them down enough to make the game doable. There was a lot of 'friendly' checking going on, everyone getting several whacks and shoves with the sticks, turning it into a wrestling hockey combination towards the end. Male machoism taking full throttle, they eventually ditched the nets after a couple games and full out wrestled. Virgil was good, but Birdy was the best. Everyone left that night with bruises and smiles on their faces.

Saturday was the Halloween party at the Omegas house, Virgil cheaply got his costume ready with help from branches and leaves at the edge of the forest surrounding campus. The Omega mansion was packed with people, everything above the second floor off limits to the guests, unless escorted by a brother. Louie was hilarious, a six-foot-tall Asian man walking around in a diaper with a bonnet on his head and a binkie in his mouth. Dante was the sperm, he wore all white compression gear, with a long slinky put into a sock hanging off his back side. The party was fun, Virgil spent the night socializing with all the brothers and new friends he had met. There were more people he didn't know there; he'd never been great with crowds and did his best to mingle. Blair showed up as a sexy warrior princess, dressed in a skimpy outfit. She looked different than her normal tomboy self, putting a lot of effort into her hair and makeup. She gained a lot of attention from guys that night, Louie teased Virgil that she'd get picked up if he didn't swoop in, but he wasn't jealous. Virgil and Blair were like siblings, they had instantly connected from the first moment they met. It was not a romantic connection, at least Virgil didn't think it was.

The Sweethearts both went as Disney princesses, Ariel dressed as the Little Mermaid for obvious reasons, and Raven dressing as Snow White. TK and Selene had collaborated with them and each took a Disney princess as well. TK chose the Jasmine look, pulling it off perfectly with her tanned skin and dark hair. Selene went as Belle, her usual classy and elegant demeanor shining through in her yellow dress. The other women at the party didn't take too kindly to TK and Selene. They saw it as them trying to get in with the Sweethearts and become one themselves. Virgil didn't understand why girls had to be so caddy and vicious where the Sweetheart position was concerned. TK and Selene didn't let it phase them, maintaining their poise, they didn't acknowledge the dirty and envious looks other girls at the party gave them. Gabriel stayed close to his girlfriend, his jealous streak evident as all the men eyed up TK, one of the most beautiful women at the party, save for Selene.

Sunday afternoon was the philanthropy fundraising event Omicron had put together at Bennigan's in Saginaw. Virgil and the other candidates all went, they had a very good turnout, and hundreds of students from campus had showed up throughout the day with the coupons Nolan had made. They would be making a nice donation to St. Jude's Hospital when the day was over. Afterwards, the candidates met up together at the pledge dorm on the second floor of the Omega house to study for their final quiz for their last Education. There were only five days left until they were initiated into the fraternity and became brothers. Everyone was excited and nervous. The experience had been like a roller coaster, fast paced, with lots of excitement. It was fun, though not something Virgil ever wanted to do again. He was ready to be a brother and experience the next Chapter of what the Omegas had to offer. The candidates talked about their battle with the Betas candidates, it was one week after their initiation, and everyone had been training hard for it. Gabriel had been pushing them at practice, not saying it out loud, he wanted to win, all the brothers did. Their reputation was on the line, who had the better, stronger Nephilim. Virgil was confident in his friends' abilities, they all were, yet they had never seen what their competition was like and therein laid their doubts. The fear of the unknown is always greater than that of the known.

Omicron walked upstairs to wait outside the meeting room, in their line. Gabriel welcomed them in, and everyone took their seats handing in their pledging materials for Gabriel to go over, while they took the quiz over last week's Education. After their quiz Gabriel handed them back their pledge binders and leaned against the desk at the front of the room.

"Nolan's the only one who has all the interviews done," Gabriel said sounding disappointed. "There are a lot of the brothers you guys have not reached out to or gotten to know like you should. This process is about bonding with the brothers and training as a Paladin. So far you guys are doing okay at both. But we don't want just 'okay' in our fraternity. Omegas are alphas!" Gabriel said, pounding his chest with his fist. "I need you guys to really bust your ass these last few days and show the brothers you want this!"

Gabriel's final Education was about leadership and scholarship, two of the most important parts of being an Omega. Omegas and Paladins were leaders, in life, at their jobs, in the community and in the human government. Paladins, had been helping shape the course of human history for thousands of years, secretly living alongside them, and protecting them. Gabriel told them all the point of being at BVSU was to get an education, which can't be done by flunking out of school. Gabriel said the easiest way to pass classes is to go to them. The classes people end up failing, generally, were the ones they skipped. Gabriel asserted that to be an Omega they needed to be students, the real reason they were all at college was to improve their thought process, open their minds, and expand their knowledge of a subject or field of study. From the very beginning one of Omegas primary goals was high scholastic attainment, and if they weren't in college to meet this demand, then Omega was not for them. Gabriel told them that if they were struggling with their grades, to take the rest of the semester after initiation and focus solely on their education. Gabriel stated that while some Omegas did join the main Paladin military, most stayed on as a low-level reserve Paladins. Living normal human lives, as watchful protectors of the people.

Gabriel said, "Leadership is a Challenge, not a Reward." Positions in the fraternity and the Paladins were not honorary posts that should be taken lightly or rewards for previous endeavors. Any leadership position, whether in Omega, the Paladins, or in the community or government should always be viewed as a challenge. A challenge to develop goals and plans, in conjunction with the duties of the office, and to demonstrate the qualities necessary to motivate others to help achieve those goals. Successful leaders should possess a thorough knowledge of human nature. Men cannot hope to be effective leaders unless they evidence a great and genuine sincerity, honest and apparent. Such sincerity demonstrates a certain selflessness showing no desire for personal reward. A leader must also know his job, what is expected of him, what resources are at his command, what methods he can use, and what his predecessors have done. Above all else a leader models good behavior, enable others to act, and encourages the hearts of others. A great leader lets people feel like heroes, letting others take credit for their accomplishments, motivating people to make a difference. A leader builds a winning team with spirit and cohesion.

Lastly Gabriel talked about being an Alumni, once a frater graduated from Omega, they were given the Alumni status, the most prestigious honor bestowed to a frater. Alumni helped the Chapter by giving advice, sometimes financial assistance, banding together for large scale Paladin operations, and coming around occasionally for fun.

"Here is how the last week is going to run," Gabriel said switching gears. "Monday night will be our last Devil Arms practice, and Tuesday will be our last Brotherhood. Brotherhood this week will be Impress Me, you have from now till then to come up with something to impress the brothers, I've arranged to give you guys $40. What you choose to do is up to Omicron. You need to make or show the fraternity something that will impress the brothers. Wednesday will be The Last Supper. Wednesday night is for you guys, to show OUR appreciation for all the hard work you've put into this process. We'll have dinner together, as a family, relax and enjoy one another's company before the Final Test. Thursday, that's the day that matters people. Anything that we have gone over on Educations or Brotherhoods, or anything found in your Omega Guides given to you at the start of this process is free game. Know all of it!" Gabriel fiercely said.

Virgil's eyebrows rose, The Omega Guide was a small book covering the history of the fraternity, an overview of the Paladins, a section on demons, Death Dealers, and Fallen. Virgil hadn't spent much time reading it. Virgil felt a panic begin to rise in him, he didn't know a quarter of what was in The Omega Guide. He looked around seeing the same panic in his friends faces, everyone but Nolan seemed worried.

"If, and this is a big if people, IF you all pass the test on Thursday, Friday will be your Initiation into the fraternity. You will succeed or fail as a group," Gabriel warned.

"Wait," Nolan said interrupting Gabriel. "What if eight of us pass and one guy messes up, it isn't fair for the eight who studied hard to be punished," he argued.

"You are one pledge class, if one of you fails, you all fail. I suggest if you are worried you make sure that everyone gets prepared. You only know as much as the person who knows the least," Gabriel shrugged feeling no sympathy. "Sunday nights are our meetings and I expect all of Omicron to show up for the first one. The whole point is to become a member of this organization. You can't contribute if you aren't at meetings letting your voice be heard." Gabriel dismissed them. Omicron went to the pledge dorms to spend the night at the Omega house.

Once all of Omicron were in the bunk beds, they devised a plan to impress the

brotherhood. In the end they decided to make a set of large portable fraternity letters that could

be taken to different events and set up next to where the Omegas were. The next day Omicron

headed to Home Depot and gathered supplies they needed to make their giant wooden letters.

They set up shop in the pledge dorm laying down newspaper on the floor. They put up a sign on

the door telling brothers not to come in as they were working on their project. Everyone pitched

in, Omicron worked as a cohesive team, they had pride in their group, and wanted to be brothers

more than anything.

Chapter 17
<u>The Final Test</u>

Monday night was Omicron's final Devil Arms practice, and spirits were high among everyone. Virgil had practiced using a few fire spells, though he longed to summon his Creation Devil Arms. Vahn and Virgil had been trying to make it work with no success.

"I suck at this!" Virgil yelled frustrated. "I'm never going to learn how to use this thing! I should be able to understand my own Devil Arms." Virgil felt like slamming his right hand against a tree, stupid symbol was a mystery to him.

"Stop being so self-critical," Vahn's heated words reflecting no patience for self-pity. "Devil Arms are complicated things, learning how to use them is a path of self-discovery."

"I know but what am I doing wrong?" Virgil asked.

"Maybe we are going about it the wrong way," Vahn suggested. "Your emotions have a big part to play in using Devil Arms, what kind of things help you to focus on Soul Reaver?" he asked Virgil.

"When I'm mad, or angry, when I want to fight, it is just there, I feel its power ready to use," Virgil said.

"Well Soul Reaver is a Chaos Devil Arms, so that makes sense. Your other symbol is a Creation Devil Arms though, perhaps a purer emotion needs to be invoked to wield it," Vahn said thoughtfully lost in concentration. "Creation is the element of life, of healing, and protection. I know you'll get the hang of it," Vahn said with a smile, putting his arm around Virgil. "You're a smart guy, I have faith."

"Thanks," Virgil said smiling back at his Big. Devil Arms practice was over, the candidates headed back inside to work on their project for tomorrow's Brotherhood. They had borrowed tools from the Omega's garage and had cut out the letters from the wood they had bought. They had spent a little more money than Gabriel gave them, so everyone chipped in a few bucks. Hector, Boyd, and Troy were heading to Mt. Pleasant the next day to pick up the paddles Omicron had ordered for their Big Brothers. The candidates worked on quizzing each other, reading facts out loud from The Omega Guide so everyone could get some studying in while they worked. None of them felt ready for their Final Test on Thursday.

The next day after Virgil's classes were over, he went to the gym. He was feeling stressed about the Final Test, and needed to work out, get his mind off things. After he was done Virgil was walking back to the entrance of the fitness center when he ran into Magnus.

"Virgil nice to see you, what are you up to?" Magnus asked him.

"I'm headed back to the house to work on our Impress Me project," Virgil said.

"There are only a few days left of pledging, and we never got our interview done," Magnus pointed out. "I'm a little disappointed you never reached out to me, I'm not like the Prytanis or anything, not really important or vital to this Chapter. It isn't a Big deal if we don't know each other I guess," Magnus said sarcastically.

"Oh!" Virgil exclaimed feeling embarrassed. "Uh, are you free now?" Virgil asked. "I would love to sit down and talk."

"Nope, sorry too busy," Magnus said, turning around and walking away. Virgil was left standing there feeling awkward and not sure what to do. Magnus took a few paces away from him and paused turning his head slightly, he asked, "Are you coming or not?"

"Yes sir!" Virgil said hurrying to catch up. They went to the main gym at the top of the bleachers, they had privacy to speak plainly.

Magnus had blond hair that he kept short, buzzed down so it was almost not even there. He had fierce blue eyes that betrayed his high level of intelligence. His usual sarcastic and arrogant personality was gone. Magnus showed a surprisingly different side to himself. He was humble, well-mannered, gracious in his speech. Virgil wasn't sure if the bravado he wore was the real Magnus, or if this kind and intelligent man was, perhaps both sides were equally part of him.

Magnus grew up in Croswell, a village, with not much to do. Magnus stated he had an older brother and sister. Growing up they hadn't known their father and mother were Nephilim. They worked day jobs, while secretly staying on part time as Paladins. Magnus stated that his older brother was extremely competitive and made his life hell. He developed a cocky and competitive attitude as a way of protecting himself from his brother's constant antagonizing behavior. Magnus saw himself as a quiet and reserved man, only putting on the mask act of a confident social guy because that was what was expected of him. The people who knew him best knew that he wasn't an asshole as some people thought of him, but he didn't care about people's perceptions. Magnus told Virgil he was good at showing people what they wanted to see and getting what he wanted from people.

Magnus told Virgil he'd joined the Omega's as his older brother had before him. Magnus and Gabriel's older brothers had been pledge brothers, and so in turn had their little brothers. Magnus said that he didn't really want to join, but felt it was what was expected of him. He'd turned eighteen before joining and his Devil Arms had already appeared. He knew he was different and wanted to be around others like himself. Magnus had made fast friends with Gabriel and his other pledge brothers.

"We need more leaders in this fraternity," Magnus said seriously. "So many of our brothers want to just let everyone in, but it is about quality over quantity. You'll hear a lot of guys argue that we can 'fix' guys or 'help' guys out that might not necessarily fit us. They worry too much about what we can do for them, we need to worry more about what they can do for us," Magnus said firmly. "We are only as strong as our members, if we let in lots of run of the mill guys, because we can 'help them' we in turn become weirder or less social, those men become who we are seen as, who we are."

Virgil asked Magnus about his Devil Arms, he had an amethyst symbol that was a straight line on his left hand. "It's the Tempest Staff, a powerful staff with wind properties," Magnus said. "My older brother often makes fun of me for having a staff when he has a lance. I wish I had something different, though I have worked hard to gain harmony with this thing. In return I've mastered my Devil Arms and that makes me a force to be reckoned with. My older brother rarely wins when we spar, and it drives him crazy," he said with a deep laugh. "Never underestimate the power of your Devil Arms, the more you learn to control its power, the greater warrior you become."

"I can't even summon this one," Virgil said waving his right hand.

Magnus shrugged, "I see a lot of potential in you, in Nolan, in Louie, and in Dante. This is a good pledge class, you guys are going to lead this fraternity when Lambda's time as the leaders comes to an end," Magnus spoke with steel conviction.

"I don't want you guys to go," Virgil looked away. "You guys are awesome!" he shouted causing Magnus to laugh.

"There was a time when I didn't see myself being a leader in this fraternity, and now I'm the Prytanis. We need intelligent and powerful men guiding us. Can I count on you to guide this fraternity?" Magnus asked Virgil staring him down.

"I will do my all for this fraternity," Virgil told Magnus his words holding a confident tone.

"Good," Magnus smiled. Magnus told Virgil the Betas were the first Paladin fraternity on campus, and when the brothers who founded Omega were looking to join the Betas, they didn't like their fraternity.

"They were dicks," Magnus put it plainly. "Jerks who only cared about being strong, and family names. Our founding brothers at this University didn't like that it was the only Paladin fraternity, so they started their own, researching the different Paladin fraternities," Magnus shared. "They liked what being a part of Omega stood for, judging brothers for their personal worth and character rather than their rank or honors. Magnus stated that the Alpha class brothers, the twenty-one guys who founded BVSU, did so because they wanted to be a part of the Paladins, but they couldn't stand the Betas. They had help from the Omega Chapter at Northwood University in Midland, and they had their first pledge class, Beta, six years ago."

After they were done, they walked outside to Magnus' car. Virgil had immensely enjoyed getting to see another side to Magnus. Even after hours of talking, he was still the most mysterious brother in the Chapter. The more you got to know of him, the less you knew. Virgil met up with the other Omicron. Nolan and Virgil worked on creating a power point, they were going to have a short presentation on what they had learned through this process. They assigned different speaking parts between the nine of them, highlighting a lesson from the process, and then something they had learned or gained on a personal level.

They finished the wooden letters, which stood about four feet tall, within minutes of Brotherhood starting. They carried the letters down the hall to the meeting room, the letters paint was still wet in most places. The candidates set themselves up, getting the projector on with the presentation, and the letters set up at the front of the room. After a few minutes, the brothers started arriving, most in street clothes, a few had come in their work attire.

Fifteen brothers were present, Gabriel gave a nod for them to start. Omicron started their presentation, discussing their first week. The initial reaction to the big secret the fraternity hid, the existence of the Nephilim society. Omega was a part of the Paladins, and they recruited men who were descendants of Judges, no matter how many times removed. They had come to see the fraternity was a family, and the purpose of the process was to learn about the fraternity, and bond with the brothers. They went through the presentation with ease, each candidate having their turn to speak to the group from the heart.

"What do you think guys, does this impress you?" Gabriel, said motioning to the large grey fraternity letters and Omicron's presentation.

The brothers looked around sharing some shrugs, staring around trying to come to a consensus.

"I guess it's alright," Doc said with a shrug. "I mean what are we looking for, have them do a little dance number next?"

"It'll pass," Buck said halfheartedly with a sigh, lifting his hand and letting it drop.

"I think it was good," Gabriel said, nodding to them, "You guys obviously have come together as a class. You had a little bit of a rough start, but you've stepped up these past few weeks. You passed Impress Me," Gabriel declared proudly.

Omicron was dismissed, Virgil drove Boyd and himself back to their dorms so they could get some rest. They spent the night sitting in Virgil's room visiting, laughing over shared stories. They were tired, but happy. Neither one of them had ever experienced something like the fraternity. It was different than a sports team or being in an after-school club. The Omegas had become guys they looked up to, guys they were friends with. Boyd said he felt closer to the brothers than Omicron, he told Virgil he was his closest pledge brother, and maybe Troy or Nolan. In truth Virgil didn't feel Boyd was his closest pledge brother, he told Boyd otherwise to spare his feelings. Virgil felt closest to Louie and Birdy, and Dante too more so lately. The great thing about being in the fraternity, everyone was friends, though it was overwhelming at times, it made college exciting. He'd never had such a large social circle before.

It was the night of The Last Supper, a tradition of a formal dinner with the brothers, the night before their last as candidates. Everyone was dressed in their best, with black dress pants, nice button up shirts, and tie colors that matched. Virgil had a silver shirt, and a sapphire blue tie his mother had bought him that matched the color of his eyes.

Omicron was seated first, and the Bigs served their Little Brothers. The mood was energetic, everyone was having fun. Virgil visited with the brothers and Sweethearts, kind words of encouragement and praise from even people he didn't know well. Ariel, Buck, Thiago, Zender, and Jace were the people he talked to most. He hadn't interviewed most of them, and they were pouring on the guilt. Virgil kept apologizing and he started to feel like a broken record. Ariel was the last person he had to talk to that he felt guilty for not getting to know better. Her attitude was completely different. She didn't make passive aggressive comments to Virgil, she told him how excited she was to have him in the group. She told him that he had to promise they would hang out and cook dinner, like he had with Raven. Apparently, Raven had gushed to her about him, and Ariel really wanted to spend time together once the process was over. Virgil had a stupid grin on his face the whole time, Ariel had an uncanny ability to empower and build up your self-esteem. Virgil kept nodding like a bobble head, he felt a goof before Ariel's graceful and friendly demeanor.

Gabriel called the dinner to a close. Virgil and the others made a quick escape to the second floor. Omicron changed into some comfortable clothes, then began the arduous task of studying the Omega fraternity. They quizzed each other, read to themselves, looked over Education notes, everyone switched what they did as time passed on, but they studied as a group. Virgil had never felt more a part of something then he did that night. Omicron came to the agreement that no matter what happened tomorrow, pass or fail, they would remain friends. Virgil knew that he'd keep in touch with most of the guys if they failed, over the past few weeks they had bonded in such a way, it felt like they'd been friends for a lifetime. Everyone ragged on Birdy, like the goofball brother that always messed up, Louie was a constant source of laughter with his mannerisms and jokes, Dante was cool and funny as well, always confident and driven.

After an hour had passed Gabriel showed up with Brody, Jace, and Reece. Gabriel quizzed them on random facts, who was the first Grand Prytanis of the Paladins, where was the 75th Conclave held, what year did the first founding brother of Omega pass away? Virgil started writing down one fact after another, his head swimming with all the knowledge. As the night went on into early morning, Virgil and the others became more tired and less confident. The more they learned, it seemed the less they knew. People started falling asleep, and they agreed to take a nap to get through the day.

Omicron was at the library studying with Abe that afternoon, for a last-minute cram session. Virgil was surprised at how much new information he was gaining, after having studied all night with Gabriel. It caused a little bit of panic to rise within him, Virgil felt himself start to shake slightly, his mind ready to freak out.

"It's okay Virgil. It is them that should make you nervous," Nolan said nodding across the table to Louie and Boyd. They were the two guys in the group that had the poorest memories. Louie still couldn't seem to get questions right when asked, even though he'd been drilled on the same ones all night.

"Gabriel said if one of us fails, we all fail right?" Virgil pondered

"Yup," Nolan said going back to his Omega Guide in front of him.

Virgil got up and moved next to Boyd, "Let me help you buddy," Virgil said with a friendly smile. Virgil spent the rest of his time trying to make Boyd feel more confident, he looked pale and sweaty.

"Boyd don't worry about it," Virgil told him, "I'm confident in you. I know you'd never let Omicron down. I trust you."

"Thanks," Boyd said, Virgil's words seeming to lift a little weight from his shoulders. "You're the smartest one here, you don't have to worry about a thing, I'm just not like you, this stuff is hard to remember. I am trying like hell to do my best," Boyd said earnestly.

"Well between you and me, I think Nolan's the smartest. Listen I know you're working hard Boyd. So, take a deep breath, and be nicer to yourself. Pass or fail, we'll make it through the night," Virgil said patting Boyd on the back. "We'll stay friends no matter what."

"Yeah!" Boyd said with a big grin.

Hector and Darius showed up and soon it was time to start heading out.

"Don't worry guys you got this!" Abe told them, as they gathered their things and headed out. "I have faith in all of you!" Abe encouraged. They thanked Abe for taking the time to help them.

Omicron had to wait outside while the Brothers prepared, they piled into Hector's old creeper van, held together by cardboard and duct tape, a kiddie pool eerily visible in the back window. The nine of them were crammed inside, uncomfortable but together. Virgil sat on the floor near the door, Troy sitting next to him.

"I want to say no matter what happens, I'm proud to call all of you brothers," Dante spoke form the front, his voice holding more emotion then normal. "At first I thought most of you were weird, now I'm really proud we are friends."

"Aww thanks man," Louie grinned, "You going to whack off to the thought of us now?" he asked sweetly.

"Shut up Louie," Dante said rolling his eyes.

"I-I-I think," Hector stuttered. "That if we bomb this test, we should go buy a bunch of beer and get wasted!"

"Yeah!" a few of Omicron cheered out.

"If those guys don't let us in, we should start our own fraternity," Dante said.

"Yeah!" more of Omicron cheered.

"Gabriel told me Lambda almost quit, and they were going to start their own fraternity," Virgil said thoughtfully to the group.

"Man, I'm really nervous," Troy said speaking up. "My stomach is upset, like I'm going to throw up."

"No shame in that son," Louie beamed. "Just do it out the window," he suggested.

"Don't puke in my van!" Hector exclaimed.

"Oh, shut it," Dante retorted. "Like it would even be noticeable in here. We're all there with you Troy. We have each other to rely on, and that makes me confident." Dante sharing a look with Troy, then Birdy, then Virgil, then Louie. "I know I'm not the smartest guy here, that's why we have Nolan and Virgil. We all have different strengths, and as a group, we make each other better for it. We WILL get through this, all of us, as one," Dante said, his words causing Virgil's insides to tingle slightly. Virgil felt touched by what he said, Dante was right.

There came a loud rap against the van, "We're ready," Jagger announced.

Omicron followed him around the house to the back yard, he led the way into the woods. They weren't blindfolded so they could make their way through easy enough. They walked for some time, Virgil's anticipation growing with each step. Where were they headed? Why weren't any of the brothers around? The night sky was filled with stars, and the moon hung bright, illuminating the dark forest around them. The chilly November air nipped at their faces. Virgil had on a light jacket over his dress clothes, the cool air seeping into his skin. They kept a fast pace, Jagger confident in his stride knowing where they were going. They came to a small clearing, the sound of running water could be faintly heard.

"Heads down, no talking," Jagger gave them each a candle.

"Whats the candle for Jagger?" Louie asked the Pylortes.

"No talking Louie!" Jagger barked. "Darius, you're up first."

Zender walked into the clearing and led the first member of Omicron away. Within a few minutes, Zender reappeared taking Nolan away next.

"Good luck," Louie called out.

Jagger came to stand in front of the big loveable Asian, "I swear, one more word out of you, and you're going to be duck taped," Jagger threatened.

"Really?" Louie asked in a high pitched voiced. Virgil heard the unmistakable sound of tape being pulled from the roll, he didn't look up, Louie got the message. Standing still they weren't generating body heat to combat night air. The time between candidates seemed to last forever, but it was always punctured by a loud wail in the distance from their pledge brother, shortly after Zender would reappear for the next one. Virgil prayed they weren't performing some dark ritual, too horrific to be observed they had to only do one candidate at a time or risk having the others flee in fear.

Eventually Troy was called up, Virgil would be next. The nervousness sank in deep at that moment, Virgil knew that he would be seeing what the others had seen. His Final Test was at hand. Virgil started quizzing himself on different facts in his head, trying to keep his mind busy. Troy's yelp came to them from the distance, and Virgil knew Zender was coming for him.

"Let's go," Zender said within a minute. Virgil raised his head up and followed Zender. They walked a short distance and approached the mouth of a cave, it was dark inside, with a faint light glowing towards the back.

"Head on in," Zender told Virgil. "Light your candle first."

Virgil took out his draw string bag, grabbing the lighter he kept on him, and lit his candle. He put his bag back on, put the lighter in his pocket, in case the flame flickered out, walking into the cave. It was tall enough he could walk upright, the cave seemed to bend at the back, light could be faintly seen on the cave wall from around the corner. Virgil walked slowly, his candle in his right hand, guiding his way. There was a small stream that ran at the back of the cave leading out through the bend. He came to the corner and turned to the left following the small tunnel. Ahead he saw what had been casting a faint glow upon the dark stone walls.

Gabriel, Magnus, and Tarek stood surrounded by candles, dressed in silver robes. The water running through the middle, and out the back end of the cave in what sounded like a small waterfall.

"Kneel, and place your candle in front of you," Gabriel instructed him. Virgil did as he was told.

"Candidate Virgil Pitcher, tonight is your Final Test for entry into the fraternity of the Omegas, Upsilon Delta Chapter of the Paladins. Are you ready?"

"Sir, yes sir," Virgil responded feeling warm, and on edge.

"Please begin and end your responses with sir," Gabriel stated. "Question one, why was our fraternity founded?"

Gabriel, Magnus, and Tarek all stared down at Virgil their gazes piercing him like bullets. "Uh," Virgil knew this, "Sir, the first Chapter of Omega was founded in the late 1800's because the men did not like the way fraternities were recruiting. Back then it was all about who your daddy was, how much money you had. The men who founded our fraternity wanted it to stand for something more, wanted their members to be judged on something more, for their personal worth and character, who the men were, sir." Virgil felt like he was babbling, his hands grew sweaty.

"Valiant, effort," Gabriel responded, each word pronounced slowly and purposefully. "Next question," Gabriel said looking down at a small piece of paper in his hands. "What are the triple obligations of every Paladin, and therefore every brother in Omega?"

"Sir, the triple obligations of every Paladin are first to protect humanity and guide it to prosperity, and away from self-destruction. Secondly to fight against the evil of the Death Dealers, the Fallen, and demons. Lastly, to protect our brothers in arms, our fellow Nephilim, recruit them to our cause and train them in the ways of our people, sir," Virgil answered.

Gabriel's eyes looked straight into Virgil's own. "Valiant, effort," Gabriel told him. "Last question, what does Brotherhood mean to you?" he asked.

These were the questions? Virgil had been expecting dates, important events, people's names.

"We're waiting," Gabriel said. Virgil realized he hadn't said anything lost in his own thoughts.

"Sir, Brotherhood means a lot to me. It isn't something that can really be captured in words. The Omegas, the brothers, the bond you all share…you guys are family, even though you aren't blood related, you guys feel, act, think, and talk like you are. Brotherhood is this overwhelming feeling of love and respect, a mutual adoration and kinship that is developed over time with trust. I can only hope that someday I'm worthy enough to be a part of this family. My words don't do it justice, but Brotherhood is all these things and more, sir," Virgil said.

Gabriel nodded, his face never moving from its serious composure, the same with Magnus and Tarek. "Valiant, effort," Gabriel told him. "Rise candidate Virgil." Virgil stood up. "Remove your clothes, save for your undergarments," Gabriel told him.

"Excuse me?" Virgil asked surprise overcoming his face.

"Remove your clothes Virgil, you can leave your underwear on," Gabriel said firmly.

"Why?" Virgil asked suddenly suspicious. He'd seen enough fraternity movies and heard enough jokes; people thought some fraternities made their guys do 'weird' things.

"Tighty whities, or boxers?" Tarek joked, asking the other two.

"We're not going to rape you," Gabriel said with a sigh. "Do you trust us or not?" Gabriel asked leaving no room for any argument.

"Sir, yes sir," Virgil said hesitantly, removing his clothes. Virgil stood in his black boxer briefs, his Dreamstone on its silver chain around his neck, unsure of what would happen next.

"This way Virgil," Gabriel motioned, the brothers parted for Virgil to go between them.

"Nice bubble butt," Tarek joked.

"Enough!" Magnus snapped, though it sounded like he had almost laughed.

Virgil didn't think he could get any redder in the face wanting desperately to put back on some clothes. He came to the end of the cave, the water falling over the side.

"Jump off," Gabriel instructed Virgil gesturing with his hand, "and complete your Final Test."

"Jump?" Virgil asked looking out. "What am I supposed to do then?" Virgil asked nervous not seeing anyone in the forest down below.

"Jump and you will see," Gabriel told him.

Virgil looked back at the three men, they were leaders in the fraternity, but more than that they had become mentors to Virgil, people he looked up to, people he admired.

"Trust me," Gabriel said warmly, a friendly smile softening the serious demeanor. That was all he had to say, Virgil looked at Gabriel and knew that he did trust his Hegemon, he trusted the brothers and this fraternity. Virgil nodded and turned towards the small waterfall, he jumped over the side letting out a small shout as he did, plunging into the cold water below.

Chapter 18
<u>Initiation</u>

The icy water chilled Virgil down to his bones, his drop plummeted him to the bottom of the small pond. Virgil kicked the mucky bottom and sprang back to the surface. The night air felt even colder against his wet skin. He swam to the edge to get out, as he did, over a dozen brothers revealed themselves, they'd been hiding behind trees. Vahn carried a long-sleeved black shirt with embroidered letters on it, along with a hoodie with letters on it, and a pair of plain sweatpants. Everyone reached out to help Virgil up out of the water, Boyd giving the towel to Virgil. Virgil happily covered himself with the towel, wiping away the cold water.

"Men of Omega, welcome Virgil to the Brotherhood!" Vahn shouted and there was a chorus of cheers that rang out.

"You come to us naked and alone, now we cloth you and name you our brother," Vahn said, draping the long-sleeved black shirt, with red letters and white stitching, across his back. "We welcome you into our Brotherhood, we are here for you to lean on now," Vahn said with a big smile his eyes becoming glossy with moisture. Vahn embraced Virgil in a big bear hug, crushing the wind out of him.

,"Thanks Big!" Virgil strained out.

"Alright enough of the gay Big and Lil shit," Doc barked stepping up. "Save some of that cute ass for the rest of us. I want a hug too," Doc choked up sounding a little emotional.

Virgil really wanted to put on some clothes. "Hang on a second," Virgil said as Vahn let go of him. Virgil hastily put on the clothes Vahn had brought, not wanting to hear anymore comments. Once he was clothed again, everyone who was present, including the five Omicron guys who'd gone before him came in for a hug. Virgil noticed the Omicron guys had also changed into Omega letters, he assumed this was part of this Chapter's ritual of initiation. He had never experienced anything so overwhelmingly…cool.

"Alright cupcakes get your panties in gear! We got three more new brothers coming down the pike," Doc said getting their attention, and everyone went back into hiding. Virgil followed Vahn.

"Thank you so much for these letters," Virgil said looking down at his sweatshirt, it was grey with blue Omega letters on the front with orange embroidery. Underneath the letters, Omicron Class was written in cursive, a nice touch.

"Oh, those are mine, I'm going to need them after this is over," Vahn whispered to Virgil.

"Oh gotcha," Virgil said his face falling.

"Kidding," Vahn said elbowing Virgil. "You're a great Lil so I wanted to make sure you had good letters. They're a reward for working so hard these past six weeks," Vahn said giving Virgil a pat on the back.

"I have a present for you too. I got you an awesome paddle, I can't wait to show it to you!" Virgil said getting excited his voice raising.

"Ladies!" Doc called out from a little way away. "Let's not spoil the fun for the next new brother to come down," he admonished them.

"Shut up," Vahn called back. "You were like a giddy school girl after you were clothed by the fraternity, we had to practically sit on you to be quiet!"

"Not ringing a bell," Doc mumbled.

"My Lil's coming up, everyone be quiet!" Thiago said.

Within minutes Hector could be seen approaching the mouth of the cave, the small waterfall emptying into the pond below. The fall was at least ten feet, but it looked much more intimidating standing nearly naked, being told to jump. It was too dark to see Hector's face, he

seemed apprehensive, in the end Magnus gave him a solid push on the back that sent him over

the edge and into the water below. Virgil and the rest of the brothers rushed out to greet him once

he surfaced and made his way to the edge. Hector started balling once Boyd handed him a towel,

and Thiago handed him a set of letters. Thiago's words were like Vahn's, then Hector became a

brother of the fraternity. It was the same process for the rest of Omicron. The symbolism behind

the brothers clothing them, had moved him more than most anything, his brothers protected him.

Once Louie had gone, all of Omicron had completed their final test. They'd done it! Gabriel,

Tarek and Magnus came down with everyone else once it was over.

"How was it?" Gabriel asked still dressed in the silver robes. Omicron answered in

cheerful and enthusiastic responses. "Tonight, is an Upsilon Delta tradition, every Chapter has a

different way of running their Final Test, this is our way. It is a secret, and under no

circumstances are you to ever reveal it to someone outside of this group, or to any new

candidates!" Gabriel said harshly. "Let them experience it, the way all of you did. Tomorrow

report to the meeting room on the second floor, there we will induct you officially into the

fraternity." Gabriel said with overwhelming pride.

"Enough chit chat let's get our stuff and go home," Magnus said, and the group obeyed.

The night seemed a blur to Virgil afterwards, but looking back on it he remembered it

with fondness. The brothers all went back to the house, staying up the rest of the night telling

stories about Omicron's process. Dante, Birdy, Louie V, and all the others were glowing with

excitement. The past six weeks had been hard work, the brothers had been demanding, and they

had all learned more about themselves then they knew possible. They talked and ate into the early hours of the morning, people one by one peeling off for bed as they could no longer fight back the tiredness that was taking over.

The initiation ceremony lasted an hour. The Omegas taught Omicron the secrets of their fraternity. It all seemed surreal to Virgil that this moment had come. It was too much information to remember it all in one go. At the end, they were called up to sign the scroll of the fraternity. The top had a copy of the fraternity's Declaration of Principles, underneath were numbers one through two hundred. Next to the numbers were signatures of various fraters, Virgil knew most of the newer ones, Vahn was #98, and Magnus, #100. When it was his turn to sign the scroll, Virgil had an empty space next to #123. Virgil signed his name on the empty space, forever linking him to #123. He was the one hundred and twenty third member to join this Chapter, and he'd never felt such pride. After he'd signed the scroll, Tarek, handed him a silver ring, with a blue gemstone. Virgil placed it on his finger, to protect him from demons, and to remind him of his commitment to the Omegas and the Paladins. Afterwards the lights were turned back on and the brothers rejoiced! The Little Brothers gave their Bigs the paddles they had ordered for them, Vahn's had turned out beautifully.

"This means a lot to me Virgil," Vahn said getting misty eyed. "It looks like it cost a lot."

"You are a great Big, I wanted to make sure you had a great paddle," Virgil said with a shrug of his shoulders, letting Vahn know it wasn't a big deal.

"No one is going anywhere!" Gabriel called out as guys shook hands and hugged. "We need pictures!"

"The Sweethearts are anxiously waiting outside, can I let them in?" Jace asked.

"Let 'em in," Magnus nodded, "They've been waiting long enough."

Jace opened the door, and Ariel and Raven burst through, bringing new life and energy to the room. With hugs and compliments they came around making everyone feel special and loved. Raven was dressed in all white, she told the brothers she had just been initiated into the Alphas with Blair and Helene, earning a thunder of applause from her boys. They spent forever taking pictures, seemingly getting every arrangement possible. After they'd taken enough pictures to crash social media, they finally were dismissed. Omicron agreed to head to the cafeteria to get some dinner, as a group. A few brothers tagged along, not wanting to let the new brothers out of their sight.

"Tonight, is all about you guys!" Vahn said raising his glass of apple juice to the men at the cafeteria. "We are going to have the party of the semester tonight, in honor of your accomplishment!"

"I'm dying for a beer!" Hector sighed earning a few laughs.

"Hey boys!" a familiar voice called out to them. Blair and Helene walked in, dressed in all white with skirts and blouses.

"Blair, you ladies get initiated too?" Louie asked.

"Yup! We just got done!" Blair said with a big grin. "We're officially sisters!"

"Congrats!" "Awesome!" "Woot woot!" the boys called in response.

"Have a seat with us!" Virgil invited them.

"Will do!" Blair called back. Virgil and Blair caught up over dinner, Blair telling him about her sorority's initiation, without spilling the secrets.

"What are you ladies up to tonight?" Vahn asked them.

"Um duh!? We're coming to the Omega's party!" Blair shouted. "This girl is thirsty and ready to party."

"Good deal," Vahn nodded pleased with her response.

"The Betas are having an initiation party as well, but most of our girls are coming to the Omega's party instead," Helene said cheerfully.

"Good!" Boyd said in response. "You ladies will have much more fun with us anyways."

"Who do you think is going to win the banner?" Helene asked off handedly.

"The what?" Louie asked.

"You know the banner, that thing everyone signs at the party?" Helene asked. "Landon told me about it, apparently all the guys compete over it, but the winner never actually gets it," she told them.

"What?" Louie asked still not getting it.

"Dude, it is not rocket science," Vahn told them. "We buy a big white sheet hang it up at the party, and everyone who comes signs it, saying congratulations and such to Omicron. The last guy still standing, who is drinking, gets to keep the banner. Kind of a victory trophy," Vahn said.

"I'm going to win the banner," Hector said confidently.

"Shit!" Louie drawled out. "Ain't nobody winning that banner but me ladies!"

"I'll take you on," Hector said. "You eighteen-year old don't have nothing on me," Hector said. "I've been legal drinking age for three years."

"Don't overdo it though," Vahn cautioned the guys with a stern voice. "It doesn't matter who wins the dumb banner. All that matters is that you have fun, enjoy yourself, and celebrate your initiation into our brotherhood. It isn't worth getting sick over, so don't make an ass of yourselves!" Vahn demanded.

"I'm going to win the banner," Virgil said to Blair.

"Uh yeah right, I'm going to win the banner!" Blair joked.

"What?" Louie asked.

"I'm like an honorary Omicron anyways," Blair said tossing her short hair back with a small grin on her face. "If I was a boy, I would have pledged with you guys, and been the best fighter in our class. I should get a shot at the prize as well," she suggested.

"You guys don't want Blair competing with you," Helene cautioned them. "She'll drink all of you under the table. Blair's a warrior, when she sets her mind to something, she'd rather die than give up!"

"You're on!" Virgil grinned to Blair.

"Lil, you're not going to win the banner, so don't kill yourself trying," Vahn cautioned Virgil.

"What?!" Virgil cried out not believing his Big had just knocked him down like that. "You don't have faith in me Big?"

Vahn waved Virgil off, "I have the utmost faith in you, but we don't need alcohol to have fun. You're not a drinker besides, and all of you guys will have no tolerance with this dry process these past six weeks. Its best to go with an attitude about having fun, not about who can drink the longest," Vahn admonished. "I'll cut you off if you get irresponsible."

After dinner they all went to get changed into some casual clothes for the party. Omicron's initiation party was smaller than the rest of the Omegas' parties. Less than two hundred people, but this time Virgil and the others were in the spotlight; everywhere they went came a chorus of cheers from the brothers and the guests. The banner hung in the living room, written in big letters across the center read, Welcome to the Family, Congratulations Omicron!

Virgil woke up the next morning face down on the couch in the living room. He was in his sweatshirt Vahn had given him. He felt terrible, slowly getting up, his head hurt worse than any headache. He stretched and realized his whole body ached, he smelled like vomit, taking off his sweatshirt he realized his long-sleeved undershirt underneath had it all over it. Virgil groaned and looked around. Louie was crashed out in the living room not far from him. Virgil got up and went to the bathroom. Once he came out, he ran into Vahn, Tarek and Gabriel who were in the kitchen.

"Well hello gorgeous," Gabriel called out to him with a shit eating grin on his face.

"Hey guys," Virgil said his voice hoarse.

"You sir are an animal!" Gabriel said pointing a finger at Virgil and laughing a little bit.

"What happened?" Virgil asked.

The three of them shared a laugh. "What do you remember?" Vahn asked him.

"Uh I don't know," Virgil said trying to remember the night. "I don't remember much after I got here, I must have passed out around 11:30pm or midnight," Virgil said feeling a little down that he'd crashed so early.

"Dude you were one of the last people awake," Gabriel said correcting him.

"I was?" Virgil asked surprised, clearly not remembering anything a half hour into the party.

"Yeah! You were in a shot competition with Hector at 4 am!" Tarek told Virgil. "You won too, you bastard," Tarek said jokingly. "I lost my twenty bucks because of you. Damn Magnus won it all. He was the only one who bet on you."

"I won the banner?" Virgil asked surprised.

"You don't remember?" Vahn asked Virgil.

"You were blacked out!" Gabriel told Virgil. "No one thought you were going to be the last man standing. I'll give you this Virgil, you are a stubborn ass. You kept babbling about the banner and refused to go down," Gabriel said shaking his head.

"I won, that's cool," Virgil said still feeling like shit, his stomach queasy. "Where is my banner then?"

"Dude after you won, we draped it over your shoulders, we picked you up, carried you to the living room. You laid on your side, and passed out," Gabriel told him.

"But it was gone when I woke up," Virgil sighed.

"No one ever gets their banner," Vahn shook his head. "I won mine too, someone stole it in the morning before I realized it."

"No!" Virgil said getting a little mad. "If I won the damn thing, I should get to keep it!"

"Take it up with the thief, no one but an Omicron would want it," Vahn said with a shrug. Tarek was awfully quiet on the matter and did his best to avoid looking at Virgil.

Virgil was hung over all day, he ate and slept to recover, finally waking up on Sunday feeling back to his old self. Virgil made a promise to himself never to drink that much again. Virgil rode with Boyd to the Omega house for their first fraternity meeting. The meeting was different than Virgil had thought it would be. Including the nine Omicron brothers there were only twenty-two brothers present, with Omicron, the Chapter now had thirty-two active brothers. Virgil was disappointed more guys didn't show up. Gabriel told them the meetings had low attendance, not everyone wanted to do the work necessary to keep the fraternity running. He told them they were full brothers now, and the fraternity needed them to step up and be an active part of the Chapter.

The meeting was conducted using Robert's Rules of Order, it ran professionally, though the brothers worked plenty of humor, jokes, and random farts into the equation. It broke the group into occasional laughter, though the farts did nothing for Virgil except gross him out. The Jeweled Officers started the meeting by giving reports on what they had done that week to contribute to the Chapter. Afterwards the meeting moved to open, where anyone could bring up new or old business, or make motions. At the end, everyone had a chance to speak out on anything they wished for the betterment of the fraternity. Every brother had to say, Yours in the Bond, when they were finished. Vahn told Virgil fraters often signed emails and letters to one another with a shortened version, YITB. Vahn said it was a sign of respect and adoration for the fraternity, Omega was the fraternity for life, and the Bond brothers shared was eternal, lasting until death. It was a summation of everything the Omegas held dear, a commitment to their fraternal pledge of brotherhood to one another.

The meeting lasted an hour and a half, by the time every brother had a chance to say a few words. The Big Brothers gave out nick names to their Lil's. Dante's nickname was Schizo. Birdy was nicknamed Doggie Style by his Big Lamar. Lamar said that during his Final Test, when he was told to kneel, he got down on all fours, causing Magnus, Tarek, and Gabriel to burst out into laughter. Vahn bestowed the nickname of Cherry onto Virgil, as Vahn's nickname was Sprinkles and his Big's nickname was Cupcake. Vahn also pointed out Virgil was 'sweet, and innocent' and still a virgin. Virgil's face grew flaming red, he was mortified the whole Chapter knew. Virgil thanked the brothers, when it was his turn, for allowing him into their family, he told them how grateful and blessed he felt to be considered their friend. Virgil also asked the thief of his banner to return it to him promptly.

"Get over it!" Doc called out jokingly, letting the truth of it sink in, Virgil would never see the banner again.

During the meeting Gabriel had a short report, much of his job now accomplished with Omicron initiated into the fraternity. He was prepping his things to turn over to the new Hegemon, who'd be taking over after elections took place at the end of the semester. Omicron wasn't allowed to run for office till next year, they could vote though, giving them power, being a third or half of the voting members if the older brothers didn't show up like usual. Gabriel closed his report with reminding Omicron they had the competition with the Betas Friday. Gabriel told them he'd be holding a practice for them Thursday night, which wasn't mandatory since they were brothers.

Virgil's week felt so different, the freedom of suddenly having so much time to do things, nothing he *had* to do. Virgil looked back over his planner realizing just how full his days had been over the past six weeks, thankful he finally had time to himself. Virgil spent the first several days, doing a whole lot of nothing. He stayed in his dorm, enjoying not having to be anywhere or spring into action when a brother asked him. Virgil did go to Brotherhood Tuesday night. Omega always had a brotherhood once a week. They went to a bowling alley in Bay City, at one time the city had more than any other in the state of Michigan. Twenty brothers came to bowl, they got four lanes next to each other, and ordered food and drinks. Virgil found himself falling into the company of his friends with ease, there was no longer a power difference between Omicron and the brothers. Sure, they were older, but Virgil and the others were treated as equals now. Truthfully Virgil sucked at bowling, he still liked using the bumpers finding it to be a more enjoyable game. The guys made fun of him for asking to use them, telling him to learn how to play the game.

Thursday night, minus Hector and Darius, the rest of Omicron showed up like Gabriel had wanted. He was a little peeved, putting it mildly, the other two had ditched, and they ignored his texts and calls. Gabriel took out his frustration on Omicron, making them work their asses off for him. They were no longer his pledges, but he'd always be their Hegemon. Omicron had the utmost respect for Gabriel, and they didn't talk back when he made them practice hard. They spent several hours scrimmaging, breaking into two teams, and practicing against each other. Once they were all tired and sweaty, Gabriel called it a night.

"Thanks for pushing it out there," Gabriel said honestly. "I really appreciate all of you. You guys make me proud to have been your Hegemon. Tomorrow, win or lose, I will be happy because I know we have a great group of brothers here. Use tomorrow night as a learning experience, it isn't about killing them, so don't go overboard. Be the bigger men and display good sportsmanship."

"What if they are taking cheap shots and not having good sportsmanship?" Dante asked.

"We will NOT stoop to their level," Gabriel commanded. "We are Omegas and damn proud of it. We'll take them on, and come out the same way we went in, on top, as gentlemen. If they want to be poor sports, that is on them. They aren't my pledge class, you guys are. I expect you to respect me, yourselves, and this fraternity by showing all of them what kind of men we are," Gabriel said speaking from the heart.

"Sir yes sir!" Omicron responded in unison.

"Thank you. Now get some rest, tomorrow is a big day," Gabriel said clapping his hands and dismissing practice.

Virgil and the others were brothers now, Gabriel told them that they would be getting rooms at the Omega house once the winter semester ended in April of next year. Since most of

Omicron were freshmen, they had housing on campus and weren't in need of housing at the fraternity house. Gabriel told them if anything happened in between then, if they needed a place to live the house was always open. Virgil hung out with Birdy, Dante, and Louie that night over at Birdy and Dante's room. They talked about their upcoming fight with the Betas and listened to music until it was late in the morning.

Friday night the Omegas and the Betas were gathered in the woods outside campus, behind the Greek housing. There was a clearing close to the Beta's territory where the two fraternities met each other. The Betas were gathered on one side of the clearing and the Omegas on the other. The new brothers from both sides stepped up to the front, Omicron had nine guys, the Betas had ten. Virgil saw Damian among the Betas, but Damian refused to make eye contact with Virgil. Though they were outnumbered by one, Virgil and his comrades weren't intimidated. Dante and Birdy were tough, Gabriel said they were just as good as any of the older brothers with melee Devil Arms combat. Virgil knew that they'd be able to contend with Beta's best fighters. Virgil was more worried about Hector, Boyd, and Troy. They were great brothers, but as warriors they were lacking. Hector and Boyd had weapons with short range, Hector was rather slow with his large club leaving himself open for frequent attacks. Boyd's throwing axe was small and not effective at warding off attacks. Troy wielded a short thin rapier, he was adept at using it, just lacked an aggressive attitude. He needed to gain a fiercer approach; it was something he had to learn for himself.

"Three brothers from both sides will act as the judges in this fight," Malachi called out. "Once a man is down and unable to continue fighting, he will be escorted off the field. The fighting will end when one side no longer has any men who can continue. When a man is down, we ask that you refrain from attacking him, until he has the strength to get back to his feet. The boundaries have been set up by four flags, we ask that brothers from either side DO NOT intervene, unless it is a life or death situation. Omegas who will be your judges?" Malachi asked.

"Tarek, Gabriel, and myself," Magnus said. "Who will be Betas three judges?"

"Jamal, Paul, and myself," Malachi said to Magnus.

"Agreed," Magnus nodded. "All Paladins will be required to keep the 'Dull' spell on their Devil Arms at ALL times. Removing the spell and engaging in combat will be grounds for immediate forfeit of the match," Magnus warned.

"Agreed," Malachi said coldly his thin lips almost disappearing into a small line, his face betraying his disdain for the Omegas.

"We will begin momentarily, men prepare yourselves!" Magnus commanded. The brothers from both fraternities had spread out across the outlined field, which was roughly the size of a football field. Trees, fallen logs, and small uneven dips in the ground were abundant through the area.

Omicron gathered up in a huddle, off in the distance the Betas were doing the same, they were led by Damian. He seemed confident leading the group a streak of arrogance marring his features, it looked so foreign upon his face Virgil thought. Damian had been a humble and kind person, and Virgil knew that was still a part of him.

"Alright, we're outnumbered but not outgunned," Dante said trying to hype up the men. "Birdy and I will take point, we'll need Darius and Hector with us up front, to stop the bulk from pushing past," Dante said, drawing a diagram in the dirt with a twig.

"You think that is a good idea?" Hector asked nervously. "I'm no good in a fight."

"Knock it off," Virgil said getting irritated. "We've never been in a real fight, so you wouldn't know that. And you can always get better with practice!" Virgil asserted.

"Hector you're the biggest guy in our group," Dante sighed looking up at the big man. "You're tall and heavy, when you're swinging that big club around it is intimidating," Dante admitted. "This is about saboteur. They don't know the extent of our skill or abilities. You'll be a deterrent, we'll have you between Birdy and I, and do our best to keep them off ya, okay?"

"You can count on me," Hector said confidently slamming a fist into his other hand.

"Louie is our trump card," Dante asserted drawing an overly large X in the dirt to represent Louie in the back. "With your bow, you can help fight from the back, and you're the only one who knows how to use Will to heal," Dante said.

"I'm not very good at it," Louie shrugged. "But I can toss a few spells out when needed. If any of you are in need of some healing, give me a shout," he told the others.

"The rest of you fill in where needed and do your best to take down as many of those jerks as you can!" Dante shouted.

"We can do this!" Virgil shouted in return.

Omicron put their hands in and on three shouted, "Omicron!" They broke from their circle and everyone cast the 'Dull' spell on their respective Devil Arms, a faint blue outline glowing around their symbols indicating their weapons had a protective barrier around them. The ten members of the Betas fanned out from across the woods, their men placing the same spells on their Devil Arms. Magnus sent a bolt of lightning into the air that cracked with a loud thunder, signaling the start of their battle. The two groups of men summoned their Devil Arms to their hands and charged at one another, eyes blazing!

Chapter 19
Soul Reaver

Dante ran at the incoming Betas, yellow light flowing from his hand, solidifying into a mighty battle axe. Dante used the momentum of his body, and swung his axe in an arc, knocking an oncoming Beta clean off his feet, he didn't get back up. Without the Dull spell he'd have been dead. Birdy, Darius and Hector clashed blades with five Betas. Birdy and Dante roared with fierce determination, their lance and axe never halting, sparks flying as their blades clashed against incoming blows from their rivals. The Betas wielded an array of swords, spears, lances, one guy had an axe. Hector fought bravely swinging his thick club at the men who approached, screaming at the top of his lungs. The Betas were hesitant to go near him, which gave him even more confidence. Two Betas fought in unison their coordinated blows threatened to overwhelm Birdy, after several of their strikes landed on his body. If it wasn't for the 'Dull' spell, Birdy would have already suffered heavy, if not fatal wounds. Birdy used his lance with electricity coursing through, to fiercely parry their blows, desperate to get some hits of his own.

"Louie!" Virgil shouted, "Help Birdy!"

Louie drew his left hand back along the string of his majestic ice bow in his right, an arrow of blue energy and ice formed along the bowstring. He let go and it sailed through the air slamming into one of the men attacking Birdy, knocking the air out from him.

"Get the fat Asian!" Damian commanded his men from the distance.

"Hey!" Louie cried in protest, continuing to shoot arrows out to help his comrades. Nolan was slightly ahead of Virgil and Louie, wind whipped up around him, his hair flying wildly, as he held firmly onto his staff. Nolan threw a wind spell at a Beta who had slipped past the front line to attack the Omicron who were holding back. The spell looked like a small tornado tearing across the ground in an intimidating show of power, it slammed into the Beta, and he went sailing through the air, landing hard on his stomach. Nolan sent a bolt of electricity at a different Beta, who wielded a mean looking earth polearm, that was quickly overwhelming Darius in the front. The purple energy crashed into the Beta stopping him in his tracks, painful cries coming from his lips, giving Darius the opportunity to hit him hard with his lance taking him down. Nolan's spells and Louie's arrows were helping enough that the guys up front could handle the Betas now. A few Betas had already made themselves comfortable on the ground and weren't getting up. The judges ran onto the field and helped them off, and out of danger.

Then a large man from the Betas barreled through the front, the one with the axe for a Devil Arms. Hector did his best to stop him, but the Beta's skill with his Devil Arms was breathtaking in its deadly beauty. He effortlessly dodged Hector's clumsy swings, and with a powerful swipe of his giant axe he hit Hector in the chest, hard, knocking him down. Hector's club faded from existence, and he didn't get back up. The large man sprinted past the open hole in Omicron's front line and charged through. His eyes were locked on Louie, his battle axe on his shoulder. Nolan shot a bolt of electricity from his hand at the large man, the Beta rolled forward, the spell zapping the ground making a large scorch mark.

"Nolan look out!" Virgil yelled. A sword yielding Beta with a ruby Devil Arms came at Nolan from the cover of a nearby tree almost stabbing him in the side. Nolan had just enough time to turn and use his staff to catch the attack. Another Beta came forward moving towards Nolan, this one wielding some sort of flail with an amethyst colored Devil Arms. Troy stepped up moving to meet him, to protect Nolan from being overwhelmed.

The tall and heavily muscled man with the battle axe was getting close to Louie, Louie shot an arrow at the man, and he swung his axe, destroying the arrow in midair.

"Oh no you don't!" Boyd said charging the big man.

"No Boyd!" Virgil yelled. The Beta had over a foot of height and at least a hundred pounds on Boyd, he didn't stand a chance. Boyd leapt at the bigger man, jumping into the air swinging his small throwing axe with all his might. The Beta used his massive blade to deflect Boyd's hit, Boyd was flung backwards to the ground, and the Beta literally ran over him, a sound of intense pain coming from the motionless Boyd. His small axe disappeared as his friend lost the concentration to keep his Devil Arms materialized.

"Boyd!" Virgil yelled.

"Virgil!" Louie called out, panic in his voice.

"You're mine archer!" The muscle man thundered.

Virgil's grip on his scythe tightened with a fierceness. "Stay back!" Virgil called out, running forward then throwing the scythe as hard as he could at the Beta. His connection strong with his scythe, he commanded it to fly low aiming for the man's thighs. The man let out a fierce and mighty roar, the scythe came at him slamming into his thighs, he tried to use his axe to deflect the sickle blade. He managed to stop the scythe from making full contact, but the force of the scythe had caused him to stop. The scythe circled back around in the air like a boomerang, the man's arm had burnt where the flames of the scythe had licked at his flesh. Virgil caught the scythe with his left hand spinning it around and grabbing it with both hands, readying the blade at his advisory.

"You're going to pay for that," the Beta spit at Virgil. Virgil's anger at the man fueled the flames on the scythe causing them to rise, his entire left arm was ablaze. Virgil ran and leapt forward bringing his scythe down. The muscle man used his axe to deflect the scythe, parrying it to Virgil's left, and almost knocking it out of Virgil's hands completely with his overwhelming strength. He swung his axe around swiftly, bringing it straight down Virgil's middle. Virgil didn't have time to deflect the attack, instead he fell backwards, the axe slamming into the ground inches from his pelvis.

"They said you were the one to watch out for," the Beta said to Virgil, his voice deep and masculine. "I have to say the hype is disappointing, I was looking forward to some competition," he said smiling slyly.

Virgil tried to get to his feet with his scythe, the man swung viciously at Virgil, Virgil desperately crawled backwards barely missing blows from his axe. A stream of blue light flew overhead hitting the man square in the chest as his hands were raised above his head. One of Louie's arrows struck him, causing him to lose his stance. Virgil used the chance to get to his feet. He had to take this beast down, and quickly get back to helping the others. Virgil let go of the scythe and commanded it to spin, the scythe began to rotate in the air, spinning faster becoming a circle of fire and metal.

"Firelance!" Virgil shouted and from his hand sprang two enormous arrows made of fire that rocketed to the Beta. Virgil felt his aura's circumference shrinking causing him discomfort. The large man attempted to deflect the flaming spell with his axe, it plowed into his chest, sending him onto his back. That didn't stop him though, flames still ablaze on the ground around him, he slowly rose to his feet. Virgil commanded the scythe to attack the Beta. The spinning spiral of flame and metal sailed through the air, grinding against the man's chest. He screamed in agony as the black flames and metal spun against him, the flames burning away his aura as it touched him. The scythe came spinning back to Virgil, slowing down as it approached his hand. Virgil grabbed the scythe, its black flames spreading up his arm. The Beta fell, he didn't get back up. The flames of the scythe having burnt too much of his aura to move.

"Virgil!" Dante's voice held panic. Virgil's focus snapped back to the battlefield, most of Omicron had been beaten. Only Dante remained standing, save for Louie behind him. Dante was locked in a fierce fight between three guys, two of whom had attacked Nolan and Troy, the third was Damian. Damian looked like he was attacking Dante with his bare fists. Dante wielded his axe like it was made of air, swinging it around with precision and grace. He was outnumbered though, and the Betas were beating him mercilessly landing hit after hit upon him. Dante was calling to him for help! Dante never asked for help.

"I'm coming!" Virgil shouted sprinting.

A Beta charged Virgil from behind a tree, almost running Virgil through with the sword Devil Arms he wielded. Virgil pivoted on his left heel, swinging his scythe up to meet the man's sword. Virgil became locked in a vicious battle with the Beta, parrying the man's blows, the two weapons grinding against each other, the muscles in Virgil's arms shaking from the force. The man's sword was infinitely swifter than the scythe, Virgil had run into this same problem when dueling with Vahn. The scythe was clunky, big, not meant for close quarters combat, Virgil needed room to swing it around. The man pushed hard against Virgil, causing him to back up, aggressively hitting Virgil on his right forearm with enough force the arm went numb. Another of the sword's blows landed on Virgil's side, he knew there would be a bruise.

Virgil heard Louie's arrows sail through the air, trying to keep the guys off Dante. If Louie's arrows weren't being muffled by the Dull spell, they would have downed the guys and saved Dante. Virgil knew his friend couldn't last forever against them. Virgil needed to get some space he concentrated hard and cast a spell he'd heard Vahn mention.

"Fira!" A pillar of flames erupted from the ground consuming the Beta attacking him. He yelled out in a mixture of pain and panic. The spell took a toll upon Virgil's aura, his chest feeling tight. The spell was a second tier, stronger than anything he'd practiced with. The Beta recoiled from the spell, the flames lasting several seconds before they began to dissolve. Virgil had an opening swinging the scythe in an arc in front of him, black flames flying from the sickle blade, slashing a line of fire across the Beta. He screamed as the black flames burnt his flesh and his aura, his very life force. Virgil went on the attack willing his body to keep fighting through the fatigue that had set in, using the man's lapse in concentration he spun the scythe through his hands with fury, it slashed at his body eager for another taste. The Beta brought his sword up to block the attack, Virgil's scythe and his sword clashed, and his enemy's sword was flung from his hand. Virgil sliced the man's stomach with the metal sickle, if not for the Dull spell he would have been gutted. He cried out in pain and fell to the ground, his sword disappearing in a shimmer of light.

Virgil looked to Dante, Damian swung a heavy fist at his friend, hitting Dante square on the jaw. Dante spun from the force of the blow, losing his balance he fell to the ground, his axe, Gaia's Wrath fell, fading from existence into yellow light, then nothing.

"Take down the archer!" Damian commanded.

"Like hell you will!" Virgil spat, adrenaline coursing through his veins reinvigorating his body with energy.

Virgil ran to intercept the three men who charged for Louie, Louie shot arrow after arrow at the men, but they worked as a unit to deflect his attacks. Virgil was fast, fast enough to get in their direct path to Louie, the three men came to a stop in front of Virgil. The two men wielded a sword and a flail. Damian's Devil Arms were a pair of white gauntlets, a Creation Devil Arms symbol was on both of his hands. Damian's Devil Arms were unlike anything Virgil had seen, their design was artistic, beautiful, and deadly.

"You think you're the only one who is aligned with Creation?" Damian asked Virgil. "Unlike you, I can actually use my Devil Arms," Damian said, raising his fists to show off the powerful metal gloves that covered his hands.

"We got the archer," the man with the sword said to Damian.

Virgil lifted the scythe in the air above his head, letting go it hovered above him. He made it spin viciously with his mind, black flames gathering around it.

"The first Beta to step past me, will taste the flames of Soul Reaver," Virgil threatened.

"You can't throw the scythe at all three of us," Damian said in an arrogant tone, clearly not intimidated. The three men spread out, so Virgil's attack wouldn't hit more than one at a time. "You're less of a match for us then Dante. He was a fiercely brave warrior, not afraid to take on all of us at once. You stand behind your Devil Arms cowering in fear. Your show of power will not be enough to make us back down, we are BETAS!" Damian shouted. The two men beside Damian stomped their feet and chanted back, then charged forward. Virgil sent the scythe at the warrior with the flail, it rammed into his stomach sending him airborne. The other man swung his sword at Virgil, the blow landing across his chest. The force of the swing felt like it cracked a rib, Virgil fell to a knee gasping for air. The man with the sword ran past Virgil to Louie.

"Blizzard!" Louie yelled. Shards of ice and cold wind shot from his extended left hand pelting the oncoming Beta who groaned in pain, it did not halt his advance.

Virgil struggled to his feet, looking up Damian was standing there, he brought his right fist down with a punitive look in his eyes. It connected with Virgil's face sending him onto his back. Virgil's vision swam, dots clouding his sight, it felt like he was suffocating, the taste of copper thick on his tongue. Virgil's connection with Soul Reaver snapped, the scythe losing its physical form disappearing.

"You're so weak," Damian spat at him. "Malachi talked you up, making you sound like some great warrior. You've been ill trained Virgil! What have you been doing these past six weeks? The Betas trained us night and day! We are the superior Nephilim here!" Damian shouted.

Virgil heard Louie groaning in pain behind him, the Beta beating him down. Virgil struggled to get up, Damian's foot stomped onto Virgil's abdomen.

"I don't think so," Damian said pushing Virgil back down.

"GET OFF HIM!" Boyd shouted out fiercely coming out of nowhere. Boyd leapt at Damian knocking him off balance. Boyd fought fiercely, his small axe slashing at Damian. Damian was lithe on his feet, dodging and weaving through Boyd's swings, his fists raised like a boxer. For all his faults, Boyd was one of the most loyal friend's Virgil had ever had. Boyd's swing was caught by Damian's left gauntlet, sparks flying from both weapons, the sound of metal grinding filled the air. Damian brought his right fist around, upper cutting Boyd straight to the throat sending him to the ground.

"I've been waiting for this," Damian smirked a cruel smile sparking a dark gleam in his eyes. "I was hoping I'd have a chance to beat that undeserved ego out of you!" Damian shouted charging Boyd. Boyd didn't even get to fully stand up before Damian began to pummel him. The other Beta who had beat down Louie came to join in, they beat on Boyd with impudence.

"Stop it!" Virgil screamed struggling to his feet. "Leave him alone!" Damian pummeled his white gauntlets into Boyd's stomach, Boyd cried out, blood spraying from his mouth onto the ground.

Rage boiled inside of Virgil. Soul Reaver's symbol blazed with a bright black flame, he'd never seen a Devil Arms glowing with such energy. "Soul Reaver," Virgil whispered, and the scythe materialized at his side. Power was flowing from the deadly weapon. Virgil could sense a deep wellspring of hate and anger that dwelled within Soul Reaver, and in that moment their thoughts became one. Virgil let his rage consume him, it felt like liquid fire spreading throughout his body, giving warmth and power to his flesh. Virgil rose to his feet and grabbed the scythe. The dark flames that covered his scythe, spread out to cover his entire body in a flaming armor that hovered just above his skin. The black symbol of Soul Reaver glowed bright against Virgil's flesh, he'd never felt more powerful. Virgil sprinted at Damian, hovering just off the ground, his scythe floating next to him, whispering dark thoughts.

"Damian!" the other Beta cried out in warning. He ran at Virgil his sword poised for battle.

Excitement filled Virgil's mind, he wanted this, the frenzy of battle, or perhaps it was Soul Reaver's desire. Virgil leapt into the air and drop kicked the Beta hard in the chest. Virgil rolled as he fell to the ground, standing in a swift motion. Damian turned to face Virgil, a look of horror across his face.

"What happened to you?" Damian asked a trace of fear leaking into his otherwise handsome features.

"You're mine," Virgil said his voice unnaturally deep and gravely, the voice of a demon.

Virgil slashed with Soul Reaver, Damian used his gauntlets to catch the blow, the force of Virgil's attack forcing him backwards. Virgil had never wielded his scythe this way, swinging it in a blur of motion creating a humming sound. Soul Reaver had a mind of its own, and it was leading now, Virgil merely the instrument upon which it used to move itself. The black flames fell from the scythe as it whipped through the air, splashing against Damian. He cried out as some of them scorched his flesh, the two weapons clashed against one another sparks flying.

The other Beta got to his feet yelling at Virgil as he sprinted to join the battle. Virgil turned his right arm towards the Beta, it was covered in unnatural fire. Dark flames gathered in Virgil's hand in the form of a large fireball, it shot forward slamming into the warrior, consuming him in the flames' hungry embrace. He dropped to the ground screaming in agony, rolling around trying to put out the black flames that burned his life force.

"You're a monster!" Damian screamed, swinging his fists at Virgil's body trying to make a hit. They were locked in a deadly battle, Virgil's scythe clanging against Damian's metal gauntlets, both trying hard to bring the other down. Damian managed to land a blow on Virgil's right shoulder, causing Virgil to stumble back. Virgil's shoulder went numb, the black flames that covered his body dulled pain and emotion, rage was all he could feel.

Virgil's eyes narrowed, he clenched the scythe with both hands, and raised the sickle up in the air. "Soul Reaver, Soul Stealer!" Virgil cried out and slashed the scythe down in a vertical arc. From the blade a wave of dark energy blast forth cutting through Damian, toppling him over, carrying on past him into the ground exploding. Damian screamed in agony. Virgil pounced onto his downed body like a tiger, his scythe's blade at Damian's throat. Damian had been so wounded by the scythe's powerful wave of dark energy he was unable to move.

"I want to carve out your throat!" Virgil's voice, unnaturally deep and gravely, came out through his clenched teeth spittle spraying across Damian's face.

"Virgil that is enough!" Magnus commanded. Virgil looked up, the six judges were approaching Virgil and Damian.

"Get off him!" Malachi demanded sternly, then as he got closer his bravado faltered as he stared into Virgil's face.

"What, what happened to his eyes!?" Malachi stammered. "They are completely black!"

"Virgil, get off of him, now!" Magnus commanded again; his resolve not dampened by Virgil's intimidating dark gaze. They were within arm's reach, and the six of them stopped.

Virgil stared down at Damian, his rage like a thirst that parched his throat painfully. "Come after Boyd like that again, and there won't be a man alive who can save you," Virgil promised Damian, his eyes wide with fear. Virgil stood up the black flames dying down along his skin, retreating to his left arm, then only the scythe.

"Virgil?" Gabriel asked hesitantly. Virgil looked up at his Hegemon, Gabriel instinctively took a step back. Virgil's eyes were pure black. The instant Soul Reaver's flames had covered him his eyes had transformed, reflecting the darkness that had taken over his body and mind. Watching his Hegemon recoil at the sight of him, broke something inside Virgil, bringing him back to his senses. Virgil commanded Soul Reaver to leave his side and the scythe dissolved into a black smoke before disappearing completely. Virgil turned from the men and ran, running as fast as his legs could carry him.

Virgil didn't know what had happened, he just wanted to forget. He ran hard, bursting into the Omega house, up the stairs to the pledge room, he went to the bathroom. Virgil made it to the toilet and threw up. When Virgil watched Damian beating on Boyd, his anger boiled over. Virgil had felt different when the black flames from Soul Reaver covered his body, it was like Soul Reaver had taken control of him. Malachi said that Virgil's eyes had been pitch black, Virgil got up from the toilet and washed his face. He put some water in his mouth and swished it around, trying to remove the taste of bile. His hands were shaky, he shut the water off and hesitantly looked in the mirror. Dark hair messy from battle, a strong jawline, with a nose slightly too large for his face, and sapphire blue eyes staring back at him.

Virgil laid in the bunk bed that had become his over the past few months. He knew there was darkness within him, and now he had seen it show itself. He heard footsteps approaching a while later, the sounds of other people coming into the room. They came near him and stopped. They stood there, Virgil didn't raise his head, he wasn't eager to talk with anyone.

"You okay?" Louie asked kindly. "We're all worried about you bud."

Virgil didn't know what to say, so he stayed quiet.

"Hey!" Dante shouted and kicked Virgil's bed. "Don't go acting like an idiot because something weird just happened. This whole experience has been one freak show reveal after the next, but we've gotten through it together!" Dante said sternly.

"What Dante's trying to say is, we're here for you man," Birdy spoke more gently.

Virgil felt his bed sink in as someone sat by his feet. "Thanks for saving me," Boyd said sitting next to him. "We won the fight. You were the last guy standing and the judges argued that the Betas should be disqualified for wailing on me when I was down," Boyd said cheerfully.

Virgil looked up at his friends. They all seemed a little rugged, weary from their recent fight. Boyd had heavy bruises and a black eye. Someone had used some spells to help as he didn't look nearly as bad as he should.

"Thanks," Virgil said sitting up.

"What happened out there?" Louie asked.

"Louie!" Dante snapped. "We agreed we were not asking that!"

"I know, I know," Louie nodded sheepishly. "Did you do it on purpose?" he asked with genuine curiosity. Dante stepped on Louie's foot, getting a reaction from him.

"I don't know what happened really," Virgil said thinking about it. "Anger is what triggers Soul Reaver for me. Watching Damian beating Boyd up, made me feel more anger than I've ever felt. I trusted Damian; he was my friend. I couldn't stand by watching him savagely attack Boyd. You were hurt trying to protect me," Virgil said feeling guilty looking his friend in the eye.

"And I'd do it again in a heartbeat," Boyd giggled gleefully with a triumphant grin. "We're brothers man, it's what we do!"

"I wish you wouldn't," Virgil said drawing his legs up to his chest. "Please don't try to protect me next time, any of you," Virgil said looking away from his friends. "I couldn't bear watching you get hurt or worse."

"Hey news flash!" Dante interrupted in a grumpy tone. "We're freaking Nephilim warriors Virgil! Getting beat up is kind of in the job description. We're going to take a few punches every now and then," Dante asserted. "We watch out for each other, protect each other, because we care for each other. Any one of us would have done the same, we were looking out for one another, I'm damn proud of Omicron," Dante was filled with pride.

"Yeah, you tried to protect me," Louie said to Virgil.

"Tried," Virgil said with a sigh.

"Hey, knock off this hate parade already," Birdy said his eyebrows furrowing together. "You're the optimistic upbeat part of our group, we don't need another worry wart like Louie."

"I'm not that bad!" Louie argued.

"I still remember how you wanted to leave that screaming woman in Mt. Pleasant to head home," Birdy countered.

"I was scared!" Louie protested.

"Thanks guys I appreciate it," Virgil said trying not to smile, he got up from the bed. The rest of Omicron made their way into the pledge dorms, getting quiet when they saw Virgil.

"Hey guys," Virgil called out to them.

"Hey," they responded not looking him in the eyes. Virgil walked past them out of the pledge dorms, needing to take a walk to clear his head. As he came past the meeting room, the door was cracked, and he heard brothers talking inside. Virgil heard his name and stopped.

"He's dangerous!" Jagger protested. "We shouldn't have someone like THAT in our fraternity. He'd fit in better with the Betas!"

"He's already a brother!" Magnus snapped. "He's one of us, and we don't turn our backs on our own."

"Regardless of how any of you feel," Professor Ramuh's voice said speaking up, "Virgil is an Omega. If he is a threat or not, it is safest to keep him where he can be watched. His Creation Devil Arms has yet to take form. If anyone sees signs that he is starting to go Dark, we will do what we must to take care of the situation," Professor Ramuh said coldly. Virgil felt stomach acid rising in his throat at the Chapter Advisor's words.

"Virgil won't go Dark!" Vahn yelled. "And we're NOT talking about taking care of my Lil!" Vahn said angrily.

"No one's going to hurt Virgil," Gabriel asserted. "Master Ramuh is merely advising us to be cautious. I care about him too Vahn," Gabriel said his voice holding understanding. "We'll make sure nothing bad happens to him. This is Virgil we are talking about for God's sakes!" Gabriel said exasperated like it was an absurd subject. "He's kind hearted, polite, and a little naïve. He's not cruel, or malicious, Virgil is not the kind of person that would kill people in cold blood."

"There is darkness within him, as surely as there is light," Master Ramuh pointed out.

"That's another thing, what kind of Nephilim has both a Chaos and Creation Devil Arms?" Jagger asked. "Do you think he's one of the Seven Seraphs?" Jagger asked them. The room grew silent.

"He could be," Gabriel responded deep in thought. "I've never seen someone's Devil Arms with that kind of power. Imagine what the other weapon's going to be like."

"What do you think?" Jagger asked.

"I think we need to watch him closely," Professor Ramuh said thoughtfully.

"Hey!" Louie called out from behind Virgil, startling him. "What are you doing?" Louie asked him with an arched brow.

"Going for a walk," Virgil said quickly, moving towards the grand staircase not wanting the brothers to know he had been listening.

"I'm coming with you," Louie said following him.

"I don't need to be followed," Virgil said coldly, looking over his shoulder.

"I know that!" Louie exclaimed rolling his eyes. "I could use the company, you don't mind, do you?" Louie asked.

"No, you can come," Virgil agreed. Louie was one of Virgil's closest friends, and it felt good to have someone on his side. They left the Omega manor and headed down the long driveway towards the other Greek housing. Virgil and Louie didn't talk, Virgil wasn't in the mood and Louie was smart enough to understand.

Virgil broke the silence, "What are your plans for the weekend?" he asked his friend.

"Not much really," Louie shrugged. "I was thinking of going home for the weekend. I haven't gone home since pledging started and my folks are missing me."

"You should!" Virgil encouraged him. "I mean tomorrow is already Saturday, so you won't have much time there. I know I enjoy getting to see my mom," Virgil told him. "Maybe I'll go home tomorrow too. Get away for a bit," Virgil said thoughtfully.

"Getting wrapped up in school and the fraternity, sometimes it's easy to forget we still have lives outside all of this," Louie suggested.

"Agreed," Virgil nodded with a smirk at Louie's humorous dialogue. Louie was getting better at using plurals in his speech.

"Don't get too worked up about what happened tonight," Louie nudged him. "You're still Virgil, we all think a lot of you," Louie said, draping his arm around Virgil.

"Thanks bud," Virgil said a smile creeping up on his face.

"And cheer up! It is no fun seeing you all gloomy, its weird man!" Louie exclaimed.

"I'll try," Virgil nodded. They walked further down the path, passing the Alphas' sorority house, the Betas' fraternity house not far after.

"Should we head back?" Louie suggested.

"Sure," Virgil sighed. He didn't want to go back to the Omegas right now. He'd felt so comfortable and safe there from day one. Hearing his friends, the men who were supposed to be his brothers, talking about him like he was a monster, it soured his perception of what the Omega house represented…a place to belong.

Men jumped out onto the path surrounding Virgil and Louie.

"What the deuce?" Louie exclaimed.

"You're coming with us," a big muscle man said to them. Virgil recognized him as a Beta, the one who had wielded an axe in their battle not an hour past.

"I don't think so," Virgil said through clenched teeth, "Soul Reaver!" Black flames bursting into his hand, he held Soul Reaver once more.

"Watch out for him!" one of them shouted.

"There are more than enough of us to take him," the muscle man said confidently.

"Louie! We cut through!" Virgil demanded. Louie summoned Shiva's Bow to his right hand. The men moved to subdue them.

"Soul Reaver!" Virgil screamed, spinning around in a circle swinging his scythe with as much force as he could muster. The men backed off from him. Before Louie could shoot off an arrow, they tackled him to the ground.

"Louie!" Virgil yelled. Virgil darted through a hole the men created backing up from the scythe's reach. Virgil moved down the road towards the Omega house feet pounding on the pavement... he needed his brothers!

"Don't let him escape!" the muscle man yelled as he helped a few others wrestle with Louie.

Virgil wanted to rescue his friend from their grasp, he didn't have it in him to take on all of them though. There were eight guys, three of them holding down Louie. Virgil was still tired from the battle earlier, he needed to eat, and rest.

"I'll be back with help!" Virgil shouted to his friend, guilt weighing heavy upon him. Virgil ran as fast as his legs could carry him, his scythe trailing after him, floating at his side. The men chased him down the road. Virgil could feel them on his heels. Virgil aimed his right hand back at his pursuers and shouted, "Firebolt!" flames shot back at the men. They weren't expecting to be attacked, the spell hitting a few Betas, causing them to slow down.

One of the men shouted, a block of earth rocketing past Virgil's elbow narrowly missing him exploding in a shower of dirt and ground raining down upon Virgil.

"Bolt!" one closer to Virgil shouted. A stream of electricity shot at Virgil hitting him in back. Virgil's whole body coursed with pain, he stumbled almost face planting into the ground. Virgil pushed himself moving forward, willing his legs not to lock up, he was in so much pain he just wanted to stop.

"Sethos wants him unharmed!" he heard someone shout behind him.

Virgil regained speed and didn't stop running, not looking back. He'd left Louie, and that shamed him. I'm going to get help, Virgil told himself, I will not abandon my friend! Virgil ran the rest of the way, sending his scythe away before he burst into the house yelling as loud as he could for help.

"What is going on!" Gabriel asked coming around the corner from the living room.

"They took him!" Virgil shouted.

"Took who Virgil?" Gabriel asked growing fierce looking.

"The Betas! They kidnapped Louie!" Virgil cried out.

Chapter 20
<u>The Arch Demon, Abdanon</u>

Twenty-five of the Omegas were gathered in the kitchen, they were missing the six older active brothers that didn't come around. This was serious, Magnus had received a text message from an unknown number, it read: *Bring Virgil to the tree graph in the woods, in the Tobico marsh, near the second observation tower.* Everyone started arguing over the best way to handle the strange demand.

"We shouldn't go," Jagger suggested, his arms crossed over his chest leaning on the dining room table. "It's a trap."

"Damn it!" Dante said, pounding his fist on the kitchen counter. "Louie's one of our own, we can't abandon him!"

"They only want Virgil, right?" Buck asked.

"You're point?" Vahn asked giving Buck an irritated glare.

"We could send Virgil there and resolve this peacefully, give them what they want," Buck suggested.

"Piss off," Vahn spat at him in disgust.

"It was just an idea," Buck said, raising his hands up in front of him, "Don't bite my head off. I'm trying to think of the best way to put the least amount of our people in danger."

"Sounds like the chicken shit way of handling this," Vahn sneered.

"This isn't getting us anywhere!" Magnus yelled, silencing them.

"I say we go, take back our big ol' Asian, and kick the shit out of anyone who gets in our way," Dante said slamming his fists on the counter, a butcher knife held firmly in his right hand.

"Where'd you get that knife from?" Gabriel asked, standing next to Dante his eyebrow raised.

"Don't worry about it," Dante said nonchalantly brushing Gabriel's comments aside with a murmuring hand. Gabriel took the knife from Dante.

"I'll go," Virgil said speaking up tired of listening to everyone argue. "If the Betas want me in exchange for Louie, I'll do it. There isn't a good reason to endanger anyone else."

"Like hell you will!" Vahn said getting angry. "You're not going there alone, or even at all!"

"You can't tell me what to do Vahn," Virgil said confidently looking his Big in the eye. "Louie got kidnapped because of me, I should have stayed and fought them off."

"Like hell I can't!" Vahn shouted in anger. "I'll lock you up in my room if that's what it takes, we don't even know why they want you in the first place."

"It is a good thing you didn't stay," Magnus told Virgil as he paced back and forth, his brow furrowed deep in concentration. "Then they'd have what they want, and we'd have no idea what was going on. It seems our only option is to go to this meeting, and see what we can learn," Magnus said stopping and turning to face the group.

"And endanger the whole Chapter?" Buck asked disagreeing with a scowl. "I can't allow that. This crap wouldn't fly if I was Prytanis," he murmured.

"You're not Prytanis, I am!" Magnus thundered back. "The whole Chapter isn't even present! Those who wish to stay may do so," Magnus commanded.

"I'm going!" Dante said an even larger knife having found its way into his hand. "I'll teach those jerks to keep their hands off of our Louie!"

"Give me that!" Gabriel said taking the second knife from Dante with an exasperated eye roll.

"What do we do, go there and give them Virgil?" Tarek asked Magnus.

"No way," Vahn's tone left no room for discussion.

"No," Magnus said calmly. "We approach the meet with caution, find out what's going on, and get Louie back. Under no circumstance are we allowing them to take custody of Virgil. We don't know why they want him, though I can guess it is something that will have negative repercussions for us all."

"Alright people we leave in five," Gabriel said ending the discussion. "Those of you who are coming get your shit together!"

The Omegas mobilized quickly, within minutes eighteen brothers were going to rescue Louie, a few had stayed to guard the house. The brothers who stayed were to alert the Chapter Advisors if they were not back in two hours. The brothers decided against telling them before they went for fear they would forbid it. Virgil rode with Gabriel, Vahn, Tarek and Dante, Gabriel driving his black SUV flying down the campus roads. They were quiet as they drove the short distance to the Tobico marsh. Bay City's bike path met the trail passing large wooden observation towers mentioned in the message. It was a couple miles back into the woods from the parking area, to get to the second observation tower. Magnus knew an old tree graph was back in the woods not far from there.

The group parked and began speed walking, passing by the first tower in a matter of minutes. Virgil asked Magnus what a tree graph was, he was nervous and needed something to distract his thoughts. The process of inosculation, where two trees had grown together, Magnus explained. The tree graph where they were headed was a very large, very old tree. A long time ago during a thunderstorm perhaps, a tree had been struck by lightning and part of it fell into this other tree. Over the years the tree that had been struck down, began to grow again, from the other tree, an uncommon phenomenon. They approached the second observation tower, and still had not seen any signs of the Betas.

"Stay alert and stay quiet," Magnus instructed. "They are nearby."

The group of eighteen men kept a tight formation, the eldest brothers and Jeweled Officers keeping to the outside with Omicron left in the middle. Magnus led the way from the trail heading back into the woods. They had to only walk a few minutes more until they came upon the tree graph. The main tree was a large white birch tree hundreds of years old, the tree that had begun growing off it was a dark twisted thing. Black branches snaked through the massive white tree unnaturally, becoming a living work of art. The tree was enormous, stretching higher than any of the other trees in the forest. Underneath it was Louie, tied up with duct tape over his mouth. He started making noise as he saw the brothers approaching, his speech inaudible. There were no Betas to be found.

Instead two warriors, clad in full battle armor, ebony wings upon their backs, stepped forward. They came to stand in front of Louie facing the Omegas. They had on helmets, so it was impossible to tell who they were, or even their genders.

"Who are you, and what do you want with Virgil?" Magnus asked standing at the front of the Omegas. His voice held its usual authoritative tone, hard to do when staring down two powerful warriors.

"We only need some of his blood," the taller of the two warriors responded. His voice held malice and disdain, as if talking to lesser beings. This was a man used to getting his way, crushing those that opposed him.

Vahn stepped forward, "You can't have him!"

"Vahn!" Magnus snapped at him, giving Vahn a fierce look Virgil had never seen on Magnus' face before. He was usually so collected, coming off as a chauvinistic know-it-all. His look held weight, Vahn backed down, there was a reason Magnus was the Prytanis of the Chapter.

"I would have the names of those who abducted one of my men," Magnus said calmly with the force of command. "We are Omegas, an act of aggression against us, is an act of aggression against the Paladin society of free Nephilim."

The tall warrior laughed, which was strange coming from the helmet. He took off his helmet revealing his face. He was exceptionally handsome, with long black hair that was tied back, high and tight. He was tall, standing 6'3, with pale white skin. His complexion was smooth and flawless without a trace of stubble. He had a small nose, with thin lips. His eyes were dark, almost black, and cold. He appeared to be in his twenties. He looked strangely familiar to Virgil.

"I'm Sethos, Son of Lucifer, the Fourth Seraph," he declared proudly. "Commander of the Death Dealers." Everyone's jaws dropped open.

"Death Dealers," Magnus stated. In an instant all the brothers summoned their Devil Arms to their sides. The Death Dealers were the army of evil Nephilim, who lived in the Ever After, the right hand of the Fallen, and allies to demons. Virgil hadn't summoned his scythe, he was surrounded by brothers, and didn't want to burn anyone.

"Not just any Death Dealers," Sethos corrected Magnus, "We are THE Nephilim, the genetic apex of our species. I'm the Fourth Seraph, the Harbringer, and this is the Fifth Seraph, the Gatekeeper. If you knew how powerful we are, you wouldn't dare draw your Devil Arms so rudely," Sethos warned. The brothers began to sweat, most of them looked like they just smelt a skunk. This was bad. He motioned to the second warrior standing beside him. The other warrior did not move, they stayed still watching silently. This was really bad. "The Gatekeeper is not one for idle banter," Sethos said with a shrug. "You can have this weak Nephilim back," Sethos motioned to Louie, "We need the Nephilim with a Creation and Chaos Devil Arms."

"Why?" Magnus asked.

"Retrieve him," Sethos said to the Gatekeeper. A black portal with dark blue light opened behind the Gatekeeper. The warrior stepped back into the portal and disappeared. The brothers let out gasps of surprise.

Virgil felt a presence appear behind him, he turned and saw a similar black portal open behind him, in between him and another brother. The Gatekeeper grabbed Virgil yanking him through. It was like the time they'd gone through a portal to the Ever After, on the night of Tradition. Virgil felt as if the wind had been knocked out of him, pressure from every direction pushed hard against him, he began to feel like he was suffocating. In an instant he reappeared with the Gatekeeper holding firmly onto him, almost touching the large tree.

"How did you do that?" Gabriel demanded. "Nephilim can't teleport at will. There are rules to how that magic works! There are no ley lines that run through here," Gabriel said very confused.

"The Gatekeeper is Seraphim Nephilim, the Fifth Seraph," Sethos smirked as if that explained everything. "The Seven Seraphs are greater than a thousand Nephilim combined, each of us born with special gifts. The Gatekeeper has control over gravity and space. The Gatekeeper can create portals to any dimension and travel anywhere." Sethos dragged Louie to his feet, he was released and ran over to the brothers. Dante ripped the duct tape off his mouth.

"Oww! Thanks a lot Dante!" Louie complained.

"Shut up Louie!" A chorus of brothers said in unison.

Sethos walked over to Virgil producing a small knife from his belt, he grabbed Virgil's right forearm and slashed a line down his arm. The Gatekeeper held Virgil, as he struggled to stop Sethos.

"You bastards!" Vahn and several brothers shouted out moving towards Sethos.

"Stay back!" Sethos commanded, throwing an arm out, as a wave of black energy flew from his black Devil Arms symbol at the brothers. It knocked most of them off their feet and forced the group backwards several meters. Sethos' black Chaos Devil Arms glowed with power. The Gatekeeper had a Chaos Devil Arms as well.

"You are no match for us," Sethos sneered. "Ultima Weapon!" Sethos called out his Devil Arms name. A black spear of energy shot up from his hand, larger than a man. It solidified into a massive sword, that would have taken two or three people to lift. Sethos carried it with fluid grace as if it weighed nothing. The blade was like diamond around the edge of the whole weapon, the rest of the sword was the traditional celestial silver. Virgil doubted he'd ever see a weapon more terrifying. "If you provoke me to battle, you will suffer annihilation," Sethos stated confidently. The Omegas were cautious. "I once killed a hundred Paladins with a single swing from my sword, the most powerful Chaos Devil Arms in existence."

"We won't let you kill Virgil!" Dante shouted.

"We do not intend on killing him, today," Sethos replied simply.

The Gatekeeper held Virgil in place his wound oozing blood, it dripped onto the roots.

"The seal requires a special kind of blood to undo its power," Sethos explained. "We needed a powerful Pureborn Nephilim, one whose blood hadn't been tainted by the Ever After."

Then the roots began to move, the tree made a loud cracking sound, like the very wood was being ripped apart. The tree shook violently, twigs and the last few dead leaves that clung to branches fell to the ground.

"What's happening?!" Gabriel shouted.

The tree cracked down the middle ripping apart. A black ooze seeped out from the tree, bubbling and twisting it grew rising into the air becoming as tall as the tree. A large twisted demon stood before them.

"At last I am freed from my prison!" the demon shouted into the night. The demon's form was an ever-changing grotesque visage of things that people only saw in their nightmares. The demon had a thin and lanky frame, held together by thick long bones. It stood almost as tall as the tree had been, hunched over, giant tusks jutting out from its face.

"Your freedom comes at price," Sethos said to the demon.

The large menacing demon turned to face Sethos, its red eyes narrowing to slits.

"You dare make demands of the Arch Demon, Abdanon! I am the demon of fear! I do not take orders from mortals!" The demon screamed with anger. Its voice was deep and gravely, like an evil monster from a children's movie. Only this demon was the real deal, a horrifying and deadly blight upon the world.

"I freed you at the command of Lilith!" Sethos told the demon who looked like it was ready to attack him.

"The Queen Mother?" Abdanon asked his tone immediately changing. "She sent you to free me at last?" Abdanon asked delighted at the thought.

"Yes," Sethos nodded. "In return for your freedom, Lilith asks that you find the Goddess' Teardrop," Sethos told him.

"Interesting," Abdanon replied, his sharp claws for hands coming together. "And what makes you think that I am able to find such a treasure?" His words more slippery than a politician's.

"You said it yourself, you are the Arch Demon of Fear," Sethos told the demon. "The Goddess' Teardrop was said to have been a tear the Creator shed when it sealed the mortal realm from the Ever After, creating the barrier, the Greater Weirding. The Creator's fears and doubts went into the Teardrop when the spell was cast, breaking the Teardrop will break the Greater Weirding," Sethos spoke with confidence. "It stands to reason you could sense the Teardrop from the fear that was put into it, upon its creation."

"Perhaps," Abdanon cooed. "What do I get in return for finding this Teardrop?" the demon asked slyly.

"You have already been given your freedom," Sethos argued. "You now have free reign upon the world of mortals. Present Lilith that Teardrop, and she will grant you whatever you ask," Sethos suggested with a slight nod to the demon.

The demon stood still thinking for a moment. "I think I sense it," it said at last. "It is not far from here," Abdanon stood up straight. "I will find this Teardrop, because it is Lilith's desire, not because you command it," it said to Sethos with disdain.

"Naturally," Sethos agreed a bored expression upon his face. "We need that Teardrop destroyed, then demons can enter the human realm as they please."

Abdanon stretched long, ugly, tattered wings only exponentially larger with holes broken throughout them.

"We can't let it escape!" Magnus commanded. "If let loose upon the world, it will surely bring death to thousands!" he shouted. The brothers charged the demon bravely. The demon roared at the brothers, the force of its bellow halting their assault.

"I do not have time for useless mortals!" Abdanon snapped. It flapped its ugly tattered wings that surprisingly lifted it into the air. It took flight, flying south.

"No!" Magnus called, "THUNDAGA!" He screamed, raising his arm straight up and a burst of white lightning bolts shot down from the sky blasting the demon causing him to drop out of the air. The demon quickly regained control beating his wings lifting himself up before he crashed, not looking back, continuing his calculated flight south.

"What just happened?" Dante asked very confused.

"You can have your Nephilim back for now," Sethos said throwing Virgil into the ground towards the brothers. "We got what we came for. Enjoy the havoc Abdanon will surely unleash upon your world." Sethos's massive sword glowed a dark blackish purple fading from existence. The Gatekeeper nodded, and opened a portal, the two warriors stepped through and disappeared. The brothers were alone in the forest, darkness and silence surrounded them.

Tarek held his hand over Virgil's cut, a blue light flowing over his wound. Virgil felt warmth spread through his arm, his skin knitting back together, then closing completely in seconds.

"I got some scrapes too bro," Louie exaggerated raising a hand.

"Heal yourself Louie!" Tarek barked, his usual friendly and carefree disposition absent in the solemn aftermath. The group stood there, wondering what had just happened, knowing the ramifications of this were going to be far reaching.

Gabriel turned to Magnus, "What are we going to do?" he asked the most intelligent brother in the fraternity.

"I'm not sure," Magnus said staring at the destroyed husk of the once mighty tree graph. "Things are going to get complicated," Magnus sighed kicking at the ground a frustrated look coming over his face.

"Let's get back to the house," Tarek suggested. "We need to alert Internationals that the Death Dealers just unleashed an Arch Demon upon the tri cities."

The men made their way back to Omega house, the Chapter Advisors were waiting in the living room with the brothers who stayed behind.

"What happened?" Professor Ramuh demanded looking angrier than Virgil had ever seen.

"The Fourth and Fifth Seraph, the Harbinger and the Gatekeeper, revealed themselves to us," Magnus said, as the brothers came into the room taking seats and finding spots to stand. "They are in command of the Death Dealers."

Master Ramuh did not appear shocked, "Buck filled me in on what happened before you left, what did they want with Virgil? I see Louie and Virgil have made it back safely," he remarked, eyeing up Virgil. His gaze staying on him for an uncomfortable amount of time.

"They used Virgil's blood to unleash an Arch Demon, Abdanon they called him. Sethos, ordered him to search for the Goddess' Teardrop," Magnus told them.

"An Arch Demon!" Chapter Advisor Ezekiel cried out. "Gabriel how did you allow this to happen!" he admonished his younger brother.

"There was nothing we could do!" Gabriel shouted feeling frustrated. "Before we had a chance to fight them, Abdanon had been unleashed, and was flying south!"

"Perhaps it is just as well, the small group you had wouldn't have survived a fight against two Seraphs, let alone Sethos," Professor Ramuh looked defeated.

"With an Arch Demon on the loose this area is going to turn into a war zone," Chapter Advisor Ifrit said speaking up. "We must notify the Grand Prytanis, Paladins need to be sent here to help us resolve this matter swiftly."

"Ex-squeeze me!" Louie said impersonating a childish tone. "All this is just a little confusing, who are the Harbinger and the Gatekeeper? What's a Seraphim Nephilim? And what is this Teardrop the Death Dealers want so badly?" Louie asked.

"Didn't Gabriel teach you this during Education?" Professor Ezekiel asked giving his younger brother an inquisitive stare.

"I went over it!" Gabriel protested to his brother crossing his arms over his chest.

"He mentioned something about it, but there was a lot of information being thrown at us, and I didn't really understand it then either," Louie scratched his head.

"After Diablos and his followers were sent into the realm of the Ever After, the Demon King's spirit was cut into three pieces and sealed away. The husk of his body was sealed in the Ever After along with his followers, with a protective barrier, held together by the Goddess' Teardrop," Master Ramuh told them.

"The Death Dealers unsealed that demon asking him to find the Goddess' Teardrop!" Nolan interjected getting excited.

"They seek the Teardrop of legend to unseal the Ever After," Master Ramuh said softly.

"The point," Master Ifrit sighed giving Master Ramuh a gruff look. "While they're still young," he added.

"Yes, yes," Master Ramuh nodded. "The Creator spoke to the Judges warning them Diablos would rise again, in a Great War to be known as Ragnorak. The Creator foretold seven special Nephilim would be born, heralding the coming of Ragnorak. These Seraphim Nephilim, or Seraphs, the blood leaders of our kind, would be given powers unknown to any other being. Two of the seven belong to the Paladins," Master Ramuh boasted confidently.

"Our Grand Prytanis, Aseril, is the Second Seraph, the Oracle, and our Grand Pylortes, Rasler, is the Third Seraph, the Doppelganger," Master Ifrit added.

"Tonight, we met the Harbinger and the Gatekeeper," Magnus said his brow furrowed in deep concentration.

"The board is being set," Master Ramuh remarked, "The Demon King stirs, and we do not yet know of the other three Seraphs, each gifted with unique abilities making them more powerful than an army of Nephilim."

"The Gatekeeper, that warrior teleported, it disappeared and in an instant was behind me," Virgil shivered, "Then it dragged me through."

"The Fifth Seraph, the Gatekeeper is the only being capable of opening portals at any location," Professor Ramuh nodded, concern covering his old and worn face.

"What about Sethos?" Gabriel asked Master Ramuh. "The leader of the Death Dealers."

Master Ramuh's face took on a grave and frightened look. "The Harbinger of destruction, as the prophecy called him. Gifted with the most powerful Chaos Devil Arms in existence, Ultima Weapon. His abilities lie in death and mass destruction. Supposedly he and he alone is capable of using the forbidden dark magic…" Master Ramuh trailed off not finishing his statement.

"We got two Seraphs on our side, right?" Nolan asked. "The Grand Prytanis and the Grand Pylortes, what about them?"

"The Grand Prytanis, is the Second Seraph, the Oracle. Like the title implies he has a powerful gift of divination, able to concentrate and see visions of possibilities for different futures," Professor Ifrit explained.

"Sounds too good to be true," Nolan said plainly.

"I have known King Aseril since my younger days," Master Ramuh said staring Nolan down. "Believe me, he is the real deal. King Aseril is the most powerful Nephilim alive today," Master Ramuh said with fondness. "Thankfully he is on our side. Rasler, the Third Seraph, is the Doppelganger. The Doppelganger has the Devil Arms, Quicksilver, a rapier sword."

"What, everyone else gets special powers and the Doppelganger gets a dinky sword?" Louie joked.

"I wouldn't make light of the Devil Arms Quicksilver," Master Ramuh admonished Louie. "While the rapier isn't much to look at on its own, Lord Rasler is perhaps one of the deadliest Nephilim alive today because of it. Quicksilver has the ability to absorb the power, of any Devil Arms it encounters, forever learning that weapon's unique form," he explained earning some surprised responses. "Rasler can transform his rapier into any Devil Arms that Quicksilver has ever touched while in combat. While Rasler fights, it is said he shifts his rapier into the form of dozens of other weapons, his blade has touched over the years. Starting off on the defensive he utilizes the agility of the rapier's lightweight form, learning his opponents fighting techniques, and absorbing their soul weapons' form in the process as he deflects his opponent's blows. Then he goes on the offensive and summons the best weapon counterpart to whatever he is fighting at the time. Every other Nephilim in existence, can only use their individual Devil Arms. The bounds of Rasler's power are virtually limitless," Master Ramuh remarked.

"That sounds awesome!" Dante said his eyes bright. "Imagine what that would look like in a fight."

"It is a sight to behold," Master Ramuh agreed.

"We need to inform the Grand Prytanis of the Arch Demon, and his mission to find the Tear Drop for the Death Dealers!" Master Ifrit said firmly, losing his patience with Master Ramuh's rambling.

"We'll go at once," Professor Ezekiel said in agreement, "Gabriel come with us. You can fill in with the specific details when needed. The Grand Prytanis, will not be pleased. I'm sure he'll have more questions than we will have answers," he sighed.

The Chapter Advisors left save for Professor Ramuh, he turned to Magnus, "We need to notify the other Paladin fraternities and sororities in the surrounding cities, will you take a few brothers and start making the calls?" Master Ramuh asked.

"Yes sir," Magnus told Master Ramuh, who nodded joining the others upstairs. Magnus took Tarek and a few of the older brothers with him to the meeting room to start making phone calls. The rest of their brothers were left sitting around, in shock, not sure what to do. To Virgil it felt like he'd been run over, he was suffering from information overload. He looked to Louie who was seated next to him on the same couch. "You alright?" Virgil asked Louie, who looked more confused and overwhelmed than Virgil felt.

"Yeah I'm fine," Louie told him.

"What did the Betas do to you?" Virgil asked him.

"Not much," Louie shrugged. "They knocked me out and when I came to, I was tied up near that ugly tree. Malachi and that Death Dealer were talking, the Betas are definitely working with them," Louie said.

"Those bastards!" Dante said getting angry. "They are supposed to be Paladins, they've betrayed us!"

"Internationals need to know," Birdy said. "They need to know the Betas Chapter at our school can't be trusted."

"I'm sure Gabriel is filling in the Grand Prytanis about all of it," Doc suggested.

"What are we going to do?" Virgil asked.

"We'll take care of this situation," Landon said speaking up. "It's what we do. We're Paladins, our job is to protect people and rid the world of demon filth. The first step is to organize a joint effort with other Paladins in the area, find out where this Arch Demon is at, then take him out," Landon said confidently.

"It isn't going to be that easy," Jagger said a frustrated look on his face. "We've never had to fight an Arch Demon before. Those things are as strong as a Judge, maybe stronger. This is going to be dangerous, people are going to die," he said getting upset.

"Lighten up," Brody said pacing nervously. "We can't go freaking out now. We'll get help from Internationals at the Capital, we won't be doing this alone," he said.

"I suggest we all get some rest," Zender added. "It's getting late, and this is going to be a long weekend. We have no way of knowing what the Betas are up to, and they won't be able to enter this house with all the protective spells upon it. Everyone should stay here for the time being."

"I can't get to sleep, I'm too hungry," Louie said rubbing his stomach.

"Me too," Zender agreed. "Let's make some food first."

"Yes!" Lamar exclaimed. "All that serious crap and listening to Professor Ramuh ramble on gave me an appetite."

The brothers headed into the kitchen, making sandwiches and eating some fresh fruit and veggies. After everyone had filled their stomachs, the brothers turned in for the night. Though they'd been told to get some rest, none of Omicron was tired. They went to the pledge dorms to relax until they crashed. Nolan had his laptop and several of them were huddled around it watching a movie. Virgil had to take a shower to clean himself up from the fight earlier. There were plenty of generic cheap clothes available in the large room, for emergencies. Virgil changed into some sweat pants and a white t-shirt.

"Things sound like their getting serious," Louie said to Virgil as he came to sit next to Louie on his bed. Louie, Dante, Birdy, and Troy were playing a game of Euchre.

"Looks like we'll be putting our training to use," Virgil suggested.

"Did you guys ever hear about the mission that took place in Detroit this past summer?" Dante asked them.

"No, what happened?" Troy asked.

"Apparently it was a large-scale operation, all the Paladin organizations in Michigan got involved. Remember hearing about the rioting and gang violence in the news back in July?" Dante asked.

"Yeah," Louie said. "My folks live in Sterling Heights and we were getting worried it was going to spread to us."

"The demon activity and numbers had swelled to great numbers, driving the people in the area mad as the demons fed off their emotions and auras. Death Dealers were also making a foot hold in the area. Our Chapter went as well, we lost a few brothers," Dante said his face growing sad.

"What's your point?" Birdy asked his roommate.

"My point Birdbrain is that this is going to be dangerous, it isn't likely we will all make it out of this alive," Dante said uncharacteristically worried.

"That's part of being a Paladin," Nolan said, speaking up from a few beds over, watching the movie with the others. "We all know the risks, just as any soldier does when he joins the military."

"But this is different," Dante sighed. "People aren't born into the military, it's a choice. We ARE Nephilim, it is in our blood, and we don't have a choice."

"Yes, we do," Birdy argued. "Before any of us joined Omega, we weren't any different from regular men, at least that we knew of. Being a Paladin, IS a choice. We don't have to be a part of this world if we don't want to," Birdy stated.

"I guess," Dante shrugged. "But once you know about it, how could you want to go back?" he asked. "Anyways the point I was trying to make was, things are going to get dangerous, and we all need to be on our A game. I don't want to lose any of Omicron," Dante told them a serious look of concern marring his face as he looked out at the group.

"Aww you're worried about us, aren't you?" Boyd said teasing Dante from across the room.

"Shut up Boyd," Dante said instantly irritated, his shoulders holding tension.

"As long as we stick together, and look out for each other, we'll handle whatever comes our way," Boyd assured them.

Virgil wasn't so sure, there was so much uncertainty now. No one had spoken to him about it yet, but Virgil hadn't stopped thinking about it since it happened. Why had his blood unsealed the demon? Why had the Death Dealers needed him? Who was he? Virgil looked at the Devil Arms on his hands, the power he held in these weapons was daunting. The blood that ran through his veins, was the source of his power. Who am I? Virgil wondered as he had since he started pledging for the Omegas. His entire identity had changed since all of this began. He knew he'd been adopted, as his mother had told him his biological mother had died giving birth to him. If that was true, who was his father? He had to be a Judge, or else why would Virgil be so powerful? He wanted to know who his father was, yet a part of him was scared to know the answer. Virgil prayed that his father was a kind and benevolent Judge, one who still resided in Nirvana, flying on white wings. Secretly he feared his father was a Fallen, a Judge who had been cast down into the Ever After for betraying the Creator. Virgil decided some truths were better left unknown. He liked being an Omega, he didn't need a Fallen trying to persuade him to join the Death Dealers.

Chapter 21
Chaos Descends on Saginaw

The next day the media was flooded with reports of violence, murder, and destruction taking place in the neighboring city of Saginaw. Overnight Saginaw had descended into madness, seemingly regular people snapping and attacking their loved ones. Hundreds of similar cases were happening, the media was blaming most of the deaths on gangs and criminals. Unbeknownst to the human populace, Abdanon had descended on Saginaw, causing an exponential increase in the number of demons in Saginaw. Magnus warned the situation was likely going to get much worse in the days to come. If the Paladins didn't intervene the human authorities were likely to call for backup through SWAT if this went on for too long. Humans were powerless to fight an army of demons, most humans couldn't even see them.

Gabriel informed them that the Grand Prytanis, Aseril Diamond, was aware of the situation and was sending the Grand Pylortes, Rasler, to exterminate the Arch Demon. Rasler would be arriving at the Omega house Sunday night with a small team of elite Paladin troops, to take over leadership of the operation. Gabriel stressed that it was very important everyone treat the Grand Pylortes with the utmost respect, he was the Third Seraph and Grand Jeweled Officer. Until Sunday night the brothers could do as they pleased, Zender and Vahn volunteered to go to campus with Omicron. They'd been stuck at the Omega house since the events of Friday night.

Virgil spent the rest of the night passing the time with the brothers, playing cards or games, trying to stay busy. The news was left on the TV's in the first and second floor living rooms, the situation was getting worse, brothers had a hard time prying their eyes from the screens. The people that were among the missing was rising, as was the body count. The police force in Saginaw, barely able to handle the large amount of crime that regularly took place was overwhelmed. Vahn spent most of his time with Virgil, Virgil could tell his Big was worried about him. Virgil appreciated Vahn's concern and enjoyed his company.

Sunday the house was buzzing, Paladins from universities in the area were coming along with Rasler and an elite squad. The south side of Bay City had a spike in crime, for reasons unknown to the public, seemingly normal people were becoming unhinged and committing atrocities, attacking others and harming themselves. The hospitals were slammed with a constant flood of injured. The demons were getting out of control, spreading, they consumed auras for sustenance, driving normally stable people into a frenzy, the ones they didn't kill outright. Wherever there were high crime rates in the world, there were high demon populations.

Some of the Alpha sisters arrived early, TK and Terra Peoples were their leaders, Blair and a few others with them. Magnus and Master Ramuh left for the stone temple out in the woods. The structure was built over an intersection of powerful ley lines, which could be utilized in teleportation spells. The spell needed for traveling across space was complicated, involved a lot of energy and power. The Paladins from other areas, used these much like telephone lines, jumping into the ley line, moving at the speed of light to a destination set by the spell. Members from the Paladin fraternities and sororities from the neighboring cities of Midland and Saginaw arrived shortly after. Midland had two Paladin fraternities at Northwood University, one of them being a Chapter of Omegas. Saginaw Valley State University had two Paladin organizations, a fraternity and a sorority. A handful of officers from each organization came to the meeting, representing their groups.

Everyone was gathered in the meeting room on the second floor. Though people were cordial, beneath the thin veil of polite pleasantries, fear marred the faces of those present. This situation had to be resolved and soon. Along with the leaders of local Paladins, there were almost sixty people present. There came the announcement that the Paladins from the Capital had arrived, and the room grew quiet. Most of them had never been to the Capital, let alone met one of the eight Grand Jeweled Officers. Gabriel and Magnus led the men from the Capital inside, chairs were set aside at the head of the room for the honored guests. The Grand Pylortes came into the room with his twelve men in silver uniforms. They were adorned with white cloaks that hung at their shoulders from their left side, with Alpha symbols at their shoulders, designating their rank within the Paladin army. Rasler, the legendary Third Seraph, the Doppelganger looked rather normal. Rasler stood 5'9, average height for a man, thin and lanky, he was pale with wispy blond hair. He was twenty-nine years old, with a face worn from stress that made him look like he was in his mid-thirties. Rasler had a Creation Devil Arms on his right hand. Rasler sat with his men. Magnus and Gabriel took their seats next to the Chapter Advisors.

Professor Ramuh began the meeting. "Ladies and Gentlemen, I thank you all for arriving on such short notice," Professor Ramuh welcomed them with a warm smile. "We have come together to tackle the dire sickness that has befallen our community. An Arch Demon is terrorizing Saginaw, it seeks something of great importance. If left unchecked, it will continue to ruin countless lives, and draw more unwanted attention from human society. We WILL NOT," Ramuh said firmly, "Tolerate its presence in our world. The Grand Pylortes has come from Alexandros to quell this matter, before any more damage can be done. Fellow Nephilim, I give you the Third Seraph, Rasler Daedra!" Master Ramuh announced proudly.

Rasler rose from his seat to a round of polite applause, he waited for the room to grow quiet. His voice was soft and calculated. "Fellow Nephilim, I have come here as a representative of your Paladin government," Rasler's tone was that of a politician. Virgil thought he sounded like someone who was used to giving speeches. "It is my job to evaluate and handle risks that present themselves to our people, threatening our way of life. With the cooperation of everyone present, I am confident we can resolve this matter swiftly and with minimal casualties," Rasler stated and then sat back down.

"Thank you, Grand Pylortes Rasler," Professor Ramuh said getting back up. "Now the objective for this operation is clear, neutralize the Arch Demon. We are confident their numbers will dwindle without him. The Arch Demon is in Saginaw on the east side, we aren't certain of his exact location."

"That's where all of us come in," Magnus said, getting up and walking up to the white board at the head of the room. A simplistic diagram of Saginaw had been drawn, focusing on the Saginaw River, and the east side. "This is where we will begin our operation," Magnus said pointing to several X's next to the different bridges that were entry points into the east side of the Saginaw River. "We will be splitting our forces into three main groups, we will sweep east from the bridges, leaving behind small groups as we advance, to keep our flank from being overwhelmed. The three forces will move east, to flush out the Arch Demon. Once he is located, a signal is to be sent out alerting the rest of us. Junior members will be stationed at the safest points near the bridges to hold our line, while the more experienced Paladins will be on the front lines."

"This operation hinges on our ability to stay organized, and communicate effectively," Professor Ramuh pointed out. "The fewer soldiers we have on the ground, the lower our odds of success are," Professor Ramuh stressed.

Magnus came to stand in the center of the room, filled with impassioned charisma. "We need as many Paladins as you can contribute. It will exponentially decrease our likelihood of casualties. I understand not all your active members may be ready for battle. All who are able and willing, should be encouraged to participate," Magnus urged. "We have the chance to do something important here," Magnus said looking the men and women in the eye. "This is OUR neighborhood, these cities belong to US, not them. The people need help that only we can give," Magnus added going back to his chair and sitting down.

"We can't pledge many girls to your cause," Terra Peoples asserted, her words steel. Her hands shook nervously, "Not all of our girls are equipped to handle a situation like this."

"We can offer it to the Sisters and see how many are interested," TK offered, speaking up. "I will personally lead the members I can bring, we may not have a big group, but we'll handle our own," she said confidently. The room was inclined to believe her, TK was easy going on the surface, with a fierce strength beneath. Virgil was interested in seeing TK and Blair using their Devil Arms in combat.

"Our active roster is low," the Prytanis of the Omegas, from Northwood University said. "We have less than twenty guys and we'd be lucky to have half that be able to help with this."

"Our guys are swamped," said a Paladin from the Delta fraternity at Saginaw Valley State University. "We don't have the luxury of not choosing to help, this is in our backyard!" He yelled out frustrated. "Every available man we have is in on this," he said, locking eyes with Lord Rasler.

"Guys we understand everyone has their own hang ups, and personal problems going on. What we need is action and a commitment from the people in this room," Gabriel said going up to the whiteboard. Writing each organization's name on the board. "If you can only send five, we'll take it," Gabriel asserted firmly. "Go back to each of your Chapters, call an emergency meeting. Get a head count of the people willing to take part, we'll be waiting to hear how many men or women you can pledge to the operation. Our Chapter will be doing the same," Gabriel said. "We'll formulate the specifics once we know who will be participating. Be here by 6pm tomorrow night to go over the strategy with Lord Rasler before we head out," Gabriel said setting down his marker.

"You can put thirteen down from Internationals," Rasler said with confidence. "All twelve of my men are Alpha rank Paladins, the best of the best."

"That's a great start," Gabriel said nodding his thanks to Rasler.

"We need you to go back to your Chapters and argue for this cause," Magnus said getting back up. "Thank you for your time," he ended the meeting.

"We will let you know by midnight then Magnus," the Prytanis from the Omegas in Midland said.

"I have a question," a guy said from the Delta SVSU fraternity. "How did this Arch Demon get loose in the first place? And why aren't the Betas from Bay Valley represented at this meeting," he remarked.

"We were also wondering why the Betas aren't here," Terra Peoples said speaking up.

"The Betas turned down the offer to assist with this operation," Magnus answered matter of factly. "We respect their decision and go into this operation with their support and blessing."

"Shit's getting deep in here," Louie whispered.

"Get your boots," Dante whispered back.

"As for the release of this Arch Demon, our Chapter had a run-in with Death Dealers," Master Ramuh explained, drawing the room's gaze. "They kidnapped one of our own," he said which drew a few gasps. "Our men got there just as they destroyed the seal on the tree that kept this monstrosity imprisoned."

"It was Sethos, the Fourth Seraph, Commander of the Death Dealers." Gabriel added.

People erupted into conversation around the room, "Just what are you getting us into!" A brother from the Delta's yelled outraged.

"The Death Dealers are everyone's problem," Rasler pointed out. "That is the charge of every Paladin," he stated firmly.

"I guess," the Delta guy said still looking shaken up. "My men can't take on the son of Lucifer," he added. "We're just regular guys, not gods."

"I am Seraphim Nephilim!" Rasler spoke with conviction, silencing everyone in the room. "You will not be fighting alone. I will be there to strike back against what comes our way," he said confidently.

"Well I guess it makes us more confident that YOU'RE the one to be standing up to people like that. My guys wouldn't mind fighting alongside the legendary Third Seraph, the Doppelganger! It isn't every day you meet a celebrity," the Delta guy gushed.

"Our girls would be excited to meet you as well," Terra Peoples said, with a fun and flirty smile playing across her face.

"I will be here, available and happy to talk with any Paladins who want to take part in the operation," Rasler said with a small smile and courteous nod.

That earned pleased nods from the members around the room. The meeting was adjourned, and Professor Ramuh walked the Paladins who had come from other schools, back to the stone temple. Rasler and the twelve Alpha Paladins had been shown to guest rooms on the fifth floor. After they had their own meeting, the Omegas had twenty-four brothers willing to participate. Virgil was surprised the whole Chapter wasn't helping, Vahn assured Virgil that not all Omegas were as involved with this aspect of things as everyone else. They sat around waiting to hear back from the other groups. They'd have six Chapters including themselves. The Alpha sorority were the first to respond an hour after they'd left, they were bringing a dozen girls. The Omegas from Northwood messaged Magnus, pledging ten brothers to the operation. They had six dozen Paladins volunteering by the end. Virgil was surprised there were so many Nephilim in the area. That wasn't even all the people each Chapter had, just the ones who were skilled enough to handle themselves on the field.

Magnus and Zender spent the day working with the Chapter Advisors and Rasler. Having so many people to juggle wasn't easy, especially since they weren't aware of everyone's capabilities. Rasler suggested breaking the groups up into six people, allowing them to cover more ground. Three of the groups would be kept back, the least experienced with one senior member in each. Rasler and his men were taking point, separating into two elite teams. They would cut a path for the rest of the Paladins to follow. Rasler was polite to the Omegas, though he wasn't one for small talk.

Of the nine groups the local Paladins had advancing east, Virgil and his friends were placed in the group furthest back. They weren't guarding the area around the bridges, though they weren't patrolling much further. Their job was to move forward a couple blocks and secure the perimeter for the brothers that were advancing, so their retreat could be swift if they had to abort the mission.

Virgil's squad consisted of Dante, Birdy, Louie, Blair, Virgil and Zender as the more experienced Paladin in their group. Virgil thanked Magnus for their group, he nodded and waved him off, too busy organizing to pay much attention. Besides Zender, Virgil felt lucky to be with his group. He knew how to communicate and work well with his friends. Now that he thought about it, Magnus and Zender organized everyone according to how they knew each other, placing Paladins from the same Chapters together. Magnus argued that people would be more effective on the field that way. Vahn told Virgil he'd been teaming up with Gabriel and Magnus for years, Tarek becoming a staple in their small team since he joined last fall. They were squad Gamma, first in line after Rasler and his team being Alpha and Beta squads. The last three groups Mu, Nu and Xi where to head to the three bridge points guarding their flank. Virgil and his friends were Kappa squad, the group several blocks down from Mu who were stationed at the Walgreen Ave Bridge. Dante was disappointed they weren't closer to the main action while Louie was visibly relieved. Magnus assured them they didn't need to be in the front to battle demons.

Once everyone was given their groups and shown on a map where they were to patrol, the large group of men and women walked to the stone temple to head to Saginaw. The sun had set fifteen minutes ago, and the sky was getting darker with every passing moment. Gabriel pulled Omicron to the side as people made their way through the worn trail. "Just wanted to say, be careful," Gabriel cautioned. "Don't be reckless guys, I mean it!" he shouted getting a little grumpy with them. "Be cautious and watch each other's backs, I will kick every single one of your asses if I have a missing or wounded Omicron after this is over, ya hear?" he said staring down every one of them, his demeanor taking on that of the badass drill instructor once more.

"Sir, yes, sir" They nodded and told him.

"Stick to your group," Gabriel added. "And when in doubt, fall back. Don't push forward," Gabriel said firmly. "If the order for withdrawal is given, everyone is to obey it without question," he finished with a somber tone. After he was done with his pep talk of sorts they started walking once more with the throng of people.

"And guys keep an eye on my Lil!" Vahn added, as Lambda class and Tarek started walking ahead.

"Aww don't worry we'll watch the Lil guy," Blair called after them, teasing Virgil.

"We'll make sure to keep him out of trouble!" Dante yelled, clapping Virgil on the shoulder.

"Knock it off guys!" Virgil said moving forward and pretending he did not know them.

"And don't worry ladies, we'll watch Blair for you!" Birdy called out to TK and Terra Peoples, they were stationed in Zeta squad, in the middle directly behind Gabriel and the others in Gamma squad.

"Kay!" TK laughed, leading her girls ahead through the trees. "Blair, I expect you'll be the only one to survive in that group. Look after the boys, will you?" she asked sweetly.

"You know it!" Blair said confidently.

"We're worried less about Blair, and more about you clowns," Terra joked. "She could kick all of your butts, so don't be talking shit about my girl!" Terra said defensively. Their sorority called out a group chant that was familiar to them. This caused a chain reaction and all the groups were shouting different fraternity and sorority rhymes. The energy among the group was high, as they walked into the stone temple. Rasler was on the center stage, near the archway. The groups all came in and spread out making room for the fourteen squads, the small amphitheater was full.

"Leave the strong foes to Alpha and Beta squads," Rasler advised. "I am more than a match if the Harbinger or Gatekeeper appear," he said with confidence. "We will take down this Arch Demon!" he shouted to them. "When you go out there tonight, I want you to fight with pride! Fight with confidence! Rely on each other's strengths! We will prevail!" Rasler turned towards the archway, carving symbols in the air before it. A portal of black energy with dark blue spirals ribboning through appeared.

"The entry point is the bus station, spread out to your positions and await instructions!" Gabriel added.

Rasler and his men went first, the rest quickly following. Virgil and his squad approached, Zender in the lead. Zender's short black hair was spiked up in the front, his black chin strap beard trimmed perfectly. Zender was the definition of calm and collected. He sauntered up to the front with confidence and led Kappa Squad through the portal. Everything stopped and compressed together, then it all came rushing back, like going down a hill on a roller coaster. They stepped onto the pavement near the bathrooms. Rasler and his men all unsheathed their wings, every one of the Alpha and Beta squads had a pair with white feathers. The few in the rest of the squads who had them did the same. TK and Terra were the only girls present who had wings. All of Gamma squad, Lambda class and Tarek, had wings. It quickly became apparent why they were the front line. The three top squads took flight and quickly disappeared into the night. They were fast. Everyone on the ground looked up with envy, only the most powerful Nephilim or Purebloods, were gifted with retractable angel wings. The ground units had no chance of keeping up.

Xi Squad was left to guard the bus station area, Virgil and his friends headed east on foot, thankfully there weren't many people out. It was eerily quiet. They made it a few blocks east, kept their eyes vigilant, and their formation tight. Virgil and Blair in the center, Dante and Zender at point, Birdy and Louie at the rear. Their hearts pounded, trying to move swiftly and carefully, ever watchful. The air was thick, an uncomfortable silence seemed to bubble around them, almost as if they weren't alone.

"They are close," Zender said, causing the hair on Virgil's arms to stand up.

"I can feel it too," Dante said whispering, "Gaia's Wrath," his axe solidifying into existence from a shimmer of yellow light.

"Oh shit," Louie said, gripping on to his ice bow as it elegantly floated into his hands from a wisp of light, a concerned frown tugging at his normal sunshine smile.

"We gotcha big guy," Blair said confidently to Louie. "Flametongue!" she commanded, a shortsword landing in her left hand with a blaze of ruby light and crackling fire. Her sword looked orange red towards the tip of the blade, a ruby encrusted on her pommel. It was powerful, and short enough for her to wield efficiently. Zender's Earth Devil Arms produced a halberd, with a shaft like a lance, and an axe at the end. The night seemed to shrink around them, the dark did not seem so empty anymore. From the shadows, figures seemed to be coming closer...

A soldier demon leapt from the darkness at Zender, he swung his halberd slashing through it, the demon fell back dissolving into ash. A swarm of them appeared surrounding their squad. They were like the demons they had fought back at the casino. Twisted creatures as tall as children, they ran on all fours snapping their snarling razor teeth, eager for blood. Louie drew his bow string back, an ice arrow sailing straight into the torso of the nearest creature, it dissolved into ash. They charged the demons, attacking with their Devil Arms! Blair fought like a wild woman, her sword leaving trails of fire as she swung it. They killed several demons each, and more materialized from under porches, beneath cars, from within shadows. When one was cut down, two more came out to replace it.

"We'll be overcome!" Zender cried out. "Fall back!" The group kept their formation tight backing away from the horde of approaching demons. Dante wielded Gaia's Wrath with impunity, however he was getting further from the group, demons filling in the gap between their squad and him.

"Dante!" Virgil called out to his friend his scythe hovering above his hand.

"I got him!" Louie cried pelting the demons circling him, disintegrating them into ash.

Blair left Virgil's side running for Dante. "Blair!" Virgil yelled. Blair charged the demons with confidence, she whispered to her blade, and it burst into flame. She swung it over her head, the blade breaking apart extending into a fiery whip. She brought it forward, a painful sounding strike as it lashed through two demons at once, destroying them instantly. She wielded the whip with even more grace than the sword. Dancing forward she began to spin around, her long fire sword whip flying around, cutting a line through to Dante. Dante turned towards Blair fighting his way to her. They reached each other and went back to back. The others from their squad pushed forward. The unending swarm of soldier demons finally began to dwindle, fierce seconds of intense battle raged on. The demons that were left suddenly cowered back, and fled, leaving them alone as quickly as they appeared. The squad regrouped, breathing hard, they were unharmed.

"That was awesome!" Virgil yelled grinning from ear to ear. He lowered his scythe's blade to rest on the ground. "I've never seen anyone fight like that!" Her sword was broken up into fragments, connected by flames, she cracked the whip and the segments came back together, the flames disappearing, a whole sword once more.

"Thanks," she said with a big smile, the guys crowding around her to get a look at her impressive Devil Arms.

"Was that your first time?" Birdy asked curiously.

"Is that what the boys like to hear?" Blair asked Virgil, who shrugged not getting the joke. "Oh, yeah, of course it was," Blair said with a sly smile batting her eyelashes.

"Really?" Louie said believing her. "My first time seeing a demon I was scared stiff!"

"Louie there is no way that was her first time!" Dante said snapping at his friend. "She's too damn good."

"I've gotten a little practice in with TK," Blair admitted. "For the few sisters who actually wanted to develop some skill with their Devil Arms, she's been secretly working with us."

"Yeah, yeah," Zender interrupted. "If you guys are done kissing her ass, we have an area to patrol. Weak soldier demons will be crawling all over the place!"

They got back in formation their weapons disappearing in flashes of light, walking to the boundary of their area. Once they had gone as far as they should, Zender suggested they circle around.

"Why?" Dante asked. "Let's just push ahead," he suggested.

"No," Zender left no room for arguing, turning around to head back. "We need to circle our area a few times. We're supposed to make sure the path back to the bus stop is clear for evacuation. Leave our area and we're not doing our job!" Zender yelled.

"They could need us!" Dante urged.

"If they do, they'll let us know," Zender said walking away. The others followed him, Dante was frustrated, following the group. They circled back taking different streets, their area was wide, and they had plenty to explore. They didn't run into anything else as they neared the bus station. Screams could be heard in the distance, as could police sirens, the city was unsafe, and every shadow hid a potential battle. Once they got within a block of the bus station, they saw Mu squad, Boyd and Nolan were a part of it along with some of the Alpha sisters.

"We picked off a couple small ones," Boyd called out to them as they approached, "Nothing we can't handle."

"Those boys behaving themselves?" Blair asked her sisters.

"They're trying hard to show off," Helene told Blair, "But we haven't seen too many demons over here."

"This area seems pretty secure," Dante pointed out. "Let's walk towards the next squad and see if there is any need further ahead." Zender grunted in agreement and their group moved east. They ran into a small group of soldier demons a few blocks ahead crawling along a house, looking to feed upon its occupants. They made quick work of them, no reinforcements coming this time. They ran into a group of young men after that, normal humans. They sized up the six of them, their eyes paying close attention to Blair. Zender and the others stared them down, they were fighting demons, some hoodlum punks weren't intimidating. The strangers started walking on a path to intercept them, as a police siren drew near, they quickly changed their path, walking away from them. Soon they came back up the street, that was the end of their territory.

"What should we do now," Dante asked sounding bored.

"Circle back to the bus station," Zender suggested.

"Again?" Dante asked incredulously. "We could be of a lot more use here. This is one of the more talented groups, we should be helping Gamma squad!" Dante argued.

"Gabriel doesn't need our help!" Zender said firmly.

There came a loud rumble from up ahead, followed by shouting, and the sound of demons. Flashing lights of exploding magic could be seen a few blocks down, another squad was fighting something up ahead.

"Should we help?" Blair asked, her ruby Devil Arms glowing on her left hand, ready for battle.

"Let's check it out," Zender nodded, and the six of them ran for the sounds of battle.

Chapter 22
The Goddess' Tear Drop

Virgil's squad emerged onto a business street, there were small shops that were closed, and a gas station at the end. Epsilon squad was embroiled in battle against bat demons, with lanky frames suspended by leathery wet wings. The creatures had red eyes and dark skin, they were shorter than an average person, their small bodies masking their enormous strength. They were dive bombing and clawing at Epsilon squad. The main problem was a massive demon, who stood over ten feet tall, large horns twisting out of it head. It stood on two legs and ran on its arms and legs like a gorilla. It looked like a gorilla with a bear head, and huge clawed hands. It was picking up cars and throwing them like they were rocks.

"Great! A troll demon, on top of bat demons," Zender cursed his luck, bringing his halberd to his hand. "They're going to need our help," he said pointing out the obvious.

"How do we take down something that large?" Birdy said staring at the troll demon.

"Like anything else!" Dante responded with confidence.

"Louie and Virgil, concentrate on taking down those flying bastards," Zender locked eyes with them, they nodded. "The rest of you help me to whittle away at that beast, it's very fast so watch out!" Zender warned, charging into the fray, the others at his side.

Virgil grabbed his scythe, throwing it like a boomerang at the nearest flying demon. The demon managed to dodge the flaming sickle, the scythe spun back around, cutting right through its middle, it exploded into ash. Louie was getting in great shots with his bow, his hours of target practice were paying off. The flying demons were dropping like flies. The six Epsilon squad members were exhausted, two of them knocked unconscious fiercely guarded by the other four.

Zender, Birdy, Dante, and Blair bravely took on the troll demon, mostly dodging its mighty blows, and stabbing it when they had an opening. Two of the Epsilon squad helped in taking down the flying demons. When they got close to their squad the men would fire off a well-timed spell blasting the demons out of the sky. Their numbers began to thin.

Virgil shouted, "Firebolt!" A beam of red energy shot from his hand erupting on impact with the troll demon, burning and stunning it for a second. While his friends all got a strike at its body, it turned to Virgil. The spell had pulled its power straight from Virgil's aura, the price to pay for the benefits of Will. The demon roared loudly, using its fists it thrashed wildly at Dante, Birdy, Blair and Zender pushing them away, then charged at Virgil.

"Get out of the way!" someone shouted. The troll demon was almost upon him, Virgil threw his scythe at the oncoming demon, dodging hard to his right as he let go. The scythe nicked the troll's side. The troll swatted Virgil with his hand as he barreled past, sending Virgil rolling across the ground. He got to his feet and the scythe came spinning back to him. The troll had sprinted right into a building. It quickly regained its composure, shaking concrete dust from its fur, glaring at Virgil. It roared fiercely, an angry look in its eyes. It came running at him once more. Virgil raised his hand and shouted, "Explosion!" A blast of fire erupted in front of him, like a bomb blast, flinging the troll backwards into a broken car.

Virgil fell back onto his butt, his head hurt, and vision went blurry. He felt his aura literally hurt for the first time, his spiritual energy weakened from the spell, his whole body ached.

"Enough with the spells!" Zender shouted to Virgil. "You're no use to us if you're passed out!" Blair lashed out at the troll demon, now laying butt deep in a smashed car like it was a Layz-boy, her sword now a flaming whip. Her Devil Arms sliced the demon creating deep cuts. Louie V pelted an arrow into its chest, then another. It rose to its feet letting loose a might roar.

"A little more!" Dante shouted, sprinting to get in range for his axe. "It looks like its slowing down."

The troll swiped at Blair, she nimbly ducked under its fist, dodging its attack. It became infuriated and started chasing her, tired of getting smacked around.

"Get it off her!" Dante demanded, charging the troll demon. Birdy got close enough and gave it a deep jab with his lance. The demon threw an arm at Birdy as it moved past him, catching him directly across the torso sending him airborne with the wind knocked out of him. Birdy was flung several yards and rolled across the cold road gasping for air, his body aching from the harsh impact.

"Damn you!" Dante screamed, swinging his axe catching it in the thigh, knocking it into a slumped position, nearly taking it off its feet. Zender swung his halberd, catching the demon's arm with a slash before it could counterattack Dante. Dante rounded on the creature running up to the troll demon, raising Gaia's Wrath into the air, smashing its blade into the demon's side with a roar of his own! The demon crashed onto its left side. The group descended on the demon like a pack of starving wolves, everyone using their weapons to beat at the massive creature's body. It was struggling to its feet, both arms on the ground pushing itself to a standing position, still alive after all the damage it had suffered. Dante leapt onto its back and swung his axe down on the creature's head with a powerful blow, it disintegrated into a pile of ash and black blood.

Dante sunk to the ground landing in a large puddle of demon gore. "Gross!" Dante exclaimed, getting some on his precious axe. "What happened?" he asked.

"The larger ones' bleed demon blood," Zender shrugged, "Its gross."

With the demons neutralized they quickly checked on Birdy, he'd gotten to his feet and made his way over to the six other guys. They were from Saginaw Valley's Delta fraternity.

"Birdy you okay?" Dante asked him concerned, putting a hand on his back and checking him over.

"I'm fine," Birdy said, sitting in the grass next to the sidewalk.

"Our friends need medical attention," One of the Epsilon squad said. "We're pulling back, we have to get them out of here!"

"The path back should be clear," Blair assured them. "Get back to the bus station!"

They thanked the others for their help, the four men helped carry the two wounded. The street they were in grew quiet, sounds of battle and panic still rose up from the city around them. They started to collect themselves, no one had put away their Devil Arms yet, their adrenaline still pumping hard from the fight. Birdy went to get up and let out a cry of pain. He was holding his right arm; he'd landed on it when he fell to the ground. It was the arm with his Devil Arms hand, it was broken.

"Damn Birdy, that thing got you good," Louie commented softly.

"Well don't just look at it, fix him!" Dante snapped.

"I can try," Louie V said nervously, looking at Birdy's arm. "I've learned the spell, just takes a lot out of me,' he said looking around.

"Well try it out," Blair suggested. Louie knelt down, setting his bow on the ground, he held both hands near Birdy's arm and closed his eyes concentrating. He took a few deep breaths,

"Ply," he said keeping his Devil Arms symbol close to Birdy's arm. A soft blue glow came from Louie's symbol coating Birdy's arm in its gentle light. Birdy grimaced and groaned in pain, Louie held onto his arm as the spell healed his limb, and Louie put it back into place. Birdy moved his arm afterwards, having full range of motion. Louie was sweating profusely, he looked pale and swayed as he tried to stand falling back down. Virgil came over to his friend, "The drain spells take on your aura is exhausting," Virgil said.

"It takes a lot of experience to push yourself to be able to use more Will," Zender huffed. "It will take time before only a couple spells make you want to sit down for a nap," he laughed.

"Can you use Will?" Birdy asked him.

"Most idiots can throw a spell or two, it takes a warrior to know what to do with it. I can use a few spells, but even I get tired after a couple. I try to save them for when it counts," he said uncharacteristically modest.

"When's that?" Louie asked, getting to his feet, leaning on Virgil for support.

"When my life's in danger," Zender said simply with a shrug.

"What now?" Virgil asked his group. "One more fight like that, and we'll have to pull back."

"I'll take down another troll, no problem," Dante said, lifting his axe onto his shoulder, flexing his biceps.

Blair smirked and rolled her eyes saying, "Show off!"

"We should stick to this area," Zender said, "We're now responsible for two areas, we can't let anything slip past us and get near our exit."

A dark fog began to roll along the ground, unnatural and menacing. They could see the glow of demon eyes faintly in the distance. Demons scuttling across the ground getting closer…

"What do we do?" Virgil asked.

"Let's get away from this!" Zender shouted, clearly alarmed and not familiar with what was going on. The six of them turned and ran, the dark fog seeming to have already surrounded the area. They went to fall back west, but the fog had covered the area, blocking their way, the shadows of dozens of demons lurking in its protection. Demons swarmed in the dark fog moving closer to them. They ran eastward away from the fog, trying to stay out of its reach, the amount of demons lurking in it was too many for them to face. They continued westward for a several blocks gaining a slight lead. Their way forward was swamped with black fog up to their knees as they approached a major street, so they veered sharply south looking to escape from the approaching darkness. The darkness was swallowing everything, hundreds of demons began to surround them.

"We're being cut off!" Blair shouted to her friends, a look of concern coming across the fierce warrior's face.

"Look there!" Virgil pointed out. A large church was close, the darkness was slightly distant from it. "Are we safe in a church?" he asked them.

"Demons can't set foot on holy ground!" Zender shouted running for the church steps. They followed closely at his heels sprinting up the many large steps to the doors. The front door was unlocked, and they ran inside slamming the door shut behind them. They anxiously waited for the monsters to emerge from the shadows or come crashing through the windows. Nothing happened. They could hear them outside, close by, but for the time, it looked like they were safe.

The church was very old and grand in scale with a large main hall, and tall ceilings. This was a church that had a lot of money pumped into it. The group dissolved their weapons, walking to the front of the room. There were candles all over, some used down to nothing, people had been coming here to pray. A war had broken out in their streets, people were feeling frightened, lost, in pain…sometimes faith was the only thing holding people together. There didn't appear to be anyone in the main hall, they spread out. There were several doors at the back, offices, a large hall, and some steps leading to the basement. Virgil felt a strange presence near the podium, though it wasn't malicious like the demons. This was a powerful entity, and it exuded warmth. At the front of the church there was a large statue, Virgil drew closer. It was of exquisite design and stood as tall as the room.

Virgil felt comforted by the statue, it calmed his mind, stilled his racing heart. He smiled at the statue and patted it lightly, turning to look elsewhere. A pulse beat out from the statue upon touching it, almost auditory. "What?" Virgil said staring at the statue. The ring on his right hand responded, the small Dreamstone reacting. There's something here, more magicite? Virgil wondered what it was when he saw a jewel embedded in the statue, a single tear crying from its face.

"Wow!" Virgil exclaimed surprised. It was the biggest piece of magicite he'd ever seen. "Guys come take a look at this!" Virgil called out.

Louie got there first, "Oh shit man!" he cried.

"That might be what it's after," Virgil said whispering out loud, wondering why they had been led here, what was the dark fog on the ground?

"What are you babbling about?" Louie asked. "Mumbles speak up!" Louie barked at Virgil.

The front door burst open. Gamma squad stormed into the building with the same urgency as Virgil's squad. Led by Gabriel were Magnus, Vahn, Jagger, Landon, and Tarek. They looked worn but still whole. Wings on their backs they turned off their Devil Arms noticing the danger had temporarily subsided in the safety of the church.

"What are you guys doing so deep in?" Gabriel asked them not happy.

"We got caught up rescuing other people, no biggie," Dante shrugged. "We're all alive, so don't make a fuss about us having milk time early," Dante grumbled.

"What in the world did you just say?" Tarek laughed.

"Don't worry about it," Dante quipped crossing his arms over his chest.

"This is getting us nowhere!" Vahn said sounding annoyed. He walked up to Virgil and Blair. "I'm glad you are alright! How was it?"

"Not what I expected," Virgil said honestly. "I was excited to see some action but," Virgil couldn't think of the right words.

"It isn't what you thought it would be?" Vahn nodded understanding what Virgil was trying to say. "Sounds really cool, swinging around powerful weapons, demons, spells, but when it happens its more…" he trailed off.

"Visceral, frightening, makes you feel sick to your stomach?" Virgil filled in.

"Or a pain in the ass?" Dante sighed. "It's not easy keeping these kids safe," he told Gabriel and the others.

"What?!" Louie and Blair cried out.

"Were you led here by the black fog?" Magnus asked them.

"Yes," Zender said. "We tried falling back, but the fog rolled in quickly, pushing us further east, then south. Virgil pointed out how it wasn't approaching the church."

"We were chased here too," Landon remarked. "There are too many demons out there to fight at once."

"We got separated from Rasler," Gabriel told them. "He will come looking for us."

"Have you found the Arch Demon?" Zender asked.

"No," Magnus answered curtly, "But I'm beginning to think he's found us. Strange this demon has refused to show himself. He must want something close by."

"I'm guessing that's it," Virgil pointed out. Lambda class came closer to look at the statue, noticing the jewel on its face. Magnus and Tarek beat their wings, flying up to get a closer look. They carefully wedged it out of the statue and brought it down. The jewel was as big as a hand, a perfect tear drop shape in an iridescent gemstone.

"This is a powerful piece of magicite," Magnus remarked holding it in his hand.

"Do you think this is the mythical artifact, the Goddess' Teardrop, the Arch Demon is seeking?" Gabriel asked sounding impressed.

"Most likely," Magnus nodded. "But now that we have it, I'm wondering if we should even take it from here. It may be safer in this church, where demons can't enter," Magnus said staring down at the treasure.

The door opened again, this time Rasler and his two squads came in. A few members of Beta squad looked exhausted, most of their white and silver uniforms were stained with ash and blood. Virgil thought Rasler looked worn and underwhelming when he first met him. Seeing Rasler now, his eyes held a strong fierceness, his blond hair was whipped up giving him a wild and dangerous look. He didn't seem phased at all from the battles he had faced, looking stronger than when the night had begun. This was a man in his element.

He came close to the group, "I gave the order for withdrawal in the sky, we must make our way to the exit," Rasler announced. "What are you all doing here?" Rasler asked them

"The darkness that is swallowing the city," Magnus told him.

"It's the Arch Demon," Rasler assured them. "He is toying with us."

"He is after this," Gabriel said taking the Teardrop into his hands.

"What!?" Rasler asked surprised walking up to Gabriel, his white wings tucked in. He took the jewel and looked it over, thinking to himself for a few minutes. "This is why you were pushed here," Rasler nodded. "He couldn't get it himself," Rasler guessed.

"I think it is wise to leave it where we found it," Magnus said earning a frown from Rasler. "Probably can't be seen by normal humans either, won't have to worry about it getting stolen," Magnus guessed.

"If Nephilim can come in, then a Death Dealer could just come back once we leave," Rasler pointed out. "We are taking this into Paladin custody," Rasler declared to Magnus.

"We'll gladly assist," Gabriel offered. "I'll personally carry it back to the portal we have open," Gabriel stated.

"Very well," Rasler nodded, handing it back to Gabriel. "We'll form an arrow formation and punch a hole through!"

"Let's go!" Magnus called out. They had four squads, Rasler's two were in front, Virgil's group was the only one without wings, so Gamma squad was sticking with them. The plan was to barrel out the door and run the gauntlet back to the bus station, where they could travel back to the stone temple in the safety of their woods. Rasler gave his men a nod once everyone was in position. They opened the doors and poured out of the church. Lambda class went next, Virgil and the others hot on their heels. They ran down the church stairs after Rasler and his men. In the sky an Omega symbol hung in the air, the sign to end operations. The black fog couldn't touch the church. Rasler and his men slashed a way forward, some of the fog seeming to dissipate. The looming fog began to gather as Gabriel got closer to the street with the jewel. A funnel spun like a tornado made of shadow and darkness, as it dissolved the menacing form of the Arch Demon, Abdanon blocked their path.

"Thank you for retrieving the precious magicite, I will gladly take it now," Abdanon's voice made Virgil's insides tremble.

Rasler's men bravely took flight, flying at the Arch Demon with coordinated aerial strikes. The Omega's charged on foot cutting through demons on the ground carving a path west, to the river. Rasler assaulted the Arch demon mercilessly, his silver rapier white Devil Arms symbol let out a flash of light transforming its symbol to an amethyst Devil Arms. A large bow was now in his hands, which shot powerful blasts of lightning. He used it from a distance letting out massive charged up forms of arrows that slammed into Abdanon with great force. Once Abdanon grew closer and looked to attack him, his weapon let out another flash, and transformed into a massive two-handed sword that should've been impossible for Rasler to even lift. Rasler grabbed onto the mighty blade and swung it at Abdanon as they came to a head. The blade allowed Rasler to pass by him, taking a chunk of the demon with him, also blocking any counterattack with its colossal blade.

Rasler flew past the demon and his weapon flashed, pulsing with white light. The weapon became a glowing lance of mythical power, Gae Bolg. Rasler's weapon overflowed with Creation energy and light. His men lead the next assault, Rasler at the back, the long silver lance, glowing with pure light poised for attack. Abdanon clawed at the Paladins as they descended, black smoky chains materializing from the black fog rising to entangle them. Rasler narrowly dodged the demon's claw and tusk, slashing him with the lance. The right tusk of the Arch Demon was severed, his torso was deeply cut. It fell to a knee black demon blood coming from its wound. Rasler went to the ground and stabbed the lance into the dark fog rolling along the ground, the darkness and chains immediately dissipated, the spell broken.

"You are not the wielder of Gae Bolg!" Abdanon spat at Rasler standing back up to its full height.

"No, but I have crossed paths with it before," Rasler mocked the Arch Demon. "That's enough to make its power my own."

"You're a Seraph!" the Arch Demon acknowledged. "Just like the others. You are gathering for our master's awakening!"

"Not that you'll be there to see it," Rasler challenged him.

"You haven't won yet Doppelganger," Abdanon mocked, his form twisted into a black spiraling tornado of darkness, melting into the sewer and out of sight.

With the dark fog gone, so were the demons lurking in it. The group ran, trying to cross a great distance in very little time. Police cars and an ambulance went flying past them when they approached a main road. They got back to the bus station in record time, Nolan informing them that all the squads had gone through the portal. Rasler and his men went through the black portal first. Gabriel ordered Mu squad to fall back and thanked them for being the protectors of their escape home. Everyone hurried through thankful to be finished with the operation. A guy who did not look familiar to Virgil, from one of the other fraternities maybe, walked up patting Gabriel on the back. As he did, his body began to change, gaining immense height, and his hands becoming bony claws with putrid flesh. He snatched up Gabriel, crushing his wings, preventing him from flying in escape.

"Gabriel!" Vahn shouted out, flying up at Abdanon clashing his sword against Abdanon's claw. "Take this!" Gabriel said throwing the Goddess' Teardrop at Vahn. Vahn dived for the jewel doing his best to catch it gently. He caught it feet above the ground, when he too was grabbed by Abdanon. His claw squeezed Vahn, the sound of his wings snapping as they were crushed was sickening. They were both in agony, caught firmly in the Arch demon's grasp.

Vahn locked eyes with Virgil and threw the Teardrop to him. Virgil caught it and the Arch demon charged at him. The others behind him pulled Virgil towards the portal, the exit back home.

"No! I must have that Teardrop!" Abdanon cried out.

"NO!" Tarek, Dante and many of the other brothers cried out charging the Arch demon.

"If you want your friends left alive, you will do as I say!" Abdanon growled, stomping the ground, making it quake beneath Virgil's feet. "Bring the Teardrop to my tower. I'll have a portal waiting where I was sealed, your friends' lives depend on it," Abdanon demanded disappearing in a black funnel of fog and energy taking to the night sky.

"Wait!" Virgil screamed, the Teardrop in his hands. He felt an immense warmth and power emanating from the jewel, unlike anything he'd felt before.

"Get through the Gate, now!" Magnus demanded.

"We gotta save them!" Dante demanded.

"This mission is over!" Magnus shouted. "We must return to the house!"

Virgil was rushed through to the bathrooms where the black portal awaited. Virgil stepped in and was pulled through the ley line. After several uncomfortable moments, Virgil emerged from the archway at the stone temple of the Omega temple. More guys poured in behind him, a few men were in the temple, most headed back to the house.

"It is safe!" Rasler exclaimed taking the Teardrop from Virgil.

"The Arch Demon took Gabriel and Vahn!" Virgil yelled to Rasler. "We have to rescue them!"

"What happened?" Rasler asked, his smile falling into a serious mask. "I only stepped through a minute ago."

"Abdanon appeared," Virgil told Rasler his speech rapid, panic starting to set in. "He grabbed them and said he'd free them in exchange for the Teardrop."

"It is true," Magnus said, walking up to them from the portal. "He wasn't able to get the Teardrop, so he took a few of our men as hostages, in hopes to bargain for it."

"We don't negotiate with Arch Demons," Rasler said with a note of finality.

"But we have to do something here," Virgil said getting upset. "We have to storm his location and fight for them."

"Fight for them?" Rasler asked curiously. "My boy, we have fought for them, for all of us, this whole night. Every man knows the dangers of going into a mission, sometimes we don't make it out. Your brothers fought bravely tonight. Gabriel was a finer Paladin then I've seen in a long time."

Was? Virgil seethed with anger. "Your point?" Virgil asked, not liking what he was hearing.

"My point," Rasler said, getting defensive, a snarl crossing his lips. "Is that to throw men at a rescue mission would endanger dozens, maybe even hundreds, with no promise of rewards. And the benefit is possibly saving two lives in the process," Rasler argued. "The needs of the many must be weighed against the needs of a few."

"It is still worth trying!" Virgil yelled getting into Rasler's face.

"Who are you to say whose life is worth more than the rest?" Rasler asked Virgil. "The Arch Demon would likely not let them go, even if you gave him what he wanted. The moment he left with them in his hands, their fate was sealed," Rasler told Virgil.

"You're one of the Seven Seraphs, the Doppelganger! You're strong enough to take down that demon and save them!" Virgil told Rasler. "Please!" he begged grabbing onto Rasler's uniform, desperation and hysteria beginning to take hold over him. "I saw you fight against him, you wounded him without getting a scratch on you. You're powerful enough to take him on!"

"I'm heading up to the house, this discussion is over," Rasler said shaking Virgil off walking to the exit.

"Wait!" Virgil said walking after him.

"Virgil stand down," Magnus commanded him.

"He can't just dismiss them like this!" Virgil yelled.

"He is the Grand Pylortes, a commanding officer in our government! As your Chapter Prytanis I am telling you to stand down!" Magnus told Virgil.

Rasler continued walking leaving the temple, Virgil stopped following him, heeding his leader's command.

Magnus waited until Rasler had gained some distance, the only people left in the stone temple were Omegas, milling about the temple in shock, standing, sitting, dazed.

"Virgil, he could bring you up on charges! He is a very important person and can't be spoken to out of turn," Magnus advised. "I know you're upset about Gabriel and Vahn, we all are!" Magnus yelled, getting emotional for the first time since Virgil had known him.

"Can we get 'em back?" Jagger asked Magnus.

"We can try," Landon nodded.

"Not with Rasler's permission, perhaps not with Internationals blessing either," Magnus said. "He'd never allow us to attempt something like that, even without the Teardrop."

"Why does he care what we do?" Dante asked angrily, "this isn't his Chapter, we run it, not him. He can take his pompous ass back to the Capital, we don't need his help."

"Dante!" Jace reprimanded. "We have to do as Internationals says, we go against them we get shut down, and then we aren't a fraternity anymore!"

"Are we going to rescue our guys or not?" Birdy asked.

"I say we do what we can for them," Magnus nodded. "But this needs to stay between us. If anyone else learns of this they could stop us, or even shut down our Chapter."

"I say we all go back up to the house and put our game faces on," Dante said. "First chance we get I'm going after our boys, anyone who wants to come can."

"I got your back," Louie volunteered first surprising Virgil.

"I'm going," Jagger said.

"No, you can't," Magnus said.

"Bullshit," Jagger said fiercely visibly shaking.

"No, he's right," Zender jumped in. "You are the Chapter Pylortes, the Sergeant at Arms. If you got wind of a plan not sanctioned by Internationals, it would be your duty to shut it down. If you remain here while a group of us sneaks off, you have plausible deniability that you were unaware of their intentions." Zender explained.

"And that means I have to stay behind as well, I'll have to sit here while you guys go off to face the Arch Demon," Magnus said clenching his fists and turning away.

"We'll make sure to come back with them," Landon told Magnus.

"Thanks, Landon," Magnus replied, not making eye contact with anyone. "I'm counting on you."

"I won't be a part of this," Jace said disgusted. "We can't get the Chapter shut down," he said walking off. Thiago and Benson went with him.

"We'll need enough brothers to stay behind to make this half way believable," Magnus shrugged.

"We can't just send Omicron," Jagger complained, "They'll be killed!"

"I'll lead the mission," Tarek volunteered. "I need at least a dozen men, and we'll slip away first chance we get."

"We'll finalize the plans soon," Magnus nodded. "For now, let's get to the house before they wonder what's keeping us."

Chapter 23
<u>Abdanon's Tower</u>

They had a quick debriefing in the Omega's meeting room, the atmosphere was sullen, defeated. There were eight severely wounded, and two missing in action, Gabriel and Vahn. Rasler was the only one who spoke, he kept it brief. Rasler thanked everyone for their effort, he made it clear at the end no one was to attempt a negotiation with Abdanon, without the Capital's consent. He looked at the brothers of Omega when he said it, giving them almost condescending looks. It was a great speech, with all the trappings of a politician telling the citizens that they empathized with their plight, pretty words with no real feelings of conviction, like hollow brass. Virgil shared a look with some of the people in the room, Dante, Louie, Blair, and Birdy. The hell they wouldn't get involved, Virgil thought. The meeting was dismissed, and Omicron class hurried out the door and down the hall to the pledge dorms.

"Wait up," Tarek called out, walking alongside them.

"We're going to get them back," Dante said firmly.

"Damn straight," Tarek nodded.

They walked into the large sleeping quarters and gathered around in a circle. A few other brothers trickled in, Brody, Landon, Zender, Doc, and Magnus was the last. He closed the door and spoke a strange word, light going out from his Devil Arms, a purple symbol hovered over the door for a few seconds then disappeared.

"Now we can speak freely," Magnus said, turning back to the room, "The spell will break when someone enters the room.

"This it?" Virgil asked concerned with how few of them there were.

"This is everyone who is willing to volunteer," Landon pointed out taking his baseball cap off and rubbing his hand through his hair. They all looked beat, they'd just got done fighting demons, and running the streets for several hours.

"It'll have to do. Now what do we do?" Tarek asked.

"We need to get the Teardrop from Professor Ramuh's office and take it to the Arch Demon," Dante said simply with a shrug of his shoulders, like it was common sense.

"And endanger the world?" Magnus asked them.

"Why is that?" Birdy asked.

"Because Birdbrain," Zender responded with a bite to his words, "That piece of magicite is the only thing holding the barrier up that protects this world from the Ever After. If it is destroyed, the judges and Death Dealers can come and go more freely."

"Oh yeah," Birdy said looking down.

"Can't we just go without it?" Doc asked. "Show up, kick that demon's ass, get our brothers and go home."

"I don't think we'll be able to get to the Arch Demon without it in our possession," Nolan pointed out. "We won't even have a shot at rescuing them without it, it is the only way he'll grant an audience with us and them."

"Alright, so let's steal the Teardrop and get going," Louie said getting up.

"Professor Ramuh is keeping the Teardrop in his office, we'll need help to get it from him without getting caught," Brody said frustrated.

Magnus had mainly been removed from the conversation, his face guarded and his thoughts reticent. "Is saving our friends worth this risk?" Magnus asked them to voice his own conflicting feelings out loud.

"What do you mean?" Tarek asked defensively.

"This is a big gamble we're taking," Magnus said carefully. "This is a small and inexperienced group, we have no guarantee any of you have the strength to stand against an Arch Demon," he said, trying not to laugh then going serious faced. "How the hell can we expect you to come through this operation with success," Magnus pondered the group, his mind filled with doubt.

"We won't know unless we try," Tarek said optimistically. "I'll be leading the group, I can take on a lot by myself, and with everyone's added help, I think we can make it," he said turning to look at the other men in the room.

"You truly believe that?" Magnus asked Tarek.

"Yes," Tarek said staring Magnus down. The two men's eyes were locked in a battle of wills. Finally, Magnus conceded defeat and nodded. "Let's do it then," Magnus replied softly nodding and looking off, lost in deep thought, his eyes betraying fear for his friends.

There came a knock at the door, it opened, and the spell was broken. It was Professor Ramuh, he came into the room and put the same spell on the door.

"How can I help?" he asked them.

"Help with what?" Louie asked innocently.

"Don't be coy Louie, it is obvious what the lot of you are scheming," Professor Ramuh sighed. "Professor Ifrit and our Pylortes are keeping Rasler entertained in the meeting room, I took the Teardrop from him to store in my office because I persuaded him it was the safest room in the house," Master Ramuh said. "It can only be opened with a master key, and only the Chapter Advisors have them." Professor Ramuh added thinking out loud. He reached into his pocket and produced a key, dropping it onto the nearest bunk bed. "The Greater Weirding was predestined to fall," Professor Ramuh said softly. "But Gabriel and Vahn's lives may yet be saved. Be quick about it," Professor Ramuh snapped, then he turned and left the room.

"I'll go," Virgil said, jumping to his feet and moving to grab the key. "I'm the fastest in Omicron."

"Wait," Magnus warned, "Once you get it, you must leave immediately," he spoke with such seriousness everyone was silent. "Once Rasler realizes it is missing, he will accuse our Chapter of foul play and may threaten to shut us down. The only way we can prevent this from happening is to be against this mission, but covertly for it," Magnus explained. "I leave all of you with this advice, take care of each other," Magnus said passionately. "I want nothing more than to go with you to save Gabriel and Vahn. We'll be wishing for your safe return. But know this…no one is coming for you. Your success or failure is up to all of you, the brothers at your side will be the only ones who can protect you. If you can't make it back, you will be resigned to the same fate," Magnus looked as his brothers and with a heavy heart left the room. There were fourteen of them, Virgil and the rest of them shared a look then sprang into action.

"We'll get the cars ready," Tarek told Virgil. "The moment you make it outside, we book it to the Tobico Marsh on the other side of campus."

"I'll come too," Boyd offered Virgil.

"I can handle it Boyd," Virgil said irritated, "I don't need a babysitter."

"Everyone knows that," Boyd barked grabbing Virgil's arm. "Listen I care about your sassy ass. I'm not going to let anything happen to you, alright! You may need a look out, or even a dumbass to blame if you get caught, I won't let you get in trouble for this, so I'm coming," Boyd said ending the argument.

"Thanks Boyd," Virgil said his expression softening, Boyd only wanted to protect him. The group left the room. Virgil and Boyd went to the stairs and hurried to the top floor. It was where the Chapter Advisors had offices and bedrooms. There were a few guest rooms for important visitors as well. They passed a few brothers along the way trying to not look suspicious. Not everyone was for this plan, and they needed to get in and out quickly.

No one was on the top floor. Virgil walked down a hall finding a nameplate signifying it was Master Ramuh's. He slid the key in the door and turned it, a wave of light ran down the door, like a spell had just been activated. Boyd motioned for Virgil to hurry, they pushed open the door and hurried inside, closing it behind them. The room was small yet over flowing with interesting trinkets and oddities. The Teardrop sat on Professor Ramuh's book shelf resting on a small marble pedestal. Virgil placed Professor Ramuh's key on his desk and reached out for the Teardrop with his right hand, it slipped into his palm with ease. He felt the overwhelming power stored inside. He gently put it in his pocket, and they opened the door running right into a tall man.

"Excuse us," Boyd stammered. Professor Ramuh nodded stepping aside for them to go.

"Thank you Master Ramuh," Virgil said slipping past him.

"For what?" he asked curious, quickly closing his office behind him.

Virgil and Boyd booked it down the stairs. They ran into Rasler and a few of his men on the third-floor staircase.

"Hello boys," Rasler called to them.

"Hello sir!" Boyd called out in a goofy and suspicious tone; Virgil wanted to smack him.

"Grand Pylortes," Virgil bowed his head as he spoke. They walked past each other, the Alpha Paladins looking at them suspiciously. Rasler kept walking forward not paying them any more attention. We must get out of here! Virgil thought frantically, sweat beginning to slick his skin. Once they had made it down to the second floor and they were completely out of sight, they burst into a full-on sprint, they burst through the front doors not looking to see who was around. Three cars waited by the circular driveway, engines running. Virgil and Boyd piled into Dante's car, Birdy riding shotgun, Nolan in the backseat. They whipped down the road, speeding to the other side of the forest and campus. Virgil looked out his window wondering if he'd see Rasler and his men flying overhead on powerful white wings, looking to stop them.

They flew into the parking area near the trail that led back to the observation towers, and the ruined tree graph. Two figures were standing at the benches not far from a map of the area. Everyone quickly got out and approached them cautiously.

"What took you bastards so long?" Blair asked them.

"We had to smuggle something out," Dante barked gruffly, but he seemed relieved to see her.

"TK," Tarek said to the other woman. She ran up to him and they embraced in a fierce hug.

"I'm so worried about him," TK said trying hard not to cry. "The sisters voted that no one was allowed to go under threat of being blacklisted from the Paladins and the sisterhood," she told them.

"That's ridiculous!" Louie shouted.

Blair laughed, "You're telling me, I'm not about to let my best friends go risk their lives and not help. I wasn't given my Devil Arms so I could sit around and be told when it was okay to save people," she said fiercely.

"It's going to be dangerous. We're headed into Ever After, we can't guarantee your safety, or that you will ever return," Tarek warned them.

TK stepped back standing at her full height. She was toned with a small frame. Her golden-brown Devil Arms glowed on her right hand, as she stared furiously into the forest ahead. "No one tells me when I can, or cannot protect the ones I love," TK said with strength and conviction. Virgil felt moved by her charisma, as did many of the brothers. "Besides I should be the one cautioning all of you not to join me, but I thank you for coming to Gabe's rescue. I can't do this alone," she admitted with a defeated look on her face.

"He's our Hegemon!" Darius said like that explained everything. "We don't need a reason to look out for him."

"Let's move out!" Tarek called the order and the group began to run. Their footsteps and heavy breathing were all Virgil could hear after a few minutes. He worried they made too much noise, or that Rasler would come landing in front of them at any moment. They finally reached the second wooden observation tower, and veered right off the path into the woods, without any pursuers. The remains of the once great and beautiful art of nature lay in ruins, the tree had been spilt right down the middle. They approached the tree and Virgil could see a portal in the middle, a gate way to a destination unknown.

Tarek spoke as they approached, "We need to stay close, and work as one."

"This isn't our first rodeo cowboy," Dante jested with sass.

"Right, this is your second rodeo, because the mission earlier tonight was your first," Tarek said with a large shit eating grin on his face.

"Exactly," Dante nodded. "We're more badass now than we were then."

"That was just a few hour ago," Louie added nervously.

"Guys, focus!" Virgil silenced them. "Let's go," he said walking up to the portal.

"I'm going first Virgil," Tarek suggested moving ahead of him.

"Right behind you," Dante called out.

They ran through the portal, their friends hot on their heels. In an instant they were stepping into the Ever After, the ethereal realm inhabited by the demons. Emptiness hung all around them. They were in a massive forest with tall black trees with white leaves, reminiscent of the redwoods in stature. The environment looked like a negative photo, blacks and whites, there was little color to this world. Just beyond the scope of their vision...death permeated the air, and with every cloying breath...the rancid odor of sulfur. There were demons here, lots of them. The power of the Dreamstone magicite on their rings, kept the brothers and ladies cloaked, their auras hidden from the demons. Without them they could not hope to survive in this world.

Tarek led the group through the forest, Dante and Brody flanking him on either side, following closely. Blair and TK were just behind them with Birdy and Zender on either side, protecting the ladies. No one used their Devil Arms, doing so would be like lighting off a flare gun in this dark world. Ebony thunder clouds coated the sky, the dying sun moving across its sluggish path. The group moved swiftly through the forest, tripping over the trees' massive gnarled roots the size of cars, their destination driving them forward. A black tower loomed over the forest, higher than the redwood like trees, disappearing into the black storm clouds above, its true height indiscernible. Virgil hung at the back with Louie, Landon, and Nolan. They were the long-range hitters, and spell casters. Virgil didn't feel like he fit in any one category. He looked at the group, now sixteen strong, all of Omicron was present. They loved their Hegemon, and even though they were inexperienced, Omicron was willing to risk their lives to get him back. Virgil said a silent prayer asking for their success and safety.

The approach to the base of the tower was almost complete after what felt like an hour. The entire tower was visible now, and the closer they got, the harder their resolve became. They moved quickly, leaping over holes, stepping through the roots. They hadn't seen any demons yet, though they could hear them, scuttling in the trees above. There were things off in the distance as well, with footsteps so loud and powerful it made the ground shake. The base of the tower came into focus, a large entrance with double doors that were four stories high.

Louie was starting to shake with fear, "You think it's that big so large demons can get in and out more easily?" Louie asked the group nervously.

"Can someone back there please hit Louie for me?" Dante asked. The cover of the dense thickness of the trees gave way as they came to the base of the tower.

They cautiously approached the large courtyard that surrounded the doors, about a football field in length left for them. They caught their breath, not sensing anything nearby. The courtyard was the remains of an ancient temple, the remnants of visionary artistic splendor could be seen around them. The whole courtyard may have been roofed in at one point, a lavish place of worship, now a desecrated and forgotten place. They moved through the broken area approaching the tower. Virgil noticed on some of the columns left standing there were statues, some were of gods or goddesses, and some had wings like angels. There were others that looked like savage creatures, gargoyles were the closet explanation that Virgil's mind could make up of their appearance. They came to a long straight walk way that had tall pillars lining the path leading to the doors of the tower. The same grotesque and fearsome stone carvings rested upon the tops of the columns.

"Damn those things are uuuugly," Louie echoed Virgil's thoughts out loud.

"Guys am I seeing things or is that one staring me down?" TK asked the group, the statue in question had its body and face turned in such a way, they were focused directly on her.

"We reach the door and get inside," Tarek commanded, and the group picked up its pace turning into a full on sprint. There was a fierce cry in the air, and the carvings took flight, leathery wings coming off their backs, they launched themselves forward following the passing meal.

"Gargoyle demons!" Landon shouted as several dive bombed the group. Everyone shouted out their Devil Arms, their soul weapons materializing into their hands. The group kept its pace, a gargoyle plummeted down to pounce on TK. She gracefully leapt into the air, spinning with a long and slender lance in hand. TK fiercely slashed the gargoyle across its chest, knocking it from the air. It fell to the ground and started to move again. These demons weren't bursting into ash so easily. Blair lashed at a few of the gargoyles who got close, her sword breaking into a fiery whip, cutting up the gargoyles sending them reeling. They were getting closer to the door, and the creatures were growing in number, their cries filling the air. Suddenly fearsome roars came from within the forest, whatever it was sounded bigger, more powerful. A chorus of violent bellows resounded in response, the ground beginning to shake beneath their feet as whatever it was headed their way. They needed to get inside…

Dozens of the winged stone demons began to fly in a funnel focusing on blocking access to the doors. The gargoyles had stopped dive bombing them, instead focusing on keeping the group from their destination. The trees not far from the tower were shaking violently, the footsteps of some very big creatures echoed like grenades.

Tarek at the head of the group raised his ice lance at the storm of wings and flesh, the aquamarine symbol on his hand coming to life with energy. "Blizzaga!" Tarek commanded. Pale blue light flowed from the Devil Arms symbol, becoming ice crystals that shot forward like missiles. The crystals expanded combining into a massive jagged block of ice. Once it had reached to the size of a school bus, it shattered in every direction faster than bullets. Tarek's Master spell punched a large hole through the gargoyles knocking them all out of the sky, destroying some outright.

"Wow!" Virgil and a few others exclaimed. It was one of the most powerful spells Virgil had ever seen. It took a visible toll on Tarek, he looked like he needed to sit down though his ice lance was still held firmly in his hand. They reached the doors! Landon and Nolan whipped out zaps of electricity from their staffs, to keep the beasts repelled as everyone pushed against the massive door, struggling to make it open. Louie began shooting at the demons as there were too many for Landon and Nolan alone. The door was far too large for beings as small as mortals. They pushed with all their strength, the weight of it taking the entire party before it slowly began moving back. It took far too long for them to get it open, the ground shaking more violently beneath their feet. Everyone hurried in then they began the exhausting task of closing it shut. The ominous thunderous footsteps had reached the edge of the trees. Humanoid giants ranging from thirty to fifty feet in height came out from the trees stalking the tower, their eyes focused on the door. Their faces were ravenous with hunger, eyes showing no sign of awareness. These were not beings that could be communicated with, they were apex predators on the hunt.

"Get these doors closed now!" Dante shouted to the group. Virgil pushed against it with all his strength, muscles tense, and feeling sick to his stomach with the macabre scene that was unfolding outside. If they didn't get the door closed, they'd be eaten within the minute! The giants were in the courtyard now. They could travel great distances at alarming pace due to their enormous stature. The giants at the head of the pack were picking up pace, their teeth and humanlike tongues exposed. Their hands were outstretched, reaching for Virgil and the others. The gargoyles had fled. All sixteen of them pushed against the door giving it all they had, it was almost closed, and they could hear the stomach twisting moans and slurps the beings made gazing down at them. The giants were almost to the door.

"Push!" Tarek screamed to the others, panic setting into the group as everyone strained their muscles with all their might, their very lives at stake.

The door clicked shut, and went up in flames, the double doors completely engulfed in fire. The group stepped back, then the fire vanished, and the doors disappeared altogether.

"What's going on?" Louie asked fear thick in his voice, sweat heavy upon his brow. They looked around, they were still in the tower entrance, but the large doors could no longer be seen. The tower shook slightly, they could feel the giants slamming into the building where the doors were located, pounding on it with their fists. If not for whatever magic had sealed the door, the giants would have burst into the entrance.

"They're still out there," Birdy said nervously. His face etched in fear, covered in sweat, those grotesque abominations had frightened everyone.

"Well luckily we are not," Zender quipped.

"What are those things?" Blair asked the group, her voice shaking still out of breath.

"Probably Nephilim," Nolan suggested.

"They don't look anything like us!" Dante retorted.

"The first Nephilim were cursed by the Creator, punishment for the mingling of mortals and Judges. They were a race of giants, who could not blend in the human world. They must have been brought to the Ever After long ago," Nolan speculated.

"No use thinking about it now," Dante said, turning around and walking into the tower entrance. "This place is huge!" Dante whistled looking around.

The main hall was as wide as the tower, made of black stone, flames hung from the walls in lanterns, the flames had no source and burned the same height continuously. A spiraling staircase was near the entrance, with both sides of the room having stairs going up, stretching along the sides of the building for a quarter of the way up, the rest of the tower was obscured in shadows. Various doors were scattered about leading to destinations unknown. There was a platform at the back of the room, reminiscent of a throne area, it was at the top of a grand stair case, separate from the ones near the entrance that climbed up the tower.

"Where do we go?" Louie asked craning his head back to stare high up, trying to take it all in.

"Before we go climbing anywhere, let's secure this hall first," Nolan suggested. The group agreed and the sixteen of them cautiously walked forward, they stayed close keeping their formation tight, but kept enough space to efficiently wield their weapons. No one had turned off their Devil Arms, everyone was still shaken up from the monstrous giants that had almost devoured them. As they came to the center of the hall, and closer to the large staircase with the mock thrones at the top, a booming voice rang out.

"You've come to my tower," the Arch Demon's deep demonic voice echoed through the hall. "I sense the presence of the Teardrop. Your friends will thank you for their lives. Approach the throne, it will bring you to the apex of the tower, and the seat of my domain," the Arch Demon instructed. The throne seemed to light up slightly, the platform glowed with a faint light.

"Should we get on?" Birdy asked.

"Doesn't sound like we have much of a choice," Brody said approaching the platform.

"And I don't want to go poking around this dude's house, who knows what the hell we would find in those spare rooms," Dante suggested. Louie turned to him with a look of pure horror his over active imagination running wild.

The group climbed up the stairs and stepped onto the large platform. Once everyone had arrived it ascended like an elevator, which rose without cables through the air. The shaft the platform used to ascend was far larger than what they stood on. Likely big enough for things to fly up, like the Arch Demon. It moved quickly and it still took several minutes to reach the top. Everyone grew tense, knuckles turning white from tightening their grips on their weapons, they were about to come face to face with the thing that had taken their friends hostage. They had everything to lose, and just as much to gain. No price could be put on a life.

The throne transporter came to a stop at the top of the tower. Two small single doors were at the east and west sides of the small room the elevator stopped at. To the north and straight ahead, were doors like the ones that had stood on the front of the tower, just scaled down to fit the room. Virgil and his friends stepped off the platform and approached the doors. Virgil shared looks with his best friends, Boyd his first friend at college, Dante and Birdy, Louie and Blair. Virgil looked at everyone in their group, Darius, Nolan, Troy, Hector, Brody, Zender, Landon, Doc, Tarek and TK. Tension was high with everyone on edge, looking around, Virgil knew their resolve had not faltered. There was nothing left for them save to let fate unfold.

The doors opened with ease, Virgil and the others walked into a long hall that was reminiscent of a church with a tall ceiling. Columns rose up periodically next to the center aisle that led down the middle. There were no benches, just a large throne at the very end. Black smoke rolled across the surface of the stone floor, a dark unnatural fog. Abdanon was at the back, Gabriel and Vahn weren't far into the room, they stood staring towards the Arch Demon, their eyes and mouths open. Their expressions marred in horror, whatever nightmares they'd experienced, were still plaguing their minds. Black chains made of smoke rose from the floor encircling their bodies, they did not move.

"Gabriel!" TK screamed and ran to him, fiercely wrapping her arms around him, shaking as tears flowed uncontrollably from her eyes.

"TK be careful!" Tarek yelled.

"It's me baby, can you hear me!" TK called to him. She had touched the chains but remained unaffected.

"Your words cannot reach their enraptured minds. They can only hear and see what I want now," the Arch Demon said, its demonic voice unsettling.

"We brought the Teardrop, now let our friends go!" Dante demanded.

"You can have the mortals, they are of no importance to me," the Arch Demon said waving Dante off lazily with a massive claw. "Give me the Teardrop, and you may take your friends."

Virgil still held the Teardrop in his pocket. He got it out with his right hand, his scythe held firmly in his left. He walked forward pulling away from the group, Boyd watched him with a concerned look. Virgil walked to the middle of the room. The Teardrop floated up from Virgil's hand zooming to the Arch Demon's outstretched claw. It landed in middle of it, looking so small in its large palm. The demon curled his hand together crushing the jewel, gasps rang out from Virgil's friends. Power escaped from the remnants of the crushed magicite. The tower shook slightly, things felt strange, like something big had just happened.

"Now that the Greater Weirding is destroyed, the hunt to free the imprisoned pieces of Diablos' soul can begin," the Arch Demon said triumphantly.

"Let's get out of here!" Darius yelled edging closer to the exit. Virgil walked backwards not wanting to take his eyes off the towering monster that stood before him, and eager to be closer to his friends.

"Going so soon?" the Arch Demon asked playfully.

"You got what you wanted, now let us go!" Tarek demanded.

"A God does not bow to the insects," Abdanon said cruelly.

"You aren't going to let us go," Virgil said understanding the demon's intent.

"No," Abdanon purred.

"You bastard!" Dante yelled. "We upheld our end of the bargain!"

"How foolish," Abdanon admonished them. "There was never a bargain, you should have negotiated if you sought to receive anything from this exchange. Endangering your world for two mortal lives, I hope it was worth it."

"Let's make a run for it!" Boyd shouted. Boyd and Darius began to run for the door. Abdanon raised his claws, black energy shot from them like a cannon blast, rocketing across the room, blasting into Boyd and Darius like bombs. Their bodies were flung into the wall, a sickening crack of bones echoed out. They fell to the floor in crumbled heaps.

"BOYD!" Virgil screamed, running towards his friend. Black chains rose from the fog at everyone's feet, rooting them where they stood. The group tried desperately to break the chains, the more they struggled the faster they wrapped around their flesh. Virgil was stuck mid stride, the chains holding him still. His scythe disappeared from his hand, the chains breaking his connection with his Devil Arms. He tried to yell, to move, but nothing happened. The world faded replaced by endless water...

391

The water was vast, stretching in every direction possible. It was cold, sending icy shivers through Virgil's warm-blooded flesh. Virgil was no longer in chains. He looked up to see faint sunlight at the top, was this…the ocean? Virgil hated being in large open water, for fear of things that lurked in the deep. He had a hard-enough time swimming in the Great Lakes of Michigan, his fear was more of a borderline phobia. He felt a presence behind him, he turned but didn't see anything. He looked down and noticed a shadow below, a shadow drifted overhead when he wasn't looking. He looked up and the body of a Great White Shark swam close by. There were suddenly more in the water, circling him, Virgil looked and counted at least six in all. What the hell was this! Virgil should have drowned, he was underwater but not breathing, something wasn't right…

The closest shark swam close by, its slippery skin making contact sending goosebumps along his flesh in response. Virgil wanted to scream, heart hammered in his chest wildly, ready to break free from his rib cage. He felt like crying, he begged for this to be over, for his heart to give out and his life to be over, he didn't want to have to live through the next few minutes. The sharks were drawing in, getting more aggressive, they would be ripping him apart soon. He still hadn't drowned, why was that? Virgil's mind felt fuzzy, it was hard to think, probably because his lungs were lacking air. Or were they? How had he gotten in the ocean? Virgil concentrated hard on that thought, feeling it was important.

Reality used a combination of bottom up and top down processing. The human brain translates information from both at the same time, to give people what they see or experience. Our senses give us signals of our surroundings giving us a partial picture, and our minds filled in the blanks with what we remembered to be true of the environment to give us a complete picture. Dreams on the other hand only used top down processing, giving us images and visions, but lacking the sensory information of the five senses. That's why in a dream, if you concentrate on the step by step physical process of how you brought yourself to a location, you won't be able to remember, because it hadn't happened. Virgil couldn't remember flying or driving to the ocean. He knew he hadn't, no way in hell would he EVER get into the ocean of his own free will. That meant, this wasn't real. A shark barreled towards him, its mouth open, teeth exposed. Virgil stretched out his hands, the black symbol of Soul Reaver blazing to life. YOU ARE NOT REAL! Virgil screamed in his mind, and commanded Soul Reaver to his side.

Virgil fell to the floor gasping for air, still feeling the water battering him about. He looked up and noticed he was still in the large hall, black fog atop the floor. His friends, all of them were wrapped in black chains, their eyes and mouths open in horror staring forward. Abdanon stood at the far end of the room, watching Virgil with a look of intense interest.

Abdanon asked him. "How did you break free from the Chains of Illusion?"

Virgil struggled to regain his composure, his body and mind still shaken up from the images of the sharks, his heart was racing, "Boyd!" Virgil yelled.

Chapter 24
Ragnorak!

Virgil couldn't believe he was gone, not Boyd, he was too stubborn to die. Virgil carefully turned Boyd's face to him. His eyes were open staring blankly forward. Tears blurred Virgil's vision, and he couldn't stop himself from weeping. Boyd did not deserve to die like this, robbed of life when he was just coming into his prime as a man. Boyd would never graduate college, or have a family, all the joys of life had been taken from him. Virgil closed Boyd's eyes and mouth. Virgil felt remorse for Darius, he'd just known Boyd much better. He'd been the first friend he'd made at college, and though he was annoying at times, Boyd had been fiercely loyal.

"Boyd," Virgil whispered, "Forgive me."

"Your cries fall upon deaf ears mortal, he is an empty shell now," the demonic tone of Abdanon slithered to Virgil across the large empty hall. Abdanon watched Virgil and his friends suffer with an expression of delight across his face. He towered over Virgil and his brothers, standing as tall as the tree that had imprisoned him. Abdanon's grotesque visage was that of a lanky and bony creature. His frame was thin, with long thick bones and putrid rotting flesh hanging in many places. Abdanon used illusions to make himself more intimidating, a cloak of tentacles, tusks, arms, and bones ever changing to terrorize his opponents. Rasler had cut off his right tusk, but since that time it had grown back. His eyes were slits with flaming red eyes. Virgil looked up from Boyd to stare down the demon who had slayed his friends.

"You are the one responsible for this! You've caused so much death and destruction. You don't deserve to live!" Virgil said with conviction.

"It matters not what you think. Your time in this world is at an end," Abdanon said coldly.

Virgil looked at his friends, all of them stood paralyzed not far from the entryway, wrapped in smoky chains which induced powerful hallucinations. All of them had looks of terror across their faces, Virgil ran over to his friends.

"Louie!" he shouted, "Wake up! Birdy! Snap out of it!" They stood transfixed, unmoving, staring blankly ahead, their mouths open, silently screaming.

"They cannot hear you. Their minds are being assaulted with visions of their darkest fears. They are slaves, to live, or die as I see fit," Abdanon said.

"Let us go," Virgil pleaded, turning to the powerful demon.

"No," Abdanon coldly replied, his red eyes narrowing down to slits. "You were a fool to come here. I have no intention of allowing such powerful blood to slip through my grasp. I will drink the life force from your auras and grow stronger."

"If you won't let us go, I will have to make you," Virgil said defiantly clenching his fists.

"You?" Abdanon asked, a faint glimmer of humor in his tone. "I was surprised you were able to break free from my Chains of Illusion," Abdanon remarked. "Your blood is different from other Nephilim. I will drink you last."

"You will not take another life!" Virgil said barring his teeth, eyes blazing with rage. Soul Reaver came into existence with a burning flash of fire, his left hand holding firmly onto its familiar shaft black flames crawling up his arm.

"You cannot defeat me with a weapon of Chaos," Abdanon mused. "I am a being of darkness, death, and fear. Darkness cannot undo darkness," his words reverberating inside Virgil's mind.

"I will cut you down!" Virgil screamed running forward.

Abdanon raised a bony putrid hand and dark energy, like lightning, shot from it at Virgil electrocuting him. Pain thrived along every nerve ending, stopping him in his tracks. His reward for defiance, was agony. The dark lightning stopped, and Virgil fell forward, his muscles spasming, steam rising off his burned body.

"That isn't enough to stop me," Virgil taunted him. Raising his head to stare up at the immense stature of the twisted demon. The demon's red eyes bore into Virgil's own, he refused to look away from their malice and hatred. Virgil met the demon's strong glare with his own.

"I don't fear you demon," Virgil spat.

This brought a genuine laugh from Abdanon, a deep and horrifying sound, it sickened Virgil to his stomach.

"You reek of fear," Abdanon slyly whispered, his words were the sound of snakes slithering at your feet. "I am the Arch Demon of Fear!" he shouted with pride. "You cannot fool me mortal. Fear is to me, as that scythe is to you. The sickly-sweet aroma wafts heavily from you. I know what truly frightens you, what fears make you shake and cry like a baby," his words choked Virgil's ears like poison.

Virgil taunted Abdanon. "If you're so powerful fight me, one on one!"

"No, no, no," Abdanon said, as if admonishing a child. "Pain does not motivate you. You do not fear it as most men do," Abdanon said thoughtfully. "It will not work to bring you down. Instead I will make you watch as I slowly torture your friends, one by one you will watch them shriek in agony as they die," Abdanon sweetly told him with excitement. "But I promise you this, Nephilim," Abdanon said, his voice growing darker, deeper. "I will make it slow. I want to watch as you plead and beg for their lives."

"NO!" Virgil screamed, leaping into action, adrenaline and rage pumping through his veins like a stimulant. Black smoky chains leapt from the dark fog on the floor rooting Virgil to the floor, not far ahead from the rest of his friends. The chains coiled around his body, grinding along his left arm, breaking his connection with Soul Reaver causing the scythe to disappear. He looked back at his brothers, tears trembled down Virgil's cheeks, imagining having to watch as the demon slowly tortured them to death.

"Yessss," Abdanon sighed like a serpent, "Now we are getting somewhere. So strange you are, you fear their deaths more than your own. You care that deeply for them?" he asked Virgil with a strange curiosity. "How peculiar, mortals never cease to amaze me with your stupidity."

"I'm supposed to protect them. Please don't," Virgil whispered, a tear falling from his face to the floor.

"Now I know your deepest fear. And I will break you," Abdanon's words were steel.

Abdanon stretched a hand out and black lightning shot from his long claw like hands, connecting with Dante, his screams echoed and reverberated across the enormous hall. His cries grew louder, overwhelming Virgil's senses.

"STOP!" Virgil screamed while his friend fried behind him.

"You will learn what true fear is by the time we are done, boy," Abdanon said over the sound of his power crackling and Dante's screams. Dante's voice was worse than any pain. There was nothing in the world more precious to Virgil then his friends. They were more than that now, they were his brothers, his family.

Virgil's vision swam, blinded by the flow of his own tears. To his right a light had caught his attention he looked hoping it was reinforcements, someone coming to help them. There would be no help, no one would come for them, just as Magnus had warned them as he wished the group success in their mission. Virgil hung his head in defeat, Dante's screams were deafening. Hopelessness began washing over him, cloaking him in its weighty veil of anguish. Dante wouldn't last much longer. Virgil wished for nothing more than the strength to defend and protect those he had grown to love.

The light shone again; this time brighter. Virgil looked and was aghast at what he saw. The symbol on his right hand radiated a pure, warm white light. The shooting star glowed against his skin, humming with life. Never had the Devil Arms on his right hand even once reacted this way. Virgil could feel its power, it was a mighty weapon, greater than Soul Reaver, perhaps the greatest weapon there ever was. Virgil was overwhelmed as a mix of different emotions flooded his mind, awe, respect, gratitude, but most of all…hope. Hope was the strongest emotion emanating from his Creation Devil Arms. Fresh tears came to his eyes, not out of fear or sadness, Virgil was humbled. He did not deserve this power, no man, demon, Judge, or creature otherwise deserved such a gift. Why it had been given to a nobody such as him? It was beyond Virgil's comprehension.

All this time Virgil had been trying to summon the white Devil Arms to use as a weapon, to fight, to overcome, and to destroy. Now it was clear to him, this weapon was not a tool of war. It was a shield of peace, to protect those who did not have the power to protect themselves. A symbol of hope to those who had none. A banner to rally all those who walked in the light of Creation, all the beings who lived life with virtue, humility, and empathy.

"Why me?" Virgil whispered to himself, not believing he should be trusted with such a responsibility. Virgil realized in that instant the true name of the Devil Arms. He was afraid to say it out loud. Virgil did not feel he had the right to its glory, nor the arrogance to call himself the master to its splendor.

Dante's screams reached a fevered pitch. "Not much longer left for this one," Abdanon teased Virgil deliciously, savoring the cruelty of his torture.

Virgil would not bear the weight of the Creation Devil Arms for himself, as he did not deserve its power. But for the sake of the Omegas, his friends, and brothers, he could not ignore the power to save them. Virgil raised his right hand up to the ceiling of the room, the white symbol shining as brightly as a star and embraced his destiny.

"RAGNORAK!" Virgil cried out into the dark of the room. A bolt of white lightning crashed through the ceiling, splitting it wide open. The bolt met Virgil's outstretched hand, forming into a blade, the light became metal. A sword of irrefutable beauty materialized into his right hand. The sword's handle gleamed with silver, the blade was long and sharp, and translucent like glass. The entire sword had a golden aura visibly surrounding it, it hummed quietly, brimming with power. It fit perfectly in Virgil's hand, it weighed next to nothing. The moment he gripped the sword, the same golden light that encircled the sword surrounded him. The light began to heal the wounds on his body.

Virgil tensed as his whole body felt like it was on fire. Virgil felt the pain spread to his back, he cried out as he felt two powerful limbs burst from his flesh. They worked themselves out, instinct taking over. In a flash of light and magic, his wings unfurled for the first time, and he looked upon them in awe as they spread out to either side of him. His left wing was adorned with ebony feathers, black as night. His right wing was clothed in pure white feathers. His wings reflected the same colors as his Devil Arms. He hadn't realized a Nephilim or Judge could have one of both.

A power came over him, his whole body brimming with energy, like molten lava, only this time it did not hurt. He felt more alive, and more powerful than he ever had in his life. He looked down at his own reflection, in the blade of his sword, noticing his eyes had changed. Instead of the usual sapphire blue, the whole of his eye socket radiated pure golden light. There were no eyes, just gold light, like a Judge's. Something had happened to Virgil, something he did not understand. This power was not from Ragnorak like the golden glow surrounding him, this was a power all his own. It felt like there was another person inside of him, standing with him, wanting control of his body. His unconscious mind, a part of his soul, the part of him that was Judge, not human. The part of him that was Judge, was a born warrior. Judges were the mightiest of the races, created to maintain order, enforce it, and protect it. With the glow of his eyes his aura was suddenly stronger extending out much further, and this part of him knew spells that the regular Virgil did not. The glow of his eyes also brought the strength and speed of a Judge to his body. He had entered a state unknown to him, Virgil had Ascended.

The screams had stopped. Abdanon was no longer electrocuting Dante, with dark lightning. "What are you?" Abdanon asked, genuine curiosity had crept into its voice. "You are the Sixth Seraphim Nephilim, the…Redeemer," Abdanon said whispering the title.

Virgil swung the sword in a circle cutting the chains that had clung to him with ease. He noticed that the burns that had marred his skin were completely gone, if he held Ragnorak, its light would slowly heal whatever physical wounds he suffered.

Virgil brought the sword to his middle holding it in front of him with both hands. "You will fall," Virgil commanded, his voice holding a tone of immortal regal authority that was not his own. Virgil beat his powerful wings once and they propelled him into the air. He flew towards Abdanon, the demon shot a ray of lightning at Virgil. Abdanon's movements seemed sluggish, Virgil's perception heightened to incredible speed in his Ascended state. Virgil easily dodged the magic that crackled past him, battle instinct taking over.

Virgil flew straight for the Arch Demon, his left claw lashed out at Virgil. Virgil veered to the right, his wings trailing dusts of magic. Virgil burst forward with a surge of speed, bringing Ragnorak down in an arc, slamming into Abdanon's outstretched wrist. The demon howled as the hand was cut from its arm, falling to the ground in a spray of black demon blood. Virgil swung Ragnorak again, cutting vertically this time, hacking at the forearm that had once been attached to his severed hand. Virgil's blade cut through Abdanon's flesh with ease, sending another chunk of demon to the floor. Abdanon stumbled back slightly, fear etched in his evil red eyes as he gazed upon the glowing Nephilim attacking him.

Abdanon let out a fierce roar, the force of it sent Virgil tumbling through the air. Virgil beat his wings, and he flew away from the demon to gain some distance. Virgil came to a stop hovering in the air glaring at the Arch Demon. He was the chosen bearer of the Holy Blade, Ragnorak, its might was now Virgil's to command.

"You are nothing!" Abdanon screamed at Virgil. "I will devour you whole and absorb your strength as my own!"

Virgil flew at Abdanon his wings stretched out the full length, sending him through the air with great speed. Abdanon leapt at Virgil, fangs bared, aiming to gore Virgil with his tusks. *Soul Reaver*, Virgil thought, the scythe was once more in his hand. Virgil spun in the air throwing his scythe at Abdanon. The scythe flew straight at Abdanon's face, the demon held its arms up, the scythe slashed across his one remaining hand taking a chunk off with it. Virgil felt Ragnorak pulse in his hand like a heartbeat, he listened to the sword's desire and slashed it in an arc at Abdanon, a wave of Creation energy swam out from its blade sounding like a sonic blast.

Throwing Abdanon down with its pure force and power, he screamed in anguish as the wave of light burned everything evil in its path. Abdnanon fell to the floor, the black fog dissipating and then altogether disappearing as the wave of light pierced the fog.

The chains that had been holding Virgil's friends broke, their source of power extinguished. The Omegas, Blair, and TK began to stir regaining consciousness.

"What happened!?" Tarek called out.

"Did we die yet?" Groaned Louie.

Virgil's scythe came flying back to him, he flew to his friends landing in front of them. "He's not finished yet," Virgil told his friends "Are you guys are okay?"

"WOW!" the fifteen of them responded in unison.

"What happened to your eyes!" Louie asked first.

"Your wings," TK said softly, taking in the wings of different colors upon his back.

"You finally figured out your other Devil Arms," Vahn said nodding to Virgil, with a look of pride.

"What's its name?" Nolan asked, looking severely shaken up. The Chains of Illusion having taken their toll on the group.

"Ragnorak," Virgil said causing the sword's gold light to flicker in response. "We need to get out of here," Virgil said to the group. "Let's hurry and make our escape now!" The group turned towards the large doors behind them. They went to move towards it, and it slammed shut.

"I'm not through with you maggots!" Abdanon called out, rising to his full stature. "I am Abdanon! Arch Demon of Fear, given life by the Queen Mother of the demons, Lilith! You will all die here! Your blood with stain this hall, and your power will fuel my own!" Abdanon screamed and howled. Virgil noticed that the demon's body had begun regenerating.

"Damn it! We've got to take this thing down!" Gabriel said, summoning the sword LionsHeart to his hand.

"He's too powerful for you guys," Virgil knew he spoke the truth. "Stay back and let me take care of him."

"Fat chance you idiot!" Blair yelled coming to stand by him. "I don't care what kind of Devil Arms you wield or how freaky your eyes look, you're my best friend Virgil!" Blair said, her voice filled with emotion. "I'll always fight by your side."

"I'm with her!" Vahn agreed. "You're my Lil, and I'll be damned if I let you run off to battle an Arch Demon on your own. I'm supposed to protect you, not the other way around," Vahn summoned his sword, Furybrand, to his hand and came to stand by Virgil. Vahn summoned his own wings, stretching out from his back in a burst of light.

"Sorry we didn't have your back earlier homes," Louie winked at him. "I'm with you man! I won't stop filling him with arrows until he falls over!"

"We fight him as a group!" Tarek shouted walking up to Virgil. His own wings bursting from his back, they were white like the rest of the brothers. Tarek summoned Stiria's Lance to his left hand, placing his right hand on Virgil's shoulder, he looked him in the eyes. "You don't have to do this alone," Tarek said to him. "You're an Omega, we protect our own." Virgil felt like he could cry, he nodded to Tarek. Tarek's eyes filled with tears, as he looked at Darius' fallen body, his Little Brother in the fraternity. "I will avenge Darius' death you monster!" Tarek spat at the demon his voice thick with emotion.

The rest of the brothers came up to surround Virgil, facing off against Abdanon, their resolve impenetrable. They stood as one, ready to fight to the death.

"Thanks for coming to save us everyone," Gabriel said, sharing a look of gratitude with Virgil. "We take this thing down and go home. No heroics people, watch your six, only take the safe shots, and guard the guys next to you," Gabriel commanded them, moving to the head of the group, his wings out and ready to propel him through battle.

"I will take point," Virgil advised Gabriel. Gabriel looked at Virgil with a look of surprise. Virgil had never told Gabriel what to do before, Gabriel was the senior brother, and had been his Hegemon.

"I'm the Hegemon, it is my responsibility to protect you," Gabriel said, leaving no room for argument.

"With all due respect Hegemon sir, I can't watch another person I care about die tonight. With this sword, I know I can take him. Please! Let me, protect you," Virgil pleaded.

Gabriel looked at Virgil, their eyes locked, a battle of wills. Gabriel looked away first, and moved to the side, Virgil walked forward, taking point.

"Brothers of Omega! We stand as one!" Gabriel shouted out. "The demon's power is great, but ours is greater! Together we can overcome anything that it throws our way! Virgil!" Gabriel called out to him. Virgil looked back, the thirteen brothers had their weapons drawn, the two ladies as well, everyone looked back at him. "We have your back brother."

"For Boyd, For Darius!" Virgil cried out as loud as he could muster. He ran forward, body moving at superhuman speed. His brothers charged forward behind him, those with wings taking to the air.

Abdanon opened his mouth and from his maw poured twenty soldier demons, the ones Virgil had fought at the casino. They ran across the hall to impede the advancement of his friends. Virgil ran forward using his scythe and sword, he whirled through the demons as they charged past him. He cut down three and continued to run at Adbanon. He trusted his friends to handle them. Abdanon charged forward. Virgil rolled out of the way, as Abdanon tried to stomp on him. Virgil slashed at his leg with his scythe as he dodged the demon. The winged brothers dived at Abdanon from above, working in unison they timed their attacks to protect each other. Abdanon swung his tusks and claws at the brothers, they used their powerful wings to dodge. Virgil swung Ragnorak at Abdanon's left leg. His blade cut deep, bringing the demon down to its knee.

Abdanon swiped at Brody as he flew by, Brody used his halberd to strike at the demon. Abdanon hit him hard, knocking him down to the floor. Brody didn't get back up. Tarek yelled, and a wave of ice shot from his hand slamming into Abdanon. Abdanon swiped at Tarek, his hand about to connect. An arrow of blue light sank deep into his hand, causing Abdanon to cry out, allowing Tarek to barely miss his grasp.

Virgil took to the air, Abdanon was handling them well for missing half an arm. Abdanon was driven near the wall of the tower, keeping his back close to the wall. Virgil dived hard, running along the stone wall he propelled himself off, kicking hard, flying straight at Abdanon's thin wings on his back. Virgil sent his scythe out before him, it spun in circles creating a deadly spinning attack, he slammed it into Abdanon dragging the scythe, with his mind, along the weak flesh of his wing. Abdanon cried out lunging fully into the wall, Virgil dived hard nearly crushed by the Arch Demon. Virgil flew forward and circled around coming to the Arch Demon's side. He used his scythe to block an incoming attack and swung Ragnorak at the right wing on the demon's back. Virgil's blade severed the wing from his body.

A black aura surrounded Abdanon, he brought his limbs in, the dark energy gathering closer to his body.

"Get back!" Virgil shouted racing to gain some distance. Abdanon threw out his arms and the black aura shot out around him like a shockwave, injuring everyone it touched flinging them back from its force. Virgil watched in fear as his winged brothers were knocked from the air. Virgil fell to the ground from the force of the blow. His body felt numb, but his grip remained firm on Ragnorak. He felt its power working on his body, slowly healing the wounds that he suffered. Virgil got to his feet. Abdanon charged for the vulnerable brothers who had also been knocked down. Virgil took to the air, pushing himself to fly as fast as his wings could carry him.

Abdanon lashed at Gabriel who was lying on the ground. Abdanon's claws raked across Gabriel's body, Gabriel cried out in pain. One of his wings was ripped apart, and he had long gashes across his chest.

"Gabriel!" Tarek cried out in fear, struggling to his feet to heal his friend.

Abdanon clawed at Tarek who was moving to Gabriel's aid. Virgil threw Soul Reaver, the scythe flying in an arc, knocking the demon's claws away from Tarek. Virgil caught up to the demon and flew in front of it, barring access to his brothers. His scythe came flying back to him.

Abdanon inhaled deeply, the force of it so powerful he was drawing Virgil forward in midair, his wings working hard to keep him from flying into the demon's mouth. Abdanon then exhaled a cloud of black smog gushing from his maw, blasting forward at the brothers. The smoke b,rought Virgil crashing down to the ground. The brothers all choked and coughed, unable to breath with the foul miasma filling the room.

"Virgil!" Tarek cried out. "You must stop him!"

Virgil raised his sword at Abdanon, a spell came to his lips, only available to him in his Ascended state, he shouted, "Light Surge!" Virgil felt an enormous amount of energy being sucked from his aura to fuel the spell, greater than anything he'd cast before. From the ceiling large beams of light poured into the room, crashing down on Abdanon, he was powerless to stop the barrage of energy. Abdanon's concentration was broken, the smog from his mouth ceased as Virgil's spell hailed the demon with powerful blasts of Creation.

A black fog once again coated the hall's floor. Virgil looked around taking in his brother's conditions. Brody was coming to, Tarek was treating Gabriel's wounds, it looked like no one else had perished. The soldier demons had been destroyed, his brothers were back in formation, ready to charge Abdanon and finish him once and for all.

"Is everyone alright?" Virgil asked. Virgil had never used a Master level spell before, he was amazed at how powerful it was. He couldn't use something like that often. Ragnorak wasn't restoring his aura, the blade only healed physical wounds.

His friends answered with some grunts and a few replies. "What kind of spell was that?" Nolan asked him. "I've never seen magic like that before, it looked like a Creation spell."

"I'm not sure, the words just came to me," Virgil said not sure how to explain his Ascended state.

Abdanon regained his composure. Black smoky chains rose up from the fog on the floor and began to wrap around everyone in the room.

"NO!" Virgil yelled out in frustration. This is what he did to them the first time! They didn't have a chance, all of them were swallowed in chains, trapping their bodies.

"Virgil!" Gabriel urgently shouted. Virgil locked eyes with his Hegemon. "Finish him!" Gabriel pleaded, his eyes filling with fear, then the illusions took him.

The chains wrapped around Virgil as well, they coiled around his legs, chest and arms, his right arm was trapped in a raised position, holding Ragnorak pointed straight at Abdanon. The chains tried to ensnare Virgil's sword, they disintegrated upon touching the Holy Blade.

"You thought you could defeat me?" Abdanon growled. "I'm an Arch Demon! One of the most powerful beings in the world! I will not fall to half-breeds," he spat at Virgil.

"You're an abomination!" Virgil shouted at Abdanon. "A twisted creature of hate and darkness, there is no place for you in our world!"

"This is not your world," Abdanon said coldly. "The world belonged to Ediolons, Judges, and Fairies long before the race of mortals. The race of man is a weak, greedy, corrupt blight upon the planet they so hungrily devour. Lilith will resurrect the Demon King, and we will take your world as our own!" Abdanon cried out in delight.

"Diablos will never rise again!" Virgil yelled at him.

"It has been foretold by your precious Creator, the War of Ragnorak will come, and Diablos shall rise. Your very existence is proof that Ragnorak is approaching. The Holy Blade has made its appearance, the wheels of fate are set in motion," Abdanon told Virgil. His red eyes narrowed down, his voice growing deep with hatred. "The world you know, is at an end."

"Never!" Virgil shouted growing impassioned. "I'll destroy thousands of demons before I let you take my world!"

"You can't even protect your friends," Abdanon mocked Virgil. "I have had enough of you, Redeemer. I do not care who your father is, you will die here and now!" Abdanon sent black lightning at Virgil, his body shaking uncontrollably. Virgil cried out in pain, he struggled to break from his chains. He knew if he could just use Ragnorak, he could free himself, and undo the fog once more.

Abdanon's power burned through Virgil, he felt like he was going to pass out. He knew if he did, his friends would die, there would be no second chance. Virgil had to be the one to break free. Virgil looked at his friends, his eyes coming to rest on Vahn, who was staring straight at

Virgil. Virgil couldn't stand the thought that they'd never get to be at the Omega house again, playing games and laughing over nonsense, enjoying one another's company. Virgil thought of this place being their final resting place, the end to all their lives. He felt his eyes start to get misty at the injustice of it, his friends needed him!

Virgil roared, loud and mighty, his will to survive and protect his friends giving him strength. In response Ragnorak let out a mighty howl, the blade screaming in the dark, drawing Virgil's startled attention. It startled Abdanon as well as he stopped his attack to stare at the sword. The glass like blade shook and thrummed with power, howling like it had a voice of its own. The sword's see through blade filled with golden light, until it was full, vibrating with power. The sword radiated with such brightness it lit up the hall. Virgil stared in wonder as Ragnorak had transformed before his eyes, its howls echoing his own. The chains that had held Virgil's right arm, evaporated into nothingness in the light of the sword.

Virgil swung Ragnorak around and aimed it at Abdanon. He screamed, "Howling Blade! Judgement Bolt!" Ragnorak howled in response unleashing its Soul Scream in a deafening blast, the light that had gathered in the sword discharged out like cannon fire. A beam of gold light rocketed at Abdanon like a giant lightning strike, going straight through him, blasting a large hole. The force of the Ragnorak's light exploded Abdanon in a rain of ash, blood, and bone.

The black fog that had filled the room lifted, and the chains disappeared. It was over. The brothers of Omega stirred. Virgil fell to his knees exhausted, sapped of the last of his energy. He thanked Ragnorak for its protection, and the blade faded in a glimmer of gold, the white symbol on his right hand settling back to normal. Virgil felt his eyes lose their golden light, the superhuman strength and speed also fading from his body. The part of his unconscious mind that was Judge, faded back into sleep, and Virgil was once more himself.

"Virgil!" Louie cried out running over to him, picking him up off his feet in a big bear hug. "Thank the Creator you joined Omicron!" Louie laughed with glee. The brothers gathered around, glad to be free of Abdanon and still alive, they started hugging each other, shaking hands, and patting each other on the back.

"Virgil!" Blair said, running over to Virgil and squeezing him tight.

"Thank you!" TK said, coming up to hug Virgil next. "Thank you for saving us," she whispered in his ear, tears running down her face.

"That was amazing Virgil," Gabriel was brimming with pride. "I've never seen anything like that. Your sword, it…howled."

"A Soul Scream most likely," Nolan said with his usual all-knowing tone, hands held together is front of him.

"A what?" Dante asked.

"Soul Screams were the ultimate attacks of Devil Arms, a power sealed away after the Battle of the Fallen," Nolan said. "When the wielder's spirit was in harmony with their soul weapons, they could unleash their inner powers, letting out a powerful attack some said sounded like the weapon was screaming, called a Soul Scream," Nolan told them.

"Where the hell do you get all this information?" Dante asked Nolan, shaking his head at him.

"The library at the Omega house, it is full of really interesting books," Nolan told him.

"Alright, that's enough people," Gabriel cut in, "We need to get out of here!"

The tower began to shake throwing all of them off balance, the ceiling started to crumble falling down all around them.

"Without Abdanon this place is going to fall apart!" Virgil shouted.

"Let's go!" Tarek commanded. Virgil ran over to Boyd's body picking him up.

"What are you doing?" Louie asked him.

"I'm not leaving him here!" Virgil yelled. "He deserves a proper burial."

"I can get him," Brody offered, Virgil was tired and let his brother do it. Tarek picked up his Little Brother, Darius.

The group ran out the large double doors that ran the length of room to the device that had brought them to this floor. They stepped onto the teleporter, and nothing happened.

"Why isn't it working?" Vahn yelled in frustration.

"Abdanon was the master of this tower," Nolan told them. "This is just speculation but without him the tower no longer has its power source."

"We could fly down," Brody offered.

"We don't all have wings," Dante said crossing his arms and rolling his eyes.

"We could carry everyone down," Gabriel suggested.

A large chunk of ceiling fell from above, it crashed in front of them breaking the teleporter, sealing off their escape down through the bottom.

"Now what are we going to do!" Louie yelled out in fear.

"We'll think of something," Vahn assured him.

The tower began to shake more violently, bits of the tower falling around them. "We don't have time for that!" Louie said getting hysterical. "We're going to die in this place!"

Just then a vortex opened behind them, a spinning cloud of black and dark blue light. The Gatekeeper, the Fifth Seraph, stepped out from the portal. The Gatekeeper was dressed as it had been that night, in dark blue battle armor with a helmet covering its face, black wings adorned on its back. The Gatekeeper was the second in command of the Death Dealers, the First Lieutenant, and sworn enemy of the Paladins.

"Redeemer," the Gatekeeper said to Virgil.

"Me?" Virgil asked, not used to being referred to by such a strange title.

Gabriel, Vahn and Tarek came to stand in front of Virgil, Virgil looked at his friends humbled by the fierce protective looks on their faces.

"What do you want?" Gabriel asked the warrior.

"I came to give the Redeemer safe passage from this place," the Gatekeeper said simply.

"How?" Louie cried out, practically leaping into the Gatekeeper's arms, tears and panic in his eyes.

"I am the Gatekeeper. I can create portals to any destination I desire," the Gatekeeper said simply.

"Why help Virgil?" Vahn asked suspiciously.

"Virgil's father asked that I make sure he be returned to safety. The God Generals have plans for the Redeemer," the Gatekeeper said. The Gatekeeper threw its hand out and a portal emerged in the air spiraling in a vortex of black and dark blue energy. "This will take you to the edge of campus. Hurry, the tower will be destroyed in moments," the Gatekeeper told them.

"Is it safe?" Vahn turned to Virgil asking him.

"We don't have a choice!" Virgil said to the group. Brody went first, running into the portal, he disappeared the moment his body touched the vortex. The rest of Virgil's friends began to quickly follow suit.

"You said my father asked you to save me, who is he?" Virgil asked the Gatekeeper his heart pounding. This was the question that had been on his mind since the beginning of all this.

The Gatekeeper stood silent, staring at Virgil not responding. Virgil couldn't see any features of the Gatekeeper through the armor and helmet. It wasn't possible to tell if it was even a man or a woman, the armor made its voice sound off.

"Virgil, let's go!" Gabriel demanded. Gabriel and Vahn were the only ones left who had not gone through.

"Wait! My father, who is he!" Virgil demanded.

The tower shook violently. "We don't have time!" Vahn told Virgil.

"I have to know!" Virgil yelled. Gabriel and Vahn grabbed Virgil. "Stop!" They pulled him into the portal.

Chapter 25
<u>Redeemer</u>

Virgil appeared at the gates of the Omega house with Gabriel and Vahn landing next to him. The rest of the brothers who had gone through the portal were there. The sky was turning red in the east. Virgil and the others could hear shouting coming closer. Rasler came out of the Omega manor followed closely by Magnus and Jagger. The group opened the gates walking to meet them. Rasler was telling Magnus and Jagger that their Chapter was getting shut down.

"The Greater Wierding protecting our world from the Ever After was destroyed!" Rasler shouted. "The Battle of Ragnorak is inevitable now! YOU!" Rasler shouted at the brothers who had just gotten back from Abdanon's tower. "You fools stole the Goddess' Teardrop! Your Prytanis and Pylortes swear that you did this without the consent of the Chapter. Consider yourselves all Black Listed from the fraternity! You'll be lucky your Chapter doesn't get shut down!"

"Our friends' lives were in danger," Tarek pleaded, "We didn't have a choice."

Rasler noticed Darius' dead body in his arms and Boyd's in Brody's. "You went to save two lives and you ended up losing two in the process. What good did that do?"

Gabriel walked up to Rasler grabbing him by his shirt and picking him up off the ground. "Don't you dare make light of their deaths!" Gabriel yelled at Rasler.

"Put me down, Gabriel," Rasler said in a commanding tone. Gabriel lowered Rasler to the ground taking his hands off the Doppelganger.

"As for you," Rasler said, turning back to Tarek. "I would have expected better from someone with a family name such as yours. Your mother will be hearing how her only son was responsible for bringing about the War of Ragnorak."

"Rasler enough!" Virgil snapped his thoughts racing, overwhelmed by what had just happened. He didn't have it in him to be yelled at by a stuffy politician after the trauma they had endured.

"Excuse me?" Rasler asked incredulously, rounding on Virgil. "That's Grand Pylortes, or Lord Rasler to you," Rasler barked. Virgil stepped forward and Rasler let out a gasp. Virgil's wings were still present, he hadn't yet retracted them back inside.

"You? Those wings," Rasler muttered, shock written across his face. "You're the Redeemer!" Rasler shouted out to Virgil. "That must be…Ragnorak!" Rasler exclaimed, looking at Virgil's white Devil Arms symbol. "You dare to use the Holy Blade as your own!?" he asked, as if it was the most sacrilege thing he'd ever heard.

"Virgil saved us," Gabriel said coming to Virgil's defense. "If it wasn't for him and that sword, none of us would be alive. That Devil Arms is HIS. It CHOSE him. He has just as much right to use it as you do Quicksilver!" Gabriel said angrily.

"The Redeemer is the bringer of destruction!" Rasler said rounding on Gabriel. "He's probably in league with the Death Dealers!" Rasler shouted. "As the Grand Pylortes of the Paladins, I hereby take you into custody," Ralser rounded on Virgil. "You will come to the Capital, where you will be put in holding. Until you can be thoroughly questioned to ascertain where your loyalties lie." Rasler made a grab for Virgil. Vahn stepped in his way.

In a challenging tone, Vahn said to Rasler, "You aren't taking Virgil anywhere."

"Virgil is coming to the Capital with me!" Rasler shouted his Devil Arms glowing, most of the Omegas took a step back. Virgil had seen Rasler wield the mighty Devil Arms against Abdanon, changing its form to that of other powerful weapons.

"He is not!" a powerful voice rang out. Professor Ramuh came down from the house walking up to the brothers.

"Ramuh," Rasler said in a less than friendly tone.

"Rasler," Professor Ramuh nodded with a friendly smile.

Professor Ramuh came to stand next to Magnus. He looked at the dead bodies of Boyd and Darius, who had been laid on the ground next to one another. Then his eyes stopped on Virgil, taking in his wings of black and white.

"Virgil will not be hauled into Alexandros, his presence announced to our world, as if he is some criminal. Virgil has already joined the ranks of the Omegas, and therefore the Paladins. There is no reason he should come under suspicion for wrong doing, just for being the Sixth Seraph," Professor Ramuh said calmly to Rasler.

"How come I was not told Virgil is one of the Seven Seraphs?" Rasler asked. "How are we to know where his true loyalties lie?"

Dante rolled his eyes, holding his arms against his chest to hide his clenching fists. "Virgil destroyed Abdanon," Dante said with sass. "If Virgil was a Death Dealer, he wouldn't have taken down such a powerful part of their army."

"That boy took down the Arch Demon? Impossible," Rasler said in disbelieve.

"Saw it with my own two eyes," Louie said wide eyed and dead serious.

"It should be clear from your interaction with him and the look upon their faces, no one knew the boy's identity. As for loyalty, that is proven with time, and trust must be given first in good faith, and continued to be earned over time," Professor Ramuh said with firm conviction. "Not many of our ranks have ever been able to make such a grand claim. Gabriel's already told you he saved the men here. Be thankful we have him on our side, Doppelganger," Professor Ramuh suggested.

"What of the Goddess' Teardrop?" Rasler said, almost stomping his foot like a child. "Someone must be held accountable for endangering the world, with the destruction of the Greater Wierding!" Rasler argued.

"What kind of punishment would please you?" Professor Ramuh asked Rasler thoughtfully.

"The person accountable for stealing the Teardrop should be immediately Black Listed from the Paladins," Rasler said harshly.

"That would be understandable, considering the offense of stealing the Teardrop, resulted in its destruction," Professor Ramuh nodded in agreeance.

"Exactly, we cannot have someone untrustworthy in our order," Rasler argued, happy Profesor Ramuh was seeing things his way.

"However," Professor Ramuh said thoughtfully, as if it was just coming to him, "By doing that, we would be excommunicating a Nephilim, from Paladin society. It would only be logical for that man, to seek out the Death Dealers, if they desired to be around people of their own kind."

"What are you saying?" Rasler said with a sneer.

"By outing a possible friend, we are most likely creating a future foe. Better to keep the devious close, in plain view, then in the shadows in our adversaries' ears," Professor Ramuh suggested, staring deeply into Rasler's eyes. Rasler was quiet for a moment. "I suppose," he said calming down.

"I willingly volunteer to inform the Grand Prytanis Aseril, immediately," Professor Ramuh offered warmly. "These boys need rest, not interrogations. We can inform his eminence together. He is the Second Seraph after all, capable of seeing visions of the future. If Virgil is a threat, he will know better than anyone," Professor Ramuh nodded with confidence. "Best appeal to the wisdom of those wiser," Professor Ramuh said, turning to go back to the Omega manor. Rasler reluctantly followed him back to the house.

Virgil willed his wings back in and they retracted, painfully, with a burst of light, his wings were sheathed in his flesh once more. Two of their own were dead. They had been so confident when they left, assured that whatever came their way, as a group, they would prevail. Against the might of one of the strongest demons in existence, they had been hopelessly out classed. Virgil looked at the faces of his friends around him seeing horror reflected in their eyes. Virgil had heard from some of the brothers that seeing battle could inflict PTSD. Virgil saw that the brothers were suffering and wondered what it would take for things to get back to normal. Perhaps they never would, perhaps suffering was normal, and Virgil had just been childish, living in a daydream.

"I'll arrange the funerals," Tarek said breaking the silence. "Someone's got to get things rolling."

"I'll help out too," Louie said speaking up. "Working on food, or money, we have to contact their families as well."

"Everyone needs some time to themselves right now," Magnus told his men. "I apologize I could not come with you. I did not enjoy being left behind with Rasler, wondering if you'd come back at all." The men listened to their Prytanis, looking to their leader for guidance. "I am proud of the men I see before me. It is an honor to call you my brothers, and it is damn good to have you back," Magnus said, tearing up slightly. It was widely known that Magnus did not cry, ever. He admitted to crying zero times in his life. Magnus left the men going inside the house before anyone had a chance to call him out on it.

"Anyone who needs medical attention meet in the living room," Tarek offered, picking up Darius and carrying him inside. Zender followed carrying Boyd. Time was a blur to Virgil. It felt like he was living someone else's life. This nonsense couldn't be what things had become. People were passing out all over, some sleeping for a short time, then getting back up to wandering around aimlessly. Not sure what to be doing. Virgil was told the Chapter Advisors were looking for him. Virgil knocked on the office door that had Professor Ramuh's nameplate, he was told to come in.

"Good morning gentlemen," Virgil said to Professor Ramuh and Professor Ifrit.

"Good morning Virgil, have a seat," Professor Ramuh offered and Virgil obliged.

"We've finished talking with the Grand Pylortes Rasler and the Grand Prytanis, Aseril. We've concluded you are to stay at Bay Valley," Professor Ramuh said.

"That's good," Virgil nodded.

"Yes, better than a prison cell at Alexandros," Professor Ifrit said gruffly.

"Am I in trouble for stealing the Teardrop?" Virgil asked.

"The official word will be Boyd stole the Goddess' Teardrop," Professor Ifrit answered.

"What! Boyd can't take the blame for that, it isn't right. It is a dishonor to his name," Virgil argued getting angry.

"Perhaps," Professor Ramuh agreed with a tired nod.

"That is the way it shall be," Professor Ifrit said with finality. "You can't punish dead men. Our Upsilon Delta Chapter will receive a slap on the wrist, and our brothers will be able to continue on as before."

"Boyd's name will not be tarnished," Professor Ramuh reassured him. "The breaking of the Goddess' Teardrop was predestined. Things have been set into motion, and the Paladins will need to focus on solutions, instead of talking about the problems."

"Rasler and the other Paladins from Alexandros are going home?" Virgil asked.

"Eventually," Professor Ramuh nodded. "Rasler will be leaving two Alpha class Paladins from Internationals, to help keep the peace and restore order after Abdanon's demise."

"To spy on us?" Virgil asked.

"Most likely," Professor Ifrit shrugged.

"Also, for your protection," Professor Ramuh added in.

"My protection?" Virgil's face betraying his obvious surprise.

"Yes, your protection boy," Professor Ifrit grumbled. "Every Fallen is going to be sniffing you out now that you've made your appearance."

"Fallen? What would they want with me?" Virgil asked in surprise.

"You are the Redeemer," Professor Ramuh nodded sadly. "Being one of the Seven Seraphs, the Redeemer's fated purpose was to bestow power unto other people. The Redeemer has the gift of giving a second chance to Fallen Judges," Professor Ramuh explained. "You have the ability to give Fallen their white wings back, allowing them to ascend once more to the realm of the Judges. There are thousands on both sides of this war, who would kill for that," Professor Ramuh cautioned.

"It was said that when the Redeemer used his power, time itself would stop, he would touch their soul and mind, and watch their lifespan of memories," Professor Ifrit explained.

"Why would I want a power like that!?" Virgil asked, throwing his hands up. He was repulsed at the idea of invading others' minds, Judges minds at that, and feeling every hurt they had ever felt. These were beings that had existed for billions of years or more, Virgil didn't know if his mind could handle the memories from an immortal.

"To determine if they are worthy of Redemption or not. You are the Redeemer. You alone can give the gift of power to Fallen, and even other Nephilim. Give wings to those who have none," Professor Ramuh said in awe.

"Like the Omegas or Blair?" Virgil wondered what flying with his friends would be like, he had the ability to give them wings? "That sounds, overwhelming," Virgil said, trying to take it all in.

"Well it isn't something you have to figure out today," Professor Ramuh said firmly. "You don't have to figure out your life and destiny at eighteen years old. You will be safe here, to continue your education, learn more about yourself, and take your time to figure this out."

"Did you know that I had the Devil Arms, Ragnorak?" Virgil asked.

"Yes," Professor Ramuh replied quickly. "The night of your eighteenth birthday, the Grand Prytanis contacted us," Professor Ramuh said. "Stating the Redeemer had arrived in our care as a pledge. He ordered us to keep it quiet and keep an eye on your development."

"Wait, so he just knew that I was the Redeemer?" Virgil said. "I still don't really understand all this Seraphim Nephilim stuff."

"There are Seven Seraphs, Aseril Diamond is the Oracle, the Second Seraph," Professor Ramuh explained, "He has the gift of divination. It is clear he wishes for you to join his side in this war."

"I thought I already had," Virgil sighed.

"In time you will fight beside Aseril Diamond and Rasler Daedra," Professor Ifrit spoke with reverence. "The three of you will lead our people through the darkness ahead."

"The other Seraphim Nephilim are picking sides," Professor Ramuh explained. "The Harbringer and the Gatekeeper are the leaders of Death Dealers. Which side you join will tip the balance of power," Professor Ramuh warned Virgil, his tone serious.

"Rasler's on our side?" Virgil asked with little belief.

"Yes, he was raised in Alexandros. He may be abrasive, but battle has a way of changing some, hardening them," Professor Ramuh explained.

"Rasler said something about my wings?" Virgil asked, curious about their difference.

"They herald the mark of the Redeemer," Professor Ramuh said. "The bringer of hope or destruction, he who walks in the light of Creation and the darkness of Chaos," Professor Ramuh said sadly, "No other Judge or Nephilim before has had such wings, and none shall after."

"This is a lot right now," Virgil said, sinking into the chair, "After that Arch Demon and…Boyd," his name made Virgil depressed.

"We understand you have gone through a lot, take time to make peace with the things that have come to pass," Professor Ifrit suggested.

"The Arch Demon, he said he didn't care who my father was, the Gatekeeper said that it should be obvious," Virgil remembered. "Who is my father?" he asked them confused. "How would they know?"

"He saw you wield Ragnorak," Professor Ramuh replied simply.

"Okay," Virgil felt frustrated not understanding.

"You're the second person to wield the Holy Blade, Ragnorak," Professor Ramuh explained to Virgil. "The first was the Judge Raphael, the Angel of light, fire, and prophecy. Your father," Professor Ramuh told him, staring him straight on.

"My father? He was the Judge that wielded Ragnorak before me?" Virgil wondered.

"Virgil, it is no small feat to wield Ragnorak, it is the most powerful weapon in existence. Raphael was one of the greatest Judges," Professor Ifrit said gruffly. "It was widely thought, that none except him could be entrusted with the power of Ragnorak. Only a being who is pure of heart, and desires to protect all life may wield the Holy Blade."

"My father, he's our enemy?" Virgil asked, starting to realize the weight of the truth.

"Raphael is one of the four God Generals. They command the rest of the Fallen and the Death Dealers," Professor Ramuh said plainly. "They are trying to resurrect the Demon King, Diablos."

Virgil understood, his father was trying to bring back to life, a being who tried to destroy the world once, and would try again if given the chance.

"I don't care who Raphael is," Virgil said, tightening his fists at his side. "He is no father to me!" He yelled. "I had a father, John, he died three years ago. If a Judge wants me to side with the darkness and kill off everyone I've ever known, he's insane," Virgil said crossing his arms.

"No one is questioning your allegiance, Virgil," Professor Ramuh reassured him. "We don't see you as an enemy because you are the son of Raphael."

"I, I don't even see Raphael as a father," Virgil said shaking his head. "More like the bio dad that got me started and had nothing to do with who I became."

"It would be hard for anyone to handle," Professor Ramuh said sadly. "We are here for you, if you need us. You are an Omega, a brother of this fraternity. We have your back frater."

"Thank you, both of you," Virgil said sadly, getting up and shaking their hands. They didn't have anything more to share and Virgil wanted to be alone.

The next few days seemed almost like a dream. Virgil slept as often as he could, enjoying not having to move, to eat, to think. The funerals came and went. (Their deaths were explained to the public and their families as an automobile accident, Nephilim with the ability to alter memory and create illusions helped keep the story credible.) So many people showed up to them. The fraternity paid for the funerals. They were buried in a large cemetery on State Park Drive, near Wilder Road in Bay City. The fraternity had bought a large plot of land there, for its eventual use to bury its fallen comrades. Virgil met a lot of new people in the fraternity, Alpha and Beta class members he'd heard stories about but never seen. Friends and family of both Boyd and Darius were there, they were so broken from their loss, their pain was hard to bare. Virgil could barely handle it himself.

Virgil's classes were affected as well. The University had a policy of giving students credit, for all their current classes that semester if a roommate died. Virgil received 14 credits for the semester, next semester's grades would determine his standing with his scholarship.

Virgil's other roommates weren't nearly as affected by Boyd's death as he was. People talked about it in Virgil's dorm, it was a big deal when a college kid dies on campus. Damian wasn't around much, but one day Virgil passed him in the hall where their bedrooms were, and he stopped and stared at Virgil. They stood their staring at each other for minutes not saying anything. Damian gave Virgil a big hug and patted him on the back. Afterwards things were friendlier between them, Virgil did not trust their Chapter, he knew they were in league with the

Death Dealers. Virgil didn't hate Damian, and he didn't want to. Hate was like cancer, slowly eating away at you on the inside, Virgil didn't want it in his life.

The rest of the semester seemed to finish fast. Virgil was no longer having to study, when everyone was getting ready for finals, he had a lot of time on his hands. Virgil found that when he was most depressed, having a full schedule, with plenty of activities to keep the body and mind busy were the best way to deal with grief. Virgil tried to not spend time thinking about Boyd, or Ragnorak, or his father. Virgil played video games nonstop. They soothed Virgil's mind, letting him escape into their interactive worlds and stories. The games were different from life in that they had happy endings, most of them. It was one of Virgil's favorite past times. He lost himself in life, working out, eating with friends, spending most of his time with Blair, Louie, Birdy, and Dante. Virgil tried to find happiness in the simple pleasures of being alive and being human, well half human anyway.

Virgil made a trip home to see his mother for a few days. Going back to his hometown of Caseville helped to rejuvenate him. The demonic activity and crime rates across the globe steadily increased, it was clear the Death Dealers, and the Fallen who commanded them, had plans in motion.

Before he knew it, Virgil had developed strong friendships with people around campus, and through the fraternity. The Sweethearts were amazing through all the hardships. Ariel and Raven went over to the Omega house daily. Baking treats, cooking meals together with the guys, they were great at lightening the mood, and bringing a smile to the brothers' faces. Some of the guys' girlfriends started coming around often to; including Mu's new girlfriend, Lilly, whom he'd been dating for several months, as well as people Virgil was more familiar with like Gabriel's TK and Brody's Selene. The brothers who had fought against Abdanon were still suffering from the stress of the battle, Tarek and Magnus suggested the brothers seek counseling from the Peer Health Services on campus if needed. Many of the brothers did go, just to have someone to talk things out with. Virgil went once and had an hour-long session. It helped Virgil feel better, he talked through the things that he was trying hard not to talk or think about. He felt better afterwards but didn't think he was going to go back again. There was no real cure for the loss of life. Time was the only thing that healed all wounds. Day by day Virgil grew a little better, feeling slightly more like his old self.

The schedule of the fraternity helped to keep the weeks structured and everyone moving forward. Elections came, the eight Jeweled Officers who would lead Upsilon Delta Chapter over the next Winter and Fall semesters. The second to last meeting was elections, they were a grueling endeavor, taking anywhere from eight to over twelve hours. Out of all the Jeweled Offices, Virgil's goal was to be the Hypophetes someday.

Twenty-two brothers showed up to vote, including the seven Omicron, they had thirty-one active total after losing Boyd and Darius. The elections started with Prytanis, Magnus won the position by a landslide. Epiprytanis was next, it was between Gabriel, Landon, and Lamar. Gabriel gave the most impassioned speech of the three. He told them how he had done the Hegemon position, achieving his pledge goal. But now he wanted to lead the fraternity, help it to do different things than before. Gabriel said his success with Xi and Omicron were his evidence of follow through on commitment to his responsibilities. The ten members of Xi and Omicron were on team Gabriel, he'd been their Hegemon, and he won the Epiprytanis position. Landon won the election for Grammateus, and Thiago surprised everyone with a win of the Crysophylos, or Treasurer. Thiago spoke about how much the fraternity meant to him, and how much he wanted to give back. He also told them that he was one of the oldest actives, and the Executive Board needed mixed opinions.

The fraternity elected Abe to Histor. It meant a lot to him, he cried when he was called back in the room and it was announced. It was good to see him get something good in return. The Hypophetes position took almost three hours. Buck, Jagger, Tarek, Lamar and Jace all ran for the position. Each man was allowed a ten-minute presentation, and then a ten-minute Q & A. The race for Hypophetes came down to Tarek and Jagger. They were the older brothers, Buck was the oldest being from Eta class with Thiago, but the younger guys didn't know him. He was close with the older brothers who'd already graduated, and was busy often, one of the guys who was rarely seen outside of the meeting and brotherhood. The men wanted a Hypophetes they all could talk to. Tarek and Jagger each had strong supporters in the room. Virgil raised his hand to go on the speakers list. He had given passionate speeches for Magnus and Gabriel. He now did the same for Tarek. He told the room how Tarek was the epitome of what it meant to be a good brother. Virgil passionately defended how Tarek was the fun guy, anyone could go to if they were having a bad day, and how he'd be there to cheer you up. Tarek was simply, the coolest brother in the Chapter. After several speeches, it was time. Tarek won the position by just a few votes. Jagger took the loss personally, leaving immediately. A few brothers, Lamar, Buck, and Benson went to make sure he was okay.

Zender became the Pylortes. He was intimidating, an excellent warrior, intelligent, and extremely driven, a perfect fit. 3 am came and finally the last election, Hegemon. Vahn was running for the position against, Doc, Jace and Brody. Vahn was the clear choice. Virgil spoke passionately for the last time that night, about how Vahn was dedicated to the fraternity. How Vahn wanted to be a teacher, and this was the only position he had ever wanted. Vahn ended up winning the office, making four of the eight Jeweled Officers from Lambda class, they were the leaders of the fraternity.

As the meeting ended Magnus told everyone that they were ALL leaders of the Chapter. Just because one didn't have a Jeweled Officer position didn't mean they weren't important or have an impact on the fraternity. Magnus said that men got upset, and people's feelings got hurt when they did not win. Everyone mattered in making the fraternity successful.

Virgil spent spare time with Blair and the guys, trying to do as much as possible before the end of their first semester. Magnus elected Virgil as Advertising Chairman and Louie as the Social Chairman, placing them in the E-Board with the Jeweled Officers. Magnus saw them as future Jeweled Officers and wanted to get them a head start in leadership. The winter break would be four weeks long this year, a lucky fall of the days gave them an extra weekend off. They had a retreat planned for the weekend after New Year's, where the brothers would go away for a weekend, hang out, party, and plan for the next semester. Setting their goals and game plan for how they would run the fraternity as a new E-Board.

Finals are the most stressful part of the semester, running on little to no sleep, studying day in and out, everyone was running on empty. The people staying in the freshmen dorms had to leave twenty-four hours after their last exam. Because Virgil was an Omega, he could go to the fraternity house and didn't have to return home for the next month. People were tearful and saddened to part with friends. Virgil recognized a lot of people around campus, their faces becoming familiar from daily run-ins. It was incredible how much people had changed in just three months. Some people would leave never to return, transferring or quitting college altogether. Virgil was glad he had joined the Omegas, it gave him a sense of purpose and drive to stay at school, feeling like a part of it. Something some people lacked who didn't join any organizations. Blair was returning to her hometown of Ortonville, the same as Landon and Helene, until after the New Year. Virgil enjoyed the moments he had left with her before the break. She had become one of his best friends, as close to him as any of his brothers.

The Omegas had a big party the last night of finals, anyone was welcome to come who was still around. A lot of people were leaving the next day, most until classes resumed. It was the goodbye party that everyone showed up for. The house was packed wall to wall. Everyone was exhausted from weeks of exams and papers and cutting loose was what the young college students wanted. Virgil had more fun that night then he could remember having in a long time, and for the first time since Abdanon's defeat, he felt truly happy. Surrounded by his new-found friends, he was grateful for life. The worries about the battles and war ahead were on no one's minds, they celebrated their youth and enjoyed the fleeting beauty of living in the moment. Virgil was glad he had joined the Omegas, looking back on it for years to come, he would always tell others, it was one of the best decisions he had ever made for himself. It taught him to be more confident in himself, reiterated the finer points of being a gentleman, and gave him greater friends then he'd ever known.

About the author:

Christiano Prime, born and raised in Michigan, by age 10 was an avid reader and developed a passion for storytelling. His dream since he was a child was to become an author and captivate readers' imaginations. When Christiano isn't playing RPG video games, or daydreaming about his next story, he is saving lives as a social worker/counselor in a hospital ER doing crisis interventions and mental health evaluations. Christiano dreams of the day he can live on the West coast and return to Michigan each year for its beautiful summers, and his three dads, two moms, and seven sisters.

This is the first of a seven-book series, the second and third novels are completed, I'm currently seeking representation from a literary agent or a publishing company. If you liked this book and would like more like it, please rate my novel amazon.com/author/christianoprime and leave a review. Your support and feedback allow me to keep working hard on the next installment of the series. Thank you for taking the time to read my story, by doing so you've helped me fulfill a lifelong dream, and I couldn't be happier to share more! Those interested in being added to my mail list to receive information about upcoming releases send your email address to primechristiano@gmail.com.

www.ingramcontent.com/pod-product-compliance
Lightning Source LLC
Chambersburg PA
CBHW030540260626
47157CB00006B/2124